RESCUING MOIRA

Guardian Hostage Rescue Specialists

ELLIE MASTERS

Editor: Erin Toland

Proofreader: Rox Leblanc

Interior Design/Formatting: Ellie Masters

Published in the United States of America

JEM Publishing

～

ISBN: 978-1-952625-21-3

Warning

~

This story contains triggers, sexually explicit scenes and adult language and might be considered offensive to some readers.

This book is for sale to adults ONLY, as defined by the laws of the country where you made your purchase. Please store your files wisely and where they cannot be accessed by underage readers.

Dedication

This book is dedicated to my one and only—my amazing and wonderful husband.

Also by Ellie Masters

The LIGHTER SIDE

Ellie Masters is the lighter side of the Jet & Ellie Masters writing duo! You will find Contemporary Romance, Military Romance, Romantic Suspense, Billionaire Romance, and Rock Star Romance in Ellie's Works.

Sign up to Ellie's Newsletter and get a free gift. https://elliemasters.com/RescuingMelissa

YOU CAN FIND ELLIE'S BOOKS HERE:

ELLIEMASTERS.COM/BOOKS

Military Romance

Guardian Hostage Rescue

Rescuing Melissa

(Get a FREE copy when you join Ellie's Newsletter)

Rescuing Zoe

Rescuing Moira

Rescuing Eve

Rescuing Lily

Rescuing Jinx

Rescuing Lexi

Rescuing Eden

The One I Want Series
(Small Town, Military Heroes)
By Jet & Ellie Masters

EACH BOOK IN THIS SERIES CAN BE READ AS A STANDALONE AND IS ABOUT A DIFFERENT COUPLE WITH AN HEA.

Aiden

Brent

Caleb

Dax

Patton

Rockstar Romance

The Angel Fire Rock Romance Series

EACH BOOK IN THIS SERIES CAN BE READ AS A STANDALONE AND IS ABOUT A DIFFERENT COUPLE WITH AN HEA. IT IS RECOMMENDED THEY ARE READ IN ORDER.

Ashes to New (prequel)

Heart's Insanity (book 1)

Heart's Desire (book 2)

Heart's Collide (book 3)

Hearts Divided (book 4)

Hearts Entwined (book5)

Forest's FALL (book 6)

Hearts The Last Beat (book7)

Contemporary Romance

Firestorm

(Kristy Bromberg's Everyday Heroes World)

Billionaire Romance

Billionaire Boys Club

Hawke

Richard

Brody

Contemporary Romance

Cocky Captain

(Vi Keeland & Penelope Ward's Cocky Hero World)

Romantic Suspense

EACH BOOK IS A STANDALONE NOVEL.

The Starling

~AND~

Science Fiction

Ellie Masters writing as L.A. Warren

Vendel Rising: a Science Fiction Serialized Novel

ONE

Moira

Hard. Cold. Unforgiving.

A concrete floor, damp air, and bone-chilling cold define my existence. The pounding in my skull is unbearable, and the coppery taste in my mouth doesn't bode well.

Gently, I explore the damage to my head. Dried, matted blood greets my probing fingers. There are lumps, too many to count, but those don't worry me. Those are survivable.

What I don't feel are depressions, skull fractures, which point toward damage to my brain.

So yeah, that's good. Just peachy.

We're focusing on the positives here. There are far too many negatives, and those scare me to death.

My tongue sweeps the inside of my mouth, finding deep cuts to my inner cheeks. My lips crack as I gently probe, moving my tongue gingerly around, exploring the damage.

I'm alive, not that it's any surprise. I excel at survival; it's what I do best—my superpower.

Death would be quieter, less painful than the agony wracking my body. But no. No death for me.

Moira Stone is a goddamn survivor.

The low drone of male voices rumbles somewhere off to my left. The stench of sweat, urine, and blood fills my nostrils. I'm not sure how much of that is mine, and I don't care. Frankly, I don't care about much right now.

This isn't my first time at a shit show.

Been here.

Done that.

Got the scars to prove it.

Whatever this is, I'll survive it. I'll survive because I'm too stubborn to give up. I don't know when to quit, or when to die. I only know how to survive.

Which sucks.

I'm really tired of this shitty life.

Dad walked out when I was five. Mom shot herself into oblivion when I turned ten. Foster Pop ripped my virginity from my prepubescent body at the tender age of eleven. By twelve, I was on the streets peddling my flesh.

The point is, I know how to survive.

At first, I played the innocent little girl routine. Men paid double for that kind of sick, twisted shit, and I got those depraved assholes to feed me the cash I needed to survive one more night on the street.

But here's the problem with too much cash.

I had money left over to ease the pain. I got hooked on coke, heroine, and basically anything I could ingest, inject, or inhale. My life consisted of one high followed by another desperate low, but through it all, I continued to survive.

I guess I've found a new low. Not that it's unexpected. I was doing pretty well at the Facility, learning to live a new life and believing I could have a good life.

What a joke.

I knew it was too good to be true.

My last big low was when I turned sixteen. Too young to turn the little girl trick, I picked up the wrong John. A veritable old-timer on the streets, I should've known better. He was too nice, smelled too good, and told too many lies.

Lies I wanted to believe.

That's what happens when a moment of weakness hits. It steals your breath and destroys your life. At sixteen, I graduated from prostitute to sex slave.

Yeah, I know. It's far more glamorous than it sounds. If you haven't figured it out yet, sarcasm is my *thing*. It gets me through this hellish life.

The sex slave thing lasted five long years. Then the Guardians freed me. I thought I was done with the whole shit show. Like I could finally be normal and do normal things. At twenty-two, I'm too old for this shit, but evidently, the universe thinks otherwise. I'm right back in the thick of things.

Fear, Confusion, and Hopelessness.

Those are three bastards I know well. They rip through me, suffocate me, drown me, and devour my will to live.

Notice how I said live, not survive. I have no desire to live through this again.

None.

I've been here before. If I could end it all now, I would, but the grace of death is not mine. That kind of power lies in the hands of the monsters arguing over their cards.

The universe is one sick prick.

I'll live, and I'll endure the vileness to come. I'll do it because I'm too much of a coward to take my own life.

"Hey, she's up." A brusque voice turns my blood to ice.

I pray for death or some kind of reprieve. I won't get it. This is my fate; to hope where there is nothing to hope for and live when there's nothing left to live for.

It appears I exist only to feel pain.

"Doesn't look like she's up to me." The second man shifts his attention in my direction.

Under that glare, my body grows still. I dig deep, tunneling into the darkness, only this time, my tricks don't work. The rank stench of blood, sweat, and fear fills my nostrils, irritating the sensitive passages.

I gag. I cough. I announce to the whole damn world that I am, indeed, awake.

The first man rises. As he does, a loud fart rips and noxious gas tumbles through the room. The foul taint rolls toward me, but not before reaching his friend first.

"Holy shit, Shelly, what the fuck did you eat?"

"Don't call me Shelly."

"I'll call you whatever the fuck I want." The second man, the one I identify as the leader, waves his hand in front of his nose. "That's the last fucking time you get to pick dinner."

"You like Joe's burritos." Shelly defends himself.

"Yeah, I love Joe's burritos, but not your goddamn farts. Take that shit outside."

"Whatever." The weight of Shelly's gaze settles on me. "What are we going to do about her?" He comes over and toes my hip with the steel tip of his boot. "Have they called yet?"

"No."

"What about…"

"I'll deal with that."

Two options present themselves. I can play dead and pretend I'm not, in fact, awake. I might convince them to leave me alone.

No, you can't.

That's right. Already announced I was awake and ready to *party*.

More likely, Shelly will kick harder until pulling a groan from me. I can go with a different option.

Option number two is much more distasteful, but I'm a fucking survivor.

I curl into myself, protecting my vulnerable midsection and hack as if I'm going to vomit. Men aren't too keen on shoving their dicks in a woman spewing her guts.

I cup my head and mumble like I don't know what's going on.

I do.

I remember every goddamn thing until I blacked out. From the abduction on the beach to getting dragged into the back of the van. I remember fighting. That foolish belief the Facility actually taught me how to survive gave me courage I couldn't afford.

I fought, and I lost.

That decision resulted in a blow to the head and no memory of what happened next. Not that it matters. I know exactly what's happening now.

If these men sense weakness, they'll take what isn't freely offered. If I do that, my chances of survival drop to zero. But here's the thing. I'm not an idiot. I know how these things work.

These are not the men I need to fight. Fighting will come later.

Survival is now. I did this when I was twelve, again at sixteen, and I'll do it at twenty-two.

As for the fight to come?

I'm not looking forward to it.

"Please don't hurt me." I cower like a weakling. My hands move from the caked blood on my scalp to my stomach, and I play up the retching noises.

Shelly presses the toe of his boot to my head. It's meant as a show of strength, demonstrating what he could do, if he so chose.

I almost wish he'd cave in my skull and end this suffering. But he doesn't.

This is what I need to know. How much leeway do these men have? Can they do what they want to me? Or is there another person pulling their strings? Either option terrifies me, but I hope for the latter. Not because it saves me anything, but because it buys me time.

I allow myself to cry, to whimper, and to curl into a tighter ball. They expect it, and I deliver like a Hollywood movie star. My knees draw up and I rock on the hard, concrete floor.

"Please don't hurt me…" I mumble those words over and over again.

The men laugh at my desperation. Shelly kicks me in the back with that steel-tipped boot of his.

I'll kill him first.

But right now, I need to know what's going on.

Who controls these men?

How valuable am I to them?

Before I do anything, I desperately need to know my worth. Find that out, and I gain power.

It won't be much, but I'm a goddamn survivor. I didn't get that way by being weak.

Or stupid.

Or hasty.

Back when I was eleven, I believed I'd be saved from my foster father, but when I told his wife, she blamed me and kicked me out the front door. Twelve is too young to be on the streets, and I quickly discovered there is no humanity. My pleas for food, shelter, and safety fell on deaf ears.

But I watched the older girls, and thanks to my foster father, I understood what they did with those men in the dark alleys. More importantly, I discovered how they made money doing it. It didn't take long before I realized I could earn double because I was so young.

Youth is a commodity on the streets. I capitalized on my strengths, doubled down, and I survived.

I know I shouldn't, but I can't help but sink into that desperate place, that futile state between wishing and hoping for a better life.

At twelve, my helplessness had been unbearable, and it took digging deep to find what I needed to survive. I had to learn how to dissociate my body from my mind. I found my strength then, but now?

Now, I don't care enough to try.

That's what's going to kill me.

Apathy.

There is no hope. There are no fairy tales. I'm not the princess imprisoned in the tower. I'm simply tired of it all.

I'm nothing, and I will always be nothing.

Forest Summers and his damn Facility let me believe in a future where I mattered. Hook, line, and sinker, I fell hard and fast for that dream. Rescued from a life of sexual slavery, I believed the lies that I had been saved.

Little did I know fate would intervene. Is this what my life is worth? To go from one degradation to the next? That sliver of hope dangled in front of me, for what?

To tease and torment?

I hate how easily I fell for it.

"Get up." The harsh tones of the monster watching me pull me from my catatonic state.

I could hide within my mind, but that does nothing to ease what comes next. This is a road I've navigated before. I know what I must do to survive. The only question is whether I have the strength to walk this vile road again.

Do you?

Hell, if I know. It's the only answer I can give.

Weakness feeds the monsters and I refuse to give them what they want. If there's one thing my previous life taught me, it is how to dig in deep and survive.

Shelly kicks me with the tip of his boot again. "I said, get up!"

Knowing that this is not the time to fight, I roll over and slowly press up from the floor. He kicks me again.

"I said, get up."

"I'm trying." I grit my teeth, knowing that tiny flare of defiance is something I'll pay for later.

"I don't have all damn day." Shelly's voice turns dangerously cold.

I slowly push my shaky body up from the unforgiving concrete and avoid looking at the bloodstain that most surely is mine. With my hands trembling and my arms shaking, I slowly rise to a sitting position. My legs curl behind me, and I stare into Shelly's cold, unforgiving eyes. There's no compassion there, only death and misery.

I want to shout, but I grit my teeth. This is not the time to fight.

He shoves me, pushing on my shoulder with his broad, meaty hand. The force of his shove knocks me back to the ground. Shelly spits on me and that steel-tip toe of his boot slams into my spine.

"I said, get up."

Slowly, I rise and fight a wave of nausea as I shift back to a sitting position. Knowing this is a game for him, I grit my teeth and manage to get my feet beneath me. On wobbly knees, I rise.

I know men like him. I know what they like, and what they hate. I know what they need to feel like men. They need broken women who cower at their feet.

No problem, buddy. I'm an expert at groveling.

I've been serving assholes like him my entire life. Defiance only makes them bolder. I sink into myself, burying who I am, and begin the process of dissociating body from mind.

My chin tucks to my chest and my gaze settles on those boots I hate. I'd love to ram that steel-toed monstrosity up his ass.

My shoulders hunch and I portray myself as a meek, mild, and subdued female. It feeds their power complex and gives me time to get my shit together.

As for the seething hatred I feel for this man, I bury that shit down a deep, dark well. That's not a mistake I can make. Not if I want to survive.

The only language these men understand is power and control. Who has it and who doesn't.

If you haven't been keeping up. They have it. I don't.

"I'm sorry." The warble in my voice is not hard to fake.

I'm terrified. I don't know who these men are, and I don't know why they took me. I don't even know where my friend is.

The last memory I have of Zoe, we were walking on the beach. Dark, and well past midnight, we headed back to the house the Facility rented for its charges so we could spend a few days in Santa Monica and pretend we were normal kids.

My first night off the Facility, almost a year after my rescue, and men chased me, caught me, and now who knows what they're going to do to me. They dragged Zoe and me into a van where I tried to fight and failed.

All I remember is blackness and waking up here.

As for here, there's no way to know where I am, but I do a quick scan of the room and notice one important thing.

I don't know what happened to Zoe.

"I bet you're sorry." The man makes a slow circuit around me. He pulls at his jaw and pauses at my back. Another shiver runs through me. "You're older than our usual."

Their usual?

Well, that answers one question.

These aren't random men. They're professional kidnappers. That's not something that should give me hope, but it does. If they're professionals, that means they're working for a client. Clients don't like damaged goods.

If I play this sick, twisted game right, I might make it out of here mostly intact.

Meek. Mild. Subdued.

Those are my weapons.

I draw my hands in front of me and clasp them loosely at my waist. I continue to stare at a spot of blood drying on the concrete.

Shelly moves again, coming to a stop in front of me. My focus shifts from the blood to his boots.

"Please, sir…" I inject maximum humility and submission into my voice. "May I have some water?"

Weakness fills my body and I can't stop the tremors. My legs shake so hard I think I'm going to collapse. If I do, that'll only encourage him to hit me again, or worse. Kick me with his steel-toed boots.

I've yet to scan my body, but from the sharp, stabbing pain in my side, my ribs are cracked. That must've happened while I was blacked out because I don't remember that beating.

Shelly places his rough, calloused fingers on my chin. He yanks my head up until I'm forced to look at him, but I don't look him in the eye.

I'm meek and subdued.

Surviving this rotten game.

My gaze rises to his lips, where I leave it.

I don't need to fake the tears falling down my cheeks. I'm scared for my life.

"She's a pretty one, isn't she?" The other man scoots his chair back and stands.

I don't like two of them on their feet. The room feels ten times smaller with them standing over me. That tremor turns into shivers of fear.

"She sure is," Shelly says. "You sure we can't have a little bit of fun with her first?"

TWO

Griff

——————

"How much longer, Doc? I'm not a fucking invalid." My stony gaze, which never fails me, slides like water off a duck's back when it comes to Doc Summers.

Her patient and unrelenting expression tells me not only is she willing to go toe to toe with me, but she already knows she'll win. Her lips curve into a sympathetic smile and her eyes soften.

Her assistant moves around the room while we argue. He keeps his head down and continues stacking trays of medical instruments to take for sterilization. When I turn my attention to him, his gaze skitters away and the instruments on his tray clatter as he shakes.

Personally, I don't get it. I'm a big guy, but I'm not scary. This guy acts like I'm going to squash him like a bug. Granted, I've raised my voice, but it's a small room and I can't help if my deep voice echoes in here. With a shake of my head, I dismiss him and turn my attention back to Doctor Skye Summers.

In a moment, she'll deny me what I need.

We've been doing this dance for three days, three agonizing days which creep along at the pace of glaciers melting. Considering

Moira's somewhere out there, kidnapped and fighting for her life—with men doing God only knows what, I have to wonder what the fuck we're doing sitting around.

"My leg is good."

"You're limping." She points to my leg. "And you're bleeding again."

"It's just a flesh wound."

"A flesh wound?" Her lips curve into a smile. "Is that what you're calling that dime-sized hole in your leg?"

"It's not a hole. You patched it up."

"And sutured your vein back together. Come on, Griff, you need to stay off the leg and give it a chance to heal."

"And what about Moira?"

"We're not discussing that again. You're no use to her if you become a liability to the team."

A growl escapes me and my fingers curl.

Liability.

That's a fighting word. I feel like a caged beast, caught on Doc Summers' very short leash, and I'm tired of this senseless waiting.

"It's time to do something."

"Don't you think Forest has every hand on deck?" Her brow arches again. Unlike her assistant, I don't intimidate her.

I think Forest believes Moira's lost to us, but I would never say that out loud. I've seen that man move mountains to bring home those who've been taken.

"I need to be out there looking for Moira, not sitting on my ass doing VR sims." I may be out of action, physically, but that doesn't mean I'm not working. Around here, the work never stops. I'm either in the VR suite helping our OCD tech genius, Mitzy, with whatever new upgrade she wants to test out, or I'm on the range shooting dimes at four hundred yards.

I run my hands through my hair and pace in a circle. Moira's out there and I'm doing nothing to bring her home.

I'm her protector. Her Guardian. I saved her once. I'll do it again, but right now, I'm doing shit to save her. It's driving me fucking crazy.

Saving others defines my very existence. I should be out there, rescuing Moira, and defending her from the worst humanity has to offer. Instead, the doc makes me sit on the sidelines.

"Another couple of days, Griff." Doc Summers stares up at me with eyes that say she knows exactly the kind of hell I'm in. Her expression also tells me I'm not going to get her to budge.

"The bum leg means nothing to me." I implore her, but she only shakes her head.

"The pain?" Her gaze hardens. "You're trying too hard to hide that limp."

"Frankly, the pain's irrelevant. I've pushed through, and past, worse pain."

"No doubt you have, but that's under duress. This is healing. You need to give it time. Stay off the leg, stop pushing, and do the physical therapy."

"I'm slaying your PT like there's no tomorrow. I'm doing great."

"You grit your teeth through your sessions, then hobble back to your bunk. You refuse to take the pain medication, and your blood pressure is through the roof. Do I need to tell you what happens if you stroke out?"

"No." She's already gotten on me about that. "What do I have to do to prove to you that I'm operational?"

"Until you sit your Guardian ass down and obey doctor's orders, you're going nowhere. Your saphenous vein was ripped to shreds. It hasn't even been seventy-two hours since you lay on my operating table bleeding out. Give it time."

"You fixed it." The gunshot to my leg ripped a hole in a major vein and damaged my quadriceps on that side. She's not kidding about the limp. My leg hurts like a motherfucker.

"With stitches that take time to heal."

"How much time?"

"More than a few days." She vents a frustrated sigh. "Come on, Griff. You push too hard or too fast, and you'll undo all my marvelous handiwork. Trust me, if you go back under my knife because of your goddamn stupidity, or pig-headedness, you might come out of anesthesia one ball short. Stop testing me on this."

My balls draw up at the threat. Doc Summers doesn't fool around.

I know this. She's already explained everything to me: how long to give the vein time to heal, how long it'll take the torn muscles to recover, all the shit.

I'm lucky that damn bullet didn't hit the femoral artery, or we wouldn't be having this conversation. I'd be six feet under communing with worms.

"I am obeying orders." She's feisty, but I'm bullheaded. I'll push until I get what I want. We're locked in a battle of wills; a war I'm determined to win.

Except, I'm not—winning that is. She's won every battle between us and I'm losing the war. The doc is one tough chick, camouflaged in a pretty package, but she's tough as nails.

I fight her at every turn because I need medical clearance to get back into action. That comes when she's good and ready to give it to me. Don't care what the fuck she says, a simple bullet wound won't keep me down.

"Give it two weeks." She gives a sharp shake of her head. "You do everything I say, stop pushing the PT, and I'll sign off."

Damn, she knows I went on that run, but a Guardian is nothing if his body is weak. It takes effort to keep my body in peak physical condition.

"Two weeks!" My shout makes her medical assistant tremble. A tray of instruments clatters to the floor, and the poor guy ducks his head. He's been doing a piss-poor job of ignoring our heated conversation.

Doc Summers gives me a look-what-you-did-now expression highlighted with an exaggerated lifting of her eyebrows. She folds her arms over her chest and taps her foot.

I'm well over a foot taller than her diminutive frame, but damn if she doesn't look down her nose at me. Any second and she'll be reading me the riot act. I sit my ass down and come at her from a different angle.

"My team is a man down. They need me."

"Alpha team is on duty at the Facility. They're not missing you."

"They're not looking for Moira?"

"Relax. They just returned. Bravo team is out."

"Did they find her?" I already know the answer, but I can't help asking.

Skye Summers is the Guardian's lead medical physician, privy to our most classified missions. If they found Moira, she'd know.

"They have a lead." Her reply, like many things, is predicated by hesitation.

"What the fuck?" Back on my feet, my fingers clench, but there's no enemy to throttle. "A lead?" My voice rises in pitch, revealing how deeply invested I am in Guardian HRS's current mission.

Moira is my responsibility. I'm the one who will rescue her. A low growl rumbles in the back of my throat. Doc Summers takes a step back. Her head cants to the side and she takes a long, hard look at me.

I say nothing; this possessiveness isn't new. It's been growing over the past year as I've watched Moira recover at the Facility. Her story isn't the worst; that probably belongs to Forest Summers and the diminutive woman standing in front of me, but Moira's been through hell. She doesn't deserve the shitty hand she's been dealt.

"Bravo just reported in. If you stop arguing with me about getting off medical hold, I can tell you what I know."

"If they have a lead…"

"No positive ID, but Mitzy's confident."

Our lead technical engineer, Mitzy, is sharp as a tack. I've never met a person smarter than her.

"If Mitzy's confident, that means something." Hope stirs within me. "Are there any others?" I remind myself the world doesn't revolve around bringing Moira safely home, even if my heart only cares about her.

Moira is everything.

"Unknown." Skye places a hand on my arm. "CJ's working with Sam to preposition assets." CJ leads the teams and works for Sam, who is the head of the Guardians. We all work for Forest Summers and the woman standing in front of me.

"You gotta let me go on that mission."

"You're not operational."

"There's no way I'm staying here sitting on my ass. I *will* be on that mission."

"I don't want you to get your hopes up. Setting up a mission is going to take time, and I may have over spoke. You know how Mitzy can be. She doesn't have anything tangible. It's more of a guessing game."

"That girl's superpower is solving the unsolvable. What did she say?"

"Only that Moira was collateral damage. Zoe was taken to Colombia for a very specific purpose, for a very discerning client."

"Yeah, I was there. Both times."

Kidnappers plucked Zoe off the streets of Cancun, fulfilling a client's specific order for a snuff film. Alpha team rescued Zoe, brought her back to the Facility, where she started putting the pieces of her life back together.

She and my best bud, Axel, are together now, gloriously happy, but not after the client demanded his order be fulfilled. Zoe was kidnapped a second time, by the same men, for the same purpose, and Moira happened to get caught up in the middle of it all.

We rescued Zoe a second time but lost Moira in the process.

"I know you were, and I'm not making light of what happened or what she must be going through."

"If you know all that, then you know what she means to me. I love you like the sister I never had, but if you stand between me and any chance of bringing her home, we're going to have a problem."

"I don't respond to threats, Griff. You know better than that."

"Fine. I'm begging you. Don't keep me from this."

Her eyes narrow as she takes me in.

"You know how this works. Work with me, instead of fighting me every step of the way. Do that, and we'll talk about you going on that mission…"

"Shit yeah." I practically shout in victory.

"Don't interrupt me. You'll be on that mission, but only in a support role. Keep pushing and that bullet wound won't heal the way it should. You'll get it infected, or worse. I need you to understand what's at risk."

I know exactly what's at risk. Given a choice between my life and Moira's, there is only one answer. She's mine to protect, and I'll sacrifice everything to bring her home. A bum leg means nothing to me if it means she gets to come home and have a chance to live a happy life.

"Is Forest giving the extraction to Alpha?"

"Yes, but until the mission's a go, I need your word that you'll slow your ass down. Give your body the time it needs to heal. Stop sneaking out and pushing your leg with those runs."

Shit, I'm busted.

"And if I promise?" This is the first bone she's tossed my way.

"If you promise, I'll consider it. Support only, but if you keep pushing yourself and rip open my handiwork, you won't be on that mission." She's stern but understands my motivation to get back to mission readiness.

Moira shouldn't mean what she does to me, but I can't help it. She was under my care at the Facility. I was her Guardian, assigned to teach her self-defense. We may have overstepped Guardian and pupil roles, but what the fuck do I care about that?

"If I do everything your way, you promise to get me on that mission?" I grit my teeth asking the question, but it's clear the only way I'll be on that mission is if Doc Summers clears me.

"I'll never make a promise I can't keep. Meet me halfway, Griff, and we'll see."

"How sure is Mitzy?"

"She's not, but you know Mitzy. She's like a dog with a bone. She'll find Moira, and when she does, you can bet there'll be Guardians there within the hour to bring her home."

And I'm going to be one of them.

Doc Summers might consign me to a support role, but my team has my back. They understand.

With nothing left to say, Doc Summers leaves me to obsess over Moira and the hell she must be in.

I've never felt this helpless.

THREE

Moira

"You saw what she did to Jack." The other man huffs a laugh. He seems to be the one in charge. "Bitch bit his dick off." Bossman lets loose, cackling as he slaps his thigh.

That's not something I remember. I would never bite off a man's dick. Is that even possible? But if I did—I give myself a high five.

Something about this place feels off. A metallic smell lingers in the air, different from the coppery tang coating my mouth. It smells like diesel fuel. Industrial comes to mind. And there's a vibration, so low it's barely perceptible, thrumming through the floor.

"And you shot him." Shelly makes another circuit around me. His loose-fitting pants do little to hide his growing arousal. "I have to say, she's fine." He tugs at his crotch, creeping me out.

Shelly's examination is more than cursory. His interest grows bolder by the second. I should know. I'm an expert at reading men's filthy desires. I know exactly what it takes to get them off, and I know what he likes.

Shelly likes a woman who fights. He's one of those who can't get it up unless he causes harm.

His breaths deepen, like they always do when a man works himself into a sexual frenzy. He'll touch me in a moment. It'll be cautious, testing the waters. Shelly's not confident enough to take what he wants outright. He needs to test my defiance first. Then, he'll use my reaction to justify what he does next. Like it's my fault when he rapes me.

Been there.

Done that.

Got the scars to prove it.

If I wasn't so damn terrified right now, I'd be bored to tears.

"And your point?" Bossman's voice comes out in a low growl. "You think what I did was out of line?"

"No, Boss." Shelly puts up his hands and takes a step back.

The protrusion of his erection bobs left and then right. He's such a pussy, backing down too quickly. I know it, and Bossman does too. I'm surprised the boss doesn't shoot Shelly's balls off just to make a point.

"That's right. I'm in charge. Not you."

"Shit." Shelly practically chokes on his words. "I was just stating what happened. He got what was coming to him."

"Damn straight, and best you remember what happens when you don't follow orders. Jack was a fucking putz. I told him not to damage the merchandise, and he had to shove his prick down her throat. He had no right kicking her like he did."

"Well, she did bite his dick off." Shelly's an idiot, defending a dead man. At least, I assume Bossman really did kill Jack.

"So?" Bossman shrugs. "What does that tell you?" Bossman doesn't wait for a reply. "Don't stick your dick where it doesn't belong." He points at me. "She's not yours."

"Don't see why it matters."

"Are we having a failure to communicate?"

"No."

"Then shut the fuck up and keep your dick in your pants." Bossman closes the distance, breaching Shelly's personal space as he goes toe-to-toe and chest-to-chest. They engage in an epic stare down. It comes as no surprise when Shelly backs down.

Men are such peacocks.

Bossman struts his stuff, maintaining his position of power. Shelly has to take it, but he can't back down right away. That shows weakness. So they do that man stare thing, getting all up in each other's faces.

I read all of this in a microsecond.

Shelly gives a huff and takes a step back. "Still don't see why we can't have a little bit of fun. She ain't no goddamn virgin we're keeping clean for him."

Again, with HIM. Who is this man who claims ownership of me?

Shelly is dumb as shit. Every word out of his mouth signs his death warrant.

Doesn't he see the obvious?

"I shot Jack twice. Once for fucking shit up, and again for being a putz, and I'll shoot your fat ass if you touch the merchandise." Bossman snaps his fingers.

"This whole thing's turned into a fucking shit storm." Shelly's not getting the message. "What does it matter if we give her a spin?"

"You criticizing me?"

"No, Boss." Shelly runs a hand through his grimy hair, then pulls at his chin again. "How the fuck did those bastards find us anyway?"

"Don't know. Don't care." Bossman spits on the floor. "What happened in Colombia isn't on us. We delivered the other girl. They fucked it up."

"At least we got this one out." Shelly lunges toward me and grips my chin. He pinches down hard, waiting for my wince of pain. "You have no idea how much trouble you've caused."

I didn't cause any trouble.

I blink through my tears.

Right now, drawing any attention to myself is a death wish. Tension in the room escalates, and I'm right smack dab in the middle of it.

But I need them to keep talking. To argue and give me the tiny scraps of knowledge I need to not go insane. I need to know what happened.

Zoe and I were captured. We were on that beach in Santa Monica. These men jumped us, then somehow, they moved us to Columbia.

Colombia? Why there?

Some kind of shit went down. Zoe's no longer with them, but I am. They protected their asset.

Me.

They protected me, taking me from whatever hellhole it was that Zoe landed in to wherever this is now.

I'm meant for something else.

But what?

Or rather, who?

I need answers, and I can't ask any of the millions of questions swirling in my head. All I can do is listen to Shelly spout off to his boss.

It doesn't escape my notice Bossman doesn't say my name. Degraded and dehumanized, I'm no longer human in his eyes.

Humans deserve compassion, consideration, and respect. I doubt these men would know compassion if it bit them in the ass, or better yet, bit right through their flaccid cocks.

Honestly, I'd like to think I am badass enough to bite a man's dick off. I've never fought for myself like that. Shit, just the thought of doing something like that makes me feel a little less helpless.

I take note of every word these men say. A bonus was promised. A bonus these men lost. I'm valuable to someone.

But who?

That value will either make these men more cautious in how they handle me, or it'll piss them off.

If I'm going to get out of this alive, I'll do it on my own. Which means I need to drive a wedge between these men.

There's only one way to do that, and it turns my stomach.

No matter.

I've done this more times than I want to count. I'll do whatever it takes to survive because I don't know how to die.

Shelly forces me to look him in the eye. "You wouldn't bite my dick, would you, bitch?"

He's testing the waters, but Shelly won't do anything with Bossman around. He's dumb as a doorknob, but not that dumb.

My gaze slides away from his hellish eyes only to land on the soulless countenance of Bossman. Hunger lurks in his eyes, a dark perversion I won't escape.

"I'm gonna take a piss and get some fresh air. This stinking ship is making me sick. Keep your eye on her and hands off."

I cling to every word Bossman says.

I'm on a ship, and not that I'm any expert, but concrete floors aren't standard on any boats I know. He said ship. That may explain the sub-sonic vibrations I've been feeling.

I concentrate on that; any detail could be important. There's no obvious rolling motion. This must be a big-ass ship.

Zoe told me about her kidnapping, how she was shoved inside a shipping container for days. Is that the kind of ship I'm on now? It makes sense, but I'm hesitant making too many assumptions. I need more facts, more details.

Like the pistol shoved in Bossman's belt and the knife strapped to his leg. I take note of those as he leaves.

I didn't pay enough attention to Shelly, but I bet he's armed too. Two armed men are too much for one small female to handle. But what about one?

Come on, Moira! The Guardians taught you how to fight. Four taught you what to do.

I only know my Guardian trainer by his numerical designation; Four. One through Six, our Guardians trained us at the Facility in self-defense. The problem is I need something offensive. I wish Four was with me now. He'd shove Shelly's boot up his ass, then feed him his dick.

What I wouldn't give for a little rescue right now.

I curl my lips inward, trying to moisten them with my own saliva, but I'm dehydrated and my lips simply stick together where they crack and bleed.

My entire body trembles and tears fall. I've got enough water in me to cry, but not enough to wet my lips. I've never felt this hopeless. At least there's this, if I do have to give one of these motherfuckers a blowjob, my lips will feel like sandpaper on their dicks.

The guns scare me. Four trained me to use my body to fight, not how to handle a gun. I swallow against the thick lump in my throat and flutter my fingers.

What do I know?

Bossman killed Jack, not for sticking his dick down my throat, but for what happened next.

So, what happened next?

If I take Shelly at his word, I bit Jack's dick off. Probably not all the way *off*, that doesn't sound possible, but if I bit Jack's dick, he likely retaliated.

I lift my hands to feel along my ribs and wince when I find tender spots. Definitely cracked. Bossman said Jack damaged the merchandise.

Hitting me is why Jack died.

So how do I get Shelly to hit me?

Whatever it is, I need to figure it out soon because Bossman will be back any minute.

Think, Moira, think. You can do this.

Why am I not tied up? They are either exceptionally confident or really dumb.

With Bossman gone, Shelly continues his lusty assessment. He wants me, but he won't take me in front of Bossman, especially after being told to keep his hands off me.

I don't know if that makes things any easier for me or not.

Not knowing what to do, and with despair having a grand old time ravaging me from the inside out, I give up and collapse.

Yeah, that's my grand plan, fall down and curl into a fetal ball. Like an ostrich sticking its head in the sand, I'm going to pretend none of this is happening.

My collapse surprises Shelly. He stands over me, canting his head sideways, looking down at me. Then he squats and his fetid breath washes over me.

"You have no idea, do you?" He pokes my shoulder. "Don't be dramatic. Your Master doesn't like his property throwing hissy fits."

I uncurl, lowering my arms from my head. The thing is, he's right.

"You heard me. Your Master isn't going to like that kind of attitude."

There's a vibration in his voice, a sense of irritation and disquiet. Shelly doesn't like being low man on the totem pole. I'll use this to my advantage.

"And what about you?" I uncurl a little bit more.

"Huh?" He scratches his head and stands, towering over me once again. When he crouched before me, I took note of his state of arousal. Despite all the things Bossman said, Shelly is still eager and primed to fuck. I also glimpsed a knife tucked into his boot.

How much time do I have until Bossman returns?

What I'm about to do turns my stomach, but I need to even out the odds.

I press my hands to my eyes and pretend I'm drying my tears. This straightens me out a little on the floor. Very slowly, I arch my back and push out my tits. Wonder of wonder, I'm still wearing my shorts and tank top from the beach. Still got the bright, red bikini on too.

Shelly does exactly what I knew he'd do and watches my every move with avid fascination. I'm the delectable treat he can't have.

"What about me?" He fixates on my words, but I need him to watch my body.

Five years as a sex slave forced me to learn how to seduce men rather than get them off as quickly as possible. Men who buy sex slaves are not the same kind of men who pick up a prostitute for a quick fuck. They crave seduction and the power that comes from owning another person. It's all about mind games.

I arch my back and stretch, moaning as I pretend I'm in pain. There's actually very little pretending. Sharp, stabbing pains shoot through me, but Shelly gets off on pain, and I need him to get off on me.

"Do you like transporting women you never get to touch?" My words come out soft and hesitant, as meek and mild as I can make them while also injecting a degree of sarcasm. My goal is to push him. To piss him off, and hopefully to get him to make a very fatal mistake.

Shelly's attention focuses completely on me—on my body. I make a show of feeling along my ribs. His hungry gaze follows the fluttering path of my fingers over bare skin as I inch my top up and up and up. I hiss when I reach the tender spots. When I twist to look at the bruises, my body moves with sinuous grace. I was trained by the worst humanity has to offer to be as sensual as possible.

I lift my tank top, intentionally pulling it higher than necessary. With the bright red of my swimsuit showing, I make a show of looking at my ribs. My hands skate along my skin, fingers seductively fluttering as Shelly's mouth gapes. His breaths deepen and his hand grips the root of his cock.

I lower the fabric of my top and bite back a groan. Curling back around, I slowly turn until I'm on my hands and knees. Shelly will think I'm trying to stand, but I pick this position with intent.

Making a show of how much it hurts, I give up and lean back on my knees. It's a position I've been put in before and has one very obvious advantage. I lick my parched lips. If I have to go as far as I think, Shelly can't get distracted by the dried, chapped skin of my lips. Time to soften them up. I don't look at him.

My role is that of a broken girl, but when I look up at him, I make sure to look up through my lashes when I finally make eye contact.

His eyes widen, first with outrage that I dare look him in the eye, but I quickly avert my gaze, playing up the submissive pose. When I look at him a second time, his hand is still at his crotch, stroking his hard length through the fabric of his pants.

Shelly's eyes dart toward the door, and I know exactly what he's thinking. How much time does he have?

Hopefully, not much.

All of this depends on Bossman coming back soon.

"Please, may I have some water?"

He paces in a circle around me and cuffs me upside the head. My back is to the door. I strategically fall to the side with a scream. Hopefully, Bossman hears me. When Shelly kicks me with his boot, I rotate my body until I have a direct line of sight on the door.

Shelly tugs at his pants. "You think you're all that? That I won't take what I want? You're just a fucking cunt." He moves behind me and goes to his knees. "I'm going to fuck that fine ass of yours and you ain't going to do shit about it. I don't need nobody's permission to fuck a cunt."

"No, please." I fight him. "I'll scream."

"Nobody gives a fuck if you scream."

"Your boss. He said…"

"Don't give no fucks about what he said. You bite me, or say a fucking word, and I'll slit your throat." He grabs my hair, yanking my head back.

I grab at his hand and scramble with everything I have, moving closer to the door, crying out as Shelly paws at me and drags me back. His meaty hand covers my mouth.

"I said, not a fucking word."

I make a show of fighting Shelly, but I'm not really using everything I know. I've done this with Four before, during some of our private lessons back at the Facility, after he inadvertently triggered some of my more severe flashbacks.

Four is much larger than Shelly, and while I didn't free myself at first from Four's attacks, I did learn how to focus my counterattacks. I don't do that with Shelly, and it twists my stomach, but my goal isn't to get free.

It's to work him up, play to his desires to hurt me, and feed his rape fantasy until he acts on it. It's not the best plan, but it's the best I have at the moment.

How long does it take for Bossman to take a piss?

I squirm and cry out when Shelly grips the back of my neck. He pushes my cheek against the cold concrete and paws at my pants. He shoves them down, ripping the buttons in the front, and kicks my knees apart. His rough, calloused hand paws at my most tender bits as I continue to struggle and cry out.

I fight him off, weakly. I don't want this, but I need Bossman's rage when he sees what Shelly's about to do.

A whimper escapes me as Shelly tears at my bikini bottom and shoves it down over my hips. I'm fully exposed to him now, and there's no sign of Bossman.

Shelly huffs as he struggles to free his bulbous cock from his pants. I seriously question what the hell I was thinking.

I cry out, louder this time, and I fight as hard as I can. No holding back now; besides, I need Shelly to "damage the goods." Shelly expects a good fight, and despite this being a part of my plan, I really don't want any part of him anywhere inside my body.

He fists my hair and lifts my head back, then slams my face against the hard concrete. Pain fills my universe with concussive force and the skin of my cheek tears. Sticky wetness smears beneath my cheek as Shelly rubs my face into the floor.

Erratic and uncontrolled, his breaths turn ragged as he fumbles behind me, trying to slip the tip of his cock between my folds.

It won't be long before…

The outer door slams open with a bang.

I glance into my avenging angel's eyes. It's the visage of a devilish man with the barrel of a gun pointed at me.

He takes one look at the cut on my face and the fresh blood on the floor, then his face twists into a deadly scowl.

"I fucking told you not to touch the merchandise."

Shelly's too far gone to stop. He grips the tip of his dick and desperately tries to slam it home. His hips jerk, but I'm dry as a bone down there. His junk slides against me but doesn't penetrate.

"Fucking putz."

My insides clench as Bossman pulls the trigger.

A concussive blast makes my eardrums pop. My eyes squeeze shut as I wait to feel the bullet rip through me. No way is Bossman that good of a shot, but Shelly's grip on the back of my neck goes suddenly slack, and his dead body slumps to the floor.

I scramble to the side, acting every bit the terrified woman that I am, but I remember my tricks from the street. When I wasn't hooking, I picked pockets to stay alive for one more day.

I stealthily palm the knife tucked into Shelly's boot.

Before Bossman closes the distance, I yank up my pants and hide the knife in the cleft between my ass cheeks.

One down.

One to go.

It's just me and Bossman now.

FOUR

Griff

WITH NOTHING LEFT TO DO BUT WAIT ON MITZY'S BRILLIANT MIND to find the lead we need, I head to the gym.

Doc said to lay off the runs, but she didn't say shit about upper body and core workouts. Right now, I need to release the excess energy thrumming through my veins. If I don't, I'll take out my frustration on someone I shouldn't.

I get to the gym a few minutes before the rest of Alpha team returns from the Facility. Decked out in black tactical gear, helmets, and black hoods, they look fucking fierce. I would be with them, if not for the bum leg.

My buddy, Axel, sees me on the mat and heads over.

"Hey, how'd the check-up go?" He plops down beside me while I pound out a few more crunches. In the middle of an intense set of crunches and planks, I speak in single word sentences.

"Not. Good." The timer on my phone beeps and I spin around to plank. I've got five minutes to hang out doing nothing other than strengthen my core. "She wouldn't clear me."

"Dude, you're barely a few days out from major surgery."

"Not major. Just a bit of repair on a vein."

"If you say so." Axel joins me on the mat, moving seamlessly into working out with me.

Teamwork is imprinted on our Guardian brains. At our most base level, we buddy up in pairs. Axel is Alpha-Three and I'm Alpha-Four. On a mission, we back each other up. We're so in tune with each other that I know what Axel's going to do before he does.

As for the rest of our team, Max and Knox take positions at the chin-up bars. They jump as one, hands gripping metal and rise together. They'll do a hundred pull-ups before going to the mat for a hundred push-ups. They'll repeat that a few times, just like I shift from crunches to planks. Max is team leader. Knox is his second. Liam and Wolfe round out our team as Alpha-Five and Alpha-Six. They work in unison and begin a brutal session of free weights.

We're a tight team and do pretty much everything together, but there's more to the Guardians than Alpha team. If the operation calls for it, we double up with another team and harness what we need to succeed. I can't think of a mission when all four teams engaged, but I suspect it could happen.

We've worked with Bravo team many times, like the op in Manila, the one that went south with Forest. Talk about an ass-clenching moment. It's never good when you lose the boss on a mission, but we rescued a score of girls forced into sexual slavery.

One of those girls was Moira.

I'll never forget her vacant expression when I strapped her into the helicopter. All the other girls cried, overjoyed with their rescue. Moira simply sat there. At first, I thought she was in shock. Only later did the truth come out.

As for losing Forest, Alpha and Bravo redeemed ourselves when we extracted him a few months later. Not too long ago, just before Moira and Zoe were kidnapped, we partnered with Charlie team to rescue a dozen girls caught up in the same sex-trafficking operation that originally kidnapped Zoe.

Our teams did a HALO drop into the Gulf of Mexico and rescued those girls off a cargo container ship. We've yet to work with Delta team. It's the only Guardian team with female Guardians.

Jenny leads that team as Delta-One, while Charlene is their newest recruit as Delta-Six. They tend to work on the domestic front, often teaming up with federal agencies on high-profile kidnapping cases— cases where the government needs the help of a private organization who's able to work outside the law.

I've seen the females but never interacted with them. In general, the teams tend to be very team-centric. We don't tend to mix unless it's on a mission.

A glance at the timer on my phone reveals another three minutes to go on the plank. This is the time to dig in deep. The lactic acid burn is just starting to kick in.

"What did Skye say?" Axel is the only one of us who calls the doc by her first name. He's more familiar with her than the rest of us.

"Doc Summers said to stop pushing myself."

Axel and I exchange a look and bust out a laugh at the same time. We're Guardians. We always push ourselves.

Three and a half minutes and the burn intensifies. Axel grows quiet beside me. The last ninety-seconds are hard. The final thirty seconds are nothing short of brutal. Our conversation degenerates into short, snappy sentences.

"No run?" Axel shifts his hands. It's the only movement we allow during a plank.

"No run."

"And?"

"If I. Bust. A. Stitch…" I pause to take a breath. We're closing in on the last minute and the burn sets in. "She'll take. One of. My balls."

Axel turns his head; his eyes grow wide. He blinks as if he's trying to process what I said. When it hits him, his arms go out and he falls to the ground laughing.

I grind my teeth and hold position.

"You're kidding, right?" Axel rolls to his back and stares at the ceiling fans slowly spinning over our heads.

"No." I'm down to huffing out single words. Forty-five seconds to go.

"Well shit, I guess you won't be doing the pack run with us tonight."

Max loves his team building bullshit. If he doesn't have us hoofing a 10K run in full body armor and gear, he figures out something else to keep us occupied. Last time, he kept us scaling the hundred-foot cliffs that lead down to the beach all damn afternoon.

"Nope."

"You're not even going to try and sneak out?"

"No."

"Lucky bastard." Axel glances at the time.

I've got twenty seconds left and I'm struggling. Whoever thinks planking is for lightweights doesn't know shit.

Axel reaches out and knocks my elbow. He thinks to make me drop, but I know Axel's thoughts before his brain registers them. I brace for it and hold my position.

Ten seconds.

Axel wraps his hand around my elbow and tries to break my lock. I double-down and resist while growling at him.

Five seconds.

My shoulders are on fire. My abs tremble and burn with the exertion. My bum leg doesn't give one shit about this. Planks are all about the core and maybe a bit of shoulder girdle strength.

One second and I huff against the pain, soaking it in. Pain is a body's way of reminding us that we're not dead.

My alarm sounds an end to five minutes of torment and a new countdown begins. This was but the first of five rounds of this particular hell.

"You going to join me for the next four rounds?"

Axel rolls his eyes and gives a half-hearted groan. He glances at the rest of our team, who've naturally paired off in the gym.

"What did Skye say about rock climbing?" His gaze casts wistfully to the interior rock wall that dominates an entire side of the building. The modified hanger is forty feet tall and fifty yards long. The rock covers the entire length of the longest wall. Guardians don't just climb up rock walls. We traverse them too.

Planking isn't supposed to do shit for your quads, but my injured thigh throbs from the minimal exertion. I rub at it, conscious of Axel's gaze. His lips twist with worry.

"She said if I behave, she might let me join the team as support."

"Support?" His brow wings up.

"Yeah…"

"She does know you're a Guardian."

"She does, but she also has the final say on whether I sit on my ass here or sit on my ass supporting your ass."

"My ass doesn't need any support."

"Thank shit for that."

"So? No rock climbing, I take it?"

"Nope. I'm going to be a picture-perfect patient. What do you know about Moira?"

"I would've said something if I knew anything." He reaches out and grabs my shoulder, giving a hard squeeze. "We will find her."

"And I'll bring her home."

"And you'll bring her home." Axel gives me a look. We understand each other perfectly.

The timer on my phone beeps again. I flip back to my plank position and Axel joins me.

We don't talk about what will happen if Skye doesn't clear me from medical hold, but it's always on our minds. A Guardian is no good if he can't operate. And if I can't operate, who's going to rescue Moira?

Hang on, Moira, you're stronger than you know.

FIVE

Moira

"GET UP," BOSSMAN GROWLS AT ME.

When I don't move fast enough, he grabs me by the hair and gives a sharp yank. A howl escapes me as he hauls me to my feet. I grab at his wrist as my feet skate across the floor, trying to find purchase. I barely get my feet under me before he slams me into the corner.

"Stay there. Don't move."

Like I have anywhere to go. With fragile female tears streaming down my face, I slide down to the floor, where I draw up my knees and wrap my arms around them.

Here's where it gets tricky.

Playing Bossman is going to be much different, and infinitely harder, than what I did to Shelly. Shelly was a brute. His brain operated barely above base, primitive instincts. It's why he was more interested in raping me than staying alive.

Called that one right.

I'd give myself a high five, or fist bump, if I wasn't scared about these next few minutes. No time to mess up now. My opponent is a stalwart professional.

I huddle, knees bent, arms wrapped around myself, and force my terrified brain to think.

How do I escape my most current version of hell?

While I ponder my options, Bossman goes to Shelly's body and kicks it. The first kick is a light tap of frustration. The next is harder, more irritated than anything else, but then Bossman loses his cool.

He rears back and kicks Shelly's body in the head, the face, and the gut. He stamps down on Shelly's head, over and over again, until the bones crunch and brain matter oozes onto the floor. Bossman keeps it up, fists clenched, jaw bunched, and spit flying, as he lets the expletives fly.

"Fucking putz." Bossman's lips twist with distaste and his rage runs its course. "I told you what would happen if you touched the girl." Bossman stands over Shelly's body and props his hands on his hips. He pulls at his chin as if thinking through what comes next.

Well, I want to know what comes next too. As far as I can see, Bossman is down two men. Is this something he can do on his own? Deliver me to whichever monster ordered a sex slave to-go? Hell if I know, but right now, that's the only thing protecting me.

Bossman's a professional. Shelly was a goon. It's a vital distinction.

Fortunately, I know how to handle professional men. Goons aren't smart enough to accumulate the kind of wealth which allows for the luxury of a personal sex slave. Bossman isn't at that level—he's a step or two above a goon—but he understands what it takes. More importantly, he knows he's not there yet.

And I understand him.

Every now and again, his attention shifts to me. Each time, I cower and curl into a tighter ball.

I can't make myself look any more wretched. I'm terrified, weak, and female. Oh, and I just survived a near rape. These are things I don't need to pretend, but I'm also cold and calculating.

Bossman doesn't know that. From here on out, he'll see, and know, exactly what I want him to see and know.

I will figure a way out of this. With a sniff, I snivel like a woman terrified beyond words.

Bossman takes a step toward me. He glares and then turns away. This happens several times, until he heads to the door and slams his fist into the unforgiving metal.

Bam! Bam! Bam!

With each strike, I whimper. He expects it, and I give him everything he expects, and more.

He shakes out his fist, examines the blood on his knuckles, then stabs his fingers into his hair, smearing the blood everywhere. Bossman looks down at Shelly's body again.

"This is just fucking great." He kicks Shelly's body a few more times, then turns his attention to me.

His expression, equal parts irritation, concern, and fury would make the strongest man piss his pants. Yeah, I don't like that mix at all, but I've learned one crucial bit of information.

Seducing Bossman is off my exceedingly short list of things to do next.

The first thing on my list is hiding the knife I snatched from Shelly.

My shorts gape and practically fall off my hips. The button is gone, ripped off in Shelly's lust-blinded fury to rut and fuck. The zipper also gapes and appears to be broken after a very quick exploration with my fingers. I won't know if I can salvage it until I can get my shorts off and take a closer look.

That's not happening.

As for the knife, it's wedged between my ass cheeks right now and won't stay hidden for long. I'm thankful for the leather sheath protecting my backside from getting sliced and diced, but it's not something I can hide.

Right now, Bossman can't see it with my back to the wall, but if he does, I'm toast. The only thing keeping me alive right now are two things.

The first, Bossman is a businessman. That means while he has no soul, or shred of human decency, there are certain ethics which hold him to a standard, like not damaging the merchandise.

I'm far more valuable than the two men he killed who dared to damage the merchandise. The second, and far more important reason when it comes to my survival, is that he doesn't see me as a threat. That's my leverage right now.

It's my only leverage.

So, what am I going to do about the knife?

There's no way I can rush him. By the time I get to my feet, and remember anything Four taught me, Bossman will plant a bullet square between my eyes. He's far too dangerous to approach directly.

Think, Moira, think. What would Four tell you to do?

"Are you going to cause me any problems?" Bossman decides it's finally time to approach me.

I'm running out of time.

Normally, I would make myself as small as possible, but there's only so much cowering I can do. There's no way to tuck myself into a smaller ball. I look up with a trembling chin and tears streaming down my cheeks. The tears do nothing for Bossman, except tell him exactly what he wants. He terrifies me.

"Did he fuck you?"

I find it impossible to find my voice.

That's a lie. I have a whole hell of a lot I'd like to say right about now, but I'm too damn smart to let any of that out. He crouches down and gets in my space. Bossman displays dominance by physical intimidation. He did it to Shelly; now he's doing it to me.

He presses the pad of his fat forefinger right between my eyes.

"I asked you a question."

I give a shake of my head.

"Is that a yes? Or is that a no?" His deep voice rumbles and growls.

"N-no."

"Good." His mouth twists. "I'd hate to throw you overboard as well."

Can't help it. My lids draw back as a ripple of fear shoots through me.

Bossman tips his head back as he cackles. Laughter rips through him, but it's cold and completely devoid of emotion.

He presses on his thighs and stands. "Gotta clean up this mess or we'll be smelling Shelly's stink for the next four days."

Four days!

I practically shout with that small dribble of information. I'm on a ship for the next four days. That means I've got far more time than I realized.

With his back turned to me, I cast about my nearest surroundings. The room we're in is a bunk room with a set of bunk beds built into the wall and two storage cupboards fixed to each end. There's the tiniest crack between the bulkhead and cabinet, and it's the perfect place to stash a knife. Before Bossman turns his attention back on me, I hide the knife and breathe out a huge sigh.

I've got four days to figure something out.

"Bet you won't just sit there like a good girl."

Cruel eyes focus on me and I can't help the hitching of my breath.

"With Shelly gone, that's going to complicate things. I'm not supposed to keep you chained up like an animal. My delivery instructions are quite specific, but I don't think you'll behave if I leave you free, and there's no way I'm not chaining you up when I sleep. Tell me, Moira Stone, are you going to be a good girl? Or am I going to have to treat you like an animal?"

The lump that grows in my throat is massive, but I manage to swallow around it and find my voice. I'll do, and be, whatever it takes to survive.

"I'll be good." My voice trembles and shakes and I almost make a fatal mistake. I almost look him square in the eye.

Bossman is a businessman, a slave trader, or transporter. Honestly, I don't care what his job title is. He's the one who communicates with his clients, and he covets the power they wield. I read every damn tell, and he's telling me so damn much right now.

A song comes to mind. This is where my mind goes when the world messes with me. Instead of one hundred beers on the wall, I hum a little ditty in my head.

~

Three human traffickers to take down.
Three human traffickers to take down.
Bite a dick, shoot a prick,
One human trafficker to take down.

~

LET'S NOT JUDGE MY LYRICAL SKILLS. I'M A BIT STRESSED right now.

"And I guess I can't get you to help with this mess." He looks back at me.

I let my frightened eyes grow wider.

"Didn't think so. You're going to cost me a shit ton of money. I'd toss you over if I could." He scratches at his head. "I'm going to lock you up. I'd ask the crew to help, but since they don't know about you, that won't work. So, you're going to help me. Aren't you?"

My brows pinch together with confusion. Why would I help him?

He snaps his fingers and points to the bunk.

"Grab that blanket." When I don't move, a feral growl catches in his throat.

One of the most terrifying sounds I've ever heard, it's enough to practically levitate me off the floor. With a hand pressed against the wall for balance, I wobble on my feet and look to him for direction. I know what he's going to do, I just don't want to do it.

He points to the blanket again and I move.

Tugging it free of the paper-thin mattress, I gather it in my arms. Bossman kicks at Shelly's body again, this time with intent.

Slowly, he straightens out Shelly's legs and places the body in a straight line. He comes to me and searches for the end of the blanket. Grabbing a corner, he tugs while I continue to stare like a woman slowly losing her mind from shock.

He steps back and lowers down on his knees. Bossman tugs on the blanket, telling me what to do without words. I bend down and place a knee on the unforgiving concrete floor. The uneven surface pokes against my kneecap, but I don't mention a word about pain. There will be enough of that later.

The two of us work together like we've been rolling corpses into blankets together for years. Once Shelly's body is covered, Bossman looks down at his handiwork.

"Shit. Unwrap him."

Again, my brows tug together.

He shakes his finger at the blanket. "Need his belt to tie it all up."

We unroll the body and Bossman frees Shelly's belt from his pants. He stops for a second, then points to his boots. "Undo the laces and hand them here."

Being the absolute best body-rolling partner on the planet, I get to work on Shelly's laces. Once I get them free, I hand them over to Bossman, who makes quick work of a knot, tying them together.

He, once again, instructs me on what to do, and we re-wrap Shelly. The belt goes around the shoulders. Bossman snugs it tight. Then he uses the laces to wrap the blanket securely just above Shelly's knees.

Looking satisfied, he takes inventory of our work, then turns that hardened gaze to me.

"Time to lock you up."

In all honesty, getting tied up is not one of my favorite things. In fact, it's one of my worst memories, but now is not the time for a full-on meltdown from my traumatic past. I put to use all the techniques taught to me while at the Facility to halt a flashback in its tracks.

Bossman has skills. An expert at rope, he trusses me up before I process what's happening. He sits me on the bunk bed I stripped of its blanket.

"Hands together."

While I fight my panic attack, he loops a length of rope around, through, and over my head, securing my hands to a bottom support of the bunk overhead. Why he didn't use that to truss up Shelly's body is a goddamn mystery, but what do I know?

Without my help, he goes to his knees. With a lot of grunting, cursing, and pissed off words about what a scumbag idiot prick Shelly was, he manages to get Shelly over his shoulder.

Which sucks for me.

Bossman is much stronger than I realized. Makes that little knife seem super inadequate.

He places his hand on the doorknob and looks back at me. "If you scream, or let anyone know you're in here, I will slit your throat, and you won't know if I stand out here and wait a bit just to see if you do. Do we understand each other?"

With my hands slowly going numb from the knots he tied around my wrists, I give a very shaky nod.

And this is a fun twist.

I sweeten the pot. With a submissive gaze, eyes lowered to the floor, I throw the bastard a bone.

"Yes, sir."

As expected, he takes in a breath and appears to stand a few inches taller. No lie, but he puffs out his chest, a feat considering he's got a dead man draped over his shoulder.

Yeah, Bossman wants his own damn pleasure slave. Not an unwilling woman trafficked for her flesh, but someone like me. He wants a woman trained in the art of giving pleasure, a woman beaten into abject submission.

I really hate this shitty life, but I'm damn good at living it. As for being a billionaire's pleasure slave? Hello? I'm still alive and kicking. I rock that shit.

Just don't want to do it again.

Been there.

Done that.

Got the scars to prove it.

I say that a lot.

Probably too much.

I'm becoming a broken record—although, me and broken are two peas in a pod.

Despite what he says, Bossman doesn't stick around. He's smart. There are crew on board this ship with absolutely no clue the two men who procured passage on a steamer, or tanker, or whatever the kind of ship this is, have a stowaway on board. They also don't know one of those passengers is now dead and getting dumped into the sea—or ocean.

What does it matter? Shelly is now fodder for bottom dwellers. I think that is some awesome karmic justice.

Honestly, I'm guessing we're in the Gulf of Mexico. It seems to be a hotspot for transporting slaves from tourist destinations in the Gulf to Colombia.

Colombia.

What the hell happened to Zoe?

I say a prayer for my friend, hoping somebody rescued her.

Although, knowing her Guardian, a man I know as Three, but Zoe knows as Axel, I bet he tore through heaven and earth to find and free his girl. He did it once, and he'll do it again.

There's no stopping a Guardian in love.

But I don't have that. All I have is me.

I'm the broken doll stuck trying to save herself. What I wouldn't give for a Guardian to save me.

Right now, the key to my survival is abject obedience to anything and everything Bossman wants. A shiver of revulsion ripples down my spine. I've done sick and twisted things in the past, but this is going to take me to a whole other level of hell.

Bossman wants a willing and compliant slave? Why is it that the weakest men are the ones who do the most vile things?

I'll give him a taste of willing and compliant, at least until I kill him.

What's that going to feel like?

Bossman killed two men recently, and I sense zero remorse in my captor. It's like business as usual. He's more irritated than anything else. There's not an ounce of compassion, or regret, in Bossman. He's just pissed he's going to have to watch over me all by himself. He'd like to think he's all that, but he's nothing more than another cheap Joe.

Been there.

Done that.

Haven't we discussed this enough?

I know men like Bossman. I may have precipitated Jack and Shelly's deaths, but I didn't kill them. Bossman made that decision. Their deaths are on him.

As for me?

Bossman will be the first person, and hopefully the last, that I'll kill.

Surprised?

Don't be. With the shitty life I've been dealt, I'm due one murder guilt free.

And I wonder how it's going to change me? Honestly, I don't think it'll do a damn thing. Thinking about killing him stirs nothing inside of me.

Like, nothing.

That kind of thing is supposed to leave a mark on your soul, but I feel like I'll be leaving the world a better place.

Fuck Bossman.

Fuck me.

Fuck this shitty life.

If God wanted my soul to be white and pristine, he would've dealt me a different hand. As it is, I'll present myself at the pearly white gates with ire and spite, demanding entrance for the evil I wiped from the face of the world.

I'll begin with Bossman, and I don't care what that does to my eternal soul. I won't grieve the murder of a killer.

I give a start as I doze and jerk back awake. With my hands tied over my head, I can't lie down. I can't lean against the bulkhead. There is no getting comfortable, but I drift, and I doze. Somewhere in the wretchedness of my dreams, I dream of an avenging angel; a Guardian sent to redeem my soul.

In particular, I dream of Four.

But that doesn't happen.

Instead, some interminable time later, Bossman returns carrying two plates steaming with food. He enters the small cabin and closes the door behind him. He unties my hands and shoves one of the plates beneath my nose.

"Eat." He scoops a spoonful of slop into his mouth. "Your Master won't be pleased if you're skin and bones."

For a moment, the briefest of moments, I wonder if engaging him in conversation is worth my time, but Bossman's piss-poor attitude remains. He doesn't give a shit about me, and I couldn't care less about him.

We eat in silence, and after I'm done, the rope wraps back around my wrists.

For three days, we repeat this same routine. Bossman ties me up, disappears beyond that door, and returns sometime later to feed and water his charge. He rarely speaks and the scowl on his face deepens with each passing day.

The tension between us rises, and all I can think about is how I can cut through my bonds, and slit his throat, before he can kill me.

SIX

Moira

THREE DAYS PASS AND I'M NO CLOSER TO DEVISING A PLAN OF ESCAPE than the day Shelly died—Correction: the day he was put down like the animal he was. I prefer to think of it that way rather than "murdered on top of me."

I cling to the little things in life to save my sanity, and that is a very little thing.

I'm well aware of what awaits me at the end of this voyage. Thinking about it twists my insides into gnarled tangles I can't unravel.

With each passing hour, it becomes more urgent to do something.

The problem is, how do I take down a man nearly twice as strong as me inside the confines of a tiny ship's stateroom? Is that even the right word? Hell, if I know.

When Bossman is around, I play the role of a meek and mild female who's lost the will to fight. That first night, right after Shelly's death, I kept my eyes down and complied with every command Bossman gave. There was no fight when he ordered me to climb into the top bunk and no struggle when he tied me up for the night.

None.

And I have a phobia of getting tied up.

The morning after the whole head-bashing and brain-spilling event, I went to work cleaning up the gore after Bossman finished his breakfast. I used one of the threadbare towels from the small lavatory attached to our cabin to scoop up the gory mess and flush it down the toilet. Then I used toilet water to rinse that fetid towel and mop everything up, over and over again.

Not my best day, and I've had some pretty shitty days. As for doing disgusting things, *been there, done that, got the scars to prove it.* I should make that my little jingle.

It would be a killer tune.

I'll say this. Mopping up Shelly's brains takes the cake when it comes to disgusting things.

It took the better part of the day to scour away the bloodstains, but I'm proud of my handiwork. I can barely see the blood anymore.

Bossman watched me on hands and knees, saying nothing, fantasizing about everything. He thought to hide his arousal, but recognizing a horny man is one of my superpowers.

When he excused himself and shut the door to the lavatory, I knew exactly what he was doing, and it didn't take him long for the filthy thoughts in his head to speed his release.

I had two goals and accomplished them with five glowing stars. The first was to clean up the mess before it made the small cabin stink.

Check. Done.

My second goal was to set the stage for Bossman and enflame his desire. Me on my knees, serving him, even though he never asked me to clean up the mess, planted a seed in his head.

Bossman's tired of being the transporter and deliverer of slaves. He's ready for the main event—ready to be the monster on the other side of the transaction.

After the day Shelly died, he left the cabin several times, sometimes returning with food, sometimes not. I made it a point to never sit on the lower bunk.

That's his spot.

And since he always sits on the one small chair at the tiny desk, doing whatever he does on that phone of his, I eat on the floor, where I swallow down my pride and the slop he feeds me.

We rarely speak.

In my spare time, I relocate Shelly's knife dozens of times but never find an opening to use it. My hiding places are too secure. Getting to it quickly and easily must be a priority. I finally return it to its original hiding place. Honestly, I don't know what I'm going to do with it.

I'm high as a kite if I think I'll survive a knife fight with a man who keeps a gun tucked into the back of his pants. My hope is he'll accidentally pull the trigger and shoot his ass off. Now that would be hysterical.

Some of Four's lessons come to mind, ways to wield a knife and disable my opponent. The thing is, Bossman is much stronger than me. The cabin is small, just the bunk and the desk with its utilitarian chair. This place isn't much larger than a prison cell.

So yeah, it's problematic.

Bossman rewards my good behavior on the evening of the third day. He leaves the cabin without tying me to the top bunk.

Freedom!

I feel like William Wallace leading his Scottish clansmen on a charge down the battlefield.

Don't ask. This is my brain and this is where it takes me.

Not that I do anything with my newfound freedom except sit in his chair. Yes, I plop my sore ass on his chair. It hurts from sitting on the hard concrete. With nothing to do, my imagination fills with all kinds of fantasies.

Most of them have to do with leading a normal life. My life is a disaster. You'd think my fantasies would be pretty damn epic. But they're not. They're exceedingly normal.

I'd give anything to be boring and uninteresting, but most importantly, safe from the monsters in this world. For whatever reason, they seem to think they own me.

Seriously, that's as salacious as my fantasies get.

I've never lived anything close to normal. No first date. No night at prom. No homecoming dances. No boring high school classes or competitive sports. I never had the chance to go to school after that bitch of a foster mother tossed me to the curb at twelve.

My school education came to a sudden and frightening end, but I learned on the streets. I learned how to survive. How to manipulate men. And most importantly, how not to die.

My lack of an official education is one of many things the people at the Facility were helping me with. I still have a year, or so, left to get my GED. I had hopes of going to college. Doing *what* is anyone's guess, but after my rescue in the Philippines by the Guardians, I experienced hope for the first time.

Now, instead of learning all the impossible poses of the Kama Sutra, I know how to read at the high school level and manage my non-existent finances.

She shoots. She scores! The fans go wild.

It's my brain and my tangents. Deal with it.

Somehow, the hours pass. I don't know what Bossman does out there all day. Sometimes he comes back hot and sweaty, breathing hard. My assumption is that there's a gym on board where he works out to maintain his muscled physique. Or, maybe, he runs the decks. The man is a powerhouse of muscle. Those are the only times he changes out of his pants and into shorts. He swaps out his boots for sneakers as well. And he takes both his knife and his gun when he goes.

Oh, and the phone.

What I wouldn't give for him to leave that behind.

As for what he does leave behind, there's nothing helpful.

Bossman packs light, but I win on who packs the lightest. All I have are my bikini top and bottom, my tank top, and my shorts with the zipper I managed to fix.

As for the chair thing, the moment the door opens and Bossman returns, I slide out of the chair and go to my knees. This is how I greet him, feeding his fantasy, but like I said, Bossman is smart.

I think I'm smarter. If anything, my motivation is greater. I'm banking on that to get me out of this mess.

He glances at me and does a full sweep of my body as my gaze lowers to his feet, where my rage simmers. I never look at him directly.

"Good news, slave." He's taken to calling me that. It started two days ago and I feed his hunger as much as I can. There is a line in the sand. I found it, and it's one he won't cross. Which sucks and pretty much leaves my plans at an impasse.

"Yes, sir?" I play it up.

"Tonight's our last night together." He sounds wistful, but all I hear is *last night*.

Time is running out.

"Sir?"

"You heard me. We pull into port tomorrow."

"And then what happens?"

Meek. Mild. Subdued.

My voice comes out whisper-soft, but not so soft that it's a strain for him to hear me.

"You meet your Master."

Here I go, falling down a rabbit hole.

"And what about you? Will you still be there to take care of me?"

God, I hope not. He disgusts me.

He tugs off his shirt and stops midway as he draws it over his chest. His entire body locks up and a gleam simmers in his gaze. It's there and gone before I know it.

"Unfortunately, not." Bossman seems genuinely sad, the fat bastard.

Well, he's not fat. The man's stacked with muscle. Intimidating, hard muscles. But he's most definitely a bastard. I wonder if his mother ever loved him.

What kind of childhood did a kid like him have that turned him into a monster like this? Like, at what point does a little boy say, "'You know what? When I become a man, I want to murder, maim, and enslave?"

Like, is there a sign-up sheet for that kind of thing?

I had a pretty shitty childhood, but I'm not out there murdering and maiming.

Wait, I may have bit off a man's dick. I'm still not convinced I did that, but I'm no murderer.

"I see." I bow my head and try not to swallow my tongue as the next words leave my lips. "Thank you for taking care of me."

Modesty between us in this small space does not exist. He forces me to use the lavatory with the door open and leaves it open when he's taking a piss. The only time he closes the door is if he's taking a dump, jerking off, or using the shower.

I have not been provided that luxury, not the jerking off thing. Gross! I meant the shower. I'm still finding Santa Monica sand in very private places. That stuff is persistent. Those tiny grains are the bane of my existence. Well, next to the whole captured and transported to be a sex-slave thing—again.

This is Strike Two!

Bossman tosses his shirt on the lower bunk, then peels out of his shorts. His naked ass doesn't interest me, except in determining how to take him down. No way am I going for the dick biting thing. Bossman gets props for being well-endowed, and he's proud of his monster cock.

I think I've got things figured out. There will be only one chance to get this right.

He surprises me when he leaves the door to the bathroom open. My gaze follows and my breath hitches when he stops in front of the small shower enclosure. It's basically a coffin standing up on edge. There's no real way to turn around inside of it. He slides open the door and turns the water to hot, but that's not what really surprises me.

I gasp when he grabs the root of his cock. He, in turn, grins like a motherfucker. The man won't touch me, but he wants me to watch.

Revulsion rips through me.

He's jerking himself off because of what I said.

But I'm ready.

It's now or never.

SEVEN

Moira

OKAY, WORST CASE SCENARIO?

I mess this up and he kills me.

Best case scenario, I take him out.

I may, or may not, survive. In all honesty, if I die, is that really a major loss? My life hasn't exactly been useful. It's not like I'm Forest Summers with his Guardian Hostage Rescue Specialists out rescuing stolen people, or his sister, Skye Summers, who literally saves lives for a living. I haven't made a difference in other people's lives like they have.

If I die tonight, nobody will mourn my passing. I have no mother. She OD'd riding the lethal high of whatever substance she injected in her veins. My father walked away. Or ran. He probably ran from the waste of human flesh my mother was. My foster parents probably had high aspirations for the poor, wretched child they took in. Little did they know I was damaged goods.

It's not my fault foster daddy dipped his dick in my unwilling flesh. And it's not my fault foster mommy blamed me and then kicked me out. None of it is my fault.

But all of it is my burden to bear. Honestly, it's not fair. Mom, dad, foster dad, and foster mom, they can all screw themselves. Not that they care. Not that I matter. As for me, I'm going to take control of my existence on this wretched planet. That begins with ending Bossman's putrid life.

I'm not ready to say murder, although that's my intent.

I'm going to kill Bossman.

That's the truth I shy away from. In this shitty life, I've been pushed to this place. I'm going to take a life or lose mine. Either way, I lose. I'll have to live with the burden of—the burden of—the burden of what? Putting a monster in the ground?

For the past three days, it's all I've thought about.

Kill or be killed.

You know, I deserve a medal. The idea of taking a life is taking a toll on me, and to be completely honest, I'm pissed. Why should I care about Bossman when he doesn't care about me?

I'm going to kill him.

There are no ifs, ands, or buts. One of us is going to die. I don't want that person to be me. So, that means I need to kill him.

I'm the victim. Right?

I *am* the victim.

I feel like if I say it with enough conviction, the Choir of Angels will take notice and agree.

I repeat this again and again. As if saying it makes it so.

I am the victim!

Cue dramatic movie score.

Yeah, I hear the static.

Does it matter? My excuses? Do they justify my actions?

There's nobody to ask. Like, I have nobody to bounce these crazy ideas off of—am I a sinner?—a saint?—am I the devil incarnate?

Hell, if I know.

But I'm pissed. I'm angry and I hate God.

Why did he put me in this position? Why is he testing me like this? Thou shall not kill. It's one of the Commandments. Like top ten. Yes, there are only ten. I know this, but come on. I'm contemplating murder.

I'm rationalizing killing another human being. Where the hell is my guiding light?

Nowhere. That's where. It's just me, and I'm justifying my actions.

This is wrong. Right?

I've thought about what it will take to kill Bossman, and it doesn't look good. He's too big. I'm too small. He's too strong. I'm too weak. And what would I use to tie him up? My hair?

What I do know is one of us isn't making it out of this room.

I scoot to the foot of the bunk, staying on my knees. Bossman glances at me and the speed of his strokes ramps up. That lopsided grin on his face turns into a line of deep concentration as he chases his release. He's stroking himself, fantasizing about me, and all I want to do is puke.

I'm virtually certain he won't rape me, but it remains a possibility. I've played up to his Master/slave fantasies enough to make any sane man break. I mean, this is almost exactly what I've asked for, but Bossman's not a normal man.

He's not sane.

No one in his line of work can be, but he has standards. Bossman has standards he won't break. Whatever moral creed he hangs onto doesn't allow messing with the merchandise.

With all of this going through my head, I reach into my hiding place and slide the grip of Shelly's knife into my hand. My Guardian's words run through my head.

Four was training me in hand-to-hand combat, not the offensive kind, but rather defensive maneuvers. My sole goal was to escape Four's grasp. He never went easy on me.

Never.

God, I love that bastard's commitment to training. Four's words run through my head. His words ring crystal clear like he's right here with me—if only that were the case.

Four is formidable. He wouldn't let Bossman intimidate him. He'd go toe-to-toe, chest-to-chest, nose-to-nose, and he'd come out victorious. Four would wipe the mat with Bossman. What I wouldn't give to have him here with me now.

"Commit, Moira. Commit with every cell in your body. Commit. When you fight, you fight for your life. Don't hold back. And if you have any doubts, stand down. Wait and find your opening, then commit." His stony glare made me gulp at the time, but I remember his words.

And I remember him.

Ferociously beautiful, Four's all sculpted beauty and deadly grace. He's the living personification of what it means to be an Alpha male. Four isn't pretty. He's all hard angles with scars that speak to a challenging past. The epitome of male perfection—at least as I define it—he's rugged, brutal, and raw. Fucking perfect, and so damn yummy.

"And what about fear? How do I work through my fear?" I feared Four. How was I, a slip of a girl, ever going to get away from him?

"Fear is a mind-killer. It has no place when fighting for your life. Use your fear or abandon it. But don't you dare let it make you hesitate. Commit and follow through."

He worked relentlessly to train me, locking me in death holds, forcing me to put everything I had into the fight, capturing me time and time again.

As time passed, those holds became excruciatingly intimate and sexually fueled. I wanted him. Desired him, but like Bossman, Four has his infuriating limits. There are lines he won't cross, and boy did I tempt him.

Or tried to.

He retaliated in the worst possible way.

The first man who ever made me feel something close to real attraction, rejected my advances. It crushed me. He crushed me.

Four pissed me off. I hungered for him, yet he drew a line in the sand, placing a barrier I could never cross. For a girl who never failed to get her man, I didn't understand what the hell was happening.

Men want me. They pay for the privilege of having me, first on the streets and then in more intimate surroundings. Men desire me. They pursue me. Never in my life has a man rejected me. Yet, that's exactly what Four did. He threw up barriers I could never cross.

Crushing on the teacher much?

Most definitely.

Head over heels, I've got one major lady boner for Four. Sadly, life sucks, and mine, in particular, sucks big-assed monkey balls.

Well, Four, I'm committed. I'm terrified as all get out and fear I'll fuck this up, but I'm committed.

This is the fight for my life. So, I commit. I commit with Four's words churning through my head, coaching me, testing me, infuriating me with the stoic distance he placed between us, but most importantly with his words telling me I can do anything if I put my mind to it.

Anything?

Like kill?

Is that what he thought when he said I could do anything? *"You, sweet Moira, my little minx, you will become a killing machine."*

Is that what he thinks? If he really does believe in me, and if I do somehow manage to get out of this, the first thing I'm doing when I see him is jump the man's bones.

He's hot, and I've got the hots for my teacher. I like him, and he's the only man on the planet who doesn't want me. That makes him insanely attractive. And let's get real here. After this shit show, I deserve to ease this terrible ache within me.

The moment I see his scruffy face, I'm either going to put that scruff to use between my thighs, or demand he make good use of what's between his legs—meaning the whole sliding in-and-out thing.

But first, there's the small problem of me being a captive sex-slave waiting to be delivered to a monster thing to overcome.

I focus on the present and commit.

My fingers curl around the knife's handle and I wait.

"Commit, Moira. You're stronger than you know. I believe in you." Four's words lend me strength. I'm glad he believes in me. With Four's words of encouragement spurring me on, I do exactly what he taught me. I empty my mind and focus on my task. This time, I'm not fighting to free myself from one of Four's impossible holds.

My intent is to take a life.

Bossman makes no secret of what he's doing. At first, he keeps his back to me, but he turns around in the tiny shower and faces me. The water pouring over him hides most of the sound, but his grunts deepen as he reaches a frenzy.

I close my eyes, keeping my senses attuned to what he's doing, and maintain my submissive posture. I want him to see me on my knees. To imagine I'm there for him. To see me as weak and no threat.

His grunts and groans escalate, ending with a shout as his release takes him. He washes up. The water turns off.

I brace.

Commit, Moira. Four's words fill my mind, almost as if he's here with me, and I commit.

Bossman slides open the shower enclosure.

He dries himself with a towel.

On my knees, I position myself right beside the lavatory door, tucked up back against the wall. He must walk past me, which is exactly what he does.

Bossman takes one step. I bow my head.

He takes another step.

I lunge and draw the sharp blade over the back of his heel, slicing deep to sever his Achilles tendon on the left.

I don't stop.

I grab his other ankle and slice through that Achilles too. Disabled, and effectively hobbled, he's still a formidable threat. Bossman drops like a load of bricks, howling and clawing at me.

Commit! Four stays with me, coaching me, and pushing me to follow through. *Don't hold back! Defend yourself.*

"You fucking cunt." Bossman's eyes grow wide as I launch on top of him. With his hands wrapped around his legs, I easily pin his arms.

His throat's exposed.

Commit!

Dissociated from what's happening, l watch from outside my body.

My arm comes down. The steel edge of the knife cuts through his skin. I miss the artery but hit the jugular.

He knocks me off. One hand goes to his throat while his murderous eyes take me in. He grabs my neck with his free hand, squeezing the tender tissues and choking my breath.

Black spots swim in my vision as I try to loosen his grip on my neck. I pry one finger free and gulp air.

There's blood everywhere. It pours out of his neck. His legs kick, smearing more blood from the cuts at the back of his heels. His blood saturates my tank top and seeps into my shorts. It mats my hair as he rolls on top of me.

He reaches down with his other hand to grip my neck, but the gash in his neck reopens. Blood spills out, splashing on my face and his hand goes back to his throat to stem the tide.

One of us is going to die.

I just hope it's not me.

We knock around a bit. Each time he tries to grab me, he releases the hold on his neck. Blood pours out. He intermittently chokes me, and I nearly pass out, but his attacks grow weaker with each passing second.

In my head, as I planned this out, I imagined a much quicker death, but Bossman doesn't give up without a fight. He bleeds out, making one hell of a mess, but finally his movements slow. His hand slaps at me. His fingers curl but fail to grab. I scoot away, backing up toward the door leading out of this cabin. He tries to crawl toward me.

I don't know what happened to the knife. Somewhere in our struggle, he knocked it free. Bossman makes one last attempt to reach me, falling short by a finger's breadth. His murderous eyes stare at me with the promise of death, but then they weaken and lose their sharpness.

He swipes at my ankles, then takes a final gurgling breath. His entire body goes limp, and I sit there, leaning against the door, with my knees drawn up to my chest.

Not really sure how long I sit there, I can't believe he's dead, but eventually, I poke him with my toe. When he doesn't react, I grow bolder, and give his shoulder a little shake.

The entire room looks like a scene out of a horror show. Blood is everywhere. It's smeared on the floor and coats Bossman's body head to toe. It's in my hair and soaked through my clothes.

I poke Bossman one more time and wait for what feels like forever to see if he breathes, but there's no movement, no life left in his body. His soulless eyes stare at the wall.

Now what?

How about a shower?

I don't know if the crew outside are going to miss Bossman. I'm guessing they won't. He spends most of his time locked inside with me. I spin around and double-check the door lock.

My guess is the crew doesn't care about their passengers, which is good for me. There's no rush to do anything right off the bat.

I rip the blanket off the top bunk and lay it over Bossman's body and the floor. The blanket squishes a little as I walk over it and make my way to the tiny bathroom.

The shower is still wet from Bossman, but I don't give a damn about that. I turn on the water and crank up the heat. One look in the mirror and I look like a horror show survivor. Blood covers my face and saturates my hair. I'm a natural blond, but look like a brunette with hints of blood red. A shiver of disgust works its way down my spine.

There are very few toiletries, but I use what's left from Shelly and Bossman. With steam filling the small lavatory, I enter the tiny shower enclosure and wash all traces of blood from my body and my clothes. Yes, I enter the shower fully clothed. For the first five minutes, I do nothing other than stand under the hot stream of water while having a major meltdown.

After that, I plan out my next steps. Bossman said tomorrow morning I'll meet my Master. We're headed into a port. Where? I have no earthly clue where, but there's no way I'm meeting up with any man who claims to be my Master.

So, what next?

My first thought is to contact one of the crew, but not knowing how much they know about Bossman and his very important cargo, there's no way to know if they'll lock me up and hand me over to the monster waiting for me. At the very least, they should lock me up for murder. I might be safe in the hands of whatever local authorities exist, but police are too easily bought.

I can't count on the crew.

Between now and whenever we dock, I need to find a way off this ship.

While my brain works on the problem of how to rescue myself, I focus on washing away the blood from my body and my clothes.

Raw from scrubbing, my skin tingles as I rinse again. Honestly, I've washed and rinsed nearly ten times. It feels as if I can't wash away Bossman's blood, but my hair is once again a golden yellow and my skin practically glistens. The water gets turned off and I exit the shower. There are no towels.

I'm really glad I put the blanket over Bossman's body. The thick fabric soaks up most of the blood, and I'm able to pick a path toward the door without getting my feet bloody. My lack of footwear will be a problem, but there's nothing to do about that. Whether I lost my sandals on the beach back in Santa Monica or somewhere in transit between here and there is a moot point.

It's time to head outside and figure a way off this ship, but I hesitate. My hand rests on the doorknob, and I find myself filled with fear.

This is different from living with Bossman these past few days. It's different from the terror rushing through me when Shelly tried to rape me.

For some crazy reason, this tiny cabin is my refuge. Does Stockholm syndrome apply to places? Because if it does, I'm oddly attached to this small space and incredibly fearful of whatever I may find out there.

And what am I going to find? This is a ship, a large one. I've figured that out, and my assumption is that this is one of those cargo tankers. So where does that leave me? If I can't approach the crew, then do I stay in here?

I don't know, but I have to leave sometime. Then what? Hide?

Where would I hide?

There's still the matter of getting off the ship. I'm pretty sure I won't be able to waltz off. There will be questions, and those questions lead right back to the dead body in this room.

What I need is a rescue. Fortunately, I know a few Guardians who happen to be pretty damn good at rescuing damsels in distress.

But how to contact them?

Use a phone idiot. A quick search around the cabin and I locate Bossman's cellphone.

When I pick it up, it tries to unlock using facial recognition, but my face is the wrong face and I don't know the passcode. Over the past few days, I should've paid better attention.

But I do have one very important person's face. Hopefully, the phone will unlock with a dead man's face. Not wanting to, but having no other choice, I peel back the blanket to reveal Bossman's face.

It's a bit of a struggle, but I eventually get the phone to unlock.

Now what?

First things first, what's the time? That's easily answered without any effort. Just past nine, it's still early evening. I don't know how crew hours and shifts work, but I'm going to assume the graveyard shift is sparsely manned. No idea why I'd think that, but I'm working with very little information right now.

I need to call for help, but Bossman's phone is nearly dead.

Quickly, I type in the emergency code drilled into all our heads, but when it comes time to input my personal code, the phone shuts off —dead.

Fuck! Why can't I catch a break?

There must be a charging cord. It's not at the desk. There's no outlet there. So where would he plug in his phone and why did it never occur to me to pay attention?

I'm really not very good at this rescuing business.

I close my eyes and take a few breaths. *Come on, Moira, you can do this.*

EIGHT

Griff

AXEL AND I SPEND TWO LONG HOURS IN THE GYM, NOT AN uncommon occurrence for us, but me staying away from anything that might mess with my leg is different.

We repeat it all the next day and the next. With each passing day, my hopes for finding Moira sink. My leg is slowly getting better. It's still not fully functional, but I'm babying it every day. If something changes, I will be on that mission.

Axel and I are at the chin-up bar, on the last of five brutal cycles of one hundred pull-ups followed by one hundred push-ups.

My entire upper body is spent, muscles scream, acid burns, and fatigue saps my reserves. I can go for hours more, if the situation demands it, but CJ enters the far side of the gym and cups his hands over his mouth. His deep, resonating voice bellows across the massive Guardian gym.

"Buckle up, bitches. We've got to go." He circles his hand over his head and points to the door. Without waiting to see if we heard, he does an abrupt about-face and marches back out the way he came.

"Do you think?" I'm too afraid to hope.

"Could be, or…" Axel doesn't finish his sentence. It could be a different mission.

We get called at all hours of the day as missions pop up. As a Guardian, life's not much different from what it was during my team days. The only real difference between what I do now, and what I did in the military, is that we're well funded now.

Instead of going into battle wearing gear cobbled together with what was offered, from my helmet with its integrated electronics, to the titanium lining the tips of my boots, I'm not only a ferocious warrior, but a technological marvel. We all are.

Thanks to Forest, who created the Guardians, and his top-notch technical team, we have the best gear and the latest technological advances to ensure success.

Everyone at Guardian HRS has their role. The Guardians are the pointy tip of the spear. We're the muscle that gets hard shit done, while Mitzy and her cadre of computer whiz kids form the complex innards of the machine which launches us into action.

I drop from the chin-up bar and wince when I inadvertently land on my bad leg. Nothing tears, but I understand Doc Summers' caution. It won't take much to shred her handiwork.

"There's only one way to tell." Axel grabs his towel and wipes off the sheen of perspiration covering his face and torso. I do the same. I'm dripping with sweat.

"Let's go." I'm eager to find out if Moira's been found. Going in as support doesn't sit well with me, but I'll take that over sitting here on my ass while my team goes without me.

Axel lopes into a jog, takes a few steps, then pulls up short. He spins around and waits for me to follow. A crease furrows his brow.

"Just following doctor's orders." I understand his confusion, but I need to be on this mission. Especially if Mitzy pulled a goddamn rabbit out of her ass and found Moira.

I grab my duffel and sling it over my shoulder. We join Max, Knox, Liam, and Wolfe at the door. They all wait on me to cross the distance. I focus on each step, remembering what Doc Summers said about a limp. Not happy with being the weak link in the chain, I brace against the pain.

A team is only as strong as the weakest link, and right now, that's me. The expressions on their faces are not those of pity or concern, but rather stalwart support. All of us have been doing this for years, first in the military special ops community and now as Guardians.

I'm not the first man to have been sidelined by an injury.

"You know what this is about?" I ask our team leader, Max, as Axel and I draw near. Max always knows shit before the rest of us.

"No." He answers with an economy of words, as his astute gaze takes me in. His attention settles on my leg. "What did the doc say?"

"Not mission-ready, but I'm clear for support."

"If it's Moira…" Max doesn't need to finish his sentence.

Everybody on this team knows what Moira means to me. They'll take care of her in my place, and if there's a way to bend the rules, they'll do what they can to bring me along.

It's a concession.

Max won't jeopardize the integrity of the team, but he knows what it's like to sit on the sidelines. That lack of control can drive a Guardian batty.

"Let's do this." As for my part, I don't push.

It's not my place to ask him to take a teammate on a mission when I'm not one hundred percent functional. As team leader, if the opportunity presents itself, Max will make the final call.

My team parts, letting me lead the way. It's another silent display of support. I love these guys, and would do anything for them, just as they'll do anything for me.

We march as a group toward the command center and file into the strategy room. A large conference table dominates the space. The high polish of the wood reflects the glow of over a score of video screens which mount to the wall and surround the room. One screen dominates the far wall, spanning the breadth of the room.

CJ's already there. He and Sam speak in subdued tones. The two of them bend their heads close to keep their conversation private.

The first thing I notice is that Alpha team is the only Guardian team present. That means this will be a targeted operation.

Mitzy flits into the room with a huge smile on her heart-shaped face. Her psychedelic hair shimmers in the overhead lights, and I swear she added glitter to her signature look. She reminds me of a pixie who sprinkles fairy dust everywhere she goes.

"Hey, guys." She gives a little flap of her hand, then joins CJ and Sam.

Where CJ is the commander of the Guardians, overseeing Alpha, Bravo, Charlie, and Delta teams, she commands the technical and intelligence teams.

Mitzy would rip me a new one if I ever said that out loud. She and her techies don't like being compared to the military side of our operation. Their idea of command structure is loose as a goose, which makes no sense to me.

Alpha team take our seats at the table while Sam, CJ, and Mitzy carry on their conversation, a conversation that comes to a dead halt the moment Doc Summers and her foster brother, Forest, enter the room.

I'd say our sudden silence is due to the formidable presence of Forest. Guardians are big men. We're all well over six feet in height and in prime physical condition, but Forest towers over us all. His glacial gaze and shock-white hair remind me of a Norse god or Viking King, but the diminutive woman standing in front of him is no less ferocious. Her power comes from a silent strength imbued in every cell in her body and the sharp intelligence sparking in her eyes.

Those two founded Guardian Hostage Rescue Specialists. They survived incredible abuse at the hands of their foster father, who rented them out for sexual favors. One of those monsters was Forest's nemesis, John Snowden, who took great pleasure in the pain he inflicted on them both. Neither of those men remain among the living.

Forest waits for his sister, Skye, to take a seat, pulling out a chair for her at the other end of the table. He scoots her in, then folds his towering frame into the chair beside her. His glacial gaze sweeps down the table, taking in his Guardians, then returns to Mitzy.

"Tell me you found her." His deep voice vibrates the air, felt more than heard.

Mitzy presses her lips together and turns toward the screen. She takes the remote from on top of the table and aims it at the control panel for the AV equipment. A map of the world pops up on the far wall and quickly zooms in on the Gulf of Mexico.

"I did." She bites her lower lip, then turns to Forest. "Or at least I think it's her, but I lost her again."

A rush of adrenaline spikes, and the urge to run out of here and hop on a plane to get Moira overcomes me. Axel grips my arm and gives a sharp shake of his head. He gets me. Not too long ago, he was in the same place, rushing out to save his girl. With the muscles of my entire body locked tight, I grit my teeth and wait for this damn briefing to run its course.

"What do you mean you think you found her?" My voice might be deep, but it's not like Forest's, which rolls like thunder through the room.

"She activated the emergency alert."

"And how was that unclear?" Forest leans forward, fingers pressing against the polished wood of the conference table. Skye places her hand on his arm and gives a shake of her head. She's the only one on the planet capable of calming that man. Well, perhaps not the only person. There are two others now. "And what do you mean by 'you lost her'?"

"As we all know, 4-E-S-T is the emergency alert all our rescuees are taught to text if they find themselves in trouble. I got an alert, but she never sent her personal code. That leaves me to make assumptions, and you know how I feel about that." Her eyes spark and flare with what she leaves unsaid.

Mitzy is a stickler for facts. She lives and breathes information, making inferences all the time, based on what that information says. What she doesn't do is guess. Mitzy either knows, or she doesn't. When the facts don't line up into a pretty package, she presents them to the Guardians, and we're the ones who connect the dots, making whatever guesses we must.

Since our asses are the ones on the line, it's a compromise which works for us well. Mitzy's said time and time again that she will never be the one to send a Guardian to his death because of faulty intelligence. She's also a stickler for following protocol. The woman obsesses, and her borderline OCD doesn't help.

I'm guessing something is off about the protocol. I respect Mitzy. The woman's mind is nothing short of chaotic brilliance. Her guesses have to be ten times better than ours, but it frustrates me when she refuses to make obvious connections.

"Tell us what you know." Skye's light, lilting voice is just like the rest of her, beautiful but bolstered by steel. She's not afraid to push Mitzy to the limit of what she'll infer from the data.

"Ten minutes ago, I received the distress alert. Pretty standard there." She points to the screen which currently displays the Gulf of Mexico. "We didn't know how those men got Moira out of the building during the raid to save Zoe, and we've been going over what surveillance there is, trying to track all traffic leaving that area at the time of the raid. Nothing gave us anything concrete to act on.

Land, sea, or air. Those men moved her by one of the three, but there was no way to know for sure. Honestly, we lost her."

My teeth grind harder as Mitzy dribbles out information. It's a game with her, give the tiniest scraps to make the rest of us go insane waiting for the goddam punchline. I swear the little sprite gets off on watching us lesser humans piece together her little crumbs of information.

I'm not sure what expression is on my face, except Axel's fingers dig in my arm hard enough for me to notice. I'd say something, but Forest catches my eye. He says nothing, but there's no reason for him to say a word.

Like me, he's been in a similar position. He knows what it's like to have someone he cares about taken from him. His look tells me he understands my situation, but even he won't buck protocol. It's hard to sit still and not lose my shit, but his look tells me to have patience.

I get it. Rushing in does nothing but create chaos and places unnecessary risk on everyone involved. I hold my tongue, but anger boils inside of me. It's been nearly four days since Moira went missing. Four long days where anything could've happened. But she texted an SOS to the facility. That must mean something.

"Spit it out, Mitz. Is it Moira, or not?" Forest says the words I want to shout.

I take in a breath and try to calm the fuck down while Mitzy does her thing.

"I'm ninety-nine percent sure it's her." She points to the map and a red light pops up. "This is Goliath, a cargo container ship which left the port of Barranquilla, Colombia the night we rescued Zoe. The text originated on that ship from an unlisted number. Either she got her hands on a phone and called for help, or her kidnappers sent the text."

"And why do you think that?" My gut clenches thinking about how Moira's kidnappers would've gotten that information.

Nobody outside Guardian HRS and the Facility knows about that code.

Moira's smart, level-headed, perhaps too calm, and thinks well under pressure. I imagine her sneaking the phone from her captors and sending the text. As for retaliation, that's not an issue. The owner of the phone will never know Moira sent a text. The moment the text fires, Mitzy's technical team sends back a stream of code to the sending device, which wipes all evidence of the text and inserts tracking software on the device.

Mitzy ignores my question. Her briefing is aimed at Sam, CJ, and Forest.

"Where's the ship headed?" Forest keeps his voice low, but insistent.

"The port of New Orleans. The moment it entered the range of cell reception from land, the text sent. Which is why I'm cautious, and worried. That text could've been loaded in the phone at any time. As you know, there's no cell reception in the Gulf, and the coverage of the cell towers on land only extends so far from the shore. Most phones store any texts, calls, or other electronic transmission, sending them once the device comes within range. There's no way to know when the text was keyed into the phone and explains why it only now sent."

"So that's why you're hesitating?" Skye taps her fingers on the table, drumming a staccato beat.

"No." Mitzy gives a sharp shake of her head. "My concern is that she didn't input her personal code. There are many reasons for that, but the most concerning is she tried to send her SOS and was caught before she could input her personal code. Since the phone wouldn't have transmitted the text until back in cell coverage, who's to say that's not what happened? Moira's smart. It's unlike her to not follow our protocols. This could well be a trap. In fact, it most likely is."

I understand Mitzy's hesitation. Every rescuee is taught to text 4-E-S-T if they're in danger and to input a personal code unique to themselves for identification purposes. If Moira tried to get word to us, and her kidnappers caught her doing so, it makes sense. In addition to texting 4-E-S-T, each rescuee has two personal codes to complete the text. One to identify themselves. The other to indicate they've been compromised.

There's no reason for Moira not to follow the protocols ingrained in all of our hostage rescuees. I understand Mitzy's hesitation.

"But you think it's her?" I control myself and let the words roll out smooth and even, rather than clipped and annoyed. I'm well aware there's no way to know it is Moira, but the assumption is she's the only rescuee unaccounted for. I have no issue connecting the dots and making that assumption.

"It's the only thing which makes sense, but I'm not inclined to send a team into a trap." Mitzy turns toward the screen and taps her upper lip. "Not to mention, the phone's dead."

"Dead?" I ask.

"We inserted our code, standard protocol, but the phone failed a short time later. Or someone turned it off. That is an alternative explanation, which is why I'm even more worried about this being a trap. Why would Moira do that?"

Good question, but I've already moved past that issue.

I do a little quick math, factoring in how long it takes to spin up the jet, load all our gear on board, and fly from the West Coast to New Orleans.

"If that tanker just entered cell reception range, how long do we have until it docks?"

NINE

Moira

VISUALIZATION AND MEDITATION ARE CENTERING TECHNIQUES THE staff at the Facility taught me. I lean on their training, yet again, and walk myself through the last three days.

My eyes don't stay closed for long. I'm such an idiot. There are two cords in the bathroom. One of which is for Bossman's phone. The other hooks up to his razor.

Back on my feet again, I gingerly walk past his body and plug the phone into the charging cord.

I should head outside and get to work on the whole getting off the ship thing, but not with a dead phone.

I mull over what to do next as a large yawn escapes me. Damn but I'm tired. My attention shifts to the phone and I make an executive level decision. To escape, I need to be on top of my game rather than yawning from exhaustion. I head to the bunk bed and crawl onto the top bunk. The moment my eyes close, images of our struggle flood my mind. I relive every horrible detail, ending with his soulless eyes staring at the ceiling. I've got to get out of this room.

But I need to stick to my plan.

Step one: a fully charged and functional phone.

As the minutes creep by, I try to calm my racing heart and let the adrenaline rush run its course. More of the meditation helps, but I feel like I'm crawling out of my skin.

I'm a killer now—just like Bossman. The entire trajectory of my life took a sharp turn the moment I took his life. That's something I have to live with, and I don't know if I can.

Not sure when I gave up the ghost, I bolt out of bed and nearly trip on Bossman's body. How long did I sleep?

Like every day since I began this adventure, nobody has come knocking on the door, and I don't want to give anyone reason to come now.

Bossman said, "in the morning" we would be pulling into port. I grab his phone and navigate to settings to change the facial recognition. His phone is no good to me if I can't unlock it without him.

Evidently, to change the face thingy, you need the passcode, which I don't know, or the face of the person that it's already set to recognize. I'm back at Bossman's body. It takes a hot minute, but I get the security features to swap out my face for his. With that done, I reset the passcode and check the time.

It's midnight, we're technically in morning territory, and I still have no way off this ship. Not to mention, no cell reception to send my SOS text.

I can delay no longer. It's time to leave this cabin.

The concrete and steel deck is cool beneath my feet. The no-shoes thing sucks, but I can tiptoe without making a sound.

So, that's a positive.

I'm in some kind of corridor, but I'm really on the exterior of the ship. A massive steel wall, with cutouts every twenty feet, is the only thing between me and the sea. It's definitely a big ass ship. When I peek out one of the cutouts, the ocean seethes with massive rollers and the water rushing by the hull has to be a hundred feet, or more, below me. There will be no jumping off this ship.

After orientating myself to bow and stern, port and starboard, I work my way aft. A set of metal stairs leads downward. I check for other people before heading down.

It's dark. Occasional lights illuminate the gloom, but it's hard to see where I'm going. When I hear male voices laughing, I plaster myself against the bulkhead and take deep breaths. They're shooting the shit and don't hear me. I backtrack and look for another way down.

As I suspected, I'm on a container ship. The front of the vessel is where the crew lives. The rest is stacked with thousands of containers; talk about feeling small. I cautiously make my way down there. Thankfully, I don't encounter any other men.

My thought is to lose myself within the maze of passageways formed by the stacks, but it quickly becomes clear, there will be little hiding. If I can see down the long stretches between containers, so can anyone else.

But what if I climb up?

Salt stirred up from the wind mixes with the harsh, industrial smells of steel, oil, and metal all around me. The darkness provides coverage but also makes things harder as I scramble my way up. It's not easy climbing up the container, but thanks to Four for all the intense physical conditioning he put me through, I scale the container with little difficulty.

My bare feet come in handy here as I brace my back and feet against adjacent containers and work my way up. I make it to the second tier of cargo containers and then to the third.

It's there where I find the perfect hiding place. This stack is two containers shorter than those around it. It's like a massive hole where I can hide—at least for now.

Satisfied, I'm well hidden, I pull out Bossman's phone and get to work on the next stage of my rescue. I need to find the Guardians, but luck is not on my side. There's still no service.

TEN

Griff

An extraction at sea is safest for all involved. Technically more challenging, Guardians are well versed in overcoming challenging situations. It's what Guardians do.

At sea, we'll encounter only the forces that are currently on board that tanker. Let it dock, and others can board, swelling their ranks, and making our job ten times worse.

"Once the ship hits the mouth of the Mississippi River, it takes about seven to eight hours to reach the port of New Orleans. They're about two hours from entering the Mississippi, which gives us ten hours to work an extraction plan."

"Ten hours!" I explode out of my seat, completely ignoring my teammates' attempts to keep me under control. "What the fuck are we doing sitting here? If you found her, we should be on a plane, not sitting around a table with our thumbs up our asses."

"Sit the fuck down, Griff," Max cuts in, before I can make more of an ass of myself.

He's not happy. Not happy with my outburst and not happy with how it shows a lack of control over his men. I'm going to owe him big time later on, but fuck; it's my girl out there. I slowly rein in my temper and sit my ass back in my chair.

CJ spins in his chair. His fingers press together, and he holds them steepled under his chin. "We're not sitting around doing nothing, Griff. There's not a person in this room who doesn't think this is, in fact, Moira. Our supply team is loading the jet as we speak. By the time we're done, it'll be ready for take-off. Our people in New Orleans are already in action, mobilizing assets for any number of different contingency plans. Our task right now is to determine if we send Alpha in alone or activate another team. I won't send you into a trap without a thorough discussion about risk, and we have the time to discuss solutions. Even if you get up now, that plane won't be taking off any sooner than possible."

"Copy that." I stand down. There's nothing I can say to refute what CJ said. He's right. We still have time.

"As I was saying…" Mitzy's pinched expression speaks volumes. She's used to hot-headed Guardians, but that doesn't mean she tolerates our unique approach to problem solving. "I'm pretty certain it's Moira. She activated the Facility SOS, but didn't complete the authentication…"

"You believe she's under duress?" Once again, my voice rises, and once again, Max glares at me. I should keep my mouth shut, but that isn't going to happen. Moira's out there, alone, undefended, unprotected, and likely fighting for her life. Meanwhile, I'm sitting around a conference table shooting the shit about why she didn't input her personal code.

"No shit, Sherlock." Mitzy turns her irritated glare on me, but I meet her stare with one of my own. "For fuck's sake, Griff, back the fuck down. We're spinning up as we speak. If you'd let me finish, we can line all the ducks up in a row. Or maybe you like going into a mission hot, without a care about thinking things through?" She crosses her arms and taps her foot. Mitzy's a tiny thing, but damn is she ferocious when challenged.

"All I'm saying is that if that is Moira, this conversation should be happening on the jet as we're flying in…"

"This briefing isn't happening on the jet because Moira failed to complete the code," Sam speaks for the first time; his voice is low and far calmer than mine. "For all we know, this is an attempt to flush out the Guardians. Bravo team walked into a shit show not too long ago, or did you forget about that?"

"No, I haven't forgotten about that." Mollified, I tuck my chin. I hate that Sam's right.

Not too long ago, Alpha and Charlie teams worked together to rescue a dozen girls off a containership in the Gulf of Mexico. Initial intelligence led Bravo team to the docks in Cancun. The mission was to find the container holding the girls and free them while still in port, before the container could be loaded.

Bravo team walked into a setup. The container they thought held the girls blew up in their faces, and the container with the girls inside of it had already been loaded on a different ship which left port less than an hour beforehand.

"Someone out there is testing our organization." Sam crosses his arms. "I know what this girl means to you, what she means to all of us. Nobody in this room wants one of those we've rescued to fall back into the hands of monsters. Moira has, and the failure to protect her affects all of us. Some more than others." His astute gaze lands directly on me. "This briefing is to decide whether one team, or two, head out."

He's right. Sam is a great leader for a reason.

"I get your caution." I glance around the table, taking in Forest, Doc Summers, CJ, and Sam. Mitzy glares at me, but I see the worry in her expression. She's not that hard to read. "But we all know it's Moira. If she's in distress, it doesn't matter. We'll extract her. It's what we do. I just wanted to know why we aren't already on that plane."

"Like Forest said, the jet is spinning up." Sam scoots back and rises, taking over control of the conversation. "I will not send a team in unless I'm sure it's not a setup. If it is, we'll be prepared for them. Whoever took Zoe Lancaster went to extreme lengths to capture her, not once, but twice. Moira Stone was not their target, but she is an opportunity. I want to make sure we know what we might be facing. I won't send a team into a trap again."

"Sometimes, the best way to find out who's behind a trap is to set it off." I can't help it. Their caution is going to cost Moira her life. "Do you think she would've given over the Facility SOS?"

"It's always a possibility."

"You don't know her at all. I don't believe Moira would do that. She's smart as a tack, a true survivor, but Moira can be flighty at times. I think it's more likely she forgot. Maybe she didn't have time to enter her personal code and only the initial text? There's no way to know what's happening to her right now. If the code was extracted, she's smart enough to know that by giving an identifying code, her kidnappers might think it's a secondary distress call. I'm betting it's nothing more than an oversight on her part, or she didn't have time."

"My job is to consider all the possibilities," Sam affirms.

"And yet, I know Moira best. She was my pupil at the Facility." Axel coughs into his fist. It's his way to tell me to shut up, but to hell with that. I stand my ground and press the issue. "If you knew what she's endured…"

"Everyone sitting at this table knows what Moira endured." Forest interrupts me. The tone of his voice sends chills down my spine. Out of everyone present, only he and Doc Summers have any true idea what Moira endured. He should know, considering he lived through worse.

"Then you know that she's stressed. So, what if she forgot the code? She remembered enough to activate the system. I'm assuming that's why we know where she is." It doesn't take but a glance down the table to confirm what I already know. "There are millions of reasons why she didn't complete the code, but we all know it's her."

"Griff…" Doc Summers places her hands on the table and swivels in her chair to look at me.

I wince, knowing she's going to tell me to stand down. Most likely, she'll cut me out of this mission altogether, saying I don't meet clearance from medical hold. I brace for whatever it is she's going to say while Axel stiffens beside me.

Nothing will keep me from saving Moira, and Axel gets it.

"I think Griff's right." Doc Summers looks at me, then places her hand on Forest's arm. "We all know how the simplest things fly out of your head in situations like this."

"But…" Sam speaks up, challenging the doctor.

Skye lifts a finger, stalling him. "Our operation is at risk." She glances up and down the table. "I don't think there's a person in this room who isn't concerned about what happened to Bravo team. Somebody has taken notice of Guardian HRS. We've been targeted, not that this is a surprise to any of us. We're damn good at what we do, and that kind of thing draws unwanted attention. We took down Snowden's operation and that sent shockwaves through the entire community. It put us on the map. It's no surprise we've been targeted, but in this, I agree with Griff. That was Moira reaching out. We're obligated to rescue her. She's one of us now, and we take care of our own."

The Guardians save those who've been taken. We give victims back their stolen lives turning them into survivors.

Mitzy nods, agreeing with what Doc Summers has to say. "We have coordinates. The cell she was using is no longer functioning, but I have the ship tagged. It makes port in ten hours. It's only a four-hour flight to New Orleans. Infil will be tricky. The ship will be navigating in the Mississippi River. Air and water are our only routes for entry, and I suggest we make the acquisition before that ship pulls into port. I've got a drone on the ship. If any other boats approach it, other than the pilot, we'll know."

We all get what she's not saying. Mitzy feels this is a trap, even though her intelligence doesn't point to it being anything more than an oversight on Moira's part to complete the protocol, but that's the thing, she doesn't have enough information to sway her either way. This is the point where Mitzy steps back and lets the Guardians take over mission planning.

"I'm surprised it's New Orleans, although that might make things easier." CJ stands and faces the map. He takes a step closer and examines the projected path of the tanker. "This would've been easier at sea, but we can make this work. We've got helicopter and water transports in staging as we speak. The only question is, do we infil by boat or air? The op will be at night, pre-dawn, which works in our favor. Hit me with your ideas."

Mitzy turns toward the screen. She blows up the image of the Mississippi River and briefs us on the complicated twists and turns the ship will need to make navigating those waters. "There are several good places to come at this from the water." She marks the spots that look the most promising.

"With it being the Gulf, helicopter traffic is heavy and unlikely to arouse suspicion. We can either rappel on board or approach upstream by boat. Travel time would be less if we meet up with a helicopter as soon as we land."

"I see." CJ pulls at his chin. "We can drop a RIB and Alpha team far upstream. They'll have time to set up and approach the ship."

I rub my hands together as we get down to the nitty-gritty of mission planning. Max pipes up and makes a comment about travel times. He's not happy with dropping into the murky waters of the Mississippi, or the density of boat traffic. It definitely complicates things.

"Any reason not to rappel right on the deck? It seems the most direct route, less prone to complications by factors out of our control."

"I've been wondering something." Forest pushes back from his seat, interrupting the tactical planning going on. "I know you won't make assumptions, Mitz, but I'm going to make a few. First, her buyer is American. It's the only thing that makes sense. If Colombian, no need to put her on a ship. Same for any other Latin American country. If she was destined for Asia, they would've flown her, or at least waited to figure out something better. I'm betting their passage on that ship was preplanned. Mitzy, get your team to look at the ship's manifest and see when, or if, they contracted to transport civilians. I'm betting they did, and I'm betting it occurred sometime before Moira's kidnapping. They picked that ship with intent. This isn't a kidnapping of convenience. Orders went out for Zoe and Moira both. We messed up what they planned for Zoe, but Moira's transfer was already planned. It's too neat and tidy. Which means, we're dealing with a sophisticated operation here."

"I agree with Forest." Doc Summers rubs at her arms as if overcome by a chill, but I get it. This is all far too calculating, and I don't believe in that many coincidences lining up in a row.

"The mission is a go." Sam places his palms down on the table. His stony gaze takes in CJ, then slowly sweeps around the room. "We have work to do. Charlie's on standby for backup. Spin them up and have them on the plane. Alpha is primary for the mission." His attention shifts to me. "We will bring Moira home, and if we can dig up any intel on this new threat, we do it."

Forest and Doc Summers exchange a look. It's actually more of a full conversation, only the rest of us are incapable of understanding their nonverbal exchange. She finally gives a nod of assent. Forest reaches out and grasps her hand. She places her other hand on top of his, then turns her attention to me.

"Griff goes, but as support only." Her focus turns to Max. "Decide who you want to fill in as Alpha-Four. Bravo team is two men down for the time being, but I'm sure they can loan you a man."

"Copy that." Max gives a sharp shake of his head while I keep my mouth zipped up tight.

I'm going and that's all I care about right now. I may not be the one to rescue Moira, but I'll be there when my team secures her freedom.

"We run the op as if it's a trap. I want contingencies for contingencies. Backup plans for the backups. Keep your heads on a swivel. Expect more resistance than you'd otherwise consider. I won't lose another team because we're too focused on the primary objective." Sam, head of all of Guardian HRS, directs his orders to CJ and Mitzy, who will, in turn, advise their teams.

All I care about is that I'm on the mission. Support, or not, I'll be as close as humanly possible, and I can't wait to hold Moira in my arms again. And this time, I don't care about maintaining professional distance.

Moira is mine. It's about time I show her what that means.

"Like Griff said," CJ says, "if this is a trap, the best way to figure out who's behind it is to spring it. I don't think we'll find that on this mission. It doesn't feel right. I don't agree with Forest, but we plan for both. This feels like more of an opportunistic grab. It's too sloppy. Griff, since you're on support, that's your task. Think of all the ways this op can go wrong. Find solutions. Poke holes."

"Yes, sir." I sit a little straighter, feeling better about having a solid role in this operation.

Forest and Doc Summers leave us to strategize. He hired Sam to lead Guardian HRS. His faith in CJ to lead the Guardian teams, and in Mitzy to lead her technical and intelligence crew, is unshakeable, but damn if it isn't a shit-ton of pressure. Nobody wants to let Forest down.

He defers to Sam's expertise, as he should. Sam is a veritable legend when it comes to the black ops community, but Forest is somewhat of a savant.

Where Mitzy doesn't assume shit, Forest sees the world differently than the rest of us. If he senses there's a new player in town, there's definitely somebody out there. I have my work cut out for me. I respect Sam's leadership, but I trust Forest's gut.

Not that I care about any of that right now.

All I care about is the doc officially gave me the go-ahead to support my team. I owe her a huge favor and have a feeling she'll call in that debt.

ELEVEN

Griff

THE FLIGHT TO NEW ORLEANS FROM THE COAST OF CALIFORNIA takes a little over three hours from take-off to landing, but five hours pass before we touch down due to loading and calling Charlie team in for the assist.

I'm a bundle of knee-bouncing nerves during the entire trip. Axel alternates between giving me the eye and shaking his head. He won't say it—there's no need—but he thinks it's long past time I do something about Moira.

Unlike me, he didn't let rules and regulations get in the way when he made his move on Zoe. Granted, those two have more history than Moira and I share, but I still think he's an ass. And, he's having far too much fun at my expense.

"Don't worry, bud," he says with a snicker. "I'm going to hug your girl real tight."

"Don't be an ass."

"Want me to lay a kiss on her, or do you wanna do that yourself?" Axel's grin is a mile wide.

The guys chuckle as they listen in. Knox and Liam sit across from each other, playing cards. Max kicks back and stretches out. He reclined his seat all the way flat. He's not asleep, but rather working through the plans we settled on a little while ago.

Those plans are the reason Axel's being a shit, as they call for an unusual evacuation off the ship. I may, or may not, have had a snit when it came down to who I'd let carry Moira in my absence.

It's Axel, obviously, we're tight, and I trust him. Not that I don't trust the other guys, but Axel is the only one of us in a committed relationship. Therefore, he carries Moira out of harm's way, and watches over her until she's back in my arms.

This support role officially sucks.

"Now, you're just being a little shit." I give Axel the finger while Knox snickers.

"Stop jerking him around." Liam lays down a card and either wins or loses that hand. I've never been able to figure out what the fuck those two play, and I can't tell if he's defending me or mocking me.

"Griff's in love. L-O-V-E, love." Knox sings the words. What's worse is that he ends it by wrapping his arms around himself to pretend he's making out. Fucker uses sloppy kissing sounds and really goes to town.

"If that's the way you kiss, slobber horse, no wonder you're single." I slap him upside the head and plop down into my seat.

Like Max, I recline all the way until I'm flat on my back. Guardians travel in style and this is a far, far cry from my military days when the best seat in the house was stuck in the middle of a long row of webbed seats lining the fuselage.

We were crammed in tight enough you could sleep sitting up. The floors were cold metal, so cold I once had a water bottle freeze solid less than six hours in the air when I accidentally left it on the floor.

We didn't have real heat, just a tube of heated air overhead with far too few flaps for vents to let that heat out. It was loud as fuck. Your feet froze and your head sweated. And the webbing on those seats was so stretched out, your ass sat on hard metal bars.

Guardian life is definitely an upgrade. Plush leather chairs, first-class accommodations, a lavatory you can actually turn around in. There's a minibar stocked with water for the flight out and beer on the way back. Up front, a large conference table and several computer displays fill the fuselage.

Mitzy and her tech team sit up there where they'll direct the mission from inside the plane while it sits on the ground.

With arms crossed over my chest, and ankles locked together, I throw a blanket over my body and cover my head. I shove earbuds in my ears, pick a song track and ignore my teammates.

Which is hard. They've officially reverted to grade school shenanigans with thick, sloppy kissing noises and other, rude sounds. I tune them out and turn my thoughts to Moira.

I'm coming, little minx. Hang on a little longer.

Mission planning continued from the moment we were wheels up and concluded not too long ago. We feel good about our plan. It's solid with little room for shit to hit the fan, but we always think that until the shit hits the proverbial fan.

Charlie Team joins us. They retreated to the back of the plane once mission planning was set.

Smaug, Mitzy's drone, is in the air. She calls her drones dragons, and each one comes with a name; even her little "dragonflies." Those are tiny handheld drones we carry in our gear for close-in operational support, but we, meaning the Guardians, refuse to refer to any of them by the oddball names the tech team baptized them with.

Smaug follows the tanker as it meticulously enters the mouth of the Mississippi River. It reports back when a small boat carrying the river pilot meets up with the ship. I follow the conversation, despite the earbuds, overly attuned to anything dealing with Moira's rescue.

The pilot is standard operating procedure and, therefore, doesn't raise any red flags. He'll assist the crew in navigating the winding twists and turns of the massive river. *Smaug* sees only one man board the ship and keeps watch for any other boats bringing reinforcements.

Mitzy and her team peer over *Smaug's* readouts and try to locate Moira.

So far, Moira's a ghost.

Not that it comes as a surprise. We assume she's being kept out of sight, most likely in one of the cabins.

My team, bolstered by Booker from Bravo, who fills in as Alpha-4 for this operation, will approach from upriver. Sam activated local assets before takeoff and they'll have six-man Zodiacs pre-positioned ahead of the tanker.

From the airfield, a helicopter will take all of us near the staging area. That's where I say goodbye to the rest of my team. While they load into the six-man RIB, I'll remain in the helicopter to provide visual support from the air.

Smaug is good, but we still rely on good old humans when possible. Too much information is rarely a problem in our line of work. I shift a bit, taking tension off my injured leg. The pain settles into a dull ache. So far, I've managed not to mess up Doc Summers' handiwork.

Her team, standard practice, follows us out, but since we have Charlie with us, they do so on another jet.

Equipped to the nines, Alpha team will have no problem scaling the walls of the tanker. Getting off will be a breeze as well. They're equipped with a new device, one Mitzy's team developed. We recently implemented it in training. This will be its first use on a mission. It's a mix between a parachute and a hang glider.

All they have to do is locate Moira, secure her to one of them, and literally run off the back of the boat. The glider will deploy and they'll float to the bank of the river where a retrieval group will pick them up.

Since I won't be there to rescue Moira, I insisted Axel carry my girl and protect her for me. Which is why they're having fun with me.

He'll strap her to his harness and the two of them will glide to safety. I wanted to be with the retrieval unit, but CJ and Max, need me on the helicopter as air support. Which makes a ton of sense, not that I like it, but that's not my call to make.

Charlie will be on the water, prepared for contingencies, and of course, the helicopter is fitted with all manner of life-saving gear. We've got a wench, a cradle which can carry not one, but two people, as well as enough rope to rappel out and down in case a water rescue is required. There's also a complement of two machine guns, mounted on either side of the helicopter, as well as a nose operated weapon. I'm manning one of the machine guns. Speed, who's joining me from Bravo team on support, has the other.

We're as ready as we can be.

And we still have hours until that ship docks.

The moment we touch down, it's a race to unload our gear from the plane and load everyone up into the helicopter. I pause for a second when I notice our pilot is a female.

"Ariel Black. I'm your taxi driver for the evening." She shakes hands with Max and the rest of the team.

"This is my team, and Griff here will be riding shotgun with you." Max briefly introduces us.

"Hi." I expect a soft, feminine shake when I take her hand, but she returns my grip with strength.

"You riding with me, then?"

"Looks like."

Ariel takes one look at me and her brow arches in question. I say nothing, not feeling like I need to explain myself to a helicopter pilot. She releases my hand and moves on to introduce herself to Charlie team.

"Dude, do you know who that is?" Knox tugs me aside and I do a double take at the awe filling his voice.

"No." I've already dismissed the pilot.

"That's Ariel Black. She's a fucking legend. Ex-army, three combat tours in the desert, war decorated. My team had injured men. We were pinned down and requested medevac. She flew into that mess." He lifts a brow like that means something to me.

I give a shake of my head because I've never heard of her.

"Dude, her helicopter was hit by an RPG and went down. She landed that thing like it was nothing, all while it spewed fire and smoke. She lost her co-pilot and two of the four special ops surgical team members on board, but she fucking pulled the two injured men free of the wreck all by herself. With a shattered leg! Defended them too. They call her Battle Angel. Fucking legend." He presses forward and enthusiastically shakes her hand. "Name's Knox and fucking pleased to breathe the same damn air."

"Excuse me?" Ariel's brows quirk up.

"Desert, several years ago, you came to medevac our wounded. RPG took you out and you saved…"

"Yeah," she rubs the back of her neck, "that was a bad day in the office. I lost three men."

"And saved two others. It's a real honor to be working with you again. You joining the Guardians?"

"Naw, I've got a great job here. Still flying medevac though, off the rigs, but got a call from an old friend and couldn't say no. Feels almost like old times."

"I know what you mean." Knox can't keep his eyes off the pilot, but I see a flash of gold around her left ring finger. Knox is going to have to keep moving along. That chick is taken.

He says a few more things while everyone loads up. Ariel Black tilts her head, assessing me. I swear she's looking for something. When her gaze lingers on my leg, her eyes brighten.

Color me impressed. I swear I'm not limping but she figures everything out. No need to tell her why I'm not with my team. She gets it. While Alpha and Charlie crowd into the helicopter, Speed and I take up our positions by the twin machine guns at the open bay doors.

Dressed in black tactical gear, my teammates smear black paint on their faces as Ariel takes us up. The Zodiacs they'll soon be riding are black. My team is decked out all in black, and the muddy waters of the Mississippi are dirty brown during the day and midnight black at night.

Black on black on black.

Nobody will see them coming. Charlie team does the same.

It's after midnight, but still sweltering hot in the cloying humidity of the Mississippi Delta. We sweat like stuck pigs and draw thick, humidified air into our lungs.

My nerves buzz and jangle, which is odd for me. I'm not the nervous type. Quite the opposite. During a mission, my emotions disappear while I embrace the lethal killing machine that I am. There's no time for shit like emotions during an op. I'm damn good at my job. My ice-cold demeanor on ops got noticed and is, in part, how I was recruited into Delta Force while in the military.

Like Delta operatives, Guardians are recruited from all branches of the military special ops community. We're brothers in arms, and nearly every one of us is a former Delta operative. After what Knox said, I'm surprised Battle Angel up at the stick isn't getting recruited. We need battle-trained helicopter pilots with nerves of steel in our organization.

Axel watches me during the short flight to a seedy marina. He knows it's killing me not to be with my team. We exchange a look, and he tells me not to worry. He's got my back and will take care of my girl until he can hand that responsibility off to me.

As we close in on the marina, I inspect the ragtag fishing boats lining the docks. It's dark down there. No lights are on. I can't make out the Zodiacs waiting for our guys, but I don't expect to. They're hidden and secure.

While there's no way to hide a low flying helicopter, we perform a rapid insertion. Speed and I man the ropes as the teams rapidly rappel out of the helicopter. Alpha and Charlie are out of the chopper in less than two minutes; then we're on our way.

While they load up into their Zodiacs, Ariel will take Speed and me downriver, following the shoreline until we meet up with the tanker. We'll do a slow pass overhead, seeing if we can find where Moira might be hiding, and scout out the locations of any men on deck.

In the minority, I assume Moira's hiding and is not currently a prisoner. Mitzy doesn't like my assumptions, but I know Moira. She's strong, almost too strong, and she's resilient as well as smart.

I wish she'd lower her walls and unbottle her emotions, but the girl is a survivor. The only person she relies on is herself.

Someday, I hope she'll open up to me and let me carry some of her pain, if only for a moment. God knows she's got a lifetime of pain to unload, and there's been nobody there she could rely on. I hope she's ready because I intend to become that person.

I listen to the progress of Alpha and Charlie through the comm channel and follow along as Ariel reports our progress. In three minutes, I'll be flying right over Moira. I wish she knew we were coming. If she sent the SOS, and I believe she did, she should be watching out for our arrival.

Almost there, little minx.

T-minus one minute and our pilot piles on altitude. We're not that far from the Gulf, where helicopter traffic is as dense as fleas on a dog in summertime as they ferry offshore oil riggers to and from their rigs. Our presence should go completely unnoticed.

I check my safety strap and lean out the open bay door. Pitch black outside, wind buffets me as the rotors overhead drown out all noise with their low roar. It's only a little cooler up here, but the humidity is still thick as molasses. My night-vision goggles are linked to Mitzy's array of technical gear, reporting back everything I see.

"On first approach," I call out, not for Mitzy's team's benefit, but for my guys on the water.

"Roger. Roger." A disembodied voice replies through my headset. I grit my teeth at the bastardization of proper radio etiquette.

Ariel slows as much as she's able as we pass slantwise across the tanker. From bow to stern, I make a broad visual sweep, seeing if I find anything to add to *Smaug's* higher-level assessment. Mitzy's drone flies far overhead, cloaked, and nearly invisible to anybody who cares.

Towers of containers greet my visual inspection. Neat little rows stacked high enough I'm surprised they don't tip and fall overboard. It's a full ship. There are only a few spots where the stacks run short. For now, the enhanced night vision of my scope registers those as deep, dark pits.

"First pass complete," I report back to those watching.

"Roger. Alpha team's in the water. Charlie's holding back in reserve. T-minus ten minutes for insertion."

"Copy that."

The tech team loves their radio code, saying things like ROGER and ROGER WILCO, which is just dumb. Prior military, Guardians keep things simple. We don't tolerate any superfluous chatter clogging communications. Mitzy's team, by contrast, is bound and determined to bastardize common radio etiquette.

The pilot swings us wide, crossing to the other bank and heading downstream. We'll cross again and do another sweep coming from stern to bow. I keep my eyes on the water, looking for other craft, but there's nothing that approaches the tanker.

As for Alpha, if I see them, they're doing a piss-poor job of hiding their assault. Alpha team does nothing piss-poor.

I only wish I was down there with them.

"Second approach," I announce our progress. Beside me, Blade sweeps the machine gun back and forth as he scans the murky waters below us. I check the decks, not expecting to see Moira out in the open, but I gotta say, I'd feel better if I saw her safe and sound.

Alpha team, who's listening in, hops on the channel. "Approaching Mayberry." Max's gruff voice cuts off with a buzz of static. Mayberry signifies they're approaching the bow.

They've got it rough, approaching a ship this size from the bow means they've gotta cross the massive bow wave thrown up as the tanker pushes through the water. They've got one hell of a rocky ride ahead of them.

We hear nothing for a bit while I catch movement on top of the stacks of containers. "Four men on top of the containers."

"We see them." My disembodied technical teammate responds. "*Smaug's* on it. Can you get a closer view? See if they're armed?"

"On it," Ariel answers, and we bleed off altitude, sinking fast. My stomach slams into my throat with the gut-wrenching sensation of falling. Helicopters are pretty damn cool, but they do a job on my stomach.

Banking hard, we turn around for another sweep, then dive toward the dark river and the ship slowly pushing upstream.

I practically lean out of the helicopter to get a better look below me. Sure as shit, those men are armed.

"Four armed men walking the stacks."

"Copy that." Max keeps his reply short and sweet. We're not expecting armed resistance, so this is a red flag.

"Mitzy, you sure no other boats came alongside?"

"Sure as shit."

"Then what's up with the welcome brigade?" I watch the men, taking note of their actions. They're looking down, in between, the tall stacks of containers, which makes no sense unless... "They're searching for something."

Or someone.

No need to finish that thought. But why would the crew of the tanker be looking for Moira? In our experience, they're unaware of the critical cargo they carry.

But this is no ordinary operation.

Moira isn't trapped inside a cargo container, out of sight of the regular crew, which makes me wonder how her kidnappers smuggled her on board. If they smuggled her at all? I've got more questions than answers with no way to find them, at least not now.

"Copy that. Passing Hugo," Max calls out the progress of the team. Hugo means they've attached the RIB to the outer hull and are beginning their assent up to the deck.

"Watch your backs." I don't like my team heading into danger, at least not when I'm not in the thick of it with them.

The men on top of the stacks won't be able to see over the side of the ship, but they've got a bird's eye view of the deck below them.

Only, they're looking in between the stacks. Alert and focused, they're meticulous in their search, using a standard grid-like search pattern.

So far, they've made it a quarter of the way toward the bow. They split up. Each man checks up a bit, then crosses over to the next row and circles back toward the stern.

They shine lights down into the dark labyrinth of passageways formed by the cargo containers. Stacked as closely as possible, the space between them is barely wider than the breadth of a man.

There are about four spots where the stacks aren't the same height; one a few rows forward of the back row, two about midway, and another close to the bow.

Ariel circles around and skims off even more altitude. Soon, they're going to take notice of the helicopter circling overhead. Not that they can see us, we're running dark, but there's no way to hide the chopping of our blades through the air.

"Passing Francine," Max lets everyone know they've scaled the side of the ship. Alpha is officially in play.

I relay the positions of the four men walking on top of the containers. They're making good time and are nearly a third of the way toward the bow. None have looked up, which tells me they haven't yet heard the chop of our rotors, but that won't last long.

We swing out wide, lose another few hundred feet of altitude, and circle around for a closer look. I switch to the internal channel for the helicopter.

"I want to see those holes in the stacks." A bad feeling stirs in my gut.

"Copy." The helicopter banks hard as Ariel circles around.

Right about now, my team should be releasing Mitzy's tiny dragonfly drones. Those will scour the ship using a combination of visual, night, and infrared scans to locate positions of the crew, and hopefully, they'll find Moira. Otherwise, Max will be left to search the tanker with only six men.

He has less than four hours to complete that task before the ship enters port. After that, things get dicey, not to mention we lose the cover of darkness as the sun rises. We're prepared for a prolonged search, but this helicopter has limited airtime. At some point, we'll have to veer off and refuel.

"Charlie engaged," Tex, Charlie-One, informs everyone they've pushed off.

The armed men add a layer of complexity to this operation, and Charlie is coming in with backup. My nerves ping like little motherfuckers, sending jolts of electricity shooting through my body. Not what I need right now.

Right now, I need to find Moira, and I'm acutely aware Mitzy's little dragonflies have yet to add anything of use.

Seconds tick by.

"Eight in bunks, sleeping. Four on the bridge." Mitzy's clear voice pipes through the comms. "We're missing four men." With the ship's manifest in hand, I trust Mitzy's numbers.

"Copy. Alpha moving out, beginning sweep," Max replies and keeps everyone abreast of Alpha team's movements. Charlie is still five minutes out.

The plan is for Mitzy's drones to locate as many crew as possible. Once their positions are known, Alpha team is to sweep the crew quarters.

More than likely, that's where Moira's being held. We assume no more than a few men are with her. Too many would draw suspicion. While not common for tourists, charting passage on unused cabins is an economical way to get around the globe if you've got lots of time and not a lot of cash.

CJ and Sam think, and we all agree, that it's unlikely she's being kept below deck in the engine room or other areas. Priority is given to crew quarters, but I'm eyeing the men searching the stacks.

"Lots of interest in those stacks." I can't help but mutter my concerns out loud.

"Advise," Max responds, requesting advice, not from me, but rather CJ, who commands this operation.

"Proceed as planned," CJ's clipped voice joins the conversation. "Griff, eyes on the stacks. Report back."

I wait for Max to respond first, then reply in the affirmative, "Copy that."

Speed and I peer out of the helicopter and keep track of the men below. We're high enough, they look like ants, even with the zoom engaged on our headsets.

At some point, our random passes will draw attention, and I'm acutely aware those men carry weapons. Not pistols, but angry looking semi-automatic rifles.

I check the magazine of my weapon and watch as Speed does the same. We won't take the first shot, but we will have the last one. I'm against harming innocent civilians. As far as I know, those men are not an active threat, but damn if my gut says otherwise.

The men on deck approach the two holes in the stack, sweep down with their lights, then move on.

"We need eyes on that spot near the bow."

Still on an internal channel to Ariel and Speed only, my gut tells me that's where we'll find Moira, and I'm well aware Alpha team is toward the stern checking the cabins.

A burst of light blasts into the night, and Ariel banks hard to the left, nosing the helicopter sharply up.

"What the fuck?" If not for my safety harness, I'd be spinning through air right now.

As I right myself, more shots fire from the men on the stack.

"Shots fired," Ariel calls out through the comms.

Impressed with her skill, I'm even more in awe of Ariel's tenacity when she spins us right around and dives toward the tanker. Doing as I asked, she's going to get us an up-close and personal view of that one hole in the stacks.

"Permission to engage?" Speed calls for the go-ahead, meanwhile the men on the stacks open up on us like it's the goddamn Fourth of July.

"Go for engage," CJ's calm voice is music to my ears.

While the men shooting at us are a threat, their aim is piss-poor. Nothing hits the helicopter. However, Speed and I take them all out with shots meant to disable rather than kill.

These are civilians, after all.

Ariel aims the nose of the helicopter at the hole in the stacks while Speed and I dispatch the men.

"Found your girl." Ariel's crisp words slam right into me.

I lower my weapon and peer down into the dark stack where I see Moira looking straight up.

"Package located." Speed is on the comms while I sit and stare. Blood speeds around my body, carrying a surge of adrenaline to every cell.

It's her.

"Alpha team, go for package," CJ directs Alpha to move off their sweep of the cabins and head toward Moira.

"Negative." Max's tone is terse.

"Negative?"

"Hostiles. Engaged. No can do." Clipped and to the point, his words rip through me.

So damn close.

I don't even wonder why Alpha encounters hostiles on board. This should be a ship full of seasoned, but harmless, crew.

"Permission to pick up the package." No way in hell am I leaving her down there.

"Negative." CJ kills my joy.

"But…"

"That's a negative." He refuses to budge.

I lean back with an exasperated sigh and slam my fist into the floor of the chopper. Speed taps his headset and I flip to our internal channel.

"I'm getting static from Command." He flashes a goofy grin. "What about you, Battle Angel? Having the same problem?"

Ariel joins the conversation. "Is that your girl down there?"

"Yes." I don't hesitate.

"Then something seems to be seriously wrong with my headset. How long do you need?"

"Two minutes." One to rappel down. One to hook Moira into a safety harness.

"I'll give you three."

Speed and I exchange a look. He disengages from his weapon and walks to the back of the cabin. After I secure myself to the cable of the winch, he hands me a secondary harness.

I lean out while he keeps tension on the line. With a nod, I push off and drop through the air.

TWELVE

Moira

GUNSHOTS PULL ME FROM A RESTLESS SLEEP. I'D LIKE TO SAY I drifted off and got actual rest, but gruesome nightmares snap me awake the moment I fall asleep.

Shelly's dead eyes stare at me, judging me, as his brain matter leaks all over the floor. Bossman's blood splashes against the walls and slowly creeps upward, like a living thing, to cover the ceiling overhead.

My gut twists and my heart seizes with every horrific detail. It's a non-stop horror movie I can't escape from inside my head.

I'm a killer now, a murderer just like Bossman. Shouldn't that make me feel different? Like a smear on my soul? A mark on my life?

I don't. I'm glad Shelly died. He was a rutting pig and poor excuse for a human. I'm happy Bossman no longer walks this world. He was vile and despicable.

I'm not happy about killing him. I'm—apathetic.

That's the word I'm searching for. The whole thing makes me feel —nothing.

It's been hours since I took his life. I'm sure of it, and it must be well past midnight. I look to the East, right off the bow, and see nothing but darkness.

Maybe I'm the one who died and this is what hell feels like. It's an odd sensation because while the air is hot and muggy, the steel beneath my butt saps my heat.

I shiver and curl into a small ball, desperately trying to stay warm. My toes curl and press against the unforgiving metal of the cargo container, and my ass hurts from the hard surface. Thankfully, there's very little wind. I'm protected from that by the containers stacked in front of me.

Another pop sounds from someplace behind and overhead. I glance up to peer into the darkness but make out nothing.

At first, the gunshot doesn't worry me, but then others follow. Those are followed by a barrage of shots coming also from overhead.

Gunfire closes in on me and I suddenly realize how poor of a hiding spot I found. There's no real way up. I'd planned on climbing back down once the ship hit port and figuring out an exit plan then.

Technically, I could squeeze myself between the containers and crawl up. That's how I got here in the first place. Strong back, stronger legs, and an even fiercer determination, I scaled the stack of containers as if my life depended on it.

It made sense at the time.

Hours later, I feel the result of that exertion in the angry protests of my legs and back. Bordering on hypothermia, I don't think I can do that again. As for any adrenaline? I emptied out that reserve when I killed Bossman and fled here. Simply put, I'm too exhausted to do anything but wait.

More shots fire overhead. They're definitely overhead.

A low vibration draws closer, building to a crescendo in my chest. Well-attuned to the noises of this ship, that sound is different.

Whomp! Whomp! Whomp!

I push back to huddle in the corner, not that it's much of a corner. There's a gap on either side of this particular stack about three feet wide. Behind me, and to the front, the gap is smaller, maybe a foot wide. It's enough that I'm not keen on getting too close to it.

I gather my knees to my chest and rock. I pray the men with the guns don't make it here, where they can look straight down on me. It never occurs to me a search would come from above.

As for the men with the guns, I assume they found Bossman's body. I bet they're out looking for Shelly, thinking the two of them had a fight that turned lethal. Little do they know, Shelly's fish food by now.

But they're still looking for somebody.

They're looking for me.

Which means—getting off this ship just became an impossibility. Tears leak out of my eyes, and I brush them off my face.

I'm headed to jail, a place where I don't trust the cops. Hell, I may never make it to jail, turned over instead to the monster who bought me for a tiny exchange of cash in exchange for a favor.

I officially hate men.

That low droning draws closer. No, not a drone, it's a rhythmic chopping noise.

A helicopter?

Maybe my monster never intended for me to make port? Picking me up directly off the ship instead of dealing with port authority and all that would entail kind of makes sense.

I'm going to kill that sick prick too. I'm a killer. Why stop now?

A light shines down on me, blinding me as it pierces the darkness. I hold up a hand to block the bright beam and squint up at a helicopter hovering overhead.

Guess I was right, he's come for me.

With nowhere to run, and no place to hide, Four's words spill through my head. *Commit, Moira. Commit as if your life depends on it.*

Well, Four, I'm fucking committed.

Deafening overhead, I cup my ears against the powerful roar. Air churned into a vortex pushes down on me, a physical force I find difficult to resist.

I assume it's landing on the stacks and imagine a deep scowl set on my new Master's face as he tries to figure out how to extract me from my hiding place. Bastard will likely make me climb up to him.

What I don't expect is the tail of a thick rope to drop into the pit, or the terrifying form of a man dressed all in black who slides down it.

All I see are the whites of his eyes. As for the rest of him, black boots, black pants, black shirt, and black masking his face. My terror spikes as he prowls toward me. This man is not some simpering, weak-willed, filthy rich monster. He's the hired hand sent to retrieve me.

I'm so screwed.

My fingers curl as I rise to a crouch.

Commit, Moira.

The deafening sound of the helicopter overhead drowns out all other noise. The *whomp, whomp, whomp* vibrates my chest, making it hard to breathe. The man takes a step toward me, hand outstretched as if I would be the fool to take it.

My hair flies everywhere, whipping my face and stinging my eyes. I let it fly, more concerned with how I'll meet this newest threat than I am about that tiny discomfort.

He shouts, but the noise from the helicopter drowns him out. It's impossible to hear anything.

He advances.

I take one step back.

He moves forward, hand outstretched, grasping at the air.

I shuffle back. Not that there's anywhere to go. In two more steps, he'll have backed me up against the container behind me.

Then what?

I can't jump down. It's thirty feet to the deck of the ship. I can't shimmy my way up. That takes tons of concentration, and right now, all my attention zeroes in on the man approaching me. There is no running. I certainly picked one hell of hiding place.

It's a damn trap.

The dark cable rotates behind him. It spins around and around, the tip drawing a slow circle.

He steps forward, and this time, when I step back, my foot finds the gap behind me.

I slip. He leaps into action. I fall. He lunges and grabs me by the waist. Before I can fight him, he tugs me tight to his chest.

What the hell?

He buries his face in my neck and the hold turns—intimate.

Before I can knee him in the groin, I finally hear his shout.

"Moira! It's me, Griff!"

Griff? I don't know anyone by that name. I press against his chest and squirm in his grip. I'm not getting free, but I feel like I need to at least make a gesture.

"Dammit, Moira, it's me, Griff!" The low rumble of his voice buzzes in my ears, sounding familiar and yet not.

"I don't know anyone by that name," I scream back at him and intensify my struggle.

The man picks me off my feet and takes several steps back from the edge. He places me down and stoops until our eyes are on the same level.

"Shit. Moira, I'm Four. You know me as Four."

Suddenly there's no air to breathe. My long blond hair lashes at my face and stings my eyes as what he says hits me. All of a sudden, there's no air to breathe. It's Four?

Is this possible? He's here to rescue me?

"My Four?"

"Yes, Moira. Yours." He releases me and detaches something from his belt.

Dressed all in black, I barely make out the dark webbing crisscrossing his body. He wears a climber's seat, webbing around his legs which attaches to more webbing around his midsection, but there's also a shoulder harness with black D-rings attached to each shoulder strap.

I glance down at what he's holding.

"Put this on." He shouts to be heard above the deafening sound of the helicopter. The downdraft pushes so hard, I'm having trouble standing.

Barely able to hear him above the noise of the helicopter, I brace my hands on his shoulders as he squats down to help me feed my feet into each leg of the harness. He tugs the contraption up to my waist and pulls tight on the securing straps.

He does the same for the strap around my waist. Two more straps dangle at either side of my waist. He loops those over my shoulders and secures them together with yet another strap across my chest.

Not gentle in the slightest, he tugs that down too, until I gasp and struggle to breathe.

My mind is a bit slow to process everything, at least until he clips my harness to the rings on his chest.

He takes my hand and walks back to the rope. Chest to chest, or rather my face to his chest, Four towers over me, he lifts me off my feet and I give a terrified squeak.

"Wrap your legs around my waist." Without waiting for me to do as he says, he positions my legs until they wrap around him.

Four reaches for the cable and does something with a clip.

"Hold on!" He shouts into my ear as he wraps his arms beneath my ass, making a kind of sling with his hands.

I wrap my arms around his neck, drawing close to him. He smells of sweat, metal, and fuel, but something else as well.

Four smells like coming home.

A screech escapes me as the world tilts beneath my feet. I squeeze my eyes shut as we lift into the air.

Nothing happens for a moment, and I open my eyes to peek around. Twenty, no fifty feet below us, the tanker is lit up like a Christmas tree. Four men struggle on top of the decks, crawling to one another as they watch us fly away. Dark stains spread out beneath each man, smearing as they move toward one another…

We rise high into the air, then swing back as the helicopter angles away from the tanker. Through it all, Four holds me close. The webbing cuts into my legs. My legs shake. My arms ache, but all I feel is the slow circle Four makes at the small of my back with the pad of his thumb.

"Don't worry, little minx, I've got you. You're safe."

I've got you.

Four's words sink into me, where they brush against my heart, and sear themselves into my soul. While deafening, the noise from the helicopter means nothing to me. All I hear is Four whispering over and over again. *I've got you. You're safe.*

A man peers down at us from the back of the helicopter. He gives me a soft, compassionate smile.

I think he knows he's intruding on something because after he hauls us on board and closes the heavy sliding doors on either side, he settles into his seat, pulls his helmet down over his eyes, and leans back as if taking a nap.

His compassion socks me in the chest because it's so unexpected. He doesn't know me, but he knows me. The man is another Guardian and knows what I endured. He gives me the only space he can by closing his eyes. It's a gesture which breaks my heart.

"I've got you." Four wraps me in his arms and tugs me tight to his chest. "I've got you." Four repeats that over and over again, rocking me in his chest.

When I look up at him, there's a glimmer in his eyes. His jaw opens slightly as if he wants to say more, but then it slams shut as fury overtakes him. His entire body vibrates, resonating with that anger. I get it. He wants to make those men pay. Sadly, Four will never have that pleasure.

I killed them. I'm a murderer.

Slowly, I lower my head, overtaken with what's happened. Disbelieving this is true.

I can't be safe.

Yet I find myself rescued—again, by the same man who saved me well over a year ago in the Philippines. He's someone I've slowly grown to love even as he distanced himself from what we both feel for each other.

In the darkest depths of my despair, I made myself a promise. I'm going to grab life by the horns and take what I want. I'm tired of being life's punching bag. It's my time.

However, reality sets in. That's a promise I'll fulfill later, not here. Not now. But I will take what's mine.

I snuggle in, burying my face against his chest. My arms wrap around his neck, and I feel safe in his arms. My legs fold, knees pressing against my chest, until I curl into a tight ball. Four gathers me in his lap and holds me tight.

A deep breath inward draws his essence into my lungs, flooding my nasal passages with the memory of Four straining over me, teaching me, laughing with me as we wrestled during training. I breathe deeply, still in shock. It still hasn't hit me, but I'm sure it will, and soon.

A slow breath out follows an even slower breath in.

I'm hanging on by a thread. I feel it like I'm one second from catastrophic collapse.

I peek up at him and meet his steady gaze as he looks down at me. A silent, bolstering presence, he's my rock. Four is the voice that got me through the darkest moments. My toes curl as I struggle to piece everything together. It's an innocuous thing, me curling my toes, but there's something about it which releases the floodgates.

I survived.

I killed a man and orchestrated another's murder, but I survived.

When I tense, Four's grip tightens. His body heat sinks into me as I shiver for the first time.

So cold.

I'm so very cold.

I'm safe.

Four's large hand cups the back of my head. His fingers thread between the gnarled mess that is my hair. He tries to pull through the tangles, but that's not happening. His chest lifts and rises with a defeated sigh.

"I found you."

I tilt my head to regard him, like really take a look at the gruff man holding me in his arms.

Four's a fierce warrior. There's little that's pretty about him, definitely nothing soft. His features are coarse, a nose broken one too many times, a square jaw that's a little too big, a little too square, but damn if he doesn't have the prettiest eyes I've ever seen.

Deep violet, they're almost black, unless you really stop to take a look. And when I do, they make my skin heat and send shivers racing down my spine. Thick lashes cap the dark violet of his eyes, and when he blinks, they sweep across his coarse cheekbones like feathers.

He holds my stare but blinks first. What does he see when he looks at me? Does he see a tragic little girl? The abused woman who's been shattered and broken too many times to count? Or does he see my strength and resilience? My ability to keep on living even when all I want is to embrace death?

I don't know what he sees, but when he looks back at me, I get the first glimpse of what I've been waiting for. He wants me. This is no ordinary rescue for him. Four has feelings for me.

I don't care about stupid Guardian policies; I've had enough of keeping my hands to myself. The first chance I get...

What? What are you going to do?

Well, shit if I know! Jumping his bones comes to mind. One bone, in particular, interests me the most.

You sure about that?

Shut up!

What I want frightens me.

Like most trafficked children, I come from a home devoid of love and lacking in the most basic supervision. Dad left at five. Mom spent her life high, or chasing the next high, until she finally crashed and burned.

Love is an abstract concept for me. It's not something I understand because I've never experienced it. Whatever this is that I feel for Four… Is that love?

I stare into the violet depths of his eyes and see only warmth, compassion, and that simmering promise of something more.

Something shifts between us. Without really noticing it, my hand lifts until I cup the side of his cheek. "I never doubted you would save me. You were there with me the whole time."

"Huh?"

"Your voice." I close my eyes and push away the ghastly images pushing in. "I heard you in my head. You told me to wait until the moment was right, and when it was, you told me to commit. You were with me the whole time."

"Little minx, I wish I had been there. I wouldn't have let them hurt you."

I blink taking in what he says and give a shake of my head. "My kidnapper didn't let the others damage the merchandise."

Griff's brow draws tight and his lips press together as the tension in his body builds.

My hand draws down his face until the tips of my fingers flutter over his lips. I trace the pillowy softness and press my lips together, moistening them.

Turbulent thoughts dance in his eyes, danger with a warning. Four shifts in his seat and the movement dislodges my fingers from their exploration.

Words fail me as tension swirls around us. It comes from him, knotting the muscles of his shoulders and bunching in his thighs. His grip on me tightens as he draws me closer to his chest. I'm pretty sure the hard length pressing against my ass isn't because his tree-trunk legs are carved from granite.

Reality sets in as I understand he wants me.

The carnal hunger simmering in his eyes is a look I know well. I'm not sure what's happening to me, but a burst of adrenaline sends my heart in a frantic gallop around my ribcage. My pulse jumps and I try to rein it in, but why do I even try?

I blink, then blink again, as his stoicism holds him back. Four has always held himself on the edge, never crossing the line between teacher and pupil.

That's okay by me. I don't need a man to make the first move. Trained by the necessity of survival, I've served men from all walks of life, every ethnicity, and every social strata. I've had men in all sizes and shapes: rich men, poor men, strong men, and weak men.

At first, when I was twelve, I played a game with myself, lying about the truth. I told myself that I was in control. I chose the Johns who slaked their filthy need within my flesh. I could stop whenever I wanted.

Not once did I believe I was enslaved, but I was. A slave to circumstance, and driven by the need to survive, I catered to my very first Master, Necessity, at the tender age of twelve.

I managed four years on the streets without a pimp, but then reality set in.

A distinguished man lured me with false promises and a silver tongue. He fed me a mouthful of lies which I swallowed in my desperation. He told me I could be free of the streets. I could have a better life. I could be free if I only agreed to serve his desire for one short night.

I believed every damn word.

Desperate kids are easy prey, and I was getting more and more desperate the older I got and the more my craving for drugs drove me out to hook every day. Every hour became a struggle to stay ahead of the insatiable need and bottomless craving for just one more hit.

I thought I was in control until I had the truth shoved in my face. At twelve, I thought I was free. At sixteen, I knew the truth. First by necessity, then to the drugs which poisoned my mind, then to the man with the silver tongue. He became my first Master as I realized I'd always been a slave.

I'm older now, twenty-two, curled in the arms of a man sworn to protect and defend. Four looks at me with lust and passion, but reins all of that in, content to simply hold me in his arms and soothe me with his soft whispers that I'm finally safe.

Thanks, Four, but I need something else.

I need control.

With a deep, shaky breath, I look into the most terrifying eyes I've ever seen. This fear is new and not based on what he will take from me, or the pain he will cause.

Four will never take anything from me. He'll never force me to do anything. I sense this. I know it deep in my bones. He'll never hurt me, but he holds the power to destroy me.

The walls close in around me as I shift in his lap.

Cupping his face with both hands, his eyes widen and his pupils dilate. I feel him all around me. His body heat brushing against my skin, sinking deep to my bones. His breaths on my cheek strangle my air and flutter stray wisps of hair free from my lashes.

Time slows down.

Moments stretch to minutes.

He sits there, body tense, breaths strained yet tightly controlled. The chilling way he commands his body is new to me. I'm used to men giving into their urges, not holding them at bay.

I brush my nose against his, testing the waters, and get no response. He doesn't draw away, but neither does he take the kiss I dearly want to give.

I want to know what he tastes like, and I plan on savoring our first kiss. But even more than that, the deep ache building within me makes me crave something far more carnal.

It's beastly and wild, a craving, or maybe a desperation, but I need something I can't quite explain. I don't even know if I know what I need myself.

Sex is a part of it. I desperately want Four to fuck me, but there's more.

What will he feel like when he's inside of me? Will I come with a whimper, dissatisfied with another weak and unfulfilled orgasm? Or will his cock ignite my senses and bury me in pleasure so damaging that his cock will be the only one that ever matters for the rest of my life?

What about his lips? How will they feel when he finally kisses me, or better yet, when he kisses me where I've never had a man kiss me before?

Prostitutes and pleasure slaves serve their clients and Masters. They don't derive pleasure from the ordeal, but I have a sense Four has it in him to wrench ungodly screams from my mouth. Screams so full of pleasure that he'll wear me out until I fade into a blissfully spent puddle of ecstasy.

Is that what love feels like?

I suppose it does, but now isn't the time. While I have no issue with a little change in position, straddling Four right now isn't going to happen. He would stop me.

I'm scared to death to make a move. If he refuses me, like he's done in the past, does that mean I mean nothing to him? Am I just another one of his countless rescuees?

A job?

Maybe I've built up a false relationship in my head, but I swear the close contact drills we shared sparked passion in us both. I can't be making that up.

His fingers caress my spine. It's beyond arousing. Each press of his fingers sends me into a quivering mess. His touch loosens the tightness of my muscles, relaxing me, sending me into such a haze that if I don't do something about it soon, I'll be a moaning puddle of… Well, of something.

Four makes no further move. The tips of our noses touch. His fingers continue their mad dance along my spine. The evidence of his arousal presses hard against the crack of my ass.

I can't help it and lean into him. I loop my arms around his neck and close the distance. The heat of his mouth makes my breath stutter and my nostrils flare. He smells phenomenal, a dark, woodsy, masculine scent. His chest is firm. His thighs are tense. He's aroused and very hard, but the expression in his eyes is unyielding.

He sits there, not moving a muscle as I slowly press my lips to his. At least I think I touch his lips. It's more like a cautious graze.

I'm not really sure.

I believe he holds the skill to destroy everything I know about sex, but he holds himself with such rigid restraint it's maddening.

My insides heat and tighten with anticipation. The endings of my nerves flare and sizzle. My entire body quakes with the need flowing through me.

Dear Lord, what is he doing to me? I feel uncertain, like I've never done this before. Granted, many Johns aren't interested in kissing, but the Masters I've had craved the claiming that comes from a kiss.

Our breaths mingle and become one as I gently brush my lips against his. A moan escapes him, and he bucks beneath me, but still, he doesn't engage. I want him. I feel it in the tingling of my breasts, the way they grow heavy and tight, and in the insistent throbbing between my legs. My chest heaves, needing air, but I too hold onto my restraint.

I pull away and slide my thumb along his jaw, then sweep it up and over the pillowy curve of his lips. I gulp as he presses closer, putting pressure on my thumb where he didn't when it was my lips.

His lips part and I gulp as he sucks my thumb into his mouth. He stares deeply into my eyes and there's no doubt he wants to kiss me. Actually, it's more than that. I feel as if he wants to peel me open and climb inside of me.

The roughness of his tongue swirls around the tip of my thumb, then he pushes my thumb out, pressing hard with his tongue until I'm free.

He licks his lips and adjusts his grip. "Moira, you're playing with fire."

"And?"

"Don't start something you can't stop."

"What if I want to burn?"

"Are you sure that's what you want?" His brow arches. "You're in shock and not making the best decisions right now." He licks his lips and drives me crazy. "You should take a moment."

"I don't want to take a moment. I want you to kiss me."

"You're so damn beautiful, strong, and resilient. Your soul glows with fire, but don't confuse gratitude for something else."

"Excuse me?" Gratitude? Is that what he thinks this is?

"You're alive. Take a moment and let your freedom sink in. You don't have to thank me for doing my job."

His job?

"I don't want it to sink in." I push against his chest and would crawl out of his lap, but he doesn't let me. I vent an exasperated huff. "I want you to kiss me." I rear back as his words sink in. "You think this is gratitude? Is that what you just said?"

"Moira," he licks his damn lips, "after such a traumatic event, your emotions will be all over the place. I'm not going to kiss you. I won't take advantage."

"Advantage? You've got some nerve. I've been throwing myself at you for a year and you think this is different? That I'm too traumatized to make my own decisions? You fucking prick."

I glare at him, feeling extra stabby.

His restraint is going to kill me. Either that or I'm going to kill him.

I want to claw his eyes out, except I want this kiss more than I want to vent my frustration. "I lived through hell to get back to you. I'm getting my damn kiss."

I crush my lips against his, and he meets my fiery passion with stone-cold indifference.

Okay, that's it. I'm going with the scratching-out-the-eyes thing next.

THIRTEEN

Griff

_____

HOLY FUCKING HELL IN A HAND BASKET.

Moira's lips taste like the sweetest nectar. Ambrosia from the gods, I swear it's all I can do to sit there like a statue and let her kiss me. I want to yank her into my arms, feast upon her lips, plunge my tongue deep into her mouth, and explore all the hidden places, but I don't.

My body reacts to the dark thoughts swirling in my head because kissing leads to fucking. With fingers, mouth, and eventually my cock, I will make this woman mine.

Restraint!

I must exercise restraint. Two reasons come to mind. The first is the not so oblivious Speed sitting not more than a few feet away. The drone of the helicopter drowns out any sounds Moira and I might make, but more concerning is the second reason: Moira's current state of mind.

Our rescuees experience either a euphoric high after their rescue or sit in a dazed fog, overcome with the trauma of their abduction. A little over a year ago, Moira experienced the latter. Her dull affect worried me at the time, but that was before I knew the full extent of her troubled past.

This time, there's nothing dull about Moira. She's a ball of fucking energy, riding the high of escaping her kidnapping.

I need to be extraordinarily cautious with every move I make. No way will I layer on further damage by taking and claiming her the way I've dreamt about since the first time I saw her. I've had it hard for her from the get-go, and if I want any future with her, caution is my go-to move.

I fucking hate caution.

But still, she attacks me with the fervor of her kiss.

My fingers curl and clench as her lips erode my self-control. Barely hanging on by a thread, I want her. I desperately want to make Moira mine.

There's no denying it, not by the way my dick responds. She has to feel my hard length pressing against her ass. With the way she squirms in my lap, there's no way she doesn't know how much she makes me ache for her.

But she's traumatized, and there's no way in hell that I'll take advantage of her.

It's something ingrained in our teaching as Guardians. Hero worship and God complex are real things in those we rescue, and that's regardless of whether they're men, women, boys, or girls.

They fixate and obsess on their rescuer. Breaking that unhealthy bond often does as much, or more, damage than the trauma they already endured at the hands of those who would take without regard for the harm they inflict.

Infatuation is something we're taught to nip in the bud. It's why there are rules because God knows how easy it would be to take advantage of our precious charges.

It's why I held back from Moira. It's why I've kept her at arm's length this past year, even when things slowly began to shift between us. My intent, all along, was to make Moira mine, but not while she was a resident at the Facility. In fact, I have it all planned out in my head.

I'm going to date her like a normal guy and treat her to what it's like to be a normal girl. Not that I'm old-fashioned, but Moira isn't like any woman I've dated before. I plan to court her and take the time to build our relationship. It'll be new for me, considering the last girl I dated was Sara Snow in high school. I did everything right with her, thought we'd get married, and despite my raging hormones, I never slept with her. I wanted to do things right, and then life got in the way. Sara cheated on me the night of prom, broke my heart, and I enlisted the very next day.

Never looked back.

And I never treated another woman with the same respect I'd shown Sara. Why bother when all they were going to do was break my heart? Since then, I've slept with my fair share of women, engaged in several short flings, but never a relationship. My life as a SEAL, and then a Delta operative, wasn't conducive to relationships, but it was excellent for scoring easy women and fast hookups.

Moira's different, and for a lot of reasons, her past being only one of many, I will take things slow.

It's why I hold back now. She practically climbs up my body, twists her arms around my neck, and presses her luscious lips to mine. I must say, the girl knows how to kiss, but I refuse to take advantage of her when she's not of sound mind and body to know what it is she's doing.

All of this? This passion? It's not real. This is what I tell myself.

What she's doing is a reaction to the rescue, and the sad thing is, Moira knows only one way to express gratitude.

The poor thing has never known a man who didn't take what he wanted without any regard for what she desired.

I won't be that man. For Moira, I'll give instead of take, and right now, that means ending this before it goes too far.

I grasp her nape and force her head back. An intoxicating rush of dominance runs through me, and I soften my grip. That's the wrong road to take with her. Shit, it's hard to string two thoughts together with the taste of her coating my lips. Although I shouldn't, I run the tip of my tongue over them and hold back a groan.

She drives me crazy.

Moira glares at me with fury and frustration when I end the kiss. I drink all that ire in. Damn, but if she isn't a fighter. Nothing gets me going more than a strong woman, and Moira has that in spades. Before she can say anything, and from the look in her eyes, I expect her to spit fire, I slide my thumb along her jaw and nudge it down to her lips.

"You taste like sin, and damn if I don't want this, but now is not the time. When I finally take you, and I will, it'll be without any of this clouding your senses."

"Nothing's clouding my senses." She pushes against me and her expression darkens. "Kiss me."

"No."

She rears back, indignation flaring in her eyes.

"What do you mean by no?"

"I mean, no."

"You're a goddamn jackass. When a woman throws herself at you, you don't say no."

"This isn't right." I refuse to let her go. Moira needs to know I'm serious about this.

"If you don't want me kissing you, then you don't want me kissing you. Message received loud and clear." She tries to climb out of my lap, but I refuse to let her out of my arms.

"Let me go."

"No."

"Four, let me go."

"The name's Griff, Moira. If you're going to cuss me out, at least use my name."

"Your name is weird, and I want you to let me go."

"You've got your wires crossed, little minx, because there's nothing I want to do more than kiss you right now."

"Then kiss me! Haven't I been through enough? Don't I deserve a simple kiss?"

"You and I know there's no such thing as a simple kiss between us."

"It's just a kiss."

I push down on her hips, pressing her against my rigid length. "Does that feel like I think there's anything simple about this?"

She grows silent for a moment, but then the fire's back in her eyes. "I don't get you. I'm not ugly. I know what I look like; it's why men…" She cuts off the rest of that thought, knowing where it leads. I patiently wait her out. "I want you to kiss me, and you want to kiss me. Frankly, I don't see where the problem is?"

"You're beautiful but incredibly stubborn. I think you know that. What you don't know is what I'm going to show you."

"And what's that? That you're a jackass like all the rest? Or that you suck at kissing? Is that it? You're a piss-poor kisser?"

"No, Moira." I have to be firm, or I'll lose my shit and take what she's not ready to give. "I'm going to show you what it feels like when a man worships you, and right now, that means holding off on a kiss when it's not the right time, the right place, or the right circumstance."

"You're fucking impossible. You know that, don't you?"

"And you're my little minx."

"Don't try to change the subject on me."

"I'm holding the woman of my dreams in my lap, with a raging hard-on, and no way to relieve it, so I agree with you—fucking is impossible right now."

"All I want is one kiss."

"When I kiss you, there's no way I'm stopping at a kiss." When her gorgeous blue eyes round in surprise, I can't help but laugh. "You heard me." I shift her to a more comfortable position and bite my lower lip. "And I'm not letting you go ever again. I don't think you get what that means, but you will."

"I will once you give me a goddamn kiss."

She bites her lower lip and nearly demolishes what little control I have left. Leaning into me, she settles back and rests her hand on my chest. I'm barely able to think, but I know deep down in my soul that to give into that kiss will be the end of us. I don't want the end.

I'm ready for a beginning.

Speed tips up his helmet and we exchange a look. I thank him for giving us what privacy he could and he shrugs like it was a no brainer. He's also letting me know we'll be landing soon. With a tap to his headset, he tells me to listen in on the private channel the three of us share.

"What's up?"

"Alpha ran into resistance on the tanker. Evidently, that crew isn't an ordinary crew. They didn't take kindly when we fired on their men."

"Max said they encountered resistance." I'm pretty sure that's why we went against protocol. We being me. I disobeyed a direct order and it'll cause waves. My future as a Guardian may be a little up in the air once we land.

"Evidently, there was a scene in one of the crew quarters. Alpha took fire from our not so innocent crew, and then they saw the room." His voice takes on a strange tone and his gaze shifts to Moira. I sense there's more to what he wants to say, but I'm stuck on what he said about the crew.

"I find it hard to believe the crew was in on this."

"I'm thinking the same thing, but this is the same tanker involved in several other transports. Mitzy is looking into it."

"Well, fuck."

Moira shifts in my lap and I bite my lower lip as her tight ass brushes against my hard cock. Why didn't I let her kiss me? I just got control over the fucker and now it's standing up for business again.

"What's going on?" Her blue eyes droop with exhaustion. The poor thing's been running on adrenaline for too long and is running out of steam. Despite our fight, her head bobs and her eyes keep falling shut. She's moments away from total collapse.

"Nothing." I lay her head against my chest and run my hand over her hair. A mess of knots, there are tangles in her tangles. My heart hurts imagining what she's been through. Moira's not had an easy life. "We'll be touching down soon. Try to get some rest. It's going to be chaos once we land."

"Okay."

I'M SURPRISED SHE DOESN'T FIGHT ME ON THIS. MOIRA SEEMS TO take pleasure in resisting everything I tell her to do. Her anger, that resistance, is her strength. It's how she survives.

Hate to say it, but I like her spunk and look forward to what that promises. I need someone strong enough to stand up to my bullshit and call me a jackass when the shoe fits.

I need someone who can deal with what I do for a living, the calling I chose to accept as my guiding principle. A weak woman won't do. She won't be able to endure the long nights when I leave her alone to save others. Moira has that strength and more.

But first, there are a few bumps in the road we need to overcome. I brace for one hell of a ride.

While she rests, Speed fills me in on the details.

The muscles in my jaw bunch as he tells me what Alpha team found. I look at my woman with a great deal of respect and a shit-ton of concern. I know what it means to take a life. There was a time when I wrestled with what that meant.

Now Moira must travel down that path. I'm afraid of what she's going to find. Knowing this, it's even better I stopped that kiss.

The psychologists at the Facility need to know what Alpha team found, and I can only hope they're able to offer Moira the support she needs.

As for me, I'm not saying a word until Moira tells me herself. But if she doesn't, I'll help her process as best I can. How do I start up a romantic relationship on top of what she's endured?

The thing about Moira is that I feel her all over, against my skin and in my blood. She's the beating of my heart, the stirring of my soul. She's already a part of me.

When I touch her face, a soft caress, she settles against me with a sigh. The poor thing tries to keep her eyes open, but her lids continue to bounce. I don't think she's aware that she's dozing in and out.

Sapped of adrenaline doesn't quite describe her current state, but at least now, she's in my arms, protected and safe.

As we return to our rendezvous point, I check in with my team. They subdued the crew and are staying with the ship for as long as possible to extract information, which kind of sucks. Messing-with-people-so-they-tell-you-shit, aka torture, is my wheelhouse. I excel at getting people to spill shit they don't want to tell me.

Support sucks, but given a choice, I'd much rather be here, comforting Moira.

Ariel closes in on the airport. After she drops us off, she'll head back to pick up Alpha and Charlie teams, who joined Alpha on the ship. They're headed to exfil as we speak.

As expected, the moment the bay doors slide open, we're inundated with activity. Moira climbs out of my lap and makes her way out of the helicopter under CJ's care. He reaches up and gives her a hand down.

Forest Summers is there, watching me with a tight-lipped expression. I can't tell if he's pissed I went against CJ's orders or pleased with my actions. Not that it matters. I jump out after Moira and take her from CJ.

He'll want to have a moment alone with me, but I'll stay with Moira as long as possible.

Behind me, Ariel's clear voice rings out. "Sorry about the problem with the comms. They can be finicky."

"Finicky?" CJ arches a brow. "Is that what we're calling it?"

"Yup. I had to make a decision. I know it wasn't my place, but as the pilot, I'm used to being mission commander. I saw an opportunity and took it."

"What do you have to say?" CJ glances at me, then his gaze slides over to Speed.

"Something like that." I don't commit an outright lie. I have too much integrity for that kind of shit, but I'm not against omitting one or two things.

Speed jumps in, "Yeah, just kind of lost you for a bit. Ariel saw an opportunity. We took it." He backs up Ariel's version of the truth while I rock back on my heels.

"I see." CJ looks between us but doesn't say a word.

Our medical team joins us.

Doc Summers takes one look at me and gives a disappointed shake of her head. Her fierce gaze takes me in. "You're bleeding."

"No, I'm not." My brows draw together. Sure, my leg hurts, but…

"Griff," she points to my leg, "get in the plane and let me take a look at that. Looks like you pulled a stitch…or two."

"I didn't…" But wetness greets my fingers as I touch the back of my thigh. It's hard to see the blood in predawn twilight, but the doc's right.

"Get in the jet." She shakes her head and takes Moira's hands in hers. "You too, Moira. Both of you, get in the jet." She glances at Forest, and they exchange another one of their secretive looks.

Whatever it is they say, he responds with a flick of his eyes. Or maybe, it's Forest's version of an eye roll. All I know is I'm in deep shit.

Doc Summers leads Moira to a waiting jet. It's not the one we flew in on, but rather one specifically outfitted with a mobile medical unit. I march along behind Moira, feeling like I got away with something, and notice for the first time how much my leg hurts.

FOURTEEN

Moira

HE'S BLEEDING?

I follow Skye's gaze, and sure enough, a glistening wet sheen coats the back of Four's pants. I want to go to him, hover over him, and check out the damage, but I can't.

I'm still overly pissed at him about that lackluster, non-responsive kiss. The man has boundaries. I get it, but still? Come on, rescuing me should've stirred something in that stoic Guardian shell of his. I know he cares about me. Why the hell won't he take that final step and—I don't know—reciprocate? Is that too much to ask?

But what do I expect? Let's be honest here. He's a man. After all is said and done, all men are stupid. I'll just have to keep pressing him.

Skye ushers us to the plane. I stomp in front of Four and do my best to ignore his hovering overprotectiveness. All the while, I want to know why he's bleeding.

But I'm too damn proud to ask. Too damn angry to show him that I care.

Before I can second guess my decision to ignore him, Skye's team separates us. I'm taken to the back of the plane, beyond the in-flight surgical suite set up at the front of the airplane, where a man I don't know smiles down at me. Like Four, he towers over me. Unlike Four, his eyes are warm, welcoming, and genuinely concerned.

"Hi, I'm Ryker." His megawatt smile nearly blinds me. Ryker is a looker, the perfect blend between rough and rugged and movie star gorgeous. His face should be on a movie poster. What the hell is he doing working for Guardian HRS?

"Moira." My flat response makes his left eyebrow curve upward. The other one stays put.

I've never been able to do that. Even after many hours standing in front of a mirror practicing, I still can't isolate just the one brow and make it arch like that. I've always thought that kind of thing was cool, like really sophisticated or mysterious.

Alas, I'm not in that cool-kid club. I belong to a whole other kind of club, and there's nothing cool about it.

"We're going to do a quick exam." Is it possible for Ryker to turn off that magnetic grin? I don't suppose it is.

"Are you a doctor?" I can't help but challenge him. I'm still kind of reeling from killing Bossman, hiding out in the stacks of containers, and Four swooping down out of the sky to rescue me.

Like seriously, that kind of shit belongs in movies.

"No." His lips curve into a broader smile, as if that's possible.

"A m-urse?"

"A m-urse?" He holds his expression, but I have a feeling he's laughing at me on the inside.

"You know, male nurse?"

"I know what a m-urse is, but it's kind of derogatory, and no, I'm not a m-urse, although there's nothing wrong with that."

"Didn't mean to be derogatory and never said there was anything wrong with it. Most of Forest's team are ex-military and there are a lot of male nurses in the military. If you're not a doc, you must be a nurse."

"Well, I'm not a doc, nor am I a nurse, and for the record, there are a lot of female nurses, doctors, anesthetists, and…"

"Anes-the-what?"

"CRNAs." He casually crosses his arms over his very broad and very muscular chest. "Certified nurse anesthetists?" There goes that brow of his. Just the one, lifting like it's smirking at me.

"You're ex-military, right?"

"Sure am. Air Force."

"But not a doc and not a nurse?"

"Nope." He pops the "P" and grins. Ryker rocks back and looks down at me. "I'm an RT."

"What's that?"

"Respiratory therapist."

"And you're going to examine me?"

"Does that bother you?"

"Just didn't think it fell in the realm of what an RT does."

"Well, in the Guardians, we cross-train and multi-task. I assure you, I'm more than qualified to perform an exam."

My attention shifts from Ryker to where Skye forces Four to unlace his boots and strip out of his pants. All that masculine flesh rivets my attention. I didn't know thighs could bulge with that many muscles. My mouth goes dry as I gape at the muscles twining up Four's legs, and I kind of linger on the bulge nestled between his thighs. I miss what Ryker says next.

"I'm sorry. What were you saying?"

Ryker glances over his shoulder. Four winces as Skye forces him onto an examination table.

"Skye will take good care of your Guardian friend. In the meantime, do you have any injuries?"

"No." My clipped response makes his smile bounce.

"Do you mind if I take that look now?"

"Do I have a choice?"

"You always have a choice, but I think a little look is a good idea. Don't you?" He points to my face, where the skin swelled after Bossman got in a few good punches. It feels tight. "You've got some impressive bruising."

"It's nothing."

"And the back of your hair is matted with blood."

"No, it's not. I washed all of him off." Shit, didn't mean to say that. Now there will be questions and I'm not interested in answering any questions. I know how this works.

Been here. Done that. Got the goddamn scars to prove it.

"You did what?"

The whole Guardian HRS operation goes out into the bad, bad world, rescues the lost and the stolen, then returns them to the Facility where a team of highly skilled psychologists, life coaches, educators, and more specialists than I can count, band together to rehabilitate the traumatized. They turn victims into self-reliant survivors.

I spent an entire year at the Facility getting rehabilitated and working through my trauma. They're helping me with my education. I'll have my GED soon, and after that, I get to decide what to do next. I'm supposed to be one of their survivors, not another victim.

Ugh! I hate my life.

I spent a good chunk of that year with Four, learning how to defend myself and increase my situational awareness. It's another part of their philosophy of turning victims into survivors.

I want to be a survivor.

But the very first time I left the Facility, look what happened? Victimized—again. Seriously, I'm starting to lose count.

I must've built up a shit-ton's worth of bad karma in a previous life to deserve this shitty run I've got going now.

An exacerbated sigh escapes me as I cross my arms and glare at Ryker. He's tall, Guardian tall, and I bet he was in some sort of special ops role as well. He'd be intimidating, except for his smile and the casual way he holds himself. It's different from how Four stands.

Four's ready for battle all the time. Like ALL the time. He's—lethal.

Dangerous.

Terrifying if you don't know him and wound super tight. Like at any moment he'll explode with lethal force. I find that absolutely intoxicating.

Ryker is tall, muscular, definitely competent, but he's genuinely interested in how I feel. I suppose that's the difference between a healer and a warrior.

"So how does a respiratory therapist land a job like this?" I try to deflect and switch the topic of conversation from me to Ryker. "And are you sure you're qualified to do an exam?"

"I can show you my certificates if that helps. As for how I got a job like this, my wife is one of Forest's earliest rescuees. She and I were teammates in the military."

"And that's how you know Forest?"

"Sort of. Along with everything else that man's involved in, he manages the rock band, Angel Fire. Have you heard of them?"

"Have I? Who hasn't?" Angel Fire is only *the* band of my generation.

"Well, they did a USO tour while Tia and I were in the desert and I got to play with the band for a bit. Got to know Forest pretty well as a result. He recruited me and Tia. We're kind of a package deal."

"And what does she do?"

He points over to Four. "She's the one getting ready to stick a needle in your boyfriend there and calm him down if he keeps giving Skye trouble."

"He's not my boyfriend." I glance over at Four. He's really making a scene, but Skye's not taking any of his bluster. "I really admire her."

"Skye?"

"I wish I could do what she does." She's a badass, confident and capable. They're not victims, but true survivors. And they're kicking it at life. Unlike me who seems to be destined to play victim for the rest of my life.

"She's pretty phenomenal, and there's no reason you can't."

"Have you looked at me? I'm pretty much broken. I'll never be able to do something like that."

"You need to take another look in the mirror because all I see is an incredibly strong woman capable of doing anything if she puts her mind to it. Now, how about letting me do a quick physical exam? I'm worried about the blood in your hair."

"I told you, I washed him out."

"You may have washed someone's blood out of your hair, but there's fresh blood. I promise to be gentle." He glances over at Four, who's been forced to lie on his stomach. "Let's just make sure there's nothing serious going on under all that hair."

I give a nod and let Ryker do his exam. His touch is soft, gentle, and he doesn't poke all the places which throb. Meanwhile, I focus on Four and what's going on over there.

Skye opens up a surgical tray, which holds all kinds of silver instruments. She bends over the back of Four's thigh and paints something dark brown over his skin.

"What is she doing?"

"Are you in pain?" Ryker glances over at Four. "My bet is she's stitching him up. That's Betadine. It sterilizes the skin. Now, on a scale of one to ten, how do you rate your pain?"

My head hurts like a motherfucker. Since walking out of the helicopter, the low, dull ache is growing into a major, pulsating headache. My feet are scraped and bruised, as is the rest of my body. Bossman did a job on my ribs, my gut, and my back. My ribs hurt. Might be cracked. And Bossman got me in the belly more times than I care to remember. My eye is also swelling.

He was really going to kill me, but I fought back. I fought back and won.

But that's me. I'm an expert at surviving. I'm also now proficient in killing. It just gets better and better.

"Zero."

"Zero? Is that what we're going with? You know, we don't give out awards for how stoic our patients can be. How about you try that again?"

"Fine, it's a one." I've experienced far worse in my life.

I allow Ryker to do a quick head-to-toe exam. My left eye, which I thought felt a little tight, is well on its way to swelling to the size of a goose egg. Ryker gives me a cold pack to help with the swelling and Tylenol for the pain.

That's like water. Does nothing. But I don't need anything stronger. As a former addict, I steer clear of pretty much all pain medicines.

Evidently, the blood is fresh and all mine. Bossman nearly cracked my skull open, leaving me with a few deep cuts. Ryker explains how the scalp is rich in blood vessels, which is why I'm bleeding like a stuck pig.

There are no other major injuries, except some scrapes to my feet from walking around the ship barefoot and scaling the cargo containers. I've got bruises all over, but Ryker doesn't think my ribs are cracked or that there are any internal injuries. His exam is far more thorough than I expect, especially for a respiratory therapist.

Ryker's smooth bedside manner relaxes me, and he talks me into letting him clean up my cuts and stitch the deepest one, on my scalp, closed. He's nearly done when I realize we're in the air.

Bright lights shine down on Four and Skye as she gets to work stitching him up. She's kitted out in a surgical cap, gloves, and a mask, as is Tia and another person helping her.

"Can I go to him?" I'm starting to feel bad about my little hissy fit. It was just a kiss and probably not the best timing on my part. Did I really expect him to reciprocate in the back of a helicopter?

Yes. That's exactly what you expected.

"Not right now. They have to maintain a sterile field." It takes a second before I realize Ryker is responding to my question about going to Four and not the little conversation in my head about that kiss.

"How can anything be sterile with us in here?"

"Air flows from the cockpit back. It's how we maintain cabin pressure. All planes do that, but it works to keep any germs we may breathe out, or stir up, from moving in that direction." He looks over at Skye. "It's going to be awhile. Can I get you something to eat or drink?"

"I'm fine."

"You don't look fine. Let's get you settled. Some water? A cookie?"

"A cookie?"

"We have the best." A smile fills his face and lifts my spirits. "The chairs recline all the way back if you want to snooze for a bit. As soon as Skye's done, I'll wake you."

"You promise?" The thought of sleep doesn't appeal to me, despite the exhaustion tugging at my body, but if I can't be with Four, I might close my eyes for just a little bit.

"Promise." Ryker settles me in one of two seats near the very back of the plane. The jet is the size of a commercial airliner, with every seat a first-class experience. He adjusts the seat all the way flat, gives me a pillow, blanket, fuzzy socks for my feet, noise-cancelling headphones, and a sleep mask.

I settle into the seat and snuggle under the blanket. My entire body feels sluggish, like it's at the end of what it'll handle. Since I can't be with Four, I close my eyes for just a moment, trusting Ryker will wake me.

FIFTEEN

Moira

A SUDDEN JARRING AND THE ROAR OF THE ENGINE WAKES ME FROM A dreamless sleep. I push back the sleep mask and blink against the bright interior lighting of the cabin.

"Four, what's going on?"

"It's Griff, and we just landed, little minx."

Four's, oops, I mean Griff's, deep voice rolls across the space between us, tightening my nipples as it rumbles across my skin. How is it possible for a voice to do that?

I tug my blanket around me, hiding my traitorous nipples from Griff's gaze. Not that he's looking at my chest. My Guardian stares deeply into my eyes.

"We're landing?"

"Yes." He helps me untangle the sleep mask from the matted mess that is my hair. "We're home."

Home?

"How long have you been sitting there?" My question is more clipped than I intend, but I'm still hanging onto residual anger. I'm like a damn bulldog with a bone and refuse to let it go. Isn't it sad I find anger a comforting emotion?

"You've been asleep since we took off." Griff lounges beside me like he doesn't have a care in the world.

Thanks for nothing, Ryker.

When did Griff drift closer? Or am I somehow, unconsciously, leaning in? I give a shake of my head, dispelling the direction of those thoughts.

"What happened to your leg?" I feel every inch of him as electricity sparks in the space between us, joining our bodies with a crackling, nerve-shivering sensation. There's that odd vibration again, humming through my veins. I rub at my arms as goosebumps lift and my skin tingles. He does this to me.

Always has.

From the day he rescued me in Manila, I've had a thing for the man who saved me. Some might call it an unhealthy attachment; I call it destiny.

He makes it hard to think, especially when all I want is his body wrapped around mine. I want to feel him touch my face, soft and gentle to start, then more demanding. Maybe run his fingers through my hair until he reaches the end and gathers it all together for one sharp tug. A thrill runs through me, thinking about how that might feel.

Self-taught in the art of giving pleasure—a matter of survival on the streets—then later trained in the erotic art of sexual servitude, I not only know what gets men off, but what gets me off as well.

Dominance, in all its insidious forms, both terrifies me and drives me wild. I'm looking forward to exploring some of that with Griff because my spidey-senses tell me he's a ferocious lover.

I slip my hands between my thighs and squeeze my legs together as tingles of anticipation shoot through me.

"Doc stitched me up." He licks his lips. I swear he doesn't mean anything by it, but my mind is already on a deep dive into the gutter.

"Did you get hurt during my…um… The operation?" I refuse to mention my rescue. I'm still pissed at him, and I'm not ready to acknowledge the gratitude he deserves for saving my ass for the second time.

"If you mean did I injure it while rescuing you, the answer is no."

"Then how?"

"Let's not talk about that. I want to know how you're holding up." He looks at me with tenderness, which is a frightening expression on his gruff face.

Griff leans close, this time I'm not imagining it, and cups my cheek. His thumb rubs softly back and forth along my jawline as he presses closer, staring deep into my eyes. He's good at that, using his penetrating gaze to crawl inside my head.

I gulp as his breaths deepen, and I may be breathing a bit hard as well.

"I'm worried about you, little minx." Griff trades out his menacing scowl for true concern.

"Don't be. I'm pretty tough."

"Didn't say you weren't, but even steel breaks when pushed beyond its breaking point." He licks his lips, and I squirm in my seat.

"I'm fine."

"Let me tell you about the oak tree and the willow."

"Huh?"

His eyes gleam as he continues to delve inside my troubled depths.

"Just listen. The oak tree is a proud tree, standing strong, it lifts its limbs high to the sky. It towers over other trees, soaking in the light, growing bigger and stronger every day. It protects those beneath it, provides shade and shelter. It's resistant to fire, drought, and pests. It doesn't give in to the storms when they blow through."

It's like he's describing me. How many storms have I endured? And I'm still standing. I'm the mighty oak. It's kind of funny, but scary too.

"In contrast, the willow's roots spread wide, forming a solid foundation. Instead of lifting its limbs to the sky, it lets them droop toward the ground, not strong enough to hold them up like the mighty oak. The lightest breeze strips its leaves from its limbs and tears away its branches."

"What's your point?"

"Which tree is more resilient? Is it the oak, or the willow?"

"That's stupid. It's the oak, obviously." Why is he talking about trees? All I see are his kissable lips, the ones he refuses to lay on me.

His eyes pinch as if he's ready to dispense great wisdom on me.

"The oak weathers most storms well, making it through them relatively intact."

"Right, and the willow gets stripped bare. I want to be the oak."

"And yet, when a really bad tempest blows through, it's the oak that splinters and cracks, too stubborn to bend when it needs to most. The oak's strength is its greatest fault."

"No, you said it stands tall. It doesn't bend."

"Exactly, it doesn't know what the willow knows."

"And what's that?"

"That in order to endure the worst the world has to offer, sometimes you need to bend. You need to embrace your weakness to survive.

You need to let the wind rip away the parts of you that you don't need, and bend beneath its fury. The oak is too proud and too strong. It stands tall in the face of adversity until it either snaps and dies, or the storm moves on. Most people think the oak is the stronger tree, when in fact, it's the willow who knows that to survive adversity, it must bend."

"But it gets the shit kicked out of it. You said it loses all its leaves and branches."

"True, but it survives. The oak does not. A firm foundation, and the willingness to bend when required, is the greatest strength you can have."

"What does any of that have to do with me? Why are you talking stupid tree metaphors?"

"Because, I'm worried you're following the path of the oak, holding fast when you should bend."

"You want me to bend?"

"Not literally, but I want you to open up and let someone in. There's no shame in admitting weakness, from time to time, or that you need a little help."

"Someone? Like some random stranger?"

"No, Moira. Me."

"You?" Both my brows lift in surprise.

"Yes. I want you to let me in. Let me carry the weight for you."

"Carry the weight?"

"Yes."

"Because I'm a victim? I can't possibly have endured what I have and come out the other side with my shit intact? I need you to carry me?"

"Everybody needs someone. I want to be that someone for you."

"Because I'm a woman? And being a woman means I'm weak and need you, a man, to carry the load?"

"That's not what I said."

"No, you said I needed to fall apart and let you pick up the pieces. What if I don't want to fall apart? What if I've got my shit locked down tight? Or maybe I'm just barely holding on and need to keep hanging on by myself? You've done enough rescuing. I'm sure I can handle the rest from here on out. Besides, how can you carry me when you won't even kiss me?"

"You know the answer to that, and are you?"

"Am I what?"

"Holding on?"

Hell to the no.

"Yes, Griff. I'm totally fine."

"Right, you're F-I-N-E, and we all know what that means."

"If you dare say fucked up, insecure, neurotic, and emotional, I'm going to kick you in the nuts, then feed you your balls."

"As delicious as that sounds, I was thinking more along the lines of Feelings Inside Not Expressed. But if you want to go with fucked up…"

"Ugh! You're impossible." I punch him in his bad leg, satisfied when he grunts in pain.

He grips my wrist when I go to take another swing at him. "Don't do that again."

"Or what?"

"I'll paddle that very fine ass of yours until you express all those feelings swirling inside that head of yours. Don't tempt me, Moira." His tone deepens and sends licks of heat shooting through me. "You remember what happened last time?"

Don't I ever?

It was the most exciting, most erotic, and most frustrating non-sexual experience of my life.

Several months ago, during training, I pushed things one step too far. Thinking I could get him to budge from his no-personal-relationships-with-the-rescuees thing, I grabbed him. Like, grabbed his crotch and stimulated him.

While he turned hard in my hand, he told me in no uncertain terms what was never going to happen between us. When I continued to stimulate him, he explained in a very calm, very controlled, very professional Guardian voice that if I didn't remove my hand from his cock, he would spin me around and paddle my ass until I couldn't sit for a week.

He told me not to push my luck.

I pushed.

And he followed through. Four spun me around, flipped me over his knee, and paddled my ass.

I didn't sit properly for days, but damn if I didn't love the delicious sting of his hand and the ache that followed.

I never said I wasn't fucked in the head. I'm so damn twisted there's no hope. I hate the men who used me and hurt me but get turned on when Griff takes control.

Yeah, it makes no sense to me either.

I answer him with a blank stare, which he meets with one of his own. And just like that, we lock in a battle of wills. Which is totally fine by me. It gives me time to take in his aggressive posture, menacing scowl, and hawkish gaze, then meet him with my strength.

I won't back down.

He bugs the shit out of me because I've never been more captivated by another human being. I've never been this interested in a man, and that menacing scowl on his face should send me running.

Instead, it's a goddamn beacon, and I'm the moth drawn irresistibly to his flame. I don't care that he's more likely to destroy me than save me. I simply need to be near him, as close as he'll let me get.

Those violet eyes of his drink me in, and those sculpted lips drive me insane. I want them on me, everywhere at once, and he steadfastly refuses every damn advance I make.

It's not possible for the tension between us to get any thicker, but when he bends down and whispers in my ear, I practically detonate.

"Open up and let me in."

Oh, I'll open up all right, and I'll let him in. Only we're not talking about the same thing. I want sex, dominance, and control. He wants to shelter, protect, and emotionally support me, like a good little Guardian.

I ache for the sweet release only he can give me, but Griff wants something I've never given another human on this planet.

I don't know how to let you in, Griff. I just don't know.

So, what do I do? Why, I deflect, of course, because that's how I survive.

"I'm fine. Maybe you should just leave me alone?"

"Is that a statement or a question?"

"Does it matter?"

"Is that what you want?" His steely gaze bounces between my eyes.

No.

I cross my arms over my chest and refuse to answer him.

"That's what I thought." Griff extends his hand. "Come. It's time to go."

My heart does a double-step the way that command rumbles in the back of his throat. There's no hesitation on his part. Griff takes control in the blink of an eye, and I find myself following him out of the airplane, confused as hell and horribly turned on.

The man oozes a dark and terrifying sensuality kept under the tightest control. My fingers itch to peel him out of his clothes and explore his hard physique, but Griff being Griff, won't let his damn moral compass be swayed by physical desire.

He'll never take advantage of a rescuee.

Which means it's up to me to take advantage of him.

SIXTEEN

Griff

I grit my teeth all the way down the airstairs as I lead Moira out. My team's not back yet, not that it matters. Between Doc Summers and CJ, I'm officially on medical hold until further notice.

No more operating for me.

CJ's not dumb. He knows I disobeyed a direct order. Granted, I had help, and Ariel taking responsibility for that decision is the only thing saving my ass right now. Failure to obey a direct order is grounds for immediate termination from the Guardians. Not that it mattered at the time. Not that I'd change one damn thing. There was no way in fucking hell I was leaving Moira in that pit.

"A word." Doc Summers approaches me, pulling me up short. "Moira, do you mind waiting in the van?"

I release my hold on Moira's arm and watch her gaze bounce between me and the doc.

"Sure." Her meek reply comes as a surprise. I'm used to her fighting tooth and nail every damn step, but she's smart. Or maybe it's because the doc asked instead of me?

Once Moira's safely out of earshot, the doc turns her hawkish glare on me. "I need you to understand something."

I cut the doc off. "I know. Stay off the leg."

"I'm serious about your leg." Her eyes soften and she places a hand on my arm. "Look, I understand what you are, and how stubborn that makes you, but I need you to listen to me and really hear what I have to say."

"I promise to be good."

"No, Griff, I don't think you get it." She blows out her breath and comes at me from a different direction. "Your leg will heal, but only if you let it. I get you have this burning need to maintain peak Guardian proficiency, and that means working your body as hard as you can, but I'm here to tell you that if you do that, you'll be crippled for life."

"I got shot. It's not a career-ending injury."

"It shouldn't be, but you're pushing it. I don't have time to tell you how the human vasculature works, except to say you're on the verge of losing the main vein in your leg. Collateral vessels will form over time, but your leg will never be the same—if you continue to push it."

"What are you saying?" My gut drops because what she's saying terrifies me. I'm not ready to walk away from my job. "I thought it was just a simple stitch."

"It was until you pulled out my handiwork. I did what I could on the plane. You deserve to have a vascular surgeon take a look at you, and I'm going to put that in my official recommendation. I know why you did what you did, and I know there's nothing anyone could've said to you to not go after your girl. But she's safe now, and you need to take a step back. Let your body heal. Stop pushing it."

She runs a hand through her hair, smoothing down the flyaways. "I'm not one to overreact, and I never lie to my patients, but I'm not here to sugarcoat things either. Either you stay off that leg and let it heal, or you risk permanent damage. That will force you off the team. I need your word you'll follow doctors' orders."

"How long?" I swallow against the thick lump in my throat. "How long will I be off the team?"

"Six to eight weeks, longer if you push it. I'll schedule you to see a vascular surgeon and we'll start physical therapy in a few days. No running. Nothing that puts stress on your leg. I need you to baby that leg, or…"

There's no reason for her to finish that statement. I'll be off the team if I don't do as she says.

"Your word, Griff." Doc Summers is going to make me swear.

I both hate and respect her for that. She knows I'm a man of my word. If I swear to be good, she knows I'll follow through. I'd rather stay on the team than get tossed out on a medical complication.

"You have my word." Those may very well be the hardest words I've had to say in a really long time.

"Thank you. I'll notify Max and CJ. I'm putting in a medical leave of absence for eight weeks. Make all your appointments, work the physical therapy, and I promise we'll have you back in fighting shape in no time."

"I hear you, Doc. I'll be good." With a grimace, and a noticeable limp, I make my way to the waiting van and the woman I love who waits patiently for me inside of it.

"What was all that about?" Moira doesn't spare a moment, curious as a cat. I can't help the way my lips tick up. Moira's got more than enough spunk to keep things interesting.

"Nothing much."

"Didn't look like nothing."

"Doc just wanted to let me know I'm on medical hold for a couple of months."

"A couple of months?" Her eyes round with surprise. "So, what does that mean?"

"For one thing..." I sit on the bench seat beside her, intentionally crowding her in. She scoots as far over as she can, but I'm a big guy and the seat's not large. I lean in close and whisper in her ear. "It means I get to focus all my attention on you. Are you ready for what that means?" Her tiny squeak is music to my ears. I get the driver's attention in the rearview mirror. "Jarrod, take us home."

He glances at Moira and his eyes pinch. "Don't you want to take her to the Facility?"

"No. I'm taking her home." I place my hand on Moira's thigh and give a firm squeeze when she begins to protest. My attention swivels to her, where I capture her bright eyes in one of my hard glares. "You're coming home with me, little minx, where I can keep my eye on you, and we can discuss what happened in that helicopter."

"But..."

My grip tightens. "For once in your life, don't fight it."

She wiggles away from me, placing another millimeter or two between us and answers with a huff, but she's not fighting me. I saw the way the pulse in her neck jumped.

I'll take the win.

I should take her back to the Facility. Protocol demands it, but Moira isn't one of the Facility's kids. She's a grown woman who can make her own decisions. If anyone asks, I'll let them assume what they want.

My decision comes down to one thing. With me on medical hold, I won't be assigned to the Facility. That's the only time I would normally get to see Moira, which means there's no way in hell I'm taking Moira back there. Besides, I'm perfectly capable of taking care of her myself.

Jarrod knows where I live, so there's no reason to give him directions. He guides us off the tarmac and steers us into the morning commute. We left New Orleans early in the morning, flew three hours home, but with the time change it's still only late morning, which works well for me.

I need a shower. Moira does too. After we clean up, I'll take her to lunch, or make something from scratch. Then we'll sit down for a long-overdue chat.

During the hour-long drive, my hand never once leaves her leg. I figure she might get tired of me touching her, but then she settles in and seems content to stare out the window.

We don't talk, but that's only because the tension swirling between us is too damn thick.

When we finally pull up outside my house, I grimace as I get out of the van. My leg is not happy, and I won't be able to pick up the prescription Doc Summers gave me for a few hours.

"Thanks, Jarrod." I wave to our driver as I help Moira out of the vehicle.

"You live here?" She gawks at my cliffside dwelling. "I guess they pay you well as a Guardian."

I live a bit north from Guardian HRS in a modest three-bedroom house snuggled between much larger homes and perched over the rocky cliffs overlooking the Pacific Ocean. It's worth millions, not that I paid a penny for it.

"The pay's not bad, but not nearly enough to afford something like this." I wait while what I said sinks in.

I was a rebel teenager, too full of myself to appreciate what my parents built. Now, this house is all I have left of them. It's nothing like me, but I cherish every square inch of their dream house.

"I can only imagine what a place like this costs. The view must be spectacular."

"It is." I suddenly feel self-conscious, realizing how much I take this place for granted. For some weird reason, I want her to like it. "Want to see it?"

"I do." Moira waits for me to open the door. Whatever anger she had toward me earlier appears to have disappeared. "Funny, this is not what I imagined when you said you were taking me home."

"What did you imagine?" I usher her inside.

"Something small. A bachelor pad. You know, one room, trashy apartment…"

"I'd never take you someplace trashy."

"Sorry." She lifts her shoulders and kind of ducks. "I shouldn't have…"

"This was my parent's home."

"Was?"

"Yes, they passed several years ago. Motorcycle accident."

It was just up the winding turns of PCH-1 and why I no longer ride, but I don't share this with Moira. My parent's afternoon drive turned lethal, taking them from me far too soon.

I don't dwell on the past, but I do have regrets. I never got the chance to tell them how sorry I was for being a little shit and walking away from the life they built for me.

Now I have that life, but I no longer have them.

"I'm sorry." When she places her hand on my arm, a jolt of electricity shoots up my arm and travels down my spine.

When she's close, the very air crackles with the energy surging between us. It's enough to put a hitch in my breath and send blood rushing through my body, specifically to one part of my body in particular, which grows more engorged by the second.

"Thank you, but like I said, it was several years ago. They left me the house." As well as a bank account and other assets which still astound me. I knew my parents had money but never understood the scope of what they built.

Moira enters the foyer and gapes. "Oh my God, this is amazing." She rushes to the back of the house with its floor-to-ceiling windows. "Can I go out on the deck?"

"Of course. Just let me get the latch."

Unlike many of the homes built on the rocky cliffs overlooking the ocean, my father chose a plot of land that's more granite than soil. Whereas soil erosion threatens many stately homes that overlook the ocean, the foundation of this house is firmly rooted in granite. Not even the infamous California earthquakes can threaten this home.

And the house is beautiful. Both rustic and sharply elegant at the same time, it's full of clean lines shored up by rough-hewn timber and steel beams. It evokes a sense of being grounded in nature.

I make quick work of the locks and open the sliding door to the outside. Immediately, the refreshing scent of the ocean floods my senses. A light breeze tickles my skin and I lift my face to the sun overhead. I love the feeling of that sun-kissed glow heating my skin.

Moira runs right up to the edge of the deck. Cantilevered over the hundred-foot drop to the rocky shoreline below, I always felt like I was living in the sky when I came out here as a kid. My imagination has always been vivid and over the top, but it doesn't hold a candle to what I see now.

Moira leans over the railing, looking down at the beach below. One heel kicks up as the calf of her other leg tightens. I follow the sweep of her leg all the way to the hem of her shorts, where the skin creases at the base of her ass.

She stands before me, long blond hair blowing in the wind, the perfect mix of temptation and sin. More than the stereotypical blonde bombshell, there's something about her that draws a man's eye. I feel the pull, a carnal craving to claim her as mine.

It's a powerful force, one I fight, because she's been a victim to men's lust her entire life. When I left home at seventeen to enlist in the military, I remember feeling far too young to head out into the world. Moira's been on her own since she was twelve. I can't imagine what that must have felt like or how terrifying it must've been to a child so young. And she's dealt with the depravities of men every day since.

All the men that took from her, and stole her innocence, need to pay for what they've done. Yet, I can't help but feel exactly what they felt when I look at the pretty girl with the long blond hair.

What makes my desire any less toxic?

My lips curl back from my teeth in a sneer as I think about all the horror she's endured. I want to kill every bastard who hurt her, not become one of them.

Yet, I'm no better than any of them. I drink in the perfection of her body. My eyes take me on an erotic field trip moving from the curve of her ankles, up her long, toned legs, around that heart-shaped ass. It's there where my gaze lingers to admire the flare of her hips before moving past her narrow waist to climb up to her delicate shoulders and settle on the graceful curve of her neck.

I have no business lusting over her, but I can't help it.

I want her.

Moira props her elbows on the railing and lifts her face to the sun. I leave her there, knowing how poorly I'm holding onto the last vestiges of my restraint. All I want is to rush her, yank down those shorts, and rut into her until I find oblivion. My stomach twists at the degrading images even as my cock swells to life. It's an eager fucker, wanting every bit of that torrid fantasy.

And I hate myself for it.

SEVENTEEN

Griff

———

Once inside, I calm down a bit. I set out towels and a fluffy robe in the guest bathroom. The bed is made. I always keep it ready, but I never invite anyone into my home. That particular quirk stems from my issues with the wealth my parents passed on to me. It makes no sense, but back in my Navy days, I felt guilty that my fellow brothers in arms struggled with what the Navy paid them, where I did not.

With my Guardian brethren, it's a little better. We make good money and few of us struggle to make ends meet. It's a comfortable life, but by no means is it rich.

When I was in high school, I hated this house. I hated my parents, and I despised their wealth. Dad was an architect. Mom was a brilliant artist. They did well for themselves, buying this home when they first met. Back then, the land wasn't valued for shit. Dad designed and built the house, and they paid off the loans when I was still small. Somehow, that privilege chaffed, especially when my friends at school had so much less.

I return to the sliding door and lean against the door jamb, enjoying the view. Moira's in the same position I left her, head tilted back, face greeting the sun. She looks amazing, glowing in the sunlight like she doesn't have a care in the world. Nobody who saw her would guess at the life she's led or the horrors she's endured.

I clear my throat and she spins around.

"I set out a towel and robe for you in the guest bathroom. Your room is off the hall to the right. I'm going to take a shower. You're welcome to take one too. The fridge is well stocked. Feel free to take whatever you want. I was thinking of heading out for lunch after we cleaned up."

"Thank you." Her expression softens.

It feels like forever and a day that our gazes lock. Passion simmers between us and the need to consummate this unrelenting desire grows with each breath. But I will not take advantage of her.

I refuse to be that man.

I won't take a goddam thing from Moira. I respect her too much. But I will give her anything and everything she desires. I love her too much to ruin whatever this is with baseless sex, especially the kind of dominating sex I prefer.

"I'll leave you to it. Please, make yourself at home."

Moira tilts her head, looking at me quizzically. Before I say, or do, something I'll regret, I make my exit, practically running to the opposite side of the house. I slam the door behind me and lean against it until my heart stops racing and my breaths stop churning the air.

Bringing her to my house wasn't my best play, but there's no way I was going to drop her off at the Facility and walk away. I need her in my life like I need air to breathe. I just have to figure out how to do that without fucking everything up.

After taking my shower, and doing the five-knuckle hustle, I'm more frustrated by the uninspired release than before. Something needs to be done.

I head into the guest room to see if Moira needs anything. She left the door wide open, and I don't think twice about heading inside. If she wants privacy, she'll shut the door, but I pull up short when I hear the shower running and see her naked.

One glance is all it takes. Not only did she not shut the outer door, but Moira kept the bathroom door open as well, giving me an unobstructed view of her nude body as she showers.

Beneath the spray of water, she rinses shampoo from her hair, running her delicate fingers through her long, blond strands. Water sluices down her tight and toned body, running in rivulets between her shoulder blades and down her back.

I lick my lips as I follow the sensual path that water takes.

I should go.

I should turn around and march right out of there, but like a punch in the gut, I'm completely, and utterly, entranced. My balls draw up as blood rushes to my cock. When I reach down to make an adjustment, Moira spins around and our gazes collide and lock fast together.

Her attention immediately shifts to my hand, where I fist my engorged member over the thin fabric of my shorts. Slowly, she draws her gaze upward as I struggle to recover. I don't like that I'm standing in her room with a raging erection, my fist gripping it, while she's naked and…

I really need to leave.

Yet, somehow, my feet refuse to budge. My mouth goes dry as I breathe in, struggling with what to do. The floral scent of the shampoo I leave for guests swirls in the air, strawberries and vanilla. It fits Moira, almost as if I bought it with her in mind. Steam billows out into the room, fogging the mirrors in the bathroom and cranking up the humidity, thickening the air with potent promise and possibilities.

I lick my lips, wanting her so badly that it physically hurts. She meets my fire with desire, and no matter how hard I fight, this is a battle I'll ultimately lose.

But not now.

Not yet.

She's been through a traumatic experience and needs time.

Her gaze shifts with indecision, but then her shoulders roll back. Moira steps out of the shower, holding my gaze the entire time. Without grabbing a towel, she boldly takes another step, dripping temptation and sin all over the floor. She takes another step, and stands before me, wet hair dripping down tits a man could lose himself in forever.

"I'm sorry, but you didn't shut the door." By some miracle, I find my voice.

Riveted in place, I make no secret about the direction of my gaze. Moira stands there, completely unaffected by her nudity and lets me drink her in.

She gathers her hair over her shoulder and gives it a tug. "I guess I wanted to see."

"See what?"

"If you would check on me."

"Why wouldn't I check on you? I want to see if you have everything you need."

"Is that it? You want to see if I have everything I need?" Her shoulders roll back and her gaze hardens. When she shifts her attention to my hand, I can't help but squeeze my fully erect cock and grimace at the raging need within me. "Because it looks like something else might be up."

Instead of releasing the vice on my cock, my grip tightens as I attempt to gain control over my body. I want her. I want her deeply, urgently, and with a desperation I don't understand, but I know what she's been through.

Moira's been used her entire life. I hate how strong my hunger is to do exactly the same to her as the monsters of her past. Truthfully, I don't know how to take what I want from her, and I'm not sure how to ask. I don't even know if it's appropriate, considering what she's been through.

What's the appropriate amount of time to wait before initiating intimacy with a survivor like Moira?

She's everything I want and everything I can't have. I can't subject her to the rawness inside of me, the beast hungering for a lick, a taste. Hell, I want to devour her. Hasn't she had enough of men taking what they want to last a lifetime?

"Griff…" Her gaze shifts again and pulls me from my thoughts. Those delicate blue orbs capture my attention.

"Yes?" I clear my throat as my voice catches.

"What is it about me that you don't like?"

"Excuse me?" Her question makes no sense.

"You want me." Her gaze bounces down to my dick, where I'm barely hanging on. "You've always wanted me. I don't think I'm wrong in saying that, but you act like you don't. Or won't." This time, her voice catches. "Is it because of my past? Do you find me disgusting? Is that why you wouldn't kiss me in the helicopter? Is that why you refuse to touch me now?"

My jaw drops. "You see what you do to me." How can she not know?

"And yet, you refuse to do anything about it."

"I never want to make you do something you don't want to do."

"Does it look like I don't want this? Did it feel like I didn't want you when I kissed you in the helicopter?"

"But…"

"You and this damned honorable code you refuse to let go of. You have no idea, do you?"

"About?"

"You asked if I needed anything." She lifts her arms out to her side, exposing herself. She's every man's wet dream, and she's standing before me, offering herself.

"Do you?" My attempt to keep things professional erodes with each passing second. "Need anything that is?" I clear my throat.

"I need you, Griff. I've always wanted you. I fantasize about you all the time." She gives a flick of her lashes. "Like all the time. I can't erase my past. If that's why you won't touch me, I can't change that. But I've ached for you from the moment we met."

"You don't disgust me. It's just…"

"Just, what?" She takes another step and closes the distance between us. Her hand lifts and she presses the pads of her fingers to my chest. Her fingertips trail down to my waist and leave a blistering wave of heat behind them. Moira bites her lower lip and peeks up at me through her lashes.

She's so small. So fragile. So completely perfect for me.

"I don't want to hurt you."

"And how would you hurt me? Other than by refusing me?"

"You escaped a nightmare. And I'm not a gentle lover. I don't know if I can be, and that's not what you need right now."

"Since when do you get to decide what I need and don't need? You know what hurts the most?"

"No."

"That I want you as much as I do, yet you make me feel like shit. After everything I've endured, all the men pawing at me, not a single one of them made me feel like I wasn't good enough for them. You do that. You make me feel like damaged goods."

"Moira, you're not damaged. You're amazing. Don't you know that? Don't you know how much I care about you? All I want is to be there for you."

"Then, for the love of God, show me. Show me how you feel. Show me how much you need me. Get out of that damn Guardian headspace for a minute and stop treating me like I'm a broken doll. Or that I can't handle a little rough sex. I may have issues and shit to sort out but treating me like fine china that will shatter if you so much as look at me isn't helping. You're making things worse."

Worse?

Her finger drops to the waistband of my shorts. I still have that grip on my dick and bite back against the excruciating arousal, which only increases as her fingers splay across my waist.

"Stop making me feel like shit because of what I've been through. Can't you lower your walls and let me in?"

Lower my walls?

Isn't that exactly what I want her to do with me? To lower her defenses and let me in.

"You don't understand. I'm not a gentle lover. Never have been. I don't know if I can be. I don't want to hurt you, or activate a…"

"A trigger? Is that what you're afraid of?"

"Of course."

"Griff, in none of my hundreds of fantasies have I ever imagined you're gentle. The most arousing experience in my entire life was when you turned me over your knee. I don't know if I'm twisted in the head, or if I can't separate dominance from sex, but when you did that, it wasn't like any of the other men. With them, I was scared, or disgusted. With you… Oh, Griff, you made me burn. My entire body came alive. I don't need gentle. I need you to be you, rough and raw, hard and demanding. Uncompromising in what you take."

She removes her hand from my abdomen, but only to shift it to my forearm. My skin heats as she slides down until her fingers curve around my wrist. Her touch only serves to increase the tension running through my body. "You can take what you need from me. I won't break."

"I never want to make you feel as if I'm using you."

"There's nothing wrong with that." She nibbles on her lip again and her fingers slide down over the back of my hand, rubbing against my knuckles before she wraps her fingers around my fist. "Not when that's what I want too."

"And what is that?"

"For you to take from me."

A dangerous growl rumbles in the back of my throat. "I don't trust myself not to hurt you." I remove her hand from mine and take a step back. "The things I want…"

"Are what?"

"They're no different from what any of those men did to you."

"It's worlds different."

"You don't understand."

"What don't I understand? You're an alpha protector, with a bit of caveman inside of you. That's totally okay with me." Her brows rise in challenge.

"Are you sure?"

"Truth?" She waits for me to answer, but I'm not sure what to say and opt for silence. "The truth is, you brought me to your home, whether to protect me, shelter me, or to finally act on those filthy fantasies running inside your head. It doesn't really matter. I'm here and I'm tired of dancing around this sexual tension. You're not protecting me from anything by closing yourself off to me. Any normal couple would be twisting the sheets by now. Instead, I'm still standing here, naked and willing, and you very obviously want me."

She again closes the gap. Stepping so close her nipples graze against the fabric of my shirt. She tips her head back and looks at me. "If you want me to beg—I'll beg. If you want me on my knees, I'll go to my knees. If you need something else…"

I don't let her finish that sentence. Everything she says is true.

Moira's gotten to me. She's under my skin and in my head. She's in every beat of my heart and every breath I take. It's time I stop fucking around and take what's rightfully mine.

What she freely, and desperately, offers.

That realization slams into my gut.

But this goes beyond anything I've felt before, stretching beyond shallow interest and casual sex. With Moira, I want more than a simple night of pleasure. I want to make her mine in every way.

That awakens the darkest, most twisted, parts of my nature.

I cup her face, tilting her head back. Before she can react, I let go of my restraint.

My desire stirs and unfurls its wings, stretching wide, as my balls tighten and my cock swells even more. These feelings, now that they're unleashed, will never again be contained. They're out there, between us, dangerous, monstrous, and impossible to tame now that they finally get to taste the woman I love.

It's heady and carnal, desperate and insane, but the fuck if I care anymore.

EIGHTEEN

Griff

—————

"You're mine, Moira. All mine."

"Yes, Griff. All yours."

Whatever else she has to say disappears beneath the press of my lips. My desire surges within me as I lay claim to her lips, her mouth, and soon her entire body.

I give no fucks about giving her space to work out her demons. Not after seeing the pain in her eyes. She thought I found her disgusting. For the next few hours, I'm going to show her exactly how much I desire her body, her mind, and her soul.

My pulse careens away, galloping on the heels of the lust raging in my veins. I want to control her body, torment her with pleasure, and wreck her for any other man.

I want to lay claim to her heart.

Blood rushes to my groin, hardening my cock even more, making it ache and throb as it swells. But that greedy fucker needs to wait its turn.

This kind of desire, it's different.

Visceral, but not rooted solely in lust. It's in the way we meld together and in how her voice caresses my skin. It's in the way she settles in my arms and in the way her scent overwhelms my senses. Her entire essence settles into my brain with a comforting sense of the familiar.

Her mouth opens for me, willing and full of surrender. Our teeth clash with the urgency of the kiss and her lips will be bruised come tomorrow. The kiss is raw, brutal, and completely unhinged. All I can think about is claiming every last piece of her.

Her gasping moans urge me forward and her tumultuous pants incite the beast within me. As I cup her face, controlling that part of her body, she grabs at me. Hands groping, she scratches my back, grappling to seek purchase as the sexual tension between us rises to a crescendo.

Our lips meet in a frenzy and it won't be long before our bodies follow. I fuck her mouth with my tongue, with ferocity and madness, similar to the way I'll soon take her body, sliding my cock home where it belongs.

Moira squirms in my grip. Her movements harden me to madness. Her hands wrap around my back as she rises on tiptoe to meet my passion with her own.

I can barely take the heat of our kiss. Her fingernails dig in, scratching and clawing as she presses her body to mine. Our mouths clash, lips smashing together as our tongues tangle with maddening urgency.

This is what a kiss should be. Ferocious. Needy. Feral. Completely desperate and unhinged.

Her fingers work up my back until she grasps my nape. Her entire body writhes beneath me with pent-up need and hunger. She wrestles to obliterate any space between us when I suddenly remember she's buck-naked and I've only allowed myself to touch the sides of her face.

I draw back and ignore her mewls of frustration. Looking into her eyes, they're nearly black, blown out with lust, and I search. I seek her permission to continue and find it in the fire sparking in her gaze.

"I want you. I've always wanted you."

"Then take me, Griff. Make me yours." Her plea slams into me; pure desire and need.

Releasing her face, I glide my hands down the bare expanse of her back, feeling her damp skin shiver beneath my touch. My palms glide around the globes of her ass and stop. I pull her tight against me, driving her hips against the long, engorged length of my cock.

"You want that? You want my cock?"

"Yes, please."

"Tell me you want to be mine."

"For the love of God, will you just fuck me already? I'm dying here. Fuck me, and don't worry about taking it slow, or being gentle. I need to feel you inside of me, taking—possessing…" Her words come in shallow, desperate gasps and her arousal fills the air with an intoxicating scent. "Dammit, Griff, you know what I need."

My hand slides around her hip and I force it between us, pushing her hips back to shove my fingers between her legs. Her silky essence coats her thighs and spreads across my fingers.

"You're fucking wet for me." I can't help the awe filling my voice as her hips drive forward, seeking contact. I oblige her while fighting the demands of my body.

Her mouth is relentless, capturing mine, she sucks on my lips as my fingers reach between her legs to find her wet and ready. Silky warm, her arousal coats my fingers, and her pussy practically sucks my fingers into the warm, welcoming recesses.

Moira sighs the moment my fingers slide in. She bucks and gyrates, seeking stimulation, which I'm more than happy to provide. I thrust my fingers in and out, stretching her opening in preparation to accept my girth. The sensitive muscles inside her pussy clench with each drive of my fingers in and out.

She grinds against me, crying out as her breaths struggle and falter. Unable to concentrate on kissing, I break off the kiss to nuzzle her neck, nipping and biting, as she rides my fingers. Her eyes squeeze shut as her body trembles with the release building inside of her. Nearly on the verge, I intend to send her over that edge.

I put my thumb in play, massaging her clit as I finger her with strokes that grow harder and more demanding with each thrust. Her entire body tightens around my fingers, and then she breaks.

Moira comes apart in my arms, her body jerking in violent spasms as she screams and cries with the rush of pleasure running through her. I continue to stimulate her, unwilling to stop until her cries dissolve into moans.

While she gulps for air, I wrack my brain, trying to figure out where I've stashed the closest condom.

Her glazed eyes find mine, satisfied but nowhere near done. My heart pounds with fury and my skin heats as she licks her lips and falls to her knees, slipping through my arms as my eyes widen.

Before I register what's happening, she pulls my shorts over my hips and frees my cock. It bobs between us, hard, engorged, and demanding.

"Griff?" She sounds unsure, almost as if she needs me to… Push?

Realizing her need to be dominated sends a rush of heat to my balls. I place my hand on the back of her head and bite my lower lip.

"Open that pretty mouth," I growl out the command and nearly lose my shit as her jaw opens.

Slowly, reverently, I watch with breathless anticipation as Moira wraps her soft lips and presses her hot tongue to the crown of my… Sweet, holy fuck, I nearly come right there. This beautiful woman is a lesson in resilience. She's beyond strong. She's indestructible, and all mine.

Overtaken with need, I barely hang on as she sucks me straight to the back of her throat. Sweet Jesus, her mouth is sin incarnate. My toes curl and my hips buck involuntarily. I can't help but thrust and try to plunge my cock deeper. No way am I going to last, but I'm damn well going to enjoy myself.

"Fuck, Moira, that's… Yes, just like that." My fingers curl in her wet hair as the overwhelming stimulation of her hot mouth brings me right to the edge. I'm going to lose my shit as she traces the veins and ridges of my turgid length. And her hands. The woman doesn't stop at my dick. Her hand holds my balls as her fingers gently squeeze and caress.

Panting furiously, I grunt as I fight to hold back my release. I've never felt this much pleasure and agony at once. I'm going to come, and with the way my release builds, I won't be surprised if I black out.

Holy hell, I don't want this to end, but she's relentless and talented. She goes from sucking the sensitive glans to flicking that spot beneath the head. Then she swallows me deep, coaxing me to let go of my restraint.

My hips have a mind of their own, thrusting and crushing my groin against her face. My fingers stab into her hair, twisting and pulling, as I slam forward, cut off her air, and fuck her with the desperation of a mad man.

I need to have her, fuck her, kiss her, mark her as mine, and hold her in my arms. I've never needed any woman like this before and don't understand where these feelings come from.

I fuck her throat, mindlessly, and she takes every inch of me. Gagging, choking, she sucks harder and fondles my balls, squeezing and tugging until I lift up on my toes and my legs tremble. She drags her tongue along my length and flicks the head mercilessly.

I breathe hard, every muscle in my body clenches, as she enraptures me and holds me on the verge. I fist her hair, desperately needing some semblance of control, but there's no winning this battle. My release slams into me as warmth coils in my balls and shoots out of my dick and down her throat.

Moira sucks it all down as I gulp for air and my vision dims. Heart pounding, I pull my spent cock out of her mouth and let my knees find the floor before I pass out.

Her breathing comes fast, a staccato in my ears as my lungs heave for breath. Her lips tick up with satisfaction. I launch at her, claiming her mouth with mine.

There's no pause or hesitation.

Moira melts into me as our lips meet in a frenzy. Arms wrap. Chests collide. Our legs intertwine as I roll her to the floor and ravage her with my mouth. My fingers spear between her legs where I bring her to a second, frenzied orgasm before we collapse in a heap on the floor.

We roll to our backs and I draw her against me as our ragged breaths settle. Propping a hand over my forehead, I tug her tight and kiss the crown of her head.

"Dammit, why the fuck did I wait to do that?"

She rolls to her side and props herself up on her elbow. Her free hand draws circles around my belly, then dips down to my spent cock. "Now that's a damn good question."

I slap her hand away from my dick, knowing I need a few more moments, but we have all the time in the world.

"Up, little minx."

"Up?"

"Yes, we're moving this to the bedroom."

"Um, hate to tell you, but we're in a bedroom right now."

"Yeah, but this one doesn't have condoms."

NINETEEN

Moira

I WAKE LIMP AS A NOODLE, WITH MY BODY BLISSFULLY SATIATED after spending the rest of the day, and night, in Griff's bed. Well, mostly. Griff took me in bed, then over the back of the couch. Against the wall. On the kitchen countertop. On all fours in the living room.

We stopped only to eat and hydrate, then went to bed, where he proceeded to show me what I've always suspected.

Griff's a kinky bastard.

He's not gentle, but damn is he generous, drowning me in so much pleasure I found myself begging for a moment to recover.

He refused.

And I found myself tied to the bed.

Best hour of my life.

I rub at the chaffing on my wrists with a contented smile on my face and stretch my hand out to my side. Griff's side of the bed is warm, but empty.

I sit and rub the sleep from my eyes. My body, while sore, feels amazing. It's like he worked out all the tension I'd been carrying from my days spent in hell.

I didn't have a single dream about Bossman or Shelly. No flashes of red coating the floor, the walls—the ceiling. Hopefully, I never will again.

Griff's not in the bathroom. I take a moment for myself and look in the mirror. As I wash my hands, I try to see what's different, because I certainly feel like a different person.

My hair's messed up. I look like I got my brains fucked out. A giggle escapes me as I think about everything we did last night, then my nose lifts as the wonderful aroma of bacon floods my senses.

I grab one of Griff's shirts and pull it on. It hangs nearly to my knees and the sleeves cover most of my arms. It's weird when I think about how much bigger he is than me. He's a formidable warrior and I'm tiny in comparison. I like it. He makes me feel girly.

And it works. It works deliciously well.

Unwilling to put on any of the clothes I wore into this house, I pad barefoot to the living room and stop dead in my tracks when I see Griff standing buck-naked at the stove. He faces away from me and has on some silly apron tied around his waist. His muscular legs and that rock-hard ass shift as he moves to the music playing through the house-wide speakers. His glutes flex to the beat as he shifts back and forth.

I watch him for a moment, loving this carefree side of my ferocious Guardian, but then his body stills, and he turns around as if he senses my silent presence. The man is hyperaware of his surroundings.

"You hungry, little minx?"

"Famished. Someone forgot to feed me dinner last night."

"I remember feeding you something." He unapologetically grabs his crotch.

"And I remember your legs turning to jelly when you came down my throat."

"This is true. You, my dear, have a very talented mouth, and the things you do with that tongue…" He doesn't finish whatever it is because the bacon burns behind him. "Shit!" Griff pulls the bacon off the stove and hits the vent fan to draw out the acrid smoke.

"You better not have ruined my bacon."

"Your bacon?" His mouth lifts into a grin. "Who says it's yours?"

I love our easy back and forth. I love it even more that he's naked, and the apron, while quirky, hints to a softer side of my Guardian. A smile curves my lips as I drink him in.

"What's going on in that head of yours, little minx?"

"Just admiring the view." I clasp my hands, twisting my fingers together.

Turning away, he tries to salvage the bacon and continues with the ass clenching, timing it to the beat of the music.

"Oh my God, that's awful."

"My ass or my moves?"

"That depends on what moves you're talking about. There were several last night which brought a smile to my face."

He sets the pan aside and spins around, stalking toward me like a man on a mission. "I'm glad you like my moves. Let me show you a few more."

"I'm seriously not going to be able to walk if you keep it up."

"Minx, if you're able to walk, then I haven't done my job."

He lifts me off my feet and sets me on the counter. Towering over me, he lowers his face slowly to mine, heightening my anticipation, but the moment our lips meet, all bets are off. He loses his restraint and I'm right there with him.

After the number of times we fucked last night, I would think the urgency of it all would've worn off. How wrong I am about that.

His mouth smashes against mine, bruising my lips as our teeth clash and our tongues tangle. We go from simmering to molten hot in the space of a heartbeat, too frantic and reckless to take our time.

Raw and unhinged, his kisses are what I always thought they should be like. Hard, with an edge, but without the fear and the loathing that I experienced with other men.

In Griff's arms, I feel safe, protected, but most of all, adored and loved. He spreads my legs and notches his hips between them. Without warning, he drives into me, hips thrusting recklessly, and hitting that spot inside of me that sends me flying.

My thighs clench around him, and I pull myself closer, needing him deeper, to thrust harder. To make me fly.

Moaning sounds escape my throat as he drives harder, wilder.

Ahhh, fuck, that's the spot.

My gasps lose their rhythm as they become shallow and more desperate. My pussy grows slicker as he thrusts and fucks in a steady, determined pace.

No man has ever made me feel this way. No man has taken control of my body and possessed me the way he takes me now.

I've always had a crush on Griff. It stems from a bit of hero worship since he's the one who rescued me in Manila. I'll never forget the tenderness in his expression when he held out his hand that very first time. I remember feeling empty inside, a place beyond shock. I wanted to die, but knew I'd continue to survive, because that's what I did best.

He was a shining beacon in that darkness, and all it took was the softness in his eyes to pull me back from the brink of despair.

That was over a year ago. Now things are different, but he's still making me feel things, feelings too new and too raw to process. They're impossible to analyze. One, because he's fucking my brains out. Two, because he drives me crazy, and I'm not alone. Griff feels it too.

At my ear, he nips and sucks. His breaths pant against my neck as his body works to bring us over the edge. My thighs squeeze around his hips and my nipples harden beneath the punishing assault of his fingers as they twist and pinch and squeeze my nipples.

I feel everything.

The first signs of my orgasm flutter in my belly. Ahhh, yes, this man knows how to fuck. And kiss. And how to go down on a woman until she's mindless with need. He knows how to touch all the right places.

My orgasm builds, and I pull him closer, needing to meld my body with his. It is no hardship staying here with him. If I was at the Facility, we couldn't do this. He's given me more blissful moments in the past twenty-four hours than I've experienced in a lifetime.

We may be having sex—lots of sex—but something else is happening as well. I don't know much about love, but an unbreakable bond is forming between us. It's a connection, stronger than I've ever shared with another person, and definitely the first time with a man. Men have never been kind to me before, which makes Griff that much more amazing. He's too good to be true, and I hate to admit it, but there's a small piece of me waiting for the other shoe to drop.

Whatever this is that's building between us, it's worth fighting for, and I find myself loath to let it go. Not that I am—letting it go—but if life has taught me anything, it's that good things never happen to people like me.

Somehow, I'll pay for daring to be happy.

Griff picks up the tempo, lifting me off the counter with each maddening thrust of his hips. Each time he adjusts the angle of his attack, I tremble on the edge of bliss. Last night, I fought my release. This time, my body squeezes around his cock, eager and determined, as a scream escapes my lips.

My release shudders through me as my cries dissolve into whimpers. Lingering pleasure shoots through my body, and as I gulp for air, Griff follows me over the edge without hesitation, without restraint.

My legs wrap around his hips and we stare deeply into each other's eyes, breaths panting as our souls join.

He leans forward and brushes his lips over mine. Unlike the frenzy before, we sink into the bliss that a simple kiss can bring.

Only there's nothing simple about this kiss. It feels as if he's making a promise and sealing it with that kiss.

"We need more condoms." Griff breaks off our kiss, pulls out and disposes of what must be the tenth condom we've used.

"Do we?" It's irrational. I know this, but I don't want anything to be between us.

"What are you saying?"

"Only that I have an IUD and my tests were all clean. I haven't been with a man since Manila, and I'm pretty sure work tests you as part of routine physical exams."

"They do."

"And?"

"I'm clean. I rarely go out, and I never date. When I... Well, I always use a condom."

I wait, letting him make up his mind. It's a big deal asking him to go without protection, but I'm not worried about pregnancy or STDs.

"That's cool. I was just thinking…"

He grips my chin between his thumb and forefinger. "First chance I get, I'll get retested, but until then, we'll play things safe. Is that good enough?"

"It's good, but if we're going out to get condoms, do you think we could stop by a thrift store while we're out?"

"A thrift store?"

"Yeah, I don't have anything to wear, and unless you're taking me back to the Facility, I need clothes."

"I have zero plans to take you back to the Facility, although you should probably meet with the councilors to talk through what happened."

"I don't want to talk to them."

"You sure about that?"

"I don't want to talk to anyone." That's a chapter of my life I'd rather forget.

"What about me? Will you talk to me?"

"Griff…"

"It's good, but you need to decide. Either you talk it out with me, or I take you to see the counselors to talk with them. You know how this works. Keeping that shit inside of you only makes it fester."

"Can we just not talk about it?" That's my vote, but I have a feeling Griff is going to overrule me.

"You know the answer to that, but for the rest of the weekend, we'll take things day by day. Next week, you decide. It's either me or them, but you will work through what happened." He taps my forehead. "Get it out, little minx. Unpack your baggage. Trust me, it's for the best."

I can tell I won't win this argument, so I deflect. "Looks like you ruined breakfast."

He lifts me off the counter and settles me on my feet before turning to the stove. "Shame, I make a mean omelet. Let's get dressed and I'll take you out for breakfast. We'll grab a couple packs of condoms on the way home."

"A couple of packs?"

He grins. "Definitely. Might have to make a second run later on. I plan to spend my weekend buried balls deep inside of you."

"Sign me up."

We clean up the mess together, take a shower, fuck one more time, then get ready to leave. I can get away with wearing Griff's shirt, but we can't find anything to cover my lower half, which leaves me with having to wear my shorts. Unlike me, they're still stained by Bossman's blood.

I intend to burn them later tonight.

TWENTY

Moira

WE SPEND MOST OF THE DAY CHECKING OUT BOUTIQUE STORES, which frustrates me. I want to hit up a thrift store and make sensible purchases I can afford. Not one time in my life have I shopped anywhere else.

Instead, Griff argues with me, saying I deserve nice things. He refuses to take me to any of the places I want to go and forces me to visit nearly a dozen boutique shops before I broker a compromise.

He grudgingly agrees and we head to the closest superstore. It's not a thrift shop, nor is it a pricey boutique. I'm still uncomfortable when I see the price tags, but I'm able to get most of the things I need.

We fight over who will pay. Griff nearly wins, but I pay in the end, using a debit card with barely enough cash to cover the charges.

He shakes his head, muttering about stubborn women, while I walk out with a smile on my face.

I have a feeling there will be precious few opportunities for me to win an argument with him, so I lord this one over his head.

"You didn't need to pay for all of that." He packs the trunk of his car with my modest purchases.

"Well, you most certainly don't need to pay for my things." I don't know why this is a sticking point for me, but the idea of him paying for everything feels too much like before.

That's how I think about it; the time before Griff when I was a sex slave.

"You're my woman."

"So?"

"That means you're mine to provide for." He gives an irritated shake of his head and mumbles about strong women being a pain in his ass. But I hear humor in his tone rather than anger.

I try very hard not to compare him to the men who came before him, but with the way Griff likes to fuck, the inevitable comparisons arise.

He's an aggressive and dominant lover, like the men who hurt me, but unlike them, he's compassionate, kind, and we've already talked about how generous he is handing out orgasms.

I don't mind his aggression, or his need to dominate in bed. It's probably because this is the first time I've ever been a willing participant.

But taking that kind of control out of the bedroom and inserting it into everyday life—like buying my necessities—is a line I'm not ready to cross.

I can't.

I don't mind giving up control in the bedroom, but I absolutely will not give any man control over any other part of my life. Even if it is Griff. My sanity depends on it.

"I'll need to go back to the Facility at some point." At least there, I have more than a day's worth of clothing. I don't need much, but I do need a few small things.

"You're staying with me." Griff's determined that I stay with him at his house.

He seems reluctant to return me to the Facility. And I get it. I totally get why.

He's protective, maybe a bit overly so, not that I mind. I've had men claim me as their own, exert their dominance and overwhelming control over every facet of my life, but I've never had this.

Griff's selfless.

He's concerned about me. But most of all, he's protective without being domineering. It's hard to describe what that means to me, especially after the life I've led.

"But all my things are there."

He's going to have to relent at some point. Not that I'm in a hurry to get back, but I am anxious to see Zoe. It's been nearly a week since I saw her, although it feels like a lifetime.

She and I were kidnapped together. I need to know what happened to her, but more importantly, how she's doing now. I'm not the only one dealing with trauma, and as wonderful as the councilors are at the Facility, it's not the same as it is when talking to a person who's lived through something similar.

"I don't see why you won't let me buy what you need." Griff's shoulders slump in defeat.

"Because."

"Because, why?"

"Because." We're headed back into argument territory and I don't like it.

He shuts the trunk and turns to me. "I'm not trying to push, and while I very much want to take care of you, I don't understand why you won't let me." He glances back toward the store. "Arguing with you hurts my heart. I'm asking, honestly asking, why it matters. And not because I'm trying to be a dick about it or pissed that you won't let me help you. I really want to know why it's important. Help me to understand."

He's right about one thing. I'm pissed about the argument and irritated by his insistence that it's no big deal for him to buy stuff for me.

"I'm not sure how to explain it."

"I need you to try. I don't like fighting."

"Well, as you know, I don't have much. The Facility gives us a small stipend for the work we do as a part of our rehabilitation into the world. It's not much, but enough to buy life's necessities." I watch him closely, to see if he gets it. The confusion creasing his face tells me he doesn't.

The truth of the matter is that the Facility supplies me with everything I need. Anything I want, all I have to do is ask. Whether that be new clothes, a new computer, a tablet to put my books on and silly games, it doesn't matter. I ask and they provide.

But that's another kind of slavery, a dependence on an outside agency that I need to fight. I want to be normal. Part of that is learning how to take care of myself and being able to provide for myself.

I try a different tack.

"Let me try it this way. Most of the kids there are not self-sufficient. The Facility is their legal guardian, and therefore, responsible for providing for all their needs. The same goes for me, kind of. As long as I'm at the Facility, I don't have to worry about paying for my toothbrushes, toothpaste, and all the essential things in life, but they're not my guardian. They're not legally responsible to provide for me like that."

"Okay, but I still don't see why I can't spoil you."

"Griff…" I give him a look. "There's a difference between spoiling a girl and taking over her life."

"I'm not trying to take over." His brows draw down. "Is that what you think? I'm only trying to help out."

"You asked me to explain, and I'm trying to do that."

"I'm trying to listen. I really want to understand, but I don't get why it's such a big deal."

"Well, all the other kids there get a modest allowance, but I came to the Facility a few months shy of turning twenty-one. An allowance didn't fit my unique circumstance, but they figured out a way for me to earn a small stipend."

"And you should save that for things you want, not to buy things you need. Not when I'm perfectly capable of doing that for you."

"Griff, there's no way for this not to sound horrible." I cringe with what I need to say. It's the comparison I avoid but is always in the back of my head. "My Masters provided everything I needed."

"Oh…" He takes a step back. "I see." From the look in his eyes, he totally gets it. Finally. Like on a gut level. I see the mortification in his expression as he processes what I'm trying to say.

"I told you it sounded bad, and I'm not comparing you to them. Those men were horrible men. You're wonderful, but it's… It's not a trigger, but it is a thing. Please understand. I *need* to buy my own things."

"I would never presume to take over control like that."

"I know." I place my hand on his arm. "You're a remarkable man, and it's in your genes to help others out. But maybe you don't have to help me in this?"

"Was last night…" He clears his throat, clearly uncomfortable. "When I tied you to the bed? Was that… Did I step over the line?"

"Oh God, no." I lift on tiptoe and kiss his cheek. "You and I are wired the same way when it comes to that. Maybe it doesn't make sense that I like it. I love it, by the way. Please don't stop." I pat his forearm, trying to reassure him. "I see how throwing a fit when you want to buy my clothes can be confusing."

"It's not confusing. It makes perfect sense, and I had no idea that's how you perceived it. Can't say I'm not relieved about sex though, because you and I in bed are fucking on fire." He draws me close and plants a devastating kiss that leaves me breathless. When he releases me, he stares down at me with passion smoldering in his gaze. "I meant to sit down and talk with you about that. I don't want to activate triggers or push things too fast."

"You can tie me up all you want. Fuck me hard and as vigorously as you want. I don't even mind if you order me around during sex. You remember that spanking you gave me?"

His grin lifts into a full-on smirk. "Yes, little minx, I remember that well."

I return his smirk with a cheeky grin. "I kind of liked that too, but maybe we draw the line there? Authoritarian, domineering men are definitely a trigger for me."

"And, outside of sex, we draw the line at me buying your clothes."

"If that's okay?" My shoulders lift. I hate putting any limits on our relationship, but I'm slowly realizing I need some boundaries.

The fact that Griff doesn't fight me on any of it is a testament to how incredibly understanding and wonderful he is.

"I know nothing about your finances, and it may have been wrong to assume. I thought I was helping, not activating triggers."

"Oh, you assumed right. I'm dirt poor, but I have way more than I ever did on the street. Honestly, being able to buy the things I need for myself, by myself, is probably the most liberating thing in my life right now."

"Message received. And, Moira?"

"Yeah."

"Thank you for taking the time to explain. I appreciate your willingness to talk this through instead of bottling it up and letting it fester. I'm not used to living with another person—I've never lived with a woman before—and I'm more likely to make assumptions I shouldn't. When I do, you need to promise to call me out on it."

"Am I living with you?"

"Is that all you got from what I just said?" His face breaks into one of his rare smiles.

It lights up his entire face, softening all the rough edges. I think it's the most beautiful thing in the world when Griff smiles.

"Fine, I pinky swear to be upfront and honest with you in all things, as long as you do the same. As for living together, it might be a bit soon for that. Let's enjoy ourselves for now, but eventually, I need to get back to the Facility. I still have work to do." I have a ton of work to do on myself, like get my GED, maybe apply to a university? At a minimum, I need a real job.

I want to be a normal girl, living a normal life. It's a dream of mine, maybe too far out of my reach, but I'm hopeful.

"I can accept that. Does that mean you're going to tell me about Bossman?"

His mention of Bossman makes my blood run cold. I'm one hundred percent certain I've told no one that name, and I haven't said a thing about what happened in that cabin.

"How do you know about Bossman?"

More worrisome, what does he know about what I did to Bossman?

TWENTY-ONE

Moira

_____

"How do you know that name?" I take a step back and press my hand over the sudden queasiness in my belly.

"You were mumbling his name in your sleep. Looked like you were having a nightmare." The way Griff speaks, it sounds like it's more than a simple nightmare.

"I don't remember waking up."

"I pulled you to me, and you settled down." Again, he acts like this is normal.

It's not. What the hell did I say? What does he know? Paranoia is not my thing, but damn if that's not the first place my mind heads.

I'm surprised I settled down, but then it's Griff. I've never felt more protected than when I'm with him. And despite our tiff in the store, his concern is not overbearing. It's exceedingly kind.

I'm not used to having someone care about me. In many ways, I don't know how to handle it. I've never depended on another human being in my life. From the age of five, when my dad left, through mom's addiction and overdose at eleven, I've only ever relied on myself. Griff scares me.

"I'm not ready to talk about that."

"I'll be right here when you are."

"Why did you ask?" I cock my head, needing to know what he knows.

"I think you know."

He stares at me with those violet eyes. Violet eyes which are normally full of violence, but only ever look at me with compassion and love. And in his expression, I read the truth. It's something I've suspected for a while but refused to believe.

He knows I'm a murderer.

"Your team found him, didn't they?"

"They did."

"I see." My entire body trembles and I take a step back. An overwhelming urge to run away overcomes me.

I'm a murderer.

And yet, Griff stands by my side. He knows what I did, and he's not judging me for it. Yet again, I don't know how to handle that. I've never had someone choose to stand by my side.

Griff walks around and opens my door. "Get in, minx. We'll talk about it, but only when you're ready. I promise not to push."

I climb into his car with my lips drawn into a tight line. He knows. Griff knows I killed a man.

I'm nowhere near ready to revisit those memories, but at least it's not some dark secret anymore. Griff isn't treating me differently because I'm a killer. What does that say about him? I know what he does for a living. Griff is a trained killer.

But I'm not.

It shouldn't matter, but it's a massive, major, humongous difference.

I need to know more about what it means to be a Guardian, and more specifically, what Griff does. Until I do, I can't broach this topic with him. I settle in and draw the seatbelt across my shoulder and click it.

THE NEXT FEW DAYS PASS IN A BLUR. GRIFF AND I SETTLE IN, LIVING together like it's as natural as breathing. We meld really well together.

We fuck. We sleep. We fuck some more.

He does most of the cooking because I'm hopeless, but I've never been taught how to cook. I never had the luxury of a home, a loving mother, or a kitchen stocked with food. My meals, more often than not, came out of garbage bins when I lived on the streets. When I was a sex slave, I was fed like a dog, or not at all.

"Is this right?" Flour dusts the granite surface of the kitchen counter and puffs in the air, forming a thin haze. I'm supposed to be kneading the dough for the pizza we're making for lunch.

We spent a lazy day in bed, only crawling out when our stomachs demanded it. Griff proclaimed pizza as our meal for the day. I thought we'd order delivery. He scoffed at that notion, going on a long, over the top, explanation about the merits of home-baked pizza and why delivery was for pussies.

He looks over my shoulder as I work flour into the dough. There's a small pile of flour at the top of my workspace that I'm supposed to slowly work into the dough.

It's a sticky mess. I've got dough stuck between my fingers, all over my palms; there's some of it sticking to my wrist. Don't know how that got there. But damn if I'm not determined to accomplish the one small task Griff assigned to me. The dough sticks as I push it around the granite countertop.

"It needs a bit more flour. You're doing good, minx. Work it in gradually and let the dough breathe." He grabs a pinch of flour from the pile and tosses it on top of the dough and all over the back of my hands.

I'm not really sure how dough breathes, but I continue to knead the sticky ball while he sets out the fixings for making pizza and works on his secret pizza sauce. It's all magic to me, but damn if it doesn't smell amazing.

"You've really never had homemade pizza before?"

"I haven't had homemade anything ever." Sad truth, but I haven't.

"We're adding this to the list." Griff dusts off his hands and goes to the fridge, where a "List of Things to Show My Minx" grows day by day.

"You can't add that to the list when we're doing it now." My protest falls on deaf ears.

"I can add whatever I want to the list. This is my list, minx. You have yours."

Each time he calls me "minx," tiny shivers race down my spine. That's another thing I've never had—a nickname.

Griff works around me, mixing sauce for the pizza, laying out an assortment of meats, shredding cheese off the block, and slicing onions and green peppers. He's a kitchen virtuoso, a hidden skill I never would've considered in the gruff warrior.

I figured he knows two things. How to kill bad guys and how to rescue those who've been taken. Being a virtuoso in the kitchen was not on my radar.

But I like that. I love all the little surprises I'm finding out about him as the days pass. I could really get used to this and settle into a life like this.

So much so that it terrifies me.

He stops to check on me, standing behind me as he looks over my shoulder. His towering form closes me in, as do his arms, which wrap around me. Griff places his large hands over mine, interlacing his fingers with mine.

"You're doing great, minx. It's almost ready."

"How can you tell?"

His fingers flex, moving mine beneath his as he kneads the ball of dough. "Feel the texture? How it's different from when you started? More pliable? More willing to stretch? See how it no longer sticks to your skin but springs back?"

I feel the heat of his body and the hard edge of his arousal poking me in the back.

"Umm… Maybe?" I can't tell that it's any different from before, but Griff seems to think I'm doing a good job. I'll take that praise any day.

"You have to go slow, work the flour in. Move too fast, or get impatient, and you ruin it."

"Um…" It's hard to know if we're talking about pizza dough or something else, especially since he rocks his pelvis against my back. Each time he leans into me, the long, hard length of him pushes against the small of my back.

"Slow and steady is the way to go."

"Griff…" A low ache settles between my legs.

"Now, it's done. Feel the texture, the way the dough yields?"

"Yes…" My reply is breathless. I desperately ache to yield to him. It's quickly becoming an obsession of mine.

I lean back and place the back of my head against his shoulder. My neck arches as he leans down and drags the tip of his nose along the sweep of my neck.

"I can't seem to get enough of you, little minx."

Griff suddenly spins me around, and we forget all about making pizza. My hands rise to cup his cheeks. I kiss him as he lifts me up and settles my legs around his waist. My pussy presses against his belly and the tip of his cock presses back. The only clothing I have on is one of his tee-shirts. He declared a no-panty rule until further notice a few days ago, stating something about removing barriers between us.

There's a bit of maneuvering as he struggles to pull down his briefs. When he declared the no-panty rule, I countered with a bare-chested rule. All he has on are his boxers, but he struggles to push them down and free his cock while also holding me.

Frustrated, he spins around and places me down on the counter behind him. With one tug, he frees his cock. The next second, he's buried balls deep inside of me.

Our arms grapple as our mouths lock in desperation. Damn, but I can't get enough of this man. Despite everything he said about going slow, I love when he moves hard and fast. He knows this and pounds relentlessly into me until my orgasm crashes and breaks over me. He follows me right over the edge, and we're soon holding each other as we regain our breath.

"I'm becoming addicted to you." He draws back and lifts my chin with his finger. "Are you sure about tomorrow?"

Tomorrow is the date I set for returning to the Facility. Not to stay. I can't imagine living there again, but there are things I need to do.

Griff makes it too easy to stay here. But I have questions, and my dreams grow more troubled by the day—or night. I guess my dreams are only troubled at night.

Griff says nothing about my nightmares or how they seem to be increasing, but I suspect he holds me every night when I scream in my sleep.

I need the resources the Facility provides. There's still much I need to work on. Griff continues honing my defensive skills. We practice at least an hour a day. I'm still traumatized by how easily I was taken, although he reminds me both Zoe and I were drugged. It should help, but it doesn't.

He attacks. I defend.

I lose every damn time.

I still have yet to escape my would-be assailant.

"It's been over a week and I need to settle a few things." I'm nervous about returning to the Facility. They'll want to ask questions.

"What are you thinking? Because I have to say, I'm not ready to let you go."

"I'm not going anywhere, but I feel like…" I give a sigh. "I feel ungrounded."

"Do you need to speak to the counselors?"

"Maybe?" I squirm as he steps back and pulls his boxers back up over his hips. "I don't really know."

"You'll know when you're ready."

"You keep saying that."

"Trust the system." Griff spouts off the Facility's creed.

I'm supposed to trust in the system they developed that turns victims into survivors. I've trusted their system for well over a year, and I thought I was ready to strike out on my own. I'm not. There's still more work to be done.

He lifts me off the counter and sets me on my feet. Then Griff turns and punches down the dough. He seems frustrated. Angry maybe? I don't really know. I'm still learning about him.

"You ready to make your pizza?" His voice is strained. I hate that he's frustrated with me, but I'm not ready to talk to him about Bossman.

I can't.

I discreetly brush away a tear. My emotions, like the rest of me, are all over the map.

Side by side, Griff shows me how to flatten the dough and form it into a circle. He doesn't speak about my inability to trust him.

We make two pizzas, one for him and one for me. We're getting to know each other, the idiosyncrasies and quirks, which only come out after spending a lot of time together. Like how he doesn't like sausage on his pizza but will pack it tight with pepperoni, and how I prefer sausage with green peppers, onions, and mushrooms. He says he's a pizza purist. I just call him weird.

We're also learning how to coexist and not push the other. Although, I'm the only one holding back. I sense my reluctance to confide in Griff bothers him.

Before, I only knew him as Four, the Guardian assigned to teach me how to defend myself. We never talked about things like the kind of pizza we preferred. Or whether coffee is a necessity or the foulest drink on the planet. We're diametrically opposed on the coffee front, by the way.

As for Griff, he insists I continue to work on my self-defense training. I thought I had that shit locked down, but evidently, I have a lot to learn. When not sleeping, eating, or fucking, he drills me relentlessly in the evasion techniques I need to master. Based heavily on Krav

Maga, the premiere self-defense method on the planet, this skill is supposed to keep me safe.

I need to confide in him and extend that trust, but I can't stop beating myself up about what I did. I killed two men—one by my own hand and the other by premeditated action.

The pizzas are amazing, not that I expect otherwise. We eat, clean the dishes, and ignore all the issues we've been side-stepping around these past few days.

After lunch, I head outside, where I enjoy the California sunshine. Griff disappears to work out in his home gym. I never understood how much time and effort went into maintaining his Guardian physique, but I have a pretty good idea now.

The man's a machine.

And can I say how appreciative I am of the results?

As for our sparring, most of our sessions on the mat end with sex. There's just something supremely erotic about grappling and fighting that turns us both on. We practice in the evening, which means I have a few hours to lose myself in a book while Griff works his body down in the gym.

I've yet to take him down, which pisses me off because Griff's holding back. He protects his leg, doing his best to listen to doctor's orders and take things easy. We talk about what it may mean if his leg doesn't heal.

I worry. He does not.

I don't know if that's male stupidity or overwhelming confidence. Either way, I leave him to do what he does best while I get lost in my book.

As for tomorrow, I'm scared.

TWENTY-TWO

Griff
_____

WITH MORE TREPIDATION THAN I'M WILLING TO ADMIT, I DRIVE Moira to the Facility as the sun rises over the eastern hills. Morning is my favorite time of day. I love waking before dawn. There's something about pounding out a five or ten-mile run before the sun crests the horizon that makes me feel like I've accomplished something for the day.

It's been a week and a half since I've pounded the pavement. Doc Summers' words echo in my head; threats of permanent disability aren't something I can sweep under the rug.

In the afternoons, when Moira escapes into her books, I double-down on my upper body and core workouts. From the waist up, I'm ripped and more defined than I've ever been in my life. From the waist down, the atrophy in my legs bothers me.

"You ready for this?" I reach across the seat and grasp Moira's hand. She's been unusually quiet during the drive in.

"No."

"Do you have an idea what you're going to do?"

"Well, first things first, I'm going to my room to pack."

The smile lifting my lips isn't something I can contain. Moira could choose to return to the Facility, but she's decided to stay with me.

This trip is a necessity for her to gather her things to bring home, but there's more to it than that. With each mile we put behind us, she comes closer to facing some hard truths.

There are people there who can help her if she opens up to them. But if she does that, leaving becomes problematic. The Facility likes to keep things in-house. They're not going to be happy with her decision to stay with me. Not that they can do anything about it. Moira isn't one of their legal wards. They have no grounds on which to force her to stay. That doesn't mean they won't try.

Moira and I both worry about them pressuring her to spend just a little more time at the Facility to work through her issues.

"And after you pack?" I try to draw her out and get her to talk to me. If she won't tell me what happened on that ship, I want her to at least trust one of her counselors with that truth.

"If you're asking whether I arranged an appointment, the answer is yes. But I'm still not ready."

"We never are." I grasp her hand and give it a tight squeeze. "But I'm here, if you need to talk."

"Thank you." She doesn't make eye contact and squirms in her seat. It's going to take time, and I'm trying to lay down some context that I hope will make things easier for her to confide in me.

Over the past few nights, I've tried to give her a glimpse into what it means to be a Guardian. There are some things I can't share, which sucks. Here I am, wanting her to be open and honest with me, while I hold back crucial details about what I do for the Guardians.

But what will she think about me when I tell her I'm Alpha Team's go-to torture guy? That extracting information from unwilling participants is my jam? What about the fact I'm also the team's sniper?

My job is to kill, and I'm very good at my job.

I was excellent while I was in the military, sanctioned by the good old United States of America. It's what drew the attention of Guardian HRS. When they found out I was getting out of the military, Sam and CJ were at my front door with a contract and an impressive benefits package.

Both CJ and Sam, went to work for the FBI as hostage rescue specialists after they separated from the military. Forest recruited them and they recruited me. Those ties to the FBI ensure Guardian HRS remains an unofficially sanctioned entity by the US government.

Officially, Delta team is our link through official channels. They deploy for domestic hostage situations, which require a certain finesse the US government can't sanction. The rest of us operate in those gray areas, where legal and non-legal objectives merge.

And that is where my unique skillset thrives.

My gut says Moira meeting with the psych docs at the Facility won't change a damn thing. She's not ready to talk to anyone, which makes me worry. That kind of shit does bad things to a person's head if they let it fester inside of them. Somehow, I need to find a way to make Moira talk.

Our drive ends far too soon. I park and walk with Moira into the Facility, and thankfully Zoe is there. I'm hoping Moira might open up to her friend.

The moment Moira notices Zoe, a high-pitched squeal splits the air.

"Zoe!" Moira releases my hand and sprints toward her friend.

"Moira!" Zoe answers in kind, and my shoulders draw up to my ears with all the female squealing going on.

The girls embrace and the squeals shut off as they simply hold each other for what seems like forever. When they part, they both brush at the tears which fell.

I breathe out a sigh and realize I may have been too protective of my time with Moira. Maybe I shouldn't have waited to get the two of them together. I head over to the greeting desk while the girls talk amongst themselves.

"Hi, Four." Kaye, the Facility's receptionist and holder of all the knowledge, knows every Guardian by sight. "How's it going?"

"Pretty damn good." I gesture toward Moira and Zoe. "I thought maybe I'd get a goodbye, but…"

Kaye gives a flap of her wrist. "Don't let it get to you. You know how things work around here."

"Yes, I do." I glance over at Moira, not sure if I should interrupt, but I have appointments of my own to make. "Did Moira arrange a schedule of any kind? I'm not sure when to pick her up."

Kaye peers at her computer screen. "She's got a couple of appointments with the staff. One's at eleven, the other's at three. Not really sure why she spaced them out like that, but I'd bet she won't be ready to leave until at least five."

"That actually works well for me." I tap the desk with my finger then head over to Moira and Zoe.

Zoe notices me first, and her expression softens. "Hi, Four."

"You can call me Griff. I think we're beyond the numbers."

"I suppose so. Axel mentioned you were taking some time off. I wondered why I didn't see you during practice."

I point to my leg. "Doctor's orders."

"I bet that's killing you."

"Definitely." My attention shifts to Moira. "Do you mind if I have a moment with my girl?"

"Your girl?" Her eyebrows lift in surprise and she shares a look with Moira. "Good going, girl. You snagged a Guardian. Now we have that in common as well. We'll have to trade stories."

Moira's face turns bright red at that comment. It's funny, because I've never seen Moira blush before. She shakes her head and shoves Zoe playfully. "Yes, we will have to compare notes."

"Definitely. You know what they say about a Guardian's stamina…" Zoe lets her words trail off but not before shifting her gaze to me and giving a knowing wink.

I have a feeling these two will be comparing a lot of things over the next hour. I draw Moira a few steps away and pull her into a massive bear hug. Don't know why, but I hate leaving her alone. It feels weird, as if I'm leaving a little piece of me behind.

"You're going to pack, right?" I kiss the top of her head and take note of the way Zoe watches us. She has to know Moira's been staying with me. No way would Axel keep that information from his girl.

"I am."

"Okay, because I don't like leaving you here, and I want your word you are, in fact, coming home with me tonight."

"Griff!" She slaps playfully at my chest. "Of course, I am."

"Okay, because you know how this place can be."

"I do, and I know why you're worried. The Facility used to be my safe space, but I have that with you now, and no way am I missing out on bedtime cuddling."

"Is that what we're calling it?"

"I like it."

"What about afternoon delights or morning glories?"

"Oh, my God, I can't believe you just said that. For the record, I like those too. I promise I'll be packed and waiting for you. I see the shrink at three, so maybe five?"

"Sounds good."

"What are you going to do all day?"

"I have a doctor's appointment of my own. Doc Summers wants to see if I've been babying my leg. She still wants a vascular surgeon to check me out, and I thought I'd stop in to see the team. I want to see if they know anything new."

"Oh, I forgot all about Bossman's phone. Do you think it's helping?"

"I hope so, and if anyone can pick apart its secrets, it'll be Mitzy and her technical team."

Moira wraps her arms around my neck and lifts on tiptoe to give me a kiss. "Don't do anything I wouldn't do."

"Same goes for you, little minx." My glance shifts to Zoe. "What would you think about having Zoe and Axel over to the house for dinner tonight?"

My comment is tactical in nature. I want to ensure Moira comes home with me. My worry is that once she's back in the comforting hold of the Facility, she'll rethink her decision to stay outside in the real world. Since I can't protect her the way I want if she's a resident in the Facility, I need her to come home.

"Oh, that would be fun. I'll ask Zoe, although I'm sure she'll want to come. She's going to want to make sure you're treating me right."

"If treating you right is drowning you in orgasms, I'm going to pass with flying colors."

"Griff!"

"Just stating facts." I give Moira one last squeeze, then release her. "I'll be back at five to pick the two of you up."

"What about Axel?"

"Oh, he'll be with me." Of that, I'm certain.

"Cool. Be good, Griff."

"Behave, little minx."

She bites her lower lip and bats her lashes at me. "I can only try."

With a shake of my head, I leave her in Zoe's company and head back to my car, where I sit for the next ten minutes. I really hate leaving her behind. It feels all kinds of wrong.

But I do have an appointment with the doc, and I'm eager to see my team. More than that, and it kills me to say it, but I'm acutely interested in checking in with Mitzy and her team.

I don't know what, if any, intelligence they've extracted from that phone, but I hope to God they've found something.

TWENTY-THREE

Moira

"He's cute." Zoe makes a show of watching Griff walk away. "That man's got a swagger to match that mighty fine ass, and he knows how to fill out those jeans. I bet it's rock hard, too…" Her voice drops to a whisper. "I'm talking about his penis." She jabs me with her elbow. "I bet it's hard enough to pound nails when he's around you."

"Zoe!" I shove my best friend and ignore the heat scorching my cheeks. I noticed the prominent bulge in Griff's jeans, but didn't think Zoe would see it.

"Oh, come on, Griff's built like Axel. Solid muscle, *everywhere*. And what's with the blush?"

"What blush?" Solid muscle is an understatement. Thick, corded muscle stretches all across Griff's physique. Every inch honed to lethal effect. Griff's muscles stretch the sleeves of his shirt and the poor fabric barely contains the expanse of his chest. As for the way he wears those jeans, I'm in agreement with Zoe. Griff is fine with a capital F-I-N-E.

"Oh, come on." She shoves me back. "Your face lit up like a Christmas tree." She pinches her chin as Griff pushes on the door leading out to the parking lot. "So, is he good in bed?" Zoe arches a brow. Unlike me, she's got that look down pat.

"You're assuming we're sleeping together." I sniff and tilt my nose in the air.

"Sweetie, there's no assuming. The way your face turned fifty shades of red says it all. I just want to know if he's any good."

"Is Axel good in bed?" I spin her question around, aiming it back at her and her overly inquisitive mind.

"Phenomenal." Zoe giggles and grabs my hands. "Now, spill. What the hell are you doing playing house with him?"

"I don't know if I'd call it playing house, but…" It's then when I notice the rock sitting on her left ring finger. "When the hell did this happen?"

"That happened not long after…" She bites her lower lip. "Oh, Moira, I've been so worried about you. Those few days felt like years not knowing what happened to you. I've never felt so helpless."

"I really don't remember much that happened that night." I shift and glance around. This isn't exactly where I want to have this conversation. "Um, do you think there's someplace we can talk?" My gaze flicks up to the cameras.

Zoe's astute gaze follows the path of my gaze. She knows exactly what I mean.

Nearly all of the Facility is under surveillance. It's not the creepy kind with Big Brother watching. We have privacy in our rooms, but the cameras are there for the staff's benefit and our welfare. That might sound weird, and creepy, but many rescuees, when they first arrive, are plagued by flashbacks.

For most of us, that kind of trauma can induce a near-catatonic state. Sometimes, something innocuous triggers us. There's no telling what it might be. The staff uses the cameras to first identify those events, and then later, to help the rescuee process what happened. It's a major part of our healing process.

So, while the cameras aren't creepy, I still don't want to have this conversation where they can hear. It'll get reported to my counselor and then we'll have to discuss and analyze it to death.

Not ready for that.

And the cameras aren't intrusive. After my first few weeks, I forgot the cameras were there. I mean, I knew they were there, but I no longer worried about them.

"I know a place." Zoe takes my hand in hers. "But I don't think you're going to get away that easily. Everyone's been talking about you, worried sick about you. We heard from Forest, of course, that you'd been rescued, and were doing well, but still… We kind of all thought you'd come back here. When you didn't—let's just say everyone got really concerned."

"Okay, we'll do the hello thing, but I really need to talk, and I want to know what happened that night. There are holes in my memory."

"I don't blame you, and I'm not surprised. Not with how that asshole kicked the shit out of you."

"I don't remember that, but my ribs did seem a bit banged up. I don't understand why he'd do that, considering…"

"Moira, you bit his dick off. He was more than a little pissed."

"I did what?"

"You heard me."

"Yeah, I heard you, but when Shelly and Bossman were talking about Jack, I thought they were exaggerating."

"No exaggeration. You are one mean bitch, and don't worry about Jack."

"Oh, I know, they killed him."

"Well, I'm sure the Guardians will make sure... What did you call them?"

"Bossman and Shelly."

"Weird names." She gives a dismissive wave. "Anyway, I'm sure Bossman and Shelly will see Guardian justice."

"Not likely." I tug on my lower lip.

Zoe cocks her head, confused, but then her eyes round when it hits. "Holy shit, Moira. Did you?"

"That's what I want to talk about." I keep my voice low, not wanting the surveillance cameras to pick up our conversation. I'm not ready to talk through my shit with them, but I am ready to share with the one person who can understand best.

I drag her through a set of doors that leads into the Facility. Zoe's a smart girl and says nothing more about it.

"So, where is everyone?" I keep my voice low.

"It's just past eight. Everyone's in class."

Zoe rolls her eyes as if explaining the most basic thing to me. I get it. I know the rhythms of life at the Facility. Or, I should remember them. Somehow, after this past week, my life no longer conforms to the rigid schedule put in place by the Facility.

What does that mean?

I stop to contemplate that small, weird fact. A few weeks ago, I would've thought nothing about the schedule we kept. I got up in the morning, went to breakfast, and always felt comforted by knowing what came next.

Now that I've been away from the Facility, I see how soothing that blanket had been. Do I still need it? Do I want that level of control exercised over my life?

The thing is, I don't, but I'm also not ready to let it go. Weird, isn't it? I don't reject the process, but I feel as if I've transcended it.

The Facility is the one and only beacon of light in my life. There's nothing hidden beneath the surface. They exist for only one purpose, and that's to one day set me free.

Is that what's happening?

Am I the one who's changed? I don't need structure in my life. In fact, if I did return, it would chafe. From the way my attention keeps shifting to the cameras nestled in the walls, I feel the weight of feeling different. I'd resent the oversight and the control.

Where does that leave me?

Okay, that's all nonsense. There's no way I've outgrown the Facility. Does this mean I'm ready to live outside its walls? Shit, but that scares me. I'm not ready, and I can't do it alone.

Griff will be there. He won't abandon me.

He's a Guardian.

And?

He will leave on missions.

But he'll come back.

Maybe. You'll still be alone. Anything could happen.

Shit, I hate vacillating like this.

I have to say, the one night I spent away from the Facility didn't turn out well. I was abducted and imprisoned in less than a day. I don't think I was out for more than twelve hours before some monster paid for the privilege to ruin my life.

Stop! No reason to go down that path.

The past is in the past. We cannot change it. All we control is our future.

The words of my instructors run through my head. They're easy to say, much harder to live. What matters is that I'm free, but it's weird being here again.

Everything feels different.

"Moira!" Zoe snaps her fingers in front of my face.

"What?"

"Where were you just now?"

"What do you mean?"

"Come on, you faded out on me." Her concern does not fall on deaf ears.

I'm well aware of what just happened. It's a mental spiral I've fallen down before, and there's nothing pretty about it. The thing is, if I focus on the past, or the way I wish things could be, I'd end up in a mental fugue. A prison of my own making. It's far too easy to fall, and it's a bitch to climb out of that kind of despair. I should know. I've had to find my way back before.

Fortunately, this time, I have Zoe to lean on.

But what happens when it's just me?

If Griff's away on a mission, and I'm all alone at the house, what do I do if my mind heads down that path? I blink and force those thoughts away. Evidently, there's still much the Facility has to offer me.

How do Skye and Forest handle it? That respiratory therapist, Ryker, said Tia was one of Forest's earliest rescuees. She's a certified respiratory anesthetist. Skye is an emergency physician. They're both victims of abuse who are rocking life.

Will I ever be like them? Will there ever be a day when I feel normal?

"You're doing it again, Moira." Zoe snaps her fingers in front of my face.

"I'm sorry. I'm really fucked-up." I point to my head. "It's a mess in there."

"How about we forget about the reunion and have that chat?" Zoe's younger than me, but there's wisdom in her eyes.

She and I experienced different sides of this fucked up coin that is the world of human sex-trafficking. I bartered my flesh at first to stay alive, and then because I had no other choice. Zoe experienced something different—something far worse. Someone, or someones, paid to watch her die a horrific death. Not once, but twice.

Thankfully, the Guardians saved her twice. Kind of like me. That's the bond we share. Saved by the Guardians, not once, but twice. I've never known what it means to have a family but consider Zoe to be not only my best friend, but my sister as well. She certainly can read me well.

"Does anyone know I was coming today?" I really don't want to skip out on the others, especially if they're looking forward to seeing me.

"Nope. Well, I knew, but only because Griff told Axel, and Axel told me, but I didn't tell any of the others." She takes my hand in hers and locks her fingers with mine. "Honestly, I didn't know what kind of state you'd be in."

"Were you thinking confident and kissing ass, or broken and…"

Zoe grins. "I was thinking you might need a friend. Or maybe just a shoulder to lean on. Come on. If we leave now, no one will see us. We can meet everyone for lunch and show them how badass you really are."

"I'm not badass. I'm horribly broken."

"That may be, but sometimes you have to walk the walk for a bit and try it on for size. You're stronger than you know, Moira Stone." Zoe speaks with absolute conviction as if she knows all the answers to all the questions in the world. She points toward the classroom. "And to those kids, you're an inspiration. Walk the talk and talk the walk."

"You sound like a damn seventies commercial."

"Just trying to put a smile on your face." She beams at me, trying to get me to crack a smile. It works. I smile at her comment.

"You're the best friend a girl could have."

"Right back at you. Now, how about we get out of here?" For someone who moments ago told me I should stop in and say hello, she sure is eager to get me alone.

"What are you thinking?"

"How about a stroll along the cliffs?"

"You know I don't like heights." I love heights. That's my hesitation talking.

"Bullshit, I've seen you standing at the edge. Besides, you're going to like this." Her brows lift like she's got some amazing secret.

What I don't mention is that all of those times she saw me standing at the edge of the cliffs, I'd been contemplating hurtling myself over the edge. I wondered how long it would take to fall. How many seconds would I have to embrace death? Would I regret my decision on the way down? Was it going to hurt when my body slammed into the rocks below? Would anyone care?

Best I not spoil her opinion of me. I'd rather Zoe think I have no fear of heights rather than know the truth. All those days sitting out on Griff's deck changed my perception about heights. From the moment he told me he loved going out there as a kid, that he felt like he was flying in the clouds, it all felt different to me. For the first time in my life, I dreamed about soaring in the clouds. I believed I could do anything, be anyone.

I felt at peace.

I blow out a frustrated breath, but I'm game. Being with Zoe makes me feel like an ordinary girl.

Normal.

She pulls me through the complex, avoiding the classrooms with our compatriots, and soon we're jogging down one of the many paved walking paths which crisscross the grounds. I think she's got some special place within the Facility proper, but Zoe guides me beyond the buildings to the paths I used to avoid. They follow the edge of the cliffs.

Zoe and I are the only residents at the Facility over the age of eighteen. I think it's why we bonded so hard. Since the Facility is the legal guardian of the kids, they provide age-appropriate education for them. That means they're stuck in school most of the day. I participated in some of that, or at least what was required to study for my GED.

"Do you think they'll mind if we wait until lunch?" I can't help it. Those kids are my family, and I feel a little guilty for not going to see them first thing.

"Moira?" Zoe props her hands on her hips and gives me a look. "They will kill you if you don't show your face the moment you stepped foot on Facility grounds, but they don't need to know when that happened. Come on, we'll be back for lunch in no time. Besides," she gives me a wink, "I want to catch up with you first. Call me selfish, but I missed you. I worried about you. I've never felt so hopeless. And, if I'm being completely honest, I wish Alpha team had saved you instead of me. I can't imagine what you've been through."

"Zoe, don't ever say that again. I'd never wish what happened to me on another person."

She pulls me into a tight hug. "I'm so glad you made it home safe, and I want you to tell me as much as you can."

I wipe my palms on my jeans, confused as to why they're suddenly sweaty. Zoe asking about what happened is a trigger. I feel it buzzing in my blood and vibrating under my skin. A queasiness unsettles my belly.

But I use the techniques the Facility taught me and control my body's reactions.

I am in control. Those are just memories. They have no power to hurt me.

It's the litany drilled into all of us when we first arrive. We're survivors. Strong. Resilient. Capable survivors.

We aren't victims.

If I say it enough times, one day, I might believe it.

"Where are we going?"

"It's just a little further." The expression on Zoe's face gives me pause. She's got something to share. It's a secret, and I can tell it's a big one.

TWENTY-FOUR

Moira
___

WE KEEP OUR CONVERSATION LIGHT, AVOIDING TRIGGER TOPICS, AND I ask her about Axel and the rock on her finger.

"I can't believe you're engaged."

"Neither can I." She lifts her hand and twists the gorgeous rock on her finger. Sunlight makes it glitter like a million-faceted gem.

"I thought you hated him."

"I did."

"When Three showed up, how long did it take before you knew it was him?"

"I didn't know Three was Axel at first."

"I would've thought you would've known. You always went on and on about growing up with him, and being in love with him, since you were, what? Five?"

"Yeah. First crush. First love. First heartbreak."

"And now, he's your fiancé." I stop and hug her. "I'm really happy for you."

Getting engaged is what a normal girl would do, not broken people like me.

"I'm happy for you. You can't tell me things aren't getting serious with Four—um, Griff. You've been living with him for the past week."

"I'm not sure how serious we are. He's more overprotective than anything else. It's almost like he's keeping me under his thumb where he can watch over me. I don't know if I'd call that a relationship."

"From the way he was looking at you, I'd say he's decided you belong to him. That man is definitely interested. I practically swooned from the overprotective vibes he was putting off."

"I suppose." I place a hand over my belly. It's weird how simply talking about Griff gives me butterflies. "I kind of wish he was here, now."

"So, you like him?" Zoe's single brow arches, inquisitive and demanding an answer.

"I've had a crush on him from the day we met. Although, I never knew his real name. He was Alpha-Four when he rescued me in Manila, then just overbearing and obnoxious Four here during sparring practice. He never went easy on me."

"They never do."

"You're telling me Axel wasn't easy on you?"

"Never. And I totally get it. It pisses me off, but if they let us win without earning it, that does us no favors."

"Well, I wish I'd fought back better back on that beach."

"We were both drugged. Don't you dare head down that road. They paid those college kids to drug us."

"They did?"

"You didn't know?"

"Like I said, most of that night is foggy."

"What do you remember?"

"Getting taken. Then waking up on a cold concrete floor."

"Wow, you lost a lot of time." Zoe ducks her head and glances out over the ocean. A breeze lifts her hair, blowing it out behind her. She tucks her hair behind her ears and kicks at the rocks. She won't look at me. "I thought you were dead."

"Why?"

"Jack went to town on you. Kicked you in the gut, the ribs, and your head before one of them put a bullet in his head."

"That was Bossman. He and Shelly talked about it. I still can't believe that really happened."

"You had to have been out for a long time."

"Why's that?"

"Because they put us on a plane and flew us to Colombia."

"Colombia? I guess that makes sense."

"Why?"

"I woke up on a cargo container ship, although it took some time before I figured that out. We were headed to New Orleans."

"Well, the team tracked us and raided the building where we were being held. They rescued me, but couldn't find you in the chaos of everything happening."

"Maybe I never made it to the building? Maybe we landed and they put me on the ship?"

"No. You were definitely there."

"Oh."

"We don't have to talk about all of this if you don't want to." Zoe reaches out for me and I link my fingers with hers. Together we stare out at the ocean, silent for a time, but I need answers.

"I need to fill in the gaps in my memory. I've been avoiding it, but it's time."

"Come, it's just a little farther."

"What is?"

"My secret place."

"How do you have a secret place?"

"Long story, but Forest shared it with me. It was the day after I tried to kill myself for the first time."

I shake my head. "Girl—been there. Done that…"

"Got the scars to prove it!" Zoe finishes my little twisted litany for me.

It became a running joke between us and I think she's the only one who ever really understood what it means.

Everyone else thinks I'm this badass survivor. What they don't know is that I suck at dying. Zoe gets it. We've bared our deepest, darkest secrets to each other during our time together.

Zoe walks to the edge of the cliff and glances over her shoulder. She winks at me, then jumps off the edge. My hand goes out and a scream lodges itself in my throat. But instead of plummeting down the hundred-foot cliff, Zoe drops only a couple of feet before stopping.

She points at me and holds her midsection while she laughs. "You should totally see the expression on your face."

I move toward the edge and glance down. Zoe's standing on a ledge. It's about three to four feet wide, plenty safe, but completely invisible unless you're standing right at the edge and looking down.

"That is so uncool!"

"You should've seen Axel's face when I did that to him. Thought he was going to paddle my ass."

"Paddle?" A smirk lifts the corner of my mouth. "Didn't think you were into that kind of thing."

"Forget I said that!" Zoe's cheeks turn crimson.

"Oh, there is no forgetting that. You're a kinky bitch."

"We're totally not talking about that."

"And why not?" I cross my arms over my chest and look down at her. "We can talk about the other shit, but not the kinky sex games you and Three, I mean Axel, get to when you're alone."

"You going to admit that you and Four—um, Griff—are banging it like rabbits?" Zoe isn't above challenging me.

My lips twist. "Maybe a little."

"A little? Like holding hands? Kissing?"

"You're horrible." I jump down beside her on the ledge. "Why are we on the side of a cliff?"

"Because." Zoe points down the gradual slope of the ledge. "I want to show you the cave."

"A cave?"

"Yeah."

"You mean to tell me you were hiding a cave from me all this time?"

"Do you hate me for it?" She gives a sheepish grin. "I needed something that was just mine. Forest caught me out here when I was going to jump. Told me about the cave and that I might want to think about it." She shrugs. "I didn't mean to keep it from you, but it was…"

I put my hand on her shoulder. "Z, I'm just pulling your leg. I totally get needing something for yourself. Now show me your cave."

She leads me down the ledge until we come to a small cut in the rock. We have to stoop and half crawl inside, but the cave opens up just a few feet in. I turn in a circle, spinning around, in wonder.

"This place is incredible." Blankets stacked in the corner snag my attention, as does a lantern and what looks to be a stash of fuel. "Looks like you come out here often. How did I not know?"

"You thought I was sneaking out to be with Three." She nibbles on her lower lip. "And I kind of was. We came here a lot."

"Just tell me where I can safely sit. Someplace the two of you didn't do the nasty on."

Zoe shakes her head. She goes to the piles of blankets and returns to the low cave opening. "Here, sit down. You can hear the ocean really well right here. It kind of magnifies the sound. And if you close your eyes, you can almost feel the waves as they slam against the rock. The whole cliff kind of rumbles, especially when there's a storm."

"Oh, I bet it would be incredible to watch a storm from here."

"Sunsets are amazing too." She lays the blankets on the floor of the cave and we settle in.

For the longest time, we do nothing other than simply sit there. I take in the smells of the cave; the musty odor of damp rock and salt fills my lungs. I close my eyes and listen. At first, all I hear are our combined breaths, but then the roar of the waves as they crash upon the rocks finds its way to my ears. It's a low, nearly subsonic sound. Z's right. I feel it more than hear it.

When I crack my eye, a gull sweeps across the opening. A few seconds later, he calls out to his friends. This is easily the most tranquil place I've ever been.

"I can't believe you kept this from me."

"Well, I didn't want you accidentally walking in on Axel and me…"

"You little horn dog." I can't help but tease her.

She's had the hots for Axel since she was five years old. Axel tolerated her because he's best friends with her brother but gave Z the ol' heave-ho when she pushed things too far. He really is the love of her life—unrequited love that finally found its way.

I've never had that. Not once in my life have I had a boy, or a man, care about me.

At least, not until Griff.

I still don't understand it. I'm afraid to believe it's true. I keep waiting for the other shoe to drop.

Zoe lies back and looks over at me. "I'm really glad you're safe."

I adjust the blanket she gave me and lie beside her. Together, we stare at the granite overhead. It should feel oppressive, but I've never felt more free.

"Me too."

"Tell me what you remember, and I'll fill in what I can."

"I remember walking on the beach with you. We found those college kids." All I wanted that night was to do something a normal girl would do, like hang out on a beach, sit around a campfire, and sing stupid songs. We did all of that, and like good buddies, we set limits on the number of drinks we allowed. "You said they drugged us?"

"It was late. We were walking back to the house. We were laughing, dancing at the water's edge, and thought we were safe."

"I don't remember leaving the bonfire, but I remember being attacked."

"There were three men who approached from down the beach. It felt wrong, so we headed away from the water. That's when I realized you were drugged. You were slurring your words but had only had water. We fought them." She puts a hand on me. "We fought hard, but there were too many of them and the drugs…"

"Slowed us down."

"Exactly. I like to think we could've taken them." She snorts, then giggles. "We fought hard, Moira."

"But?"

"They took us. Ditched our phones."

"How did the Guardians find us?"

Zoe pulls out her necklace. It's the tracker the Facility gave to all of us. I feel around my neck, noticing for the first time, despite everything, that mine is gone. Zoe glances over at me.

"They found our phones and your necklace in the sand. Fortunately, I still had mine and activated the tracker. They took us straight to the airport and flew us to Columbia."

My breaths become shallow and rapid as Zoe explains everything that happened. She takes me through what happened in the van. How I actually bit a man's dick off. How he retaliated. How Bossman killed him. Then she tells me how Alpha Team rescued her in Columbia and how they lost me.

"So, you really dangled on a rope below a helicopter?"

"It was terrifying, but I was just happy Axel was there. Griff got shot."

"Is that how it happened?"

"Yeah. They exchanged gunfire. It was terrifying, and when he was pulled up… Well, Axel put a tourniquet on his leg and Skye and her team fixed him up."

"That explains a lot."

"How's that?"

I tell her about my rescue, and how I too dangled on a cable beneath a helicopter, and how the wound in his leg reopened.

"So, he's now on indefinite medical hold until it heals."

"Is that where he went?"

"Yeah, he has an appointment with Skye."

"I guess that means we have all day."

"I suppose we do."

"Now, tell me what happened on that ship."

TWENTY-FIVE

Griff

———

"So?" I stare at the back of Doc Summers as she types away on her computer screen, inputting the results of her exam. "How's the leg look? I've been babying it like you wanted." My leg bounces nervously while I wait for her answer.

"Your leg looks good."

"That's good, right?" I release the tension in my fingers. The knuckles turned white with the death grip I held on the side of the exam table.

"I still want you to meet with a vascular surgeon. We need to check the integrity of the repair, but if you continue to stay off it, I see no problem with reinstating your operating privileges."

"And how much longer?" When I look at my legs, I cringe. All I see are signs of atrophy. The quads aren't nearly as well defined as before, and the skin sags where it used to be stretched tight over those muscles.

"You still have about 6-8 weeks."

"That's what you said a week ago." To keep from sounding petulant, I practically growl out the words.

"And that's what I'm saying now." Doc Summers spins around.

"You know how much muscle mass I'm going to lose between now and then?"

"Not as much as you'll lose if that leg doesn't heal." She regards me with a long, solemn look. "I know it's hard, and I get that you want to get back to work. I also understand your concern over your physical conditioning, but you need to trust me on this. I want to see you in another three weeks. Depending on how things look and how your appointment goes with the vascular surgeon, we might be able to begin some gentle physical therapy."

"I'm going to have chicken legs by then."

"Griff, you're going to be fine. Everything looks good. No venous congestion. No clots on the ultrasound." She put gel on the back of my leg earlier and took a look at the blood flowing in that vein. Clots and strictures, a narrowing of the injured vessel, are bad. I'm not medical, but I got that much.

I blow out a breath and accept her assessment. "I guess I'll see you in three weeks."

"You know, you're still cleared for support. You can still be a vital asset to the team."

"I kind of thought maybe I wasn't."

Her soft smile eases some of the worry I had. "I know exactly what you're worried about, and we're not talking about what may, or may not, have happened during Moira's rescue. Ariel Black is sticking to her story, and Speed backs it up." The look she gives says she knows that's all bullshit, but I keep my mouth shut, not wanting to put the doc in a compromising position by speaking the truth. "You should check in with Mitzy and the team."

"Why?" That's an odd comment coming from her.

"Only because I know they're meeting in about ten minutes."

"Meeting about what?"

"About that phone." For a doctor, Doc Summers seems to know a ton about the inner workings in and around Guardian HRS.

"Well, shit." That's all she needs to say to get my gimp-assed self out of her exam room. I head out of medical and make a beeline to the main conference room for the techies. The brisk walk makes the pain in my leg flare, but I grit my teeth and double-step it. No way am I missing this, although I'm a bit concerned I wasn't called in.

Not that it matters.

I palm the door to the conference room and push it open. It's dark inside, and everyone swivels toward the door. Some lift their hands to shield against the glare from the hallway.

It takes a moment, but I slowly make out the faces bathed in the blue glow of the monitors. Mitzy with her psychedelic hair stands out. The monolithic form of Forest stands at the back of the room. He leans against the back wall with a scowl and an icy glare. Sitting around the table, Sam, CJ, and Alpha-One, my direct commander, Max, take me in. No other members of Alpha team are here. I pull to a dead stop, suddenly realizing this may not be a briefing I should be at.

"Sorry, Doc Summers said I should come."

"Did she now?" Forest's voice rumbles across the space between us, vibrating the air.

"She said I was still in a support role." I look around, confused, because the rest of my team isn't here.

"Shut the damn door." Sam, who's closest to the door, holds his hand over his face and pinches his eyes shut.

"I can leave."

"Come in and have a seat." Forest kicks off the far wall and waves me toward the table. "Another pair of eyes will help." He runs his fingers through his shockingly white-blond hair and lets the shoulder-length strands slip through his fingers. The expression on his face is grim.

Not willing to look a gift horse in the mouth, I quickly enter and make sure the door latches behind me. Max kicks out a chair, and I yank it back and sit my ass down.

"How's Moira?" Forest's low rumble surprises me. It's not a question I expect, but then I remember Forest's past. He's genuinely interested in the wellbeing of his rescuees.

"She's good."

"Is she talking?" Those three words say much about the way Forest thinks. He understands the trauma she endured, and like the rest of us, he knows what happened in that stateroom.

I desperately want to get Moira to confide in me about what happened back there. She killed the man she refers to as Bossman, and he didn't go down easy. I can't imagine the terror she experienced in those few moments, but I know she relives it each night in her dreams.

"No." I cross my arms and try to look like I haven't spent the past week fucking her brains out instead of dealing with her emotional trauma. I feel like a goddamn putz, arrogant, self-absorbed, and drunk on pussy. That changes today. "She's still clammed up, but no triggers. No flashbacks. Only a few nightmares."

"I see." Forest leans back against the wall. "I assume you've taken responsibility for her wellbeing?" It's a simple statement, but Forest lobs it out there as a challenge. I'm up for it. At least until I'm operating again. When I leave Moira, it'll only be with absolute assurance she can defend herself, and I'll get someone to watch over her. No way in hell will I leave her completely unprotected.

"I have."

"That's good. She's been at the Facility too long, and with her abduction, staying there will only increase her reliance on the place. It's supposed to be an aid, not a crutch. See to it that she continues to stay with you."

"That's my intent, but I can't make her stay if that's not what she wants." I don't mention my greatest fear. When I pick Moira up to take her home, will she let me? But I agree with Forest. She needs to get away from the Facility.

She needs to know what it's like to live a normal, happy life. My hope is she chooses to include me in that future. I have a few ideas on how to keep her safe.

I see the Facility being far more of a hindrance than a simple crutch. Somehow, I need to help Moira figure out a way to feel safe outside the Facility walls. Right now, I have no idea how to make that happen, but I will. It's just a matter of time, persistence, and perseverance.

Max gives me a look, then shakes his head. I'm not fooling anyone about our intimate relationship, but I'm not the kind of guy to talk about my woman like that. It's disrespectful.

"Where is she now?" Max spins in his chair until he faces me directly.

"I took her to the Facility. She needed to get her things, and she has an appointment with a counselor."

"Good. She needs to get it out there." Forest concludes that conversation. His sharp gaze returns to the monitors at the other end of the room, which provide the only light.

"What's going on here?" My attention shifts with the rest of those present.

"Mitzy was just about to show us what she's found." Max crosses his arms over his chest.

"If y'all are done shooting the shit, I can get back to it." Mitzy gives a little snort of indignation. She likes to play things up, like we never pay attention to her, but the opposite is true. Considering our lives depend on the intelligence she obtains, we're acutely interested in what she has to say.

I lean forward and keep my voice low, speaking only to Max. "Where's the rest of the team?"

"At the range."

"Why aren't they…"

"Seriously, Griff, can you shut up?" Mitzy taps her foot while Forest chuckles behind me.

"My apologies."

"As if." She flicks through several screens. "This is probably the biggest boon we've had in a very long time, but it won't last. I'm sure the people Sly Gabel worked for are plugging the holes in their operation, but we've been able to ascertain a few things."

I sit on my hands, eager to find out what Mitzy and her tech-savvy team discovered with the phone Moira carried off that ship.

"Who's Sly Gabel?"

"The man this phone belonged to. Seriously, keep up or get out. Stop wasting my time." Mitzy glares at me.

I lift my hands in mock surrender and keep my trap shut.

For the next twenty minutes, Mitzy drones on about how they cracked the phone, deciphered the code, and inadvertently activated a self-destruct sequence, which started a data wipe.

I cringe through this part because she's incapable of jumping to the end, where the important stuff waits. We have to endure a lengthy monologue on technical stuff I barely follow. Scratch that. It's all Greek to me.

Forest seems to have no problem keeping up, but he's a goddam genius. Sam, CJ, and Max mostly follow, but I see confusion knitting their brows here and there during Mitzy's long spiel. I wade through her briefing and follow as best I can.

"It's not much, but we have a lead." Mitzy's eyes brighten, and I swear she gives a little bounce. "I found their main server before the data wipe destroyed everything on the phone."

"How does that help?" I'm the first to jump in with a question.

"It helps us…" Forest kicks off from the wall and moves to the front of the room. "It helps because we can insert a buyer."

"A buyer?"

"Two actually. One to draw their fire and the other to infiltrate their ranks."

"How the hell do you do that?"

"I know a guy."

A guy? Of course, Forest knows a guy. Some random person whom he can insert into a billion-dollar industry that trades in human lives.

"You said two."

Max drums his fingers on the table. "He wants to send a Guardian."

"One of us?" Can't help it, my jaw drops. "Who?"

Max lifts his hand, and with a flourish, spins his finger until it points back at him.

"You?"

"Evidently." Max doesn't sound happy about his role.

"As the mole or the target?"

Max cants his head and gives CJ a long, hard look. "As the fucking target."

"How's that going to work?" I can't help it. This sounds like a shit plan. "Don't you think they'll see you coming a mile away?"

"We have to assume they do," Sam speaks for the first time. "We're drafting a backstory for Max right now."

"A back story? Like how does a Guardian jump fence to buy his own sex slave? That's a pretty big leap. How the hell are you going to pull it off?"

"That's why we're here today," Max says with a grumble. "Trying to figure out how, or why, I'd give all this up."

"It's a shit plan."

"Why's that?" Sam leans in and fixes me with a heavy stare.

"Because Max has good guy written all over him. No way will they believe he isn't a plant."

"That would be the me-being-the-target bit of it." Max swivels in his chair. He interlaces his fingers and places them behind his head. Leaning way back, Max stares at the ceiling. From the expression on his face, he's thinking through the problem.

"Look, I get the concept, but it has to have some shred of believability. And with that crowd..." I shift my attention to Max. "Are you prepared to do what might be asked of you to prove yourself?"

His lips press together and he averts his gaze. I totally get it. Chances are pretty damn high he'll be forced to cross a line none of us would ever cross.

"Does this seem like the best time to be setting up an undercover infiltration?" I ask.

"Why?" CJ turns his attention to me.

"Bravo team is down two men. Alpha team is down one with me out. Charlie and Delta are good. If you take Max out of the picture, Alpha is down two. That's half your teams not at full strength." I glance around the table, but they're all aware of the facts. I'm not presenting anything new.

"We're aware of the issues." Sam leans forward and rests his elbows on the table. "Griff's got a point. To do this right, we need a lead of at least eight weeks; longer would be better. What are the projections on Bravo team? Do we have an idea when they'll be functional?"

"Several months," CJ replies.

"Doesn't it make more sense to pull one of them?" Max is one tough son-of-a-bitch, but I know him. He won't be able to cross that line. We need someone else.

"That's what we're trying to sort out now." CJ taps the face of his watch, no doubt sending a text.

"There's always the other option," Mitzy chimes in.

The temperature in the room drops with her comment. I glance around, not knowing what that option might be, but acutely aware of the reactions around me.

Sam doesn't like it. His spine went ramrod straight, and his lips pull apart, baring his teeth as he grimaces.

CJ's less dramatic. He draws a circle on the table, too intent on pushing his finger over the polished surface.

Max's entire body shifts as he suddenly leans forward. "We nixed that when you brought it up." The ominous tone in his voice makes the fine hairs on my arm lift.

"Mitzy has a point." Forest kicks off from the wall and draws back the chair at the head of the table. "We should consider it."

"What?" I glance around the table and take note of how nobody will meet my eye. "Anybody care to share?"

"Doesn't matter." Max pushes away from the table. "We're not considering it."

"What are we *not* considering?" Silence greets me as my attention shifts from Max, to CJ, and then to Sam. When none of them will meet my eye, I direct my gaze at Mitzy. "Tell me."

Mitzy's gaze flicks to Forest. I catch her request for permission to clue me in. Forest gives a sharp nod.

"We use Moira." Mitzy doesn't even blink. When she speaks, she delivers the news in a deadpan voice.

"What the fuck?" I tug at my ear, certain I got that wrong.

"We have the name of the buyer who ordered Moira. We can set up a sting. Dirty Guardian making an exchange. It's perfect."

"No way." CJ slams his hand down on the table. "We discussed this. Moira is not an operative. That idea is tabled."

"Wait?" My gaze jumps around the room. "You discussed it? When did you 'discuss' it?"

"We discussed it. Moira's demonstrated she can take care of herself." Mitzy emphatically crosses her arms over her chest. Somehow, that diminutive woman manages to stare down her nose at CJ. Mitzy is fucking fierce. My balls draw up a bit, and she's not even talking to me. "Tell him, Forest. Tell them how it can work."

Despite the little hiccup with my balls, they're talking about my girl, and the things they're saying are flat out wrong.

"I don't know what the fuck you all were talking about before I got here, but there's no way in hell Moira will be used as bait." I kick back my chair. "No. Fucking. Way." The chair careens behind me and slams into the wall. Mitzy doesn't even flinch with my shout.

Sam, CJ, and Max agree with me. No need for words. It's obvious in the set of their shoulders and the expressions on their faces. Good to know they think it's crazy too.

Use Moira?

Mitzy's fucked in the head.

"What gave you the hair-brained idea to put Moira at risk?" My words slice through the air, cutting and sharp. "You've thought of some crazy-assed things in the past, but this takes the cake."

"Don't bite my head off." Mitzy uncrosses her arms and stands as if there aren't five angry men staring her down. "It wasn't my idea."

Forest shifts behind me, and my heart skips a beat. I turn on Forest and realize there are only four angry men in the room. The look on Forest's face is determined, fierce, and guilty.

"This is your idea?"

"Still is." He regards me dryly. "We have access to their server. Client lists. Orders. Delivery dates. Upcoming auctions. We can't sit on this. Whatever we do, it needs to be soon. The only way to tear this operation down is from the inside. And I agree with what everyone's said so far. Inserting a mole will take time. Turning one of our Guardians dirty is a plausible lie. It's just outlandish enough for them to believe."

"And what would turn a Guardian dirty?"

"Gambling debts." The muscles of Max's jaw tick. "I'm supposed to rack up certain debts that force me to break my oaths."

It almost makes sense. Max has a thing about gambling. It's why the team doesn't gamble. When we lose a bet, we exchange buttons. It's stupid, but it's what we do. The point is, there's substantial history pointing at Max's history with gambling addiction.

"Doesn't hold water. That kind of shit doesn't just happen. Your cover will never be established. It's too thin."

"Which is why I recommend using Moira." Forest continues as if his stupid plan has any merit.

"Not happening." I put my foot down. "First off, we just rescued her. Second, it was the second time she's been rescued by the Guardians. My girl deserves to live a normal life, away from any of this bullshit. Third…"

"First off…" Forest cuts me off with his glittering gaze. "Moira is more than capable of pulling this off. Secondly, she understands that world. Nobody else here has a better understanding of how they operate."

"Moira doesn't have that knowledge. She was a sex slave, passed around to the highest bidder at Snowden's parties."

The muscles of Forest's jaw tick at the mention of Snowden. That man no longer walks the world of the living, but not before nearly destroying Forest, and the ones he loves, in the process.

"You'd be surprised how much those men talk when their guard is down. She's aware of more than she knows, and now we know just what she's capable of when pushed."

"No fucking way are you putting her in danger. She's not ready."

I'm not sure why I phrase it like that. It's not that she's not ready. Moira will never be ready for something like that. It's insane and *so far* out there, I can't believe we're talking about it. My fingers curl, and the pulse in my neck jumps. A roaring rushes past my ears as my blood heats. Forest will likely kick my ass, but I'm willing to throw down with him.

For Moira, I'll do anything.

"While I realize you're all manly men, has it occurred to any of you Neanderthals that we could simply ask?" Mitzy cuts through the tension with her lilting voice, but it does nothing to change my thoughts.

"Moira's not doing it." I stand by my word.

"Says the Neanderthal." Mitzy blows out a breath and flips her hair out of her eyes. She's growing out the pixie cut and I notice for the first time she has bangs. They fall right back in her face. "Did you see what she did to…"

"No."

"No?" Max's brow arches. "I thought you reviewed the body cam footage."

"I read the reports. That was enough." I didn't want to watch the tapes because there's a part of me hoping Moira will one day confide in me. I want my reactions to be genuine, realistic, and not forewarned by the video.

"Griff, you really need to look at the tapes."

I cross my arms, digging in my heels. "Doesn't matter. Moira isn't a Guardian. She's not equipped for a mission like that. Find another way." With that, I've had enough.

The rest of my team is getting in a few rounds at the range. Right about now, I feel like shooting shit, or blowing shit up. There are still a few hours before I'm due to pick Moira up, and I need to clear my head before then.

Send Moira out?

What the fuck is Forest thinking?

TWENTY-SIX

Moira

LIKE THORNS DIGGING THEIR WAY OUT FROM INSIDE OF ME, TELLING Zoe about those few days on the ship pierce, stab, and rip with an unrelenting fury.

I wish I could say my experience made me harder and more resilient, but the memories make me shake uncontrollably and send a flood of tears pouring from my eyes. The salty essence coats my lips and flows into my mouth, no matter how hard I press my lips together, trying to keep it out.

I didn't think talking about it would bring back the shakes, or that fluttering feeling in my gut that feels like a free fall into hell. A calming breath draws in the early evening air, flooding my nasal passages with the smell of salt, sea, and brine. Those flavors combine with my tears, coating my tongue, to make me gag. It's too reminiscent of sitting in that hole between the cargo containers where all I could smell was metal mixed with the briny sea.

I rock, arms clasped around my shins, chin propped on my knees, and sob. A river of tears flow out of me as my entire body shakes. When I close my eyes, the grisly visage of Bossman's dead eyes stares back at me, damning me for my sins and judging me for the life I took. Doesn't matter that it was me or him, taking a life changed me. I'm weaker now, more fragile. The tenuous hold I keep on my emotions is a weakened, frayed thing.

"Oh, Moira…" Zoe sits beside me, lending me her strength.

Her fingers push back my long, blond curls, sweeping them off my cheeks, but they cling to the mess of tears streaming down my face. My only friend, I bare my soul to her because she understands the fear and hopelessness I experienced. She faced her own death, not once but twice. We share that horror as well.

"I'm a murderer." I curl in my lower lip, biting hard to keep my teeth from chattering. "I don't know why I'm so cold, but I feel dead inside."

"You know that's not true. You're not a murderer. You acted in self-defense and feeling dead inside is normal. You'll feel better with time."

"How can you be so sure?"

"Because I felt a little of it too. Trust me, things will get better."

"But I thought things were better. I spend a year here, learning how to be normal, learning how to defend myself, and all of it was for nothing. I'm still that same helpless girl. How am I ever going to feel safe again?"

"You will."

"I killed a man." My words come out a whisper and aren't really meant for Zoe's ears. A part of me needs to say it because I need to own what I did.

I took a life.

"In self-defense," Zoe repeats what she's already said dozens of times. "He deserved it."

Does anyone deserve death? I'm not so sure. He deserved to suffer. I agree on that, but death? Somehow, I feel cheated. Like, Bossman should have suffered more. I freed him when I took his life. I should've made him suffer.

"You don't understand. I plotted his murder for days, moving that damn knife around to find the perfect hiding place."

I'd been very methodical. Obsessive comes to mind. I killed him hundreds of times in my head before that knife ever sliced through his flesh. He should've suffered—more.

"He kidnapped you and was going to give you to a monster. You did nothing wrong."

"Then why does it feel like I did?"

"Have you talked to Griff about this?"

"No."

"And why not?"

"Because I don't want to."

"Why?" She runs her fingers through my hair, comforting me.

My eyes close as the tips of her fingers dig into my scalp and pull through the long strands. My hair is my pride and joy. It's also the root of all my problems. I know what I look like. I know what men see.

My hair only enhances my natural beauty, turning me from pretty to bombshell beautiful. I've been compared to Aphrodite, Madonna, and Marilyn Monroe—all iconic beauties.

Men covet my beauty. They yearn to own it, control it, and show off their pretty little slave to other men.

"I wish I killed the man who bought me." My fingers grip tight around my wrists as I tug my knees to my chest. The skin over my knuckles turns white.

"I know."

I squeeze my lids together, fighting off a fresh flood of tears. I lean toward Zoe, tipping my head until it touches her shoulder. She wraps her arm around me and we sit quietly, looking out over the vastness of the Pacific Ocean.

It's a calm day. The ocean's at peace. It reflects back the tranquil blue of the sky. The only distortion on its surface is the relentless march of swells as they approach the shore. I wish I was out there, lost in the vastness of it all.

"Do you ever wish you were someone else?" I wipe my nose on the fabric of my sleeve and sniff back the tears.

"Sometimes." Zoe takes in a deep breath and blows it out. "But if I were someone else, I never would've met Axel."

"He never would've hurt you." Their road to happiness was twisted and complicated.

"True, but in the end, it was worth it. Our path wasn't easy, and I definitely had to fight for it, but in the end, I wouldn't trade it for anything."

"I'm happy for you." I saw the beginnings of their romance at the Facility when Axel decided to take what he denied himself for too long. After Zoe's rescue, he decided to tie her to him forever, placing an engagement ring on her finger. She told me everything that happened the night we were abducted.

"And I'm happy for you." She gives another playful nudge and peeks at me through her lashes.

"Why?" I shift a little to find a more comfortable position. I kick my heels out and grasp the back of my thighs, still hugging my legs tight to my body, but this way, I can lean forward a little more.

"Griff," Zoe says Griff's name with surprise. "You never would've found Griff."

"Is that what I've done?"

"What do you mean?"

"I don't know if what Griff and I have is anything more than sex."

"I'm not sure what to say about that, except I have a feeling you mean a lot more to Griff than sex."

"How would you know?"

"Because of something Axel said."

"What was that?"

"That Griff disobeyed a direct order to get you."

"I don't know about that."

"It's the truth. Axel said the helicopter pilot covered, but he knows Griff. Those two are closer than brothers. From what Axel didn't say, I think Griff put his job on the line when he did that. Why would he risk his job as a Guardian if it wasn't because of something more than sex? The two of you weren't even a thing when he did that. Don't you think that means something?"

"Griff is protective to a fault. His job is more than a job. It's his creed. Rescuing others is his life's work. If you look at it like that, I was just another job."

"If you think he saved you because of some deep-seated moral imperative, you might be right, but there's more going on there than you give him credit for. He would never jeopardize the mission, go against a direct order, or place his teammates in danger, unless there was a damn good reason to do so. He risked all of that—for you."

"You're reading a whole lot into something that probably doesn't exist."

"Or maybe you're too scared to see what's right in front of you?"

"And that is?"

"Griff's in love with you, silly, and not because you're sleeping with him. Have you ever wondered why Four was always the Guardian who trained you?"

"He's not the only one. They switched things up."

"True, for everyone else they do, but somehow Griff was always your primary."

I swipe at my cheek and sniff. "Maybe I'm too broken to love? How can any man want someone like me? I'm damaged."

"I hear you, and I don't have any good answers for you. Our histories are different, and I'll never pretend that I know what you've been through, but if Griff has no reservations about putting himself out there, about risking his career, don't you think that's something you should pay attention to?"

"I'm afraid."

"We're all afraid, but if you let him in, trust him to guard your heart and to love the fierce woman you are, maybe you won't have to work through all the trauma alone. You really need to talk to him. Tell him what you told me. I'm sure he has insight that I don't have. You owe it to him." With a sigh, Zoe pushes me off her shoulder. She scoots behind me and moves to her knees. Before I can ask what she's doing, she gathers my hair and divides it into three sections. "Do you know I've never had a sleepover?"

"You haven't?" The sudden switch in conversation throws me, but I have a sense things were getting too deep.

"My dad was strict to a fault. I never had a girlfriend whose hair I could braid." She draws my hair tight and begins to weave the plaits together. "It's one of those rights of passage I feel like I missed out on."

"I missed out on everything." I blow out my breath. "If I could go back in time, I'd wish for a dad who didn't leave and a mother who didn't love her drugs more than her kid. I'd wish for sleepovers and slumber parties, dances, and dates. I'd wish for a friend like you."

"Well, you have me now. We'll just have to work on the rest. And one of the things girls talk about are boys, and you have yet to tell me all the filthy, dirty, nasty things Griff does to you."

Zoe's words bring a smile to my face. My tears stop, and a burst of laughter escapes my lips as I remember all the ways Griff introduced me to his home.

"You're a really good friend."

"You are too." She finishes the braid, but with nothing to tie it off with, she lets the ends unravel as she scoots around to sit in front of me. "Now you braid my hair, and tell me about the first time you and Griff made love."

I gather her long hair and divide it neatly into four parts. I may never have been to a sleepover, or braided my friend's hair, but I'm an expert in all things which enhance a woman's beauty, and I can plait a multitude of complex braids.

"I wouldn't call what we did as making love."

"Then what would you call it?"

"He claimed me."

A shiver races down my spine with the overwhelming memory of being taken by Griff. His unrestrained passion and unyielding dominance made sex something I enjoyed for the first time ever. He made me crave all the things he could do to my body.

"Oh, now that sounds juicy. I want all the details. Don't leave anything out."

I don't.

We spend the rest of the day in that cave talking about Griff. Zoe tells me about her first time with Axel and even points out the exact spot in the cave where he took her for the first time.

We talk through lunch and past the time I was supposed to meet with the counselor. Not that I care. Talking to Zoe does far more for me than sitting with a shrink.

I show her how to do the more intricate braids, and she practices on my hair while I talk about the ship, how scared I was, how I got Bossman to kill Shelly, and relived every gory detail of Bossman's death. Then the fear as I snuck around the ship, desperate to find a way off the cargo container and the sickening moment when I knew that would never happen.

"Then there was this light…" I mention the helicopter.

"You know, we share one more thing in common."

"What's that?"

"We've both been strapped to our man and lifted to safety dangling by a rope in the dead of night. How many girls do you know who can say that?"

We fall into a fit of laughter and spend the next hour talking about our men, sex, and the myriad of sexual positions they seem to love. Before we know it, the sun dips down toward the horizon, casting a warm glow into the cave.

Talking to Zoe helps, but there's a lingering sorrow which stains my soul, layers and layers of trauma, abuse, and the depravity of men that are now a part of me.

I may want to be normal, but I'll never be free of my past. It's a sobering truth and an uncomfortable realization. I always thought things would change for me. In my mind, I saw an end. At first, it was in the embrace of death, but I'm too good at surviving.

Some point along the way, I thought that if I just kept going long enough, all the bad things in my life would fall away, piece by piece like an onion with all its layers. Maybe that's a poor analogy, but maybe the reason I am such a good survivor is because some small piece of me clung to hope?

"Want to know something?" I push a small pebble across the cave floor with the tip of my shoe.

"What?" Zoe sits beside me again, staring out across the water as the sun sets the sky ablaze with ribbons of orange and bands of red streaking overhead.

"I want to kill the man who bought me."

How upset was he when Bossman failed to deliver me?

I bet the asshole was livid, and I'm thrilled to be the one to deny his depraved desires.

He's the man I want to rot in hell. Not Bossman, although Bossman deserves a special place there, along with Shelly. If there's a circle in hell where a man gets fucked by his own dick, then has it shoved down his throat, that's where Shelly belongs.

But the man who ripped away my illusion of being safe, he's the one I want to confront. I want him to suffer horribly for doing that, and then I want him to die.

I don't know why him, and none of the hundreds of others who took advantage of me, but he stole something precious the others never could take from me.

With the others, I knew what I was doing. I made a conscious choice, damn the consequences. I bartered my body, willingly allowing them to use it so that I might survive another night. At sixteen, I made a horrible mistake, but it wasn't like I didn't make that choice too.

If I'd stayed on the streets, I would've been dead within a year, probably far less than that. As a sex slave, I had inherent value to the men who owned me. They used me, but they kept me off the streets. They got me clean from drugs, and I never again went hungry. I always had a place to sleep.

This time, I didn't choose. That's what angers me the most, because it's the first real time something precious was taken from me.

My free will had been brutally stolen, and I think that's what I'm struggling to process. I felt safe for the first time, and I finally mustered the confidence to head back out in the world, venturing past the gates of the Facility to enjoy one weekend like any normal girl. My entire future lay in front of me. I could do anything and choose to be anyone I wanted. I felt free for the first time in my life.

That man who paid for my abduction stole my confidence. He took my security and blew it apart.

I don't want to live in fear. I don't want to constantly look over my shoulder to see who the next asshole will be who thinks he can take what doesn't belong to him. I want to walk the world with my head held high and do it with the knowledge that no man will ever hurt me again.

I'm a murderer now. I can kill that man, too. What's one more life on my hands?

Zoe nudges me in the shoulder. "The sun's setting."

"Yeah, it's gorgeous. I see why you like this place so much. It's amazing."

"I was talking more about the time." She taps her watch. "When was Griff coming back?"

"Oh shit!" I scramble to my feet and dust off the tiny bits of dirt and rock that cling to my clothes. "I'm late."

"Sorry." Zoe grimaces. "I lost track of time."

"Don't be." I take her hands in mine. "You're a gazillion times better than a stuffy old shrink."

She laughs. "I hope so." Standing beside me, she dusts off her pants, but then she stills. Zoe holds up a finger, silencing me.

When she cocks an ear, I do the same. The sound of rocks crunching underfoot is not only unmistakable, it's getting closer by the second.

Something snaps inside of me. My heart slams against my ribs, banging away as my breaths quicken.

I look around the roomy cave for a weapon, suddenly terrified. There is literally no place to run.

Zoe puts her hand back, pressing it against my stomach. She pushes me back as she takes a step away from the cave entrance.

"Who is it?" I know I should be quiet, but I can't help it.

"I don't know."

I listen again. This time, I pick up the tread of two pairs of feet. From their heavy step, I conclude they are men. My scalp crawls with dread and that sensation slithers down my spine. A rustling sound from outside the cave makes me jump. I whirl at another sound coming from outside. I know what's out there. Men who intend great harm.

Icy fear shoots through me, locking my joints and making my lungs seize on my last breath. I try to cry out, but my voice is gone, fled somewhere I can't find it.

I need to move. Every instinct screams at me to flee, but there's nowhere to go.

Backed into a corner, there is no escape. My legs feel like rubber and don't seem to want to work the right way. My eyes are wide, unblinking, but blind to everything around me.

Keep breathing.

A voice inside my head tells me to stay present and keep functioning, even though that does no good. No matter how much I fight, or how much I beg, men always come for me, and then they take.

"Who knows about this place?" Terror flows through me as I break apart, reverting to my most base instincts.

Survival.

But is that what I want? A human can only endure so much before they snap, and I'm breaking into a million pieces. I won't survive being taken again.

"Forest and Axel. I don't think Forest told anyone about it but me."

I grip the back of her shoulder and pull her to me, not sure if I do it to protect her, shelter myself, or to give me some semblance of control over the boiling fear raging inside of me. She's my anchor and I desperately need something to hang onto.

My insides twist and churn with the adrenaline spiking in my blood. Wild, rabid, and far beyond terror, my heart bangs against the walls of my chest as I wrestle with the fear triggering inside of me.

If I don't get a grip, I'll lose all grasp with reality.

My fight is a valiant one but ultimately doomed. Darkness creeps into my vision. Tingles of sensation prick my lips. And my breaths come in shuddering gasps; fast, rhythmic, panting sounds that don't draw in enough oxygen to feed my fear-filled mind. Panic rips through me and I stumble my way back until the cool surface of the cave wall presses against my back.

Zoe turns. I barely recognize her. Her fingers snap in front of me and her mouth moves, but all I hear is the howling of my blood. A vice constricts around my ribcage, making it impossible to breathe, squeezing, tightening, as violent spasms rip through me.

My mouth opens on a scream, but nothing comes out except a hoarse moan. My eyes glaze over. My heart pounds. My legs turn to rubber beneath me, and my body crumples under the inescapable pull of gravity. I wait for the hard impact with the stone floor but find myself lifted instead.

"Moira?" A deep voice tugs at the edge of awareness. "Come back to me. Let me in." While confident, there's an aggressive edge to his voice. Layered on top of that is a sprinkle of concern and fear.

"Griff, put her on the ground. Zoe, lay out those blankets." Another deep voice, this one reminding me of rocks breaking beneath a glacier, pierces through the fog of my awareness, but not deep enough to pull me from the grasp of my overwhelming fear.

"What's wrong with her?" Light and lilting, I know that voice. "Is that a trigger?"

"That is a psychologic break brought on by a trigger. Do you know what happened before she lost it?"

"The two of you were walking on the ledge outside the cave. I was worried, but then I knew it could only be one of two people. Moira freaked out, but after you announced yourselves, I didn't think anything of it until she dragged me to the back of the cave."

"We need to know why she triggered." One of the male voices states. They're both deep, but that one is more familiar. Intimate even.

My brain processes these pieces of information slowly. Sweaty and breathless, my entire body twitches. Adrenaline floods my system, firing off all my senses and putting them on high alert.

I grab at the nearest thing and stop.

A masculine essence floods my senses. I take another breath, drawing that potent aroma deep into my lungs. I hate men, but something inside me craves that smell and the amazing man to whom it belongs.

The fog surrounding my thoughts lifts, and I pull in a calming breath. I take another breath, drawing more of that scent inside of me. Damaged and traumatized, I'm normally closed off to the foul scents of my abusers, but this is different. He smells different. Dominant masculinity, aggressive protection, and overwhelming concern; it's a potent concoction, and I'm hooked.

My glazed eyes focus on the face of a Guardian.

My Guardian.

My hands rest on his biceps, and beneath my fingers, thick, corded muscles stretch the skin taut. My fingers trace the dips and valleys of those muscles; every inch honed to perfection by a job that demands excellence in all things.

Griff is a study in masculine beauty.

Before my lungs give out completely, I fight the shadows creeping in and focus on his face. Aside from the churning in my gut and the pounding of my heart, his face entrances me.

That sense of dread falls back beneath those violet eyes. With the fading sunlight, his face is cast in shadow, but I sense his concern and the bristling tension girding his frame. His eyes focus on mine with the same burning intensity as the setting sun.

"Moira." His voice demands an answer, but I'm too far gone. With fear clouding my thoughts, I struggle to piece together what I'm seeing.

As for how I feel, the very atmosphere vibrates with a buzzing electricity, cracking with white-hot energy. That current sweeps across my skin, sinks into my heart, and stands the fine hairs on my arms on end.

He brushes the backs of his knuckles against my cheek as his chiseled lips bow into a gentle smile. Our gazes lock, and licks of heat race up and down my body.

I feel him everywhere, curling warmth sinking into me. In the depths of his gaze, concern, worry, and the deepest love, shift and simmer. It's enough to know I'm safe in his arms, that he cares about me with the entirety of his soul.

My arms wrap around his neck, and I pull myself up until I can lean my head against his chest.

"Griff?"

"Glad to have you back, little minx. You had me worried."

A sigh escapes me as the heat of his body envelopes me. I'm strung out like I'm at the wrong end of a bad trip. It's a level of exhaustion that hurts. Every muscle in my body wants to surrender, and a great desire for sleep overcomes me.

"I'm tired."

"I know." He cradles me in his arms and looks up. "We need to get her out of here."

"Agreed."

My head lolls to the side as my strength flees. I snap it back, desperate to hold onto consciousness, but it's too much.

"I'm sorry."

"Sorry for what?"

"For failing at life."

"Sweet Moira, you are the strongest woman I know." Griff gets a leg under him. My body rises as he stands. Wind whispers over my skin as a ruddy light shines down on me. The sun's almost set. I feel as if this is the end.

In his arms, there are no worries. No fear. And no dreams.

Griff carries me out of the cave, and I barely register the harrowing walk along the narrow ledge before the last of my strength flees.

The light from the sun disappears as my eyes close. Consciousness fades and darkness pulls me into a dreamless sleep.

Well, not entirely dreamless. A man without a face stares down at me, arm lifted as if to strike a killing blow. I glare at him with defiance and issue a challenge of my own.

That's the man I must kill.

And I will.

I will kill again.

TWENTY-SEVEN

Griff

_____

FOREST FOLLOWS BEHIND ME ON THE NARROW LEDGE. I STRUGGLE TO climb the two feet up and growl when Forest tries to take Moira from my arms. He gives me a look, then jumps up and reaches down, hooking his massive hands under my shoulders to hoist me up as I take the step. I say nothing, but the message is received.

Moira is mine.

He puts the phone to his ear and walks beside me as we head back to the main buildings.

"Yes. Catatonic." His fingers flex as I step up the pace.

All I can think about is getting Moira to safety. Not that the cave wasn't safe. It's the prison of her mind which worries me.

"Meet us at the Facility. We're headed to her room now."

"Not going to her room." I bite out the words. It's a bit of a hike back to the Facility. Carrying Moira in my arms is the most physically taxing way to carry another person, but there's no way I'm slinging her over my shoulder, and I'm sure as shit not letting Forest hold her.

"Griff…" Forest tries to take charge of the situation, but I give a sharp shake of my head. He's not in command here, not when it comes to my woman.

I march right through the Facility and across the parking lot. Forest and Zoe follow, both hovering protectively around my girl. When I gently place Moira in the backseat, Zoe jumps in and cradles Moira's head in her lap. The glare I receive tells me she's not going anywhere. I'm good with that. I'm going to need help once I get Moira home.

What I don't expect is Forest. He climbs into the passenger seat and buckles in. "Skye will meet us at your house. The rest of your team is inbound."

My voice catches, and I'm forced to clear the lump in my throat. "They don't have to…"

"And yet, they will be there." Forest glances over his shoulder. "How is she?"

"Breathing's shallow." Zoe looks at me through the rearview mirror. "Is that okay?"

"As long as she's breathing." It's not okay. Moira is lost inside her mind and it's up to me to bring her back. "Tell me everything that happened today."

While Forest talks to his sister over the phone, I demand Zoe tell me everything she and Moira talked about.

"I can't betray her confidence."

"You can and you will." My fists grip the steering wheel as I race down PCH-1. Maybe I should've taken Moira to Guardian HQ? Doc Summers has a full surgical suite on site. But Moira doesn't need surgery. She's locked in her head, reliving a life's worth of tragedy. I know what my girl needs, and she needs me.

I need information.

"I don't care if you pinky swore or took a goddamn blood oath. Tell me everything that happened."

Over the next thirty minutes, Zoe spills, and I try to make sense of what happened.

Every cell in my body demands I protect Moira. If that means pulling her out of this fugue, I'll do whatever it takes. When we pull up outside my house, my team is already there. They sit outside the gates in four different vehicles and file in behind me when the iron bars swing open.

It's the first time any of them have seen my house. I'm not comfortable exposing this part of myself. The money my parents left, the house and all that comes with it messes with my head. Like I don't deserve nice things.

No one says a word as I carry Moira inside. Max, Knox, Liam, and Wolfe follow in behind Zoe and Forest. They say nothing as I take Moira to my room and lay her on the bed. Only Zoe follows me inside.

"Where's Axel?" Acutely aware my buddy isn't here, I reach out to the closest thing. Right now, that's Zoe.

"He's picking up Skye." Forest's voice rumbles behind me. "They'll be here in a few minutes."

I run my fingers through my hair to hide the shaking in my limbs.

"Griff," Zoe places her hand on my arm, "she wants to tell you what happened, but she's not ready. It doesn't mean anything more than that."

Nothing more than that?

This is the woman I welcomed into my home, into my life, and my bed, yet she still holds out on me. Is it a lack of faith? Trust? What do I need to do to get Moira to open up and confide in me?

I need to stay by her side, but before I can be of any use to Moira, I need to get a grip of my own emotions. I head into the living room and meet the concerned stares of my team. The front door opens and Doc Summers breezes into my house as if she owns the place.

"Where is she?"

I point to the bedroom and watch the doc disappear into my room.

Axel enters next, closing the door behind him. He walks right up to me, clasps my hand, and pulls me into a bro-hug. Axel taps my back. This is when we would normally break, but he holds me for an extra beat.

"Tell me what happened." Axel releases me and takes in our team. "How can we help?" This is who we are, Guardians to the core, but when it comes down to it, we're brothers, a family formed by choice with bonds forged in the fiercest fires of hell.

"Can I get anyone something to drink?" I clear my throat and look around.

Axel rolls his eyes and shoves me toward the bedroom. "Go to your girl. I'm sure we can figure out what to do next."

The guys stand as one and surround me. Fists out, they shove their hands into the center of our circle. I place my fist on top of the pile. One by one, they show their support, removing their fist from the bottom and tapping mine on top. When Wolfe finishes, we huddle in, head to head, shoulder to shoulder.

Forest watches the display from the kitchen, giving us what privacy he can.

Max speaks for the team. "Sworn to serve."

Knox continues. "Driven to protect."

Axel grins at me. "We are Guardians."

I clear my throat. "We stand together."

Liam shifts his feet. "Brothers united."

Wolfe grips my wrist. "We are one."

"Thanks, guys. It means the world to me to have you here."

"Go to your girl. We'll be here." Max claps me on the shoulder and shoves me toward my room.

The guys part, half of them returning to the overstuffed sofas, the others toward the kitchen. The banging of cupboard doors sounds behind me as I leave them to it.

When I walk into my room, Doc Summers looks up at me. A stethoscope is propped in her ears and the drum is pressed to Moira's chest. The doc puts a finger to her lips, telling me to be silent, then closes her eyes.

Zoe paces back and forth, wringing her hands as she goes. I lean against the doorjamb and wait for the doc to finish her assessment.

Doc Summers pulls the earpieces out of her ears and folds the tubing of her stethoscope before tucking it into the pocket of her jacket. She again puts a finger to her lips. Rising with incredible grace, she closes the distance between us.

"Her vitals are weaker than I'd like. I don't know what happened, but she's exhibiting signs of shock."

"From what?"

Doc Summers' gaze shifts to Zoe. "I'm hoping we can piece that together."

"So, what do I do?" My attention shifts to Moira.

"We tuck her in and let her body do what it's designed to do."

"And what's that?"

"Rest and heal." Her attention once again shifts between Zoe and me. "I suppose I can leave it to the two of you to get her settled in bed?" Her brow arches.

I don't need Zoe's help, but I sense there's more going on here than I realize.

"Of course." I manage to get the words out, despite my concern.

I don't know what catatonia looks like, but I'm scared. That's not an emotion I'm equipped to deal with. I fight my enemies head-on or hand-to-hand. How do I fight the demons locked in Moira's mind?

I've never felt so helpless.

TWENTY-EIGHT

Moira

I STIR BENEATH THE SOFT COMFORT OF DOWN AND FLEECE, stretching my arms overhead. My toes point and I yawn with a full-body stretch. A fog clouds my memories, and I feel tired, beyond tired. Exhaustion pulls at me, straining my limbs and sapping my strength.

Why do I feel as if I fought an epic battle and lost?

My hand goes to my chest. It hurts to breathe. No, that's not right. It's just a struggle like each pull happens only with conscious effort. Confusion crowds the edges of my thoughts and I struggle to piece together the last few hours.

How did I get from the cave to Griff's bed? I stretch my hand out, naturally feeling for him, or at least for the lingering warmth his body leaves behind.

The sheets beside me are cold and tucked tight. There's no evidence he was in bed at all.

That's odd.

I feel groggy, like waking from a long slumber, only I want to curl into a ball and drag the covers over my head. Sleep sounds perfect, but something tells me to get up.

Once again, I stretch. My toes curl. My fingers reach far overhead. Damn, that feels good. Grit coats my eyes and I rub away the sleep. Scanning my surroundings, I confirm this is definitely Griff's bed. His presence floods the room with virile masculinity, everywhere but in the bed itself.

So, where is he? And what time is it?

My gaze sweeps the room, then lands on the clock next to the bed. It's well past midnight. I brush the hair from my face and draw back the covers. Placing my bare feet on the floor, I wriggle my toes in the thick carpet.

When I get up, the sound of male voices reaches my ears—several male voices, and they're arguing. I cock my head, but I can't make out the words.

Looking down, I realize I'm nearly naked. With others in the house, I need something more than my bra and panties if I'm going to see what the commotion is about.

The voices grow louder, then drop for a beat, but they're soon back at it, arguing with indistinct words. Curious by nature, I throw on one of Griff's shirts and head for the bedroom door. I pause at the door, eavesdropping, not sure if I should stay in here or head out there.

I peek through a crack in the door and feel my breath hitch. Griff stands with his back to me facing a room of intimidating men. He takes my breath away as my gaze meanders up and around the physical perfection of his body. Thick, corded muscles strain the fabric of his shirt, every inch of him honed through intensive physical conditioning.

Warmth fills my chest as I marvel at the man who opened his home to me and welcomed me into his life. Unlike me, he has no reservation about putting himself out there, of opening himself to the possibility of something more than raw, physical attraction. He's generous and overprotective, perhaps too much, but there's a vulnerability about him as well.

His hand settles on the back of a chair. His fingers flex as his entire body tenses.

"I said no." His entire body vibrates with anger. "We're not discussing this further."

"Griff." A man I don't know pinches the bridge of his nose. "You know it makes sense."

"Did any of you see her when I carried her inside? She had a breakdown…"

A what?

"Moira is stronger than you think." With the sound of rolling thunder, I know that voice. Why is Forest here?

I nudge the door open with my toe, praying the hinges don't squeak. It doesn't take a rocket scientist to figure out who those men are. It's Griff's team, and they're arguing about me.

Why?

I smack the side of my head; maybe if I can dislodge the cobwebs clouding my thoughts, things would make more sense. I remember the cave and spending the day with Zoe. We talked about Griff and Axel. My cheeks heat at how graphic our conversation turned. Why do I remember that with crystal clarity but not how I got here?

"There's no fucking way you're using Moira as bait. No. Fucking. Way. End of conversation. She's not a Guardian. She's not trained…"

"Griff." Axel moves into view and looks right at me. He gives a jerk of his chin and Griff spins around.

"Moira—you're up." He rushes over, yanks the door open, and swallows me in one of his bear hugs.

I pull in a calming breath. His masculine scent floods my senses, causing an overwhelming sense of calm to sweep over me.

This feels right.

Griff's hand settles on the back of my head and he holds me tight against him. I surrender into his embrace, absorbing how wonderful it feels to have someone who truly cares about me. I've never had that before. He makes me feel alive, refreshed, almost electrified. The blood rushing through my veins races around blissfully free and content to run in perpetual circles like it's the best damn moment of my life. He feels like coming home, and I've never had a home before.

For some weird reason, my entire body begins to shake. It's like a release of tension flowing out of my body and into him, where he takes it all in, shouldering my burdens for me. It's a heady sensation, and I grip him tight, holding on as emotion sweeps through me.

The fog lifts, and I remember what happened.

I remember all of it.

The memories slam into me, buffeting me from all sides. My body shakes, and Griff stills.

"Moira?"

I look up at him, tears streaming down my face. "I killed him. I killed Bossman." My words disintegrate into a blubbering mess as I bury my face against Griff's chest.

"I know." He runs his hand through my hair, slowly drawing his fingers through the tangles. "I know." His grip tightens, and we slowly rock in place.

"Do you hate me?" I chase the memories as they flash in my mind's eye. Bossman's dead stare. Shelly's heavy weight as we rolled him in the blanket. Blood everywhere. In my hair. Saturating my clothes. Slipping under my feet. Squishing between my toes.

"No. God no." Griff holds me out and away from him, but only to stoop until he's eye level with me. "I'm in love with you."

"But, I'm a murderer."

"You're not a murderer. You defended yourself. You kicked ass! You made it possible for us to rescue you. If you hadn't…" He doesn't finish the sentence, but I know what would've happened. "I could never hate you."

I don't understand what the Guardians do. I mean, I know what they do, but not how they do it. I don't understand their mental state. I've watched enough television to put the pieces together. I know their job involves killing. And what Griff says is true.

Bossman would never have let me out of that room. If the Guardians had breached it, Bossman would've used me as a shield, and there's only one way that would've played out.

It was him or me.

Intellectually, I get it. I understand I'm not going to be arrested for what happened. Any judge would see the truth, and I'd get off on a self-defense plea. My mind knows this, but my heart and my soul feel differently about it.

I swipe at my cheeks. "What did you mean?"

"About what?"

"You said I wasn't a Guardian. What were you talking about?"

His lips firm into a hard line. "It was nothing, just random conversation." He smooths my hair and walks me back into the bedroom. "You need rest. It's been a long day."

"I freaked out, didn't I?" I'm still struggling to piece together what happened.

"Something triggered you." Forest leans against the doorjamb, arms crossed and glacial gaze hard as ice.

Griff blows out his breath. "I won't lie to you. You scared me, but yes, you had an episode."

An episode.

It's what the Facility calls a psychological break.

"I need to know what happened."

"You need rest." There he goes protecting me, even from myself.

The back of my neck itches because I know they were talking about me. I let Griff lead me further into the bedroom. He releases me, but only to kick Forest out. When he closes the door, I clasp my hands in front of me.

"Tell me what I walked in on?" There's no mistaking the plea in my voice, just as there was no mistaking the tension in that room. My question hangs in the air between us as Griff's entire body locks tight.

"I don't want to, but my gut tells me you have the right to know."

"What does that mean?"

"Only that I'm navigating uncharted waters here. Everything inside of me says not to tell you. That I need to protect you." He spins back toward the door. "That means keeping that from you, but we promised to talk and work things out."

"I appreciate that." For some reason, a surge of fear rushes through me.

He doesn't want me to know whatever they were talking about, but he's willing to share it with me. Not because it's a good idea. Clearly, he doesn't agree with any of them. But he's going to tell me because we've decided to be open with one another.

That hits me like a ton of bricks. Things just got real. This is a relationship. It's not just about sex. My stomach suddenly feels light and shaky.

And it sucks.

It sucks considering what I've been keeping from him. I back up to the bed because it feels as if my knees are going to give out. When the mattress hits the back of my legs, I plop down with a thud.

"What do you know about Bossman?" I look up at him, noting the tension in his body.

Griff comes to me. He knocks my knees aside and wedges his body between them. He places a finger under my chin and sweeps the broad pad of his thumb across my lips. Normally, that would feel sexual in nature, but this time it goes deeper. Like soul deep. A connection I've never felt with anyone ever.

"You say his name in your dreams." His voice is soft, tender, concerned but solid.

"My nightmares?"

"Yes, your nightmares."

"Every night?"

"Every night." He nods and his thumb sweeps to my jaw. The corners of his lips turn up into a soft smile filled with warmth, tenderness, and love.

"But you know more, don't you?"

"I know you killed him."

"Do you know how I killed him?"

"I've read the reports." His gaze shifts between my eyes, darting back and forth. He traces the angle of my jaw. A slow, leisurely exploration, like he's got all the time in the world.

"But you never asked me."

"I waited for you to tell me yourself." His violet eyes simmer with tenderness.

"Why?"

"Because I wanted you to trust me enough to confide in me. That's the easiest answer, but there's more to it than that."

"I'm sorry I didn't."

"No need to be sorry, minx." His fingers move to my hair, stroking lightly through the long curls. "I read the reports but never watched the video."

"There's video?" My voice cracks with that news.

"There's always video. We wear body cams and helmet cams. Every move is recorded and the mission debriefed afterwards."

"Oh, I guess I should've known." This just shows me how much I don't know about his world.

"Honestly, I didn't ask because I sensed you weren't ready to tell me. I didn't want to push. We've moved fast this past week and I just wanted to give you time to decide that was something you were ready to share with me."

"I told Zoe." I press my lips together.

"I figured as much."

"Is that why I had an episode?"

"I don't think talking to her triggered you."

"Then, I don't get what happened."

"You heard us approach. Or at least that's the way Zoe reports it. I think you heard the sound of men and that triggered a latent memory. Maybe it was because you told Zoe what happened.

Maybe it wasn't. That may have brought other memories to the surface."

"Maybe." Actually, I think he's right. "Griff?"

"Yes?" He spins around and sits beside me on the bed.

"I'm tired of being scared and feeling helpless." I'd say I was tired of living, but for the first time I can remember, there's something—someone—in my life worth sticking around for. There's no thought about ending things.

"I know." He loops his arm around my shoulder and we sit there for some time saying nothing.

My memory returns and I play through what happened in that cave. I remember how helpless I felt.

"I told Zoe I wanted to make him pay." I told her I wanted to kill him.

"Who?"

"The man who ordered me up like an object to be delivered on a platter."

"I understand that."

"I wish I was more like you." I lean into him, drawing strength from his presence.

"How's that?"

"You're strong. Fearless. You're in control of what happens around you. I want to feel just a little bit of that."

"You have that. You're free."

"Not as long as he's out there. What's to keep him from coming after me again?"

"The Guardians are working on that."

"How?"

"It's what we were arguing about."

"But you were arguing about me."

"Forest has it in his head to use you as bait. Flush out your buyer and find a way to get inside that organization. It's the only way to tear it down."

"Me?" I point to my chest.

"You." His jaw clenches. "But don't worry. I'll never put you in danger. That's what I was telling them."

"Because I'm not a Guardian."

"Because I want to keep you safe. What he's proposing isn't just risky, it's insane."

"But could it potentially work?"

"I'll never let it get that far. It's not something we're considering."

"We? We as in you and the Guardians, or we as in you and me?"

"Both."

"What if I want to try?" I press my lips together.

His entire body stills and it's some time before he answers.

"Moira, you can't be serious."

"I'm just thinking out loud. If I want to try, do you think it's something I could do? Like, would I be *able* to do it?"

It's not totally insane. While I don't know what Forest is thinking, Griff mentioned using me as bait. If they can find the man who ordered me off the slave menu, I can get close enough to kill him. That would make me feel... What? Powerful? Righteous?

Safe?

Or am I totally insane?

"It would be incredibly dangerous." His arm slips from my shoulders and he clasps his hands in front of him. Griff doesn't look at me.

"You didn't answer my question."

"Do I think you could do it? Shit, you're the strongest person I know. You'd need work. A lot of work. Training. We couldn't send you out the way you are now. You're strong and fit. You handled yourself well on that ship."

"But?" I wait for him to tell me I can't do it.

"Are you saying you want to do it?"

"I know women can't be Guardians, but if I can help in the smallest way, it might help me feel like I have some control over my life."

"There are female Guardians."

"There are?"

"Two. They're on Delta team. Jenny is Delta-One, team leader. She took over the team when CJ stepped up to lead all four teams. Charlene is Delta-six. She's been on the team for a couple of years."

"I didn't know that."

"Delta team works domestic issues. They're often hired by the FBI to work domestic kidnapping operations."

"So, it wouldn't be unheard of then?"

"No, but are we talking about what I think we're talking about?"

"That depends. Is this something you'd let me do?"

"Minx, it's not up to me to decide what I will or won't let you do. You can do whatever you want. I'm not here to make that decision for you."

"But what you said out there…"

"Hey, I'm not thrilled by this. Not one bit. I'm going to work you so hard that you'll want to quit."

"Why would you do that?"

"Because, if you do this, you need to know you can do it. I won't go soft on your training. No one will."

"What do you mean no one will?"

"We train as a team. Not as individuals. Max won't take anyone on an op he hasn't personally vetted. I'll never lie to you. I plan on doing everything in my power to make you change your mind."

"That makes no sense. How is that supporting me?"

"Because if you make it through what I have planned and still want to do this, I'll be right there by your side. I just don't want you to think this will be a walk in the park. Putting my woman in danger goes against everything I believe, but I'm not here to stand in your way. You need to understand what that means."

"It means you're not one of them."

No need to elaborate who *them* refers to. He knows exactly what I mean. Griff isn't here to rule my life like the Masters of my past. He's not going to tell me what to do, what not to do, or control me in any way. He's not one of the men who forced me to do as they wished, rather than what I wanted.

It's the greatest gift I've ever been given.

"Tell me one thing." I lean against him.

"Whatever you want."

"If I train and pass all your tests, do *you* think this is something I can do? Am I capable enough?"

"You're stronger than you know. More capable than you believe. Your mind and your self-doubt are your greatest weakness. If this is something you want to consider, what I think doesn't matter."

"Perhaps not, but I don't know what it takes to be a Guardian. You must have some sense. Am I too weak? Because if I am…"

"As much as I'd love to say yes, and keep you from going any further down this path, I can't lie to you. You have the capability to pull this off. As for whether or not you've got the mental fortitude to endure our unique brand of training, that's entirely up to you."

I push out a breath, realizing what's happening. Griff doesn't want this, but he won't stand in my way. He'll push me. Test me. He'll try everything he knows to get me to quit. But he'll only do it to ensure I am ready.

"If I pass your tests?"

"I'll be right by your side."

I cover my face and dig deep for what it is I want.

"And if I fail?"

"You'll fail knowing you did the best you could, and I'll still be by your side."

"I want to hurt him. I don't know about the rest of it, tearing down things from the inside out, but I want to make him pay for what he did to me."

"I have one request." He turns gravely serious.

"What?"

"If I think you're not ready, or that you're unfocused, or a danger to the team…"

"I'll tell you."

"And if I think you're not ready?"

"I trust you. I trust you'll always be honest with me. Whether to say I'm good to go, or that I need to step back. You say the word, and I'll listen."

He didn't have to be honest with me now, and yet he was. I'm new to this relationship thing, but I know what he did for me is huge. Like massively, hugely ginormous. If it's possible, I fall a little more in love with him.

It's his turn to scrub his face. "I can't believe I'm sitting here, in my bedroom, where I've waited a year to finally get you in my bed, and we're talking about putting you back in harm's way. It feels all kinds of wrong."

"But if it helps in any way, it's worth it. Right? Isn't this why you became a Guardian in the first place? To save those who've been taken?"

"It is, just never thought I'd be doing it with my wife."

"Your what?"

"You heard me."

"Griff…"

"I'm not asking. I'm putting a ring on your finger, a chip in your back, and I'm making you my wife."

"A chip in my back?"

"Damn straight."

"Um…"

"It's a tracker. Non-removable, unlike your necklace. I'm not putting you out there without a way to find you again. That's non-negotiable."

"But the ring thing? That's a joke, right?"

"Does it look like I'm joking?" He stands and holds out his hand. "Let's go tell them the good news." He says *good,* but with the way his mouth twists on the word, he's not happy about this at all.

I take his hand, but I'm not sure what good news we're sharing with his team. That we're getting married? Or that Griff's agreed to Forest's crazy plan?

Hell, I can't believe I've agreed to Forest's plan.

TWENTY-NINE

Moira

I STAGGER TO MY FEET AND WIPE THE SWEAT OUT OF MY EYES. AXEL crashes into me with a flurry of punches and kicks delivered with brute force and incredible speed. My ribs ache. My ears ring. I weave back and forth like a drunkard.

He strikes again. Pushes me back. I counter with a jab. He bats my arm aside like an annoyance. I hit and miss a dozen times while each of his powerful punches lands a direct hit.

"Break!" Griff's shout is my reprieve.

We've been going at this for what feels like hours but is really less than ten minutes. I'm wrung out with no fight left in me. I crash to the ground and hold my aching ribs while I struggle to catch my breath.

The thing is, Axel's been pulling his punches. He's not supposed to, but he's going easy on me.

"That was pathetic." Griff looms over me. "Get up."

I don't know what happened to the kind, protective man I love. Griff the Instructor is a grueling taskmaster with zero pity. He demands my best and expects I give him two hundred percent each and every day. There is no respite. He's made it his mission to either turn me into a warrior princess or force me to admit I'm in way over my head and throw in the towel.

In that, he's kept his word. He's pushing me to quit, but I'm tenacious to a fault. I want the Guardians to put me on this mission, and I'm going to fight to earn my place.

I *need* this in my life, and I've decided it's the only way I'll ever feel in control and safe. Griff gets it. He'd like to lock me up at home and never let me out again. It's the overprotective alpha male in him trying to keep me safe, but he knows I need this.

And he's not going easy on me.

The last two weeks?

They've been hell.

"I hate you." But I struggle to my knees.

"You can tell me all about how much you hate me later. Get up."

"What am I doing wrong?" I huff out my question, frustrated that I didn't land one punch. Not that it would've done much. Like Griff, Axel is taller, broader, and just plain bigger than me. There's no way I can take him down. "This is impossible."

Two weeks of this torture and I swear my defensive skills are regressing instead of getting stronger.

"You throwing in the towel?" Griff stares at me, willing me to give up. If I do that, I'm out.

"No!" I growl at him.

"Then set up." He claps his hands and points to the center of the training mat. Before I find my position, Griff claps his hands.

I dodge a roundhouse kick to my head and duck beneath Axel's fist. I dodge two more blows before Axel scores a direct hit in my solar plexus with his knee. Once. Twice. He doesn't hold back and I stagger backward until I lose my balance and crash on my ass.

I glare at Axel, but he's laser-focused on me. He glances at Griff, who shakes his head. Bastard isn't going to stop this round until what? I'm bleeding? Knocked out?

I hate Griff with righteous anger.

"Hey, boys, you picking on a girl again?"

A low, sultry female voice snaps my head up, just in time for Axel to clock me with his foot. My body careens sideways and I land in a pile of limp muscles and twitching limbs. I'm so damn tired.

"Break!" Griff calls an end to this round while I swipe at my mouth.

Yup, there's the blood. My eyes pinch in anger as Axel offers me a hand up.

"I hate you too."

"You'll thank me later." Axel gives a shrug like he doesn't have a care in the world, but the glance he gives Griff is full of concern.

"Hi, Jenny." Griff greets the newcomer. "Thanks for stopping by."

"Hey, my pleasure. When Alpha calls Delta, you know we can't refuse. Is this the one?" Her eyes cut to me, but she otherwise doesn't acknowledge my existence.

I can't help but gape at what must be the most beautiful woman I've ever seen. Her ebony skin soaks in the light. I have great skin, but it's nothing compared to her flawless complexion. And those eyes. Deep, dark, and mesmerizing, they draw me in deep. Her angular features should be harsh, but they're achingly beautiful. She's tall, standing only a few inches shorter than Griff, and while she's not stacked with muscle, she clearly works out. Nobody gets that kind of muscular definition without a lot of hard work. My mouth gapes, and I can't help but stare at her lithe body that belongs on a runway, not here in Guardian HQ.

"What's your name, kid?" She turns that dark stare on me and I feel like I want to crawl into a deep dark hole. "Did you guys knock her senseless? Or is she mute? Cat got your tongue, kid?"

"Moira, stand up and meet Jenny." Griff pulls me from my stupor and I rise on shaky legs. And that's where I stay because this woman intimidates the hell out of me.

"Is Charlene coming?" Griff keeps an eye on me while addressing the woman.

"Charlie is coming and she's bringing Mack. Word to the wise. Don't call her Charlene. She'll feed you your balls."

"Message received." Griff takes a step back.

Axel laughs and the woman turns her magnetic gaze on him.

"Laugh it up, fuzzball. Griff tells me you and I are going to spar."

I don't think I've ever seen a Guardian gulp before, but I swear Axel looks a little paler than he did a second ago.

"Actually, I thought you'd take us both on." Griff rocks back on his heels.

"Now that would be fun, but Doc Summers heard I was coming over here and she told me to make sure you babied your little boo-boo." She points to his leg. "Hear you're still on support."

Griff's jaw clenches and he rolls his eyes. "I'm beginning to hate Doc Summers."

"Chin up. It's for your own good. Now, about why I'm here."

"Moira, Jenny is lead for Delta team."

"Um, nice to meet you." My wobbly legs threaten to give out on me. I brush the dust off my hands and turn my suspicious gaze on Griff. "What's going on?"

"I want to prove a point," he says.

"Prove what point?"

"Why does Axel keep wiping you on the mat?" His expression remains tight, focused, and demanding an answer.

"Um, because he's *ginormous* and knows what he's doing."

"True, but so do you."

"Doesn't feel like it." I know what to do. Griff's been drilling that into my head for the better part of a year, but it still doesn't come naturally to me. Axel doesn't think. He just reacts. I'm still trying to figure out when to use each move. That leaves me a split second behind Axel. It's time he uses to pound me into the mat.

We've been working on hand-to-hand combat for the past two weeks, a *required* skill for my upcoming mission. And I'm failing at it.

Spectacularly.

"You're not trying."

"I *am* trying, but you're just all so much bigger than me." Not to mention stronger. Oh, and of course, they've been trained by the best of the best. Hell, they *are* the best of the best. I'm just little old me. Tiny. Puny. Wet behind the ears when it comes to this kind of thing.

"Moira, it's a pleasure to meet you." Jenny ignores Griff's and my back and forth. "Nice to see someone was finally able to sink her nails into this man. Good luck taming him though."

I'm still confused why she's here. Griff closes the distance between us. He takes my hands in his and stoops down. He does that whenever he's trying to make a point.

"You're stuck in your head, little minx." He taps my temple for emphasis.

"I don't even know what that means."

Griff pulls me out of the ring. "What I mean is you've lost before you've even begun."

"Huh?" His explanation only increases my confusion.

He taps my forehead. "The battle is fought with the mind as much as, or more than, the body. The moves we've been teaching you capitalize on momentum. They're designed to level the playing field. Size and strength mean less when you can manipulate your attacker using their body weight against them."

"Whatever."

"Not whatever." He taps my temple again. "You believe you can't win, so you've already lost."

"I've sparred against Axel, Max, Knox, Liam, and Wolfe, and I've lost to them all. I can't even get a hit in." I've also sparred with Griff at home, but that always leads to sex. Pretty amazing sex, but fighting him is different than sparring with the other guys of Alpha team.

"Kid, it's because you see these brutes and know you're smaller than them. Lighter than them. They may have more training and years of experience on you, but that doesn't mean you're helpless against them." She taps her temple. "Ninety-percent of the fight is up here. Confidence will win you more fights than raw skill. The lack of confidence will lose every damn time."

"Years of training says otherwise." I can't help the snippy comment.

"Come on." Jenny steps onto the mat. "Watch and learn." She points to Axel, who glares at Griff.

"You owe me a case, dude. A fucking case." Axel joins Jenny on the mat.

Without warning, Jenny crashes into Axel. She's a blur of punches and kicks. She moves with sinuous grace. Each motion flows into the next, like she knows exactly where her body is going to be before it gets there.

Axel defends then goes on the attack. Or tries to. Jenny's fist crunches against his nose. She dodges a blow and hits him in the gut with the back of her heel. Axel grunts and launches at her. Jenny lets Axel grab her, but then she spins and turns his attack against him, tossing him to the ground.

Placing a foot on his belly like a victorious killer, she props her hands on her hips. "That is how you fight."

"What? How? I don't…"

"Kid…" She lifts a finger. "Size has nothing to do with it. Strength only matters if you let them get a hold of you. Griff's right. You've lost because you don't believe a woman can take down a Guardian. But the fact you're female is your greatest advantage. Men will underestimate you. Use that to your advantage."

Axel grabs her ankle and lifts it off his stomach. He rolls free and dusts off his hands. Jenny flashes her pearly white teeth at him and gives a little snap. Axel just shakes his head and glares at Griff again.

"I'm sorry, but that was just for show, right?" I look to Axel. "You let her win?"

"I never throw a fight." He shakes hands with Jenny and fishes a raggedy button out of his pants. He lifts the button, showing it to Griff. "A whole case of beer."

"I don't get it. What's with the button?" I'm so confused.

Jenny snatches it out of his hand. "I've heard about these. Alpha team is weird." She tucks the button into her bra. "Now, kid, let me show you why this works. First, get out of your head. You've got a lot of preconceived notions floating around in there that we need to purge."

"Um, okay?"

"Do you mind?" Jenny turns to Axel.

302 • ELLIE MASTERS

"At your disposal." Axel gives a semi bow.

"Kid, watch closely." Jenny proceeds to reenact her fight with Axel, only this time, they move at half the speed as before.

Jenny shows me how she uses her body's momentum to flow into the next move, and how she used the same thing to take Axel's hits and let them slide right over her. When she shows me how she tossed him on the ground, my mouth gapes.

"No way! Does that really work?"

"It does, but why don't we have you practice?" She snaps her fingers. "Get in here, kid. Let me show you a thing or two."

The next hour blows my mind.

I meet two other people from Delta team. A pretty blonde that looks every bit the blonde bimbo with her double D's, perky smile, and cheerleader attitude. It's hard for me to take her seriously. When Jenny puts Charlie up against Mack, a man who looks like a Mack truck and makes Griff and Axel look small, I feel like I've entered the twilight zone. Charlie takes a licking from Mack, but she puts him flat on his back—twice.

There may be something to this momentum thing after all.

And the only good thing about all this sparring is the deal I made with Griff. Each night before I crawl into bed, he has to kiss all my bruises and rub out the aches in my muscles. Bedtime sex is quickly becoming my favorite kind of sex.

We spend four hours in the gym, Griff, Axel, Mack, Charlie, Jenny and I. At first, they let me rest, showing me—proving to me—how both women can meet the men equally in a fight. They show me one other thing that terrifies me. This momentum thing only works if I can keep my opponent from grabbing hold of me. Once that happens, brute strength wins.

That means I lose.

I practice first with Jenny. She shows me a few things, then attacks me. We do this several times until I finally spin her around and throw her to the mat.

"There you go, kid." She dusts off her hands, then points to Mack. "Now you get to play with him."

At some point, we lose Axel. Griff stays with me but allows Jenny to take over my training.

The next morning, it's just me, Jenny, Charlie, and Mack. Griff is off meeting with the vascular surgeon about his leg. Jenny and her teammates don't go easy on me, but I learn more in the next two days than I did in the past two weeks. Instead of trying to get me to quit, like Griff did, Jenny coaches me to win. I'm no expert, but I'm getting better.

The following day, Griff's not there either. He and the rest of Alpha are in some meeting. I asked but he gave me that look that said I was on a need-to-know basis. It's hard. The longer I'm here, practicing with half of Delta team, the more I wish I was one of them. Their sense of camaraderie feels like the family I never had.

At the end of practice, Jenny wipes the sweat from her neck. I'm drenched head to toe. Charlie barely broke a sweat, and Mack looks like he could go on for days. I've yet to toss Mack on his back, but I did evade his grappling hold for nearly an entire match. That's big for me. Like huge. I celebrate the win.

"Wanna join us for lunch, kid?" Jenny wraps the towel around her neck.

"I'd love to, but I've got an appointment with Skye."

"Gotcha."

"I really want to thank you for taking time to help me with this."

"No problem." Mack places his massive hand on my shoulder. "You're not horrible anymore, kid."

"Gee, thanks."

Mack is fun. He's huge, massive, and yet his smiles are the absolute best thing in the world. They take all his ferociousness and erase it, leaving only a wonderful man behind. He's like a scary teddy bear, and I love how he and Jenny flirt. They think they're not obvious about it, but there's something simmering between those two.

Charlie is simply amazing. She's a couple of years older than me, and I completely underestimated her, which is a bit disturbing. I'm blond, beautiful, and well aware of the stereotypes levied against me. Yet, I did exactly that with Charlie.

Lesson learned.

We break and I head to medical where Skye is waiting for me. I've figured out the structure of Guardian HRS, putting all the people I've met into place. At the top is Forest and his sister, Skye. They created the Guardians.

Forest is top guy, but he doesn't actually run anything. He's got his hands in too many things, like managing the rock band Angel Fire, among many other things, to really lead the Guardians. That task goes to Sam, ex-Delta operative and former FBI Hostage Rescue Specialist; he's the man who took Forest's idea and turned it into reality.

He recruited CJ to be the Delta team leader, but CJ stepped up from Delta-One, to command all four Guardian teams.

The other people who work at Guardian HRS refer to the teams as the pointy tip of the spear. But there's a lot more to Guardian HRS than the teams. For instance, Skye and her medical department.

Also recruited from the ranks of the military elite, her team of combat medics bring excellence in all things to the front of the line. Then there's Mitzy with her team of computer whiz kids, hackers, intelligence specialists, and engineers who make all kinds of cool gadgets, like the tiny dragonfly drones I've seen Griff and his team working with. Not to mention the virtual reality set up she and Forest designed together. Talk about mind-blowing.

Skye, Mitzy, and CJ report directly to Sam. Forest comes and goes, poking his nose in missions of personal interest. I thought he was the boss, but he's more like an interested party with full access. I thought he would be the one who decided if I was mission ready.

He's not. That's up to Skye, CJ, and ultimately Sam. Oh, and of course, Max. The teams work independently. Max has ultimate say in what happens on his team. If Sam says I'm ready, but Max says no, then I'm off the mission. It's a bit convoluted but important to understand. I haven't been pleading my case with Max the way I should. He's the one I have to convince.

I knock on the door to Skye's office and walk into the waiting area. The medical facilities are similar to what anyone would find apart from Guardian HRS, with a waiting room, check-in desk, and exam rooms, but there's a full surgical suite, imaging facilities, and intensive care unit as well. Basically, they run a mini-hospital and clinic.

"Hey, Moira." Skye pops her head out from a door leading off the waiting room. "You ready?"

"Maybe?" I'm so not ready.

"Relax, it's a very simple procedure."

"You sure about that? Getting a tracker implanted in my body doesn't seem simple to me."

"It really is. Come on, I'll show you." She leads me down a corridor and shows me inside a procedure room. "Have a seat."

I hop on the patient table, complete with the requisite paper barrier, and kick my heels against the edge as I fidget with my fingers.

"Look, it's super small." She holds up a small plastic pack and hands it to me. "See, a little larger than a grain of rice."

"And it goes where?"

"Well, initially we put them in the arm, but…" She looks at me squirm. "Let's just say, we place them in a much more secure area now."

I don't want to ask why they switched. "And how do you stick it in me?"

She holds up something that looks like a cross between a gun, a needle, and a medieval torture device. "It's a prick, just like getting a shot."

"That's a pretty big needle." I glance at the door because I suddenly have a very pressing need to have Griff by my side. He's with his team, doing whatever it is Guardians do when they aren't on a mission, or torturing their girlfriend on the mat.

"Trust me, it's safe."

"And where are we putting it?"

Skye pulls back the hair behind her ear. "We're putting in two."

"Two?"

"Yes, another precaution."

"I don't understand."

"One to find and one to hide."

"Stop scaring my girl, Doc." Griff's brusque tone sounds from down the hall. "Did I miss it?"

"No, you're just in time, and I wasn't scaring your girl."

My eyes round because that's exactly what's happening. The idea of anyone doing a full body search that would turn up a tracker embedded in my body is way more thorough than I realized.

"Do you think I'll really get searched?"

"People are far more tech-savvy today than ever before, but don't worry."

"I'm very worried."

"I only mean that you will also have a bracelet with a tracking device. Your story will be that the Facility hired out protection on you when you leave the grounds."

"I'm your protection, minx." Griff winks.

"Okay." I reach for Griff and he closes the distance, hugging me tight to his side.

"As your protection detail, we require our clients to wear tracking devices. You'll be outfitted with a bracelet and an earring. We anticipate those will be removed, and that's where it should stop."

"Should stop?"

"There's always a chance they'll do a sweep of your body." Griff gives a little pinch to my arm. "That's why there's a diversion embedded in your arm."

"But won't they find the one behind my ear?"

"That one doesn't transmit." Skye hands me a second plastic packet. "This one is activated by touch, specifically by tapping SOS over the device. That ensures it's not accidentally activated by touch."

"I don't get it."

"Detectors can only sense devices that are actively transmitting. The one behind your ear does not transmit. You have to activate it. The bracelet and earring transmit steadily, as does the tracker we're going to put in your arm."

"I thought I was just going to get one thing shoved under my skin. Now it's two?"

"You're not going out there unless I'm one hundred percent positive we can find you if—when you're taken."

"I'm not on the mission yet."

Griff exchanges a look with Skye.

"Little minx, what do you think I've been doing these past few days?"

"I don't know. Guardian stuff?"

"Guardian stuff is mission planning. As much as I don't like it, you're a go for the mission. Max signed off on it yesterday."

"Yesterday? Why didn't you tell me?" My brows pinch together.

"I was otherwise occupied." His brows lift, reminding me what we did last night. It was the first night we experimented with rope and can I say... *Mind blown!*

My face heats as I remember last night. Skye's lips curl into a smile and she turns her back as Griff and I share a private moment.

My heart swells with the love he holds for me. Heat and passion simmer in his eyes—last night was epic—but it's more than that. We've lowered our walls, shown our vulnerabilities, and grow closer each and every day.

He showed me a new side of himself last night and I can't wait for more. I squirm on the table, suddenly needing a bit of alone time with my man, but first, Skye needs to shoot me up with tracking devices.

Then it hits. "It's a go?"

"It is." His deep voice sends delicious licks of pleasure shooting down my spine. Protective undertones, tempered by his dominance, flare in what he doesn't say. He's not happy putting me at risk, but he's done everything in his power to make certain I'm ready to face whatever comes next.

"I'm scared."

What I love most about Griff is that I can express my fears freely. He's not here to rule my life, or control it, but he's committed to standing by my side and fighting my battles with me, rather than for me. That goes against every protective instinct he has. He does it because men have controlled me before, dictating every facet of my existence. He's a stronger, bigger, deadly partner, but a partner, nonetheless.

My partner.

My Guardian.

I'm not fooling myself about my abilities. Granted, I've been training in self-defense for over a year, but it's only been these last two weeks that I've studied with such intensity. That doesn't make my skills equal to his. Far from it.

There's no way I can compete against decades of the intensive and brutal physical training he endured as a SEAL, a Delta operative, and now as a Guardian. The one thing he's impressed upon me are the limits of what I can do.

"You can always back out."

He'd love for me to back out. He spent the last few weeks making my life a living hell, specifically to test my resolve.

"Are you okay with this?"

"I'm not. Putting you out there goes against everything I believe." His shoulders roll back. "But I accept this is something you need to do, and it meets Guardian objectives. I'll do what I can to keep you safe."

"Do you really think they'll try to make another attempt to kidnap me?"

"We think someone is sniffing around Guardian operations, and from what Mitzy's been able to determine, they have one very irate buyer. They're being pressured to deliver."

"Me." I gulp as the word slips out of my mouth.

"And that's when I'm no longer able to protect you. You'll be on your own."

"But you'll be close, right? Isn't that the plan?"

"As soon as we're done here, we're meeting with the team to start prep work."

"I thought you said it was all planned out."

"Mission planning is just the beginning. There's a lot more that goes into spinning up for an op. Your work has only just begun. The easy part is behind you."

"That was the easy part?"

"Yup. If you think I was hard on you before, you've yet to see what it really means to work. I hope this is still what you want. The kid gloves are off."

I gulp. No way has the past few weeks been easy. How can things get any harder?

By the end of the week, I will regret asking that question.

THIRTY

Griff

Preparation at Guardian HRS has been going non-stop for the past few weeks. Today is the day I take my woman out into the world and lay the groundwork for her *next* abduction.

My gut twists with that thought.

Putting her in harm's way goes against every fiber of my being, but this is what Moira needs before she can move on with her life. It's her path to walk and mine to stand by her side. Many times, I thought to step in and call an end to the craziness. If I push hard enough, Moira will cave to my demands, but what would that make me?

Just another one of the men who've used and abused her for their own purposes. I won't do that.

I won't be that.

Even if I hate everything about this operation, but Max finally set me straight, or rather he and Jenny did. They sat me down and laid it all out in front of me.

Jenny took over Moira's training because I, evidently, was "hindering" her training. I thought I was doing a pretty good job, but Max said I was brow-beating Moira. Talk about a kick in the gut.

Jenny assures me Moira is more than capable of taking care of herself. Doesn't mean I won't be by her side as much as I can, and it doesn't mean I won't be first in line to rescue her for a third time.

Please let this be the last time my woman is placed in the line of fire.

I can't deal with the idea of what might happen before Alpha team can swoop in and save the day.

As far as the operation goes, it's simple. Our objective is the man who ordered Moira off the goddamn sex-slave menu. We don't know shit about the operation. Like how did he make initial contact? *Who* are his contacts? A man like that doesn't decide to purchase a slave on a whim. He needed to have an introduction, some entry point into the slave trade pipeline. We need that entry point.

Sourness coats my mouth as I get ready to take Moira shopping. I hate exposing her to those who've been searching for her, but at least I finally get to take her shopping. No more bargain buys at a thrift store.

We don't know, but we believe, the men who've been tasked with acquiring Moira assume she's been on Facility grounds this whole time. Our security there is locked down tight, with additional protocols put in action such as extra background sweeps initiated on everyone—including me.

No one is beyond reproach.

The Facility is locked down. Guardian HRS is secure. Our threat is outside our walls. Not within it, which is how it should be.

"You almost ready?" I bellow through the house. Moira took over the guest bedroom as her closet. For a woman on a shoestring budget, she's pretty damn thrifty and has accumulated a shitload of shoes, purses, and clothes.

"I'm coming." Her light feminine voice sends shivers racing down my spine. She was coming all right, all over my fingers, my face, and my tongue less than an hour ago.

"Hurry up! Don't make me swat that mighty fine ass of yours."

Moira peeks out of the bedroom. "Promises, promises."

"Don't poke the beast." A low growl accompanies my words.

"What if I want the beast to poke me?"

"Moira! We're going to be late."

"Oh, come on. We're going shopping. There's no timetable."

"My team is going to be in position." They're already down in Santa Monica.

"Well, I guess you need to make a decision then."

"And what would that be?"

"Are you going to leave me aching all day? Or are you going to come in here and toss me over your knee for taking too much time?"

"Do *not* tease."

"Do I look like I'm teasing?" She hides behind the door but slides one long leg out where I can see it. Turning gracefully, she adds the curve of her tight ass, wriggling it seductively.

My girl is feisty. That's rooted in her uneasiness. Today marks the first day of Operation Temptress. I picked the name, and I don't give one shit what anyone thinks about it.

Right now. Moira is certainly tempting me. Damn, but I admire her inner strength. Strong in mind and body, she's fearless. Or should be. Damn, if I don't want to take the edge off her uncertainty. She's stalling, and I have a choice to make. Do I cave to her taunts, take her hard, and drive her out of her mind? Or do I shut this all down, leaving us both aching for the rest of the day?

I plant my legs wide and pull at my chin. We're going to be so damn late.

Storming into the guest room turned closet, my sudden appearance takes my temptress by surprise. Already decided on what she needs to silence her fears, I don't hold back. Her mouth opens on a squeak but I grab her throat, silencing her, and yank her against me with enough force to make her knees wobble.

"I told you not to tease me."

Her eyes round in fear, but it's not real. Already her body reacts with the rush of adrenaline flooding her system. She pushes against me in challenge.

"And what if I do? What are you going to do about it?"

Damn, but if this woman doesn't take my breath away. This is how her life should be. Wild. Unrestrained. Free. Not beaten into submission, chained and collared, waiting for monstrous men to do unspeakable things to her.

I may get rough with Moira, but it's by her request. Her demand. A deep, throaty sound rumbles in the back of my throat. It slams against her feminine whimper and wraps around her gentle surrender. My entire body tunes into the signals she gives. That's how I know how hard to push.

She begs for a display of strength.

Maybe I should be softer, gentler with her, but that's not what she needs. I remember the girl with the vacant stare I saved in Manila over a year ago.

Back then, the fight had been beaten out of her. She'd been stripped of all hope, her fire quenched as she was forced to be docile and obedient. Moira has come a long way from that empty shell of a woman.

Her fire burns hot. She's eager for a fight, stepping up to go after those who would throw her back in a cage.

And she's all mine.

I move my hand from her throat to twist in the hair at her nape. Slanting my head, I check her eyes for the tacit permission she always gives. Then my lips crash against her mouth in a mind-blowing kiss. I take from my girl. I take what I want, how I want, and make no apologies for the ferociousness with which I claim her as mine. My heart pounds like a jackhammer inside my chest, and my cock jerks, eager and ready to stand up.

Honestly, I could kiss Moira all day. The sex is amazing, but holding her in my arms is pretty damn awesome all on its own.

She opens for me the moment I place my mouth on her. No less forceful than any of our other kisses, this one feels different. We're familiar with each other now, but that's not what this is. It's us expressing our combined uneasiness with this mission. A need to unite as one, man and woman joined together.

Not that anybody expects her to be abducted the first day out, but anything is possible. This is us putting our fears and concerns out there, dealing with it the best way we know how.

Her tongue brushes against mine, so sweet, so very much mine. My hands move. I can't stop myself and I let them go everywhere. I rip off her shirt, forcing her hands up over her head. Her breath catches as I momentarily bind her there and intensify the kiss. But the fabric soon falls to the ground. Her bra follows a moment later. I break off the kiss, but only to bend my head and lower my mouth to latch onto a pink nipple.

I pull on her hair and force her head back. Her body arches, thrusting her chest forward. With her hands free, she shoves my pants down over my hips, freeing my engorged cock. Bold and confident, she fists my cock. Her small fingers wrap around the shaft and she gives a sharp jerk. My eyes practically roll to the back of my head and I bite down on her nipple, reminding her who's in charge. Not that it stops her as she continues jerking me off.

Two can play at that game. I palm her ass, then lift her leg to curl it around my waist. My fingers seek her hot, wet pussy, where I find her aroused and ready for me. I slip a finger inside, pull out, and slide two back in. She strokes me as I finger her pussy until we are both moaning with pleasure.

I can't stand it any longer. Pulling my fingers out, I hitch her leg high on my hip and slam her against the wall. She guides my dick until the tip brushes against her opening. Once there, I don't waste any more time. I slam home with a groan and bite my lower lip to keep from coming right there.

"Griff…" Her breathy moan nearly drives me over the edge. "Harder."

"You need it rough, little minx?"

"Yes, please." She lifts her fingers to my shoulders, where her nails dig in.

"You're mine."

"Yes. Show me. Griff, show me how much I'm yours."

Needing no further encouragement, I pound into my girl. The sweet sound of sex fills the room as our bodies collide in the rhythm of the ages. Hard. Fast. And punishing. I slam home, seeking heaven in her arms. So damn good. Her soft pants and frenzied cries heat my blood, setting my body on fire. Solely focused on the way I slide in and out, I know I'll never get enough of this.

Of her.

"Please." She loops her arms around my neck and grips my ass hard with her leg. "Harder. Griff, please! Ruin me."

I step up the tempo. Thrust harder. Force myself deeper. My hand grips her nape, yanking her head back. Exposing her neck where I suck and bite.

"Mine, Moira. You're fucking mine. Come for me." I pound into her, pushing harder, slamming forward. Mindless of the force I use to take her the way she craves.

Sometimes, I like to take my time and enjoy the journey. This is not one of those times. It's desperate, raw, and rough. I'm not interested in making her squirm beneath me. I want my girl to scream. Right now, it's a race to completion because I'm barely holding back.

"Griff! Yes. There. More. Almost there."

"Mouth. Now." I growl the command.

She lifts her head and I don't waste a moment claiming her mouth. Her pleasure breaks and I swallow her moans. Moira whimpers as her pussy contracts around my dick. Ripples of pleasure surge through her as I slam deep inside her wet heat. Two strokes later, I fall over the edge, joining her as our bodies crash together in shared ecstasy.

When I finally pull back from the kiss, her soft eyes take me in.

"Thank you." Her body quivers and she hugs me tight. "I needed that."

"You don't say?" The corner of my mouth tics up.

"I'm nervous."

"It's okay to be nervous."

Her head tilts forward until she rests her cheek against my chest. "Griff?"

"Yes?" I sweep her blond hair off her face.

"Will you still love me if this—if he makes me…"

No way in hell are we going there. I grip her arms and hold her a bit away from me. I want her to see the truth of what I need to say.

"First off, I love you. There's nothing in this world that will make me stop loving you or love you any less than I do right now. No matter what happens. Do you hear me?"

"But—if he…" Her gaze drops and she nibbles at her lower lip.

Her concern rocks me to the core. Have I thought about what could happen? Damn straight I have.

Is there a possibility he will take what doesn't belong to him? It's possible.

If he does, sure as shit I'll feed him his balls. But in no way will that change how I feel about Moira. Her entire life is one abuse piled upon another. That doesn't matter to me, and if it happens again, we'll navigate our way through it.

But that's not what Moira needs to hear.

"I'll never let that happen." I trace the gentle curve of her jawline and press the pad of my thumb against her lips.

"I know, but I'm scared."

"Don't be scared. You've been training hard and you can take care of yourself. I'll always be close. You're no longer alone. You've got me."

"I've got you." A smile curves her lips. Moira flings her arms around my neck and she lifts on tiptoe to give me a kiss. "You were soft on me."

"That was soft?" I arch my brow. "I'm pretty sure we put a dent in the wall."

"Maybe." Her eyes twinkle. "But you forgot to spank my ass."

"Did I now?" I grab her wrist. "Who said I forgot?" With a yank, I tug her to the bed. Yeah, we're going to be epically late for her shopping adventure.

THIRTY-ONE

Moira

GRIFF'S TAKING ME BACK OUT IN THE WORLD.

If it's not his house, Guardian HQ, or that one trip shopping that first day, then I haven't seen it. I've been safely ensconced either in Griff's house, the Facility, or Guardian HQ training for this mission.

Or rather, training for my abduction.

Before I stepped out, I needed Griff to center me. And boy did he do a bang-up job of banging my brains out. With him, I crave dominance. I love how he takes me out of my head.

It's just him and me. As for all the chaotic thoughts in my head, he sweeps them aside, and I find bliss in his arms. Or rather, his talented dick. That man knows how to fuck a woman until she can't think straight.

Or walk straight.

A grin slips onto my face thinking about the amazing ache between my legs.

And I'm out. Walking the streets, shopping like I've got plastic to burn.

I'm chipped and ready for anything.

We tested the chip in my arm as well as the one hidden behind my ear. I know how to activate the SOS beacon as well as send limited messages after a crash course in MORSE code. It's all a matter of tapping in the right sequence.

"Here you go." I exit the store and shove another bag into Griff's arms. This is the third shop I've hit today and Griff's loaded down with packages.

"Yes, ma'am." With his brusque voice, devoid of the emotion simmering in his eyes, Griff takes my packages.

To everyone else, he's nothing more than hired help, my bodyguard. Dark suit, dark sunglasses, protective hovering. He fits the job to a T.

My job is to make a splash, burn through the plastic in my brand-new purse, and either trip facial recognition software, or get the world talking. I'm to draw the eye of my abductor and convince him I'm worth another chance.

We're back in Santa Monica. Not too far from the beach where I was taken. If I said that didn't make me nervous, that would be a lie. My entire body feels strung out. My stomach's queasy. My skin is super sensitive. Each time a stranger bumps into me, I jump.

To keep up appearances, we stay at a local hotel. It's on the beach, and we share a double room suite. Only one of those beds gets used. Once we retire for the day, Griff puts me through my paces. First, with a bit of self-defense practice, then with wrestling of the more intimate kind.

Griff goes inside the stores with me but remains a respectable distance away from me. Hovering near the door. Watching all the entrances and exits. Scaring the other customers with the intensity of his stare.

It kind of sucks.

Here I am, on an epic girl's shopping adventure, and I'm basically alone. I wanted to bring Zoe, but Axel and Forest nipped that in the bud. As did Sam, CJ, Max, and the rest of Alpha team.

Until we know who's in charge of this human-trafficking ring, Zoe stays protected. There's still a man out there with an eye on her.

So, shopping?

The first day, I have a total blast. The second day is still fun, but I lose steam halfway through and beg to go back to the hotel early. Day three and four, I shop for shoes and accessories. I need that. I'm tired of constantly trying on new clothes. On and off. On and off. How many times in one day am I supposed to take my clothes off, only to put them back on?

It's day five and I move on to jewelry. I don't know what Guardian HQ is going to do with all my purchases. Hopefully, they'll use all this stuff for a fundraiser and recoup some of the money, maybe make a bit for a women's charity. I admit to one splurge. Yesterday, I found a flirty red dress with a corset bodice and flared skirt that touches just above my knees. I love the way the fabric flows around my legs but hugs me tight across my waist and chest. What I love best is the way Griff's eyes bugged out when he saw me in it this morning.

"What do you think?" I extend my arm and give a little flap of my hand. The diamond bracelet flashes beneath the megawatt lights in the jewelry store.

"It looks nice, ma'am." Griff, in private security mode, keeps his voice a level monotone. Behind his mirrored sunglasses, I know he's checking out my tits. The wonder of a corseted top is the way it accentuates my curves.

And I'm really having fun teasing him. As my bodyguard, he can't touch me. To say I'm having fun with him is an understatement, and if I'm really lucky, later on tonight, he'll show me exactly what he thinks about my behavior. I'm hoping for a little over the knee action myself, not that I'm begging for it.

But come on.

I'm *begging* for it.

A mischievous grin fills my face as I close the distance between us.

"Oh, come on." I walk over to him and flick my wrist in front of his face. "What do you think?"

"I think it looks expensive, but whatever Miss Stone wants." The corner of his mouth twitches up, but he suppresses the unprofessional emotion. We're not the only people in the store and he has an image to maintain.

"I like expensive things." I hate expensive things, but this is part of the being flashy bit of my role. I do a little twirl, letting the fabric of my dress lift and show off my legs.

When Griff groans, I give a little snicker. Definitely having fun with this game of tease.

Despite the interest I show in the bracelet, I decline to purchase it. Griff holds the door for me as I exit and joins me on the curb. I pretend like I'm trying to decide where to go next, while he closes the gap between us.

"How much longer do we need to do this?" I fix a smile to my face, knowing there's a very small possibility I'm being watched.

At some point, Guardian HQ needs to call this a bust. Maybe, my would-be kidnapper moved on to another girl. I may no longer interest him or not be worth the risk of a requisition.

"A few more days."

"More? It's already been a week." I can't help the petulance in my voice. I'm so *not* a shopper.

"More." He crosses his arms behind his back and stares out at the busy traffic. "This isn't a safe place to stand."

"Why not? You seriously don't think someone will grab me off the street in broad daylight?"

"I've learned to never assume."

"I'm hungry. Do you want to grab something to eat?"

"A bodyguard wouldn't eat with his client."

"Ugh. So many rules!"

"How about that shop?" He points to a dress boutique across the street.

"I'm done for the day."

"It's barely noon. One more shop, then you can lounge around the hotel pool if you want."

"Boring."

"Nobody said this was a glamorous job."

"Fine. One more shop."

Tired of all the shopping, I enter the boutique dress shop with a sigh. Griff follows behind me. First thing, he makes a circuit of the small shop. Behind his mirrored sunglasses, there's no doubt he's checking out all the exits.

Gorgeous dresses from evening gowns to modern cocktail dresses draw my eye. Satin chic to sequined jeweled, the store drips wealth. I disparage ever needing to wear any of the dresses, which makes shopping for one problematic.

My heart isn't in it.

Griff completes his circuit of the store. He glances down a hall leading off the display floor and pushes open the doors to each of the four changing rooms in a nook towards the back.

The older saleswoman watches him, but after his security check is complete, she ignores him in favor of me. I suppose having a bodyguard join a woman during a shopping excursion isn't worthy of her attention. From a quick glance at the price tags on the few dresses I've looked at, I bet the majority of her clients come with a security escort. Griff gives me the okay with a jerk of his chin, then takes up his position by the front of the store.

Other than Griff and myself, there are two other women shopping and just the one sales associate. They don't have fancy escorts like me, but they're flashing haute couture like it's going out of style. Which, when I think about it, is probably true. That kind of stuff comes in and out of fashion with a passing breeze.

I take my time, because I'm killing time, and make my way slowly around the store. Not pushy like some of the other salespeople I've had to deal with this past week, I'm left to myself.

I've learned there are two different kinds of shops. One filled with vultures, eager sales associates who live off their commissions, and stores like this one who leave their customers alone and wait for a signal to assist. This appears to be one of those stores.

The bell at the front dings as a man in an expensive suit walks in. He takes a quick look around, pointedly ignores Griff standing by the door, and moves to the back of the store where the cocktail dresses are gathered.

I pay him no mind, continuing my leisurely stroll around the store. Griff's over-protectiveness aside, I attempt to shed my irritation.

The two women flag the sales associate over. With their arms full of potentials, they eagerly follow the woman to the changing rooms in the back.

Honestly, this whole trip is a waste of time. What are the chances anyone notices me? Despite what everyone at Guardian HRS says, I don't believe I'm *that* special. The man who paid to have me abducted and delivered is more likely to move on to the next shiny thing than waste any more time, money, or frustration on me.

"Excuse me, Miss, but do you have this in a size four?" The man in a suit holds up a black strapless cocktail dress.

"I'm sorry, I don't work here."

"Oh, please forgive me." He takes a step back and lifts his hand in apology.

"It's okay."

"I didn't mean to offend." He glances around the store and blows out his breath. "I'm actually kind of at a loss in here."

"Excuse me?"

"Out of my element."

"Why's that?"

"It's not often I buy a woman a dress." He glances around. "There are too many choices."

"Welcome to the world of women's fashion." I give a soft laugh. I stopped looking for anything specific on day one. Why bother when it doesn't matter what I buy. It's not like I get to keep any of it.

"Agreed, I thought a smaller boutique would be easier, but I'm a bit overwhelmed." He glances around, looking for the saleswoman.

I follow his gaze around the store and notice she's no longer on the floor, but then I see her near the dressing room helping out the other two customers.

"That woman over there works here. She can probably help you."

"Looks like she's going to be busy for a while, and I am on my lunch break." His brows knit together.

I empathize with him. While not much of a shopper myself, I've been subjected to grueling shopping ordeals in the past. Paraded around by my Master of the hour, I've endured the torture that is boutique dress shopping.

Maybe that's why I'm not excited to play this role.

Been here. Done that…

Wow, it's been a long time since that phrase whispered through my head.

"Um, if it wouldn't be too much of an inconvenience, do you think you might help me?"

Cultured and smooth, he's attractive with his short, clipped hair and manicured nails, but a bit flashy with the Rolex and diamond stud cufflinks. Seems a bit pompous for business attire. If I'm not mistaken, his tie pin is a ruby. A bit flashy, but who am I to judge?

As for time, I've got the rest of the afternoon to do nothing. Might as well help him out.

"How can I help?"

"Well, I need to buy a dress for my… For a special woman." The way he says it makes me think not his wife. Mistress maybe? Only there's no ring on his finger. "I plan on collecting her later tonight. I have a very special evening planned. Elegant. Sophisticated. A new beginning for us. I want it to be spectacular. Elegant, but she should be comfortable."

"Do you normally buy her dresses?"

"No…" he shakes his head. "This is actually the first time. Tonight's a surprise. You see, I plan on tying her to me tonight. I've been chasing her for about a year now, and it's time to make things official. More permanent as it were."

"Oh, like a proposal?"

"Something like that." He holds up the black dress. "The only thing is, I'm not sure what kind of dress to buy."

"I see. It can be challenging."

"They look different on the hangers than they do on a woman's body. I don't want to take up too much of your time, but I admit I'm at a total loss here. What would you like to wear, if you were being surprised tonight?"

"Well," I reach for the cocktail dress he holds, "does she have a preference?"

"A preference?"

"You know like loose fitting clothes or ones that hug her body? Does she like short dresses or longer flowing skirts?"

"Definitely tight." The way his cheeks pink up is cute. "She's got an amazing figure and likes to show it off."

"Are you specifically looking for black, or will any color do?"

"I just figured little black dress, but honestly, red is my favorite." His gaze dips down to my red dress and lingers on my cleavage for a beat too long. Suddenly, his attention shifts back up to my eyes. "Sorry, but you are very much like her. I didn't mean to stare. The red looks pretty on you."

"Um, thank you." It's cute how polite he's trying to be. "What's her complexion?"

"Don't think this weird, but she's blond like you, fair skin with the faintest golden glow, almost the same coloring as you."

"Really?"

"Yes, and you're about the same height." His attention shifts to the top of my head as he mentally measures my height. Then it shifts to my body. This time, he doesn't apologize for checking me out. "Not sure, but probably the same size."

"So, red or black?"

"I think red." He gives a shake of his head.

"That dress is strapless. Is that what you're looking for, or does it matter?"

"Whatever is most comfortable." He's cute, like he's trying to be cool. I'm a good bit younger than him. He's at least late forties, maybe early fifties, but fit. The man has not let himself go. He's nothing like my Griff, but his girlfriend certainly has nothing to complain about.

"I'd go with something like this." I pull two red dresses off the display and hold them up. One is a form-fitting sheath dress, with off-the-shoulder sleeves. The other one is similar to what I wear; flowing skirt with capped sleeves, but it glitters with a sequined bodice.

When his brows pinch, confused, I hold the first dress up to my body to help him have an idea what it might look like on his girl. When his eyes shift to the dress matching closest to what I have on, I hold that one in front of myself.

"That one." He picks the sleeveless sheath dress.

"You sure of her size?"

"Fairly certain." He takes the dress from me, then gives a little bow. It's awkward, but cute. "Thank you so much for helping me out. I really am hopeless with this kind of thing."

"Fingers crossed it fits." I hold up my crossed fingers.

"I think it's going to be lovely." His gaze lingers on me a beat too long, but he pulls away before it gets too uncomfortable.

I move off, still absently searching for dresses. A glance toward the door tells me what I already know. Griff watched the entire exchange, his body locking tight, ready to swoop in and save the day.

Nothing here draws my eye, and I head to the front door. "Come on, I'm hungry."

Griff's gaze locks hard on the man I helped. He stands by the register, paying for his purchase.

"Come on. I was just helping the poor guy out. He looked so lost."

"He can get lost someplace else."

"Well, I'm ready to get lost and find somewhere to grab lunch. Surely we can do that."

"Protocol."

"Eating lunch with my bodyguard seems like it comes with the territory. We don't have to act all chummy. You keep your hands to yourself, and I'll keep mine to myself."

Griff flashes a cheeky grin. "I've got a better idea."

"What?"

"How about room service? Then neither of us has to keep our hands to ourselves."

"Hmm…" I twist back and forth, watching the fabric of my skirt swish just above my knees. I know what I'm doing. Each time the skirt lifts up, Griff gets a glimpse of my thighs, and he knows exactly what I'm wearing beneath this dress.

"Come on."

"Snapping orders? I thought you worked for me today, Mr. Bodyguard."

"Damn straight I'm snapping orders. Get your ass in gear, little minx; we have a lunch date."

"We do?"

"Yes, and the first thing I'm feasting on is you." Griff closes in on me. "My bed. Now." His command sends a lick of heat shooting down my spine.

THIRTY-TWO

Moira

I PRACTICALLY DOUBLE-STEP IT BACK TO THE HOTEL. WE PASS KNOX, Liam, and Axel in the hotel lobby, but don't stop. We're not supposed to know them, and they aren't supposed to know us. They're backup in the unlikely event my abductor makes an attempt to grab me, which I don't get. Isn't that the whole point?

Griff herds me into the elevator, acting like the consummate gentleman he is not, but only because of the elderly couple who share our ride to the tenth floor. When the doors open, Griff uses his arm to bar the opening while the couple, and then I, exit.

He trails me down the hall, prowling like a hunter, and drives my anticipation wild. I glance at him as I pull out the key card. He rocks back on his heels, like he doesn't have a care in the world, only Griff is horribly turned on. His hard, long length tents the front of his pants. When my gaze makes it back to his face, he winks.

"Whatcha waiting for?" He grabs himself while I lick my lower lip. "That's right, little minx, I'll be feeding this to you real soon." His eyes darken, half-hooded by his thick lashes, but they do nothing to hide the fire blazing in his violet eyes.

My eyes widen. This is when I should run away, but I press the keycard to the electronic lock and push my way inside. Griff's right behind me and he doesn't wait for the door to close before he's on me.

Gripping the back of my neck, he forces me against the wall. Without preamble, he lowers the zipper at my back and divests me of the dress. I think he's going to kiss me, but Griff only nuzzles my neck, teasing me. When I moan, needing more, his hand comes down on my buttocks.

I tense. Not from pain. Instead, my world lights on fire. He soothes the stinging bite with the sensual glide of his palm. Hypnotic in the way his hand moves, my eyes close to the sinful friction of skin on skin. The burn from his slap makes my pulse sing. The passion of it makes my legs shake, not knowing if that's all he'll give me.

"You like that?" He nuzzles my neck. "You like the burn?"

"Yes."

God yes.

But I'm no fool to ask for more. Griff will more than oblige me, drawing out screams of pleasure as he takes me to a place outside my body. My belly quivers as his talented fingers knead the stinging burn. Trickles of electricity shoot along my nerves, loosening my tense muscles and turning my body to putty in his hands.

He kisses along my neck, massages away the sting in my ass, assaulting my senses in the process. Hot and heavy, my body's under the most wicked and determined attack of a man bent on pleasure. Slowly, inextricably, he wrecks my ability to think as his hands, and those talented fingers, glide over my curves and order my flesh to heat and burn.

"Griff…" I lift on tiptoe as he coaxes out my body's response to his touch. He knows exactly how to touch me, how hard, how soft, how fast, and how slow. My entire body quivers beneath his stealthy attack.

My blood heats at the warm, wet caress of his mouth against my spine. I twist to see behind me, but he swats my ass again. This time harder, more purposeful, more threatening than before.

"Eyes front, little minx."

I press my forehead to the wall as he curls his tongue along my spine. My blood heats as he trails his lips toward the curve of my ass. Sucking and nipping at my flesh, he drives me wild, pulling my insides this way and that as I squirm with the stimulation.

Griff loves to warm up my body. I've never had that before. All men before him took what they wanted with no regard to my physical state, making sex painful more often than not. I thrash beneath Griff's greedy mouth, my body warming and heating with his idea of foreplay.

Suddenly, Griff spins me around to face him. His arresting presence catches my breath. Strong, powerful, brutally beautiful, the harsh lines of his face soften beneath the tenderness in his expression.

He turns his attention from my spine to my breasts, moving from one to the other, kissing, sucking, and nipping at my nipples until I rise on tiptoe beneath the stimulation. I burn beneath the heat of his breath. Mine rushes in and out, frenzied and growing more desperate.

"Griff—please." Not against begging, I need him to touch me.

Every nerve in my body thrums beneath his touch. Hot mouth. Wicked tongue. Devious teeth.

He licks his way down to my hips, the force of his tongue relentless as he slowly, steadily works inch by inch down my body. My fingers curl by my sides, but when I can't stand it anymore, I grasp his hair and tug on the roots.

My entire body trembles as the heat of his breath licks against my folds. When did he get... *Ahhh*. All thought stops as he buries his mouth between my legs.

The scrape of his scruffy beard burns, but I don't care. Awash in pleasure, he ravishes my pussy with the determination of a man on a mission. Plundering. Conquering. He assaults my senses, building the rhythm that drags me up, up, and up. My entire body catches fire, heat everywhere, as he licks faster and probes deeper with that wicked tongue.

"You taste like heaven." His hot breath sears my skin.

Strung out and panting, I'm unable to respond. My body jolts as a sizzling wave breaks over me.

Breaths erratic.

Pulse racing.

The first wave of my orgasm crashes over me as I scream. Raw, sexual heat washes through me, surging within me, as tears swarm in my eyes. My fingers dig into his scalp as he licks and laps me all the way through a merciless orgasm.

"Griff—that was…"

He gathers me in his arms. My legs are shaky and weak, and I don't protest him carrying me to bed. As I recover my senses, he divests himself of his clothes and notches the head of his cock against my folds.

"I love you, Moira Stone." He professes his love with his words and his body. Griff thrusts deep, burying himself to the root as my body twitches with the lingering sparks of my orgasm.

Griff stabs past my opening, pushing deep, driving hard with his hips as he takes me. A strangled groan sounds in the back of my throat as a new orgasm builds. He rocks against me, taking what he wants, picking up speed, as I hang on the best I can.

His grunts sound in my ears. The determination of a man with one singular purpose. He ravages my body, fucking me like an animal. He spreads me wide, pushing my legs as far apart as he can if only to bury himself deeper. He braces over me, not subjecting me to his full weight, but that leaves one hand free. That hand is everywhere, stroking, grasping, pinching, and mauling my breasts.

Wet for him, he glides in and out with slippery, wet strokes, building a rhythm that ignites my body for a second time. I writhe in the most delicious agony beneath him as he moves. A study in perfection and determination, he's fully engaged, but it's more than seeking a physical release.

Physically and emotionally, Griff fucks me like a madman and makes love to me with all the passion of his soul. I feel him everywhere. On top of me. Inside of me. He's burrowing under my skin, taking up residence inside my heart, and delving deep into my core.

"Goddamn, Moira, what you do to me is sinful." He deepens the fevered kisses on my neck as he buries deeper, stretching me to fit his cock. His passion renders me helpless, but I've never felt more in control.

I choose this.

I choose him.

My body jerks with the frantic thrusting of his hips.

"Christ, you're tight. Perfect for me. Hot. Wet. Are you close?"

"Yes." My fingers claw at his back as my pussy clenches around his cock.

His mouth melds with mine, grinding with maddening pressure as his hips move his pelvis against mine. He fists my hair and plunges mercilessly as he groans with the buildup of his release. My insides burn. My nerves sizzle. My skin heats as my entire body shakes. Faster and faster, he moves as pleasure sparks within me.

Our gasps mingle, twisting together. The frantic pace of his thrusts slows, and he rocks his hips differently. Slow, methodical, it's also reverent and surreal. The drag of his cock sliding out sends sparks shooting.

His body shakes. His chest heaves. I break upon him, crying out as another orgasm washes over me. He follows right behind me.

I place the back of my hand to my forehead.

"I think I just died a little there."

He nuzzles my neck. "You look pretty alive to me."

"Only because I have you." I loop my arms around his neck and meet his mouth with mine. "I want to stay here forever."

Griff rolls to his back beside me. "I should've paddled your ass harder after teasing me all day."

"Too late."

"Never too late." His grin should alarm me, but I can only laugh. From the way he's still catching his breath, I have a feeling that will have to wait for another day.

"Later maybe." He closes his eyes and sighs. "I think I'm just going to close my eyes for a second."

A second turns into a minute, then Griff's soft snores sound. I scoot off the bed, unwilling to wake him, and decide what to do about lunch. I could order in, but I decide to stretch my legs and grab something special from the bistro downstairs.

I tiptoe out of the bedroom and get dressed in the main area of the suite. Griff's a light sleeper and I don't want him to wake before I get a chance to surprise him with lunch. Closing the door softly behind me, I exit the suite and head to the elevator. It takes a bit to get to on my floor. Another gentleman joins me, standing off to the side as he checks his watch. Dressed in khakis and a dark polo, he gives me a passing glance, then silently waits with me for the elevator to arrive.

The call bell dings. The elevator doors part. I take a step, but then draw up short. Two very large men stand to either side of the man from the boutique. He smiles at me. It's a Cheshire Cat kind of grin. He looks far too pleased with himself, and boy, do I get an *off* vibe.

"Ah, there she is." A red dress hangs casually from his fingers. "I've been waiting for you."

I take a step back, but the man behind me closes the distance. He blocks my retreat. Before I can react, he grabs my arms, lifts me off my feet, and walks me inside the elevator.

All that fancy training, drilled into me over the past year and hammered into me over the past few weeks, goes right out the window. I struggle, but I'm no match for one man, let alone four. I open my mouth to scream, but the man on the left shoves cloth saturated in a sweet-smelling substance over my face. I inhale the sweet essence of chloroform, something I've experienced before.

No. No. No.

My eyes water and I breathe in the aromatic vapor. I barely register the prick of a needle in my arm. Darkness shrouds my vision as I go limp in their arms.

THIRTY-THREE

Griff
_____

I STIR IN THE BED, STRETCHING MY ARMS OUT WIDE. I FEEL FOR Moira, needing to pull her to me, but my hand finds nothing. Bolting upright, I take in the room. The bed is a mess of twisted sheets, evidence of our lovemaking, but there's no Moira.

How long was I out?

I remember feeling amazing after sex, filled with bone-deep contentment having Moira in my life, in my bed, and firmly entrenched in my heart. I see our future spreading before us and can't wait for it to begin.

"Moira?" I rub my fingers through my hair and wipe my face with my hands. Getting up, I check the bathroom. The door's open and the light's out.

"Moira?" I call out, worried this time, as a tingling sensation trickles down my spine. Rushing into the outer room, there is no sign of Moira.

As I throw on my clothes, I call my team.

"Yo!" Axel answers.

"Moira's gone."

"Copy that." Axel doesn't ask bullshit questions like "how do I know," but gets exactly what I mean. "Searching now."

He and the rest of my team will make a sweep of the lobby, checking out elevators and stairwells while I canvas the tenth floor and the floors above and below.

Once dressed, I race outside. There's not much to check. The hallway is long and devoid of any sign of Moira. I jab at the elevator and tap my foot as I wait for it to arrive. "Where are you, little minx?"

My phone vibrates. I glance at the screen and growl. Liam located Moira's bracelet in the elevator. No way in hell would she take it off, and there's no way for it to fall off accidentally.

Even though this is part of our plan, I'm not prepared for the intense fear churning in my gut. I remind myself what's important as I wait for the goddamn elevator to arrive. Why is it taking so damn long!

First things first, they want Moira alive. I take a deep breath. She's safe for the moment. Second, Moira's kickass in all things. She can hold her own.

But only if nobody gets their hands on her.

Jenny's right about one thing. Once a larger opponent, insert *man* here, gets a hold of a smaller opponent, *a woman*, the fight is all but over.

Jenny could probably work her way free of a chokehold or arm bar. Charlie could too. Some of Moira's training drilled escape from those holds as well, but when adding in fear, and there's no doubt in my mind Moira is scared to death, that kind of training rarely sticks. It's simply not ingrained into Moira's muscle memory.

Sure as shit, you can bet that's the first thing we'll work on from here on out. Finally, the elevator dings and I race inside. Stabbing the "close door" button, I once again curse about how slow the damn elevator moves.

When I get downstairs, my team is there. We exchange one look and move into operation mode. There's no breath wasted on asking how I'm feeling. They know I'm out for blood. From the way they return my stare, they're feeling lethal too.

"Situation." I press my palms to the side of my legs, wiping the nervous perspiration off. That's an emotion I don't need, and I lock it down tight. Until this op finishes, I'm laser-focused on the goal.

"Mitzy is tracking." Liam glances up from his phone. "Moira made it to the elevator. Found her bracelet there. These guys are smart and knew to look."

"Let's hope that's where they stop looking."

"Facial recognition is in play. Waiting on security footage. Knox and Wolfe went to grab it." Max fills in the gaps, letting me know what's been done. "Moira's on the move."

A low growl rumbles from my throat. "And our orders?"

"Follow. Do not engage." Max holds my eye for a beat, ensuring I hear the orders.

I know the plan. We've drilled it countless times. Our objective is the man, or men, who took Moira. Recovering her is the secondary objective. I take offense to that, but the operational goal is to gather intelligence. Moira comes second to that goal. To me, she's the priority. Max is simply giving a gentle reminder of the long game.

Bottom line, we need access to the organization.

"Axel?" My best bud isn't here.

"Bringing the car around." Max strides off toward the entrance. I follow without missing a beat.

Right now, I'm going after my girl.

We're going after my girl.

I wouldn't want any other men by my side. Brothers sealed together by the heat of battle, we've spilled beer and blood between us, depending on how shitty the day. We are a team. My problems are their problems. And their support is the only reason I'm not losing my shit right now.

Just knowing they've got their hands on her… again, tears me up inside.

The three of us crowd into the SUV Axel brings around front. Wolfe and Knox will join us later. Liam props a table on his lap. On it is a map of the city and a tiny red dot. The dot is moving.

Axel pulls out, eyes on the road, fingers gripping the wheel. He feels the same as me and knows exactly how it feels to have his woman in enemy hands. Conversation is kept to a minimum. Max talks to HQ while Axel races to close the distance. They've got a ten minute lead on us.

Meanwhile, I pull out weapons from the back of the car and distribute them to my team. The metallic sound of the slides racking a round in the chamber fills the interior of the vehicle. After the weapons, I pull out the vests, passing those out too. When we stop, wherever we stop, we'll be ready.

What we won't be is obvious. In another upgrade from military life, our body armor looks like normal street wear, courtesy of Mitzy's tech team. After putting on his gear, Liam holds the wheel as Axel shoulders into his tactical vest.

"Lost the earring," Liam calls out an update, "shifting to tertiary tracker."

"Damn, these guys are thorough." Max grits his teeth.

We all expected Moira to lose the bracelet early on, but the earring should've passed a cursory inspection. Her abductors are probably divesting her of anything that could hold a tracker. It's what I would do if our roles were reversed. Bile coats the back of my throat because *divesting* Moira of trackers means they're likely stripping her of all her jewelry, clothes, and shoes. The thought of them pawing over my girl brings on a murderous rage.

"Lock it down." Max's command snaps through the air. He takes me in, knowing exactly what's going on in my head. "Mission focus."

"Copy that."

He's right. Emotions during an op are liabilities, more likely to result in negative results than achieving mission objective. I inhale and lock up my rage. I shove that shit far back in my head where I'll unpack it later.

"You good?" he pushes.

"I'm good."

"Right." He points toward the tablet Liam balances on his knees. "Still got the tracker in her arm."

"Any idea where they're headed?"

"Airport," Axel responds. He's got an eye on the road, one on the GPS, and a third eye on Liam's tablet. I'm more interested in Axel's uncanny ability to read a situation.

"No surprise." I draw in another deep breath. Too much rage lingers in my blood. Gotta tamp that shit down or I'll be a liability to my team. I close my eyes.

"They're not in a rush," Axel continues.

I only hear what he doesn't say. We have time.

Max puts his phone to his ear and relays what Axel says. A brief exchange follows as he gets the tech team involved. He lowers the phone. "Knox and Wolfe are on their way. Five minutes behind us."

I breathe out, calming my nerves and getting a hold on my emotions. If Knox and Wolfe are inbound, they retrieved the security footage. It's only a matter of time before we know who we're dealing with.

Max glances over at me and I nod. I'm doing good. Back in control. His phone rings again. This time, he puts it on speaker.

"You're on speaker."

"Good." Mitzy's high-pitched voice rings clearly through the phone. "Four men. One waited for her by the elevator. Forced her inside. They exited on the second floor, carrying her. We tracked them to the garage. Made no effort to conceal their identities. Will have more info later. Your vehicle is a black SUV." She reads off the make, model, and tags from the security footage in the garage.

"Axel thinks they're headed to the airport. Any way to get us intel on that?"

"Any way?" Mitzy snorts. "I'll have the tail number to you ASAP." With that, she ends the call.

"How long?" Max asks.

"Fifteen minutes."

"All right. Let's go. Hit me with ideas." Max sits back while we volley different ideas back and forth. This is the tricky part. In setting up this operation, there was no way to know where Moira would be taken.

At least we have a good idea where.

The only question now is how to get to her before that plane takes off?

THIRTY-FOUR

Moira

I WAKE IN THE BACK OF A MOVING VEHICLE, LIKE THIRD ROW BACK OF an SUV. My head rests on someone's lap and pounds with the worst headache ever.

Well, maybe not the worst. Dead Man Jack gave my skull a beating. Bossman tried. Shelly kept tapping my head with his steel-tipped toe. One thing unites all those men.

They're all dead. By my hand, or my actions, they no longer walk the world of the living.

It seems I'm doomed to forever be waking up as some man's captive. It happened at sixteen, again not too many weeks ago with the Bossman/Shelly duo, and now again with this asshole.

"Ah, princess, you're waking up." A strange hand brushes the hair out of my eyes. I give a start, but he holds me down with an arm made of iron.

"Where am I?" It feels like there's a dense fog between me and the world. I have to claw my way out, but I swear I recognize that voice. There's something else I recognize as well; the feeling of my hands zip-tied together.

I hate this shitty life.

But I'm no longer alone. I feel for my bracelet and squeeze my eyes together when I notice it's gone. No way for me to check my ears, but from the way this bastard has my head pressed into his muscular thigh, I have a feeling my earrings are gone too. And the fabric of my dress is different. A quick check reveals what my brain already put together.

"Where are you taking me?"

"Why, princess, I'm taking you home." He releases me from the lock of his arm and gives a light swat to my ass. Like, a really light swat. "Let's try to mind our language, shall we?"

Language? I didn't swear, curse, or ask anything but a simple question.

His comment is not only weird, it's creepy. Smooth and cultured, there's no anger in his voice. In fact, he sounds like a creepy Mr. Rogers, only I'm one hundred percent sure I want nothing to do with his *neighborhood.*

"Who are you?" I should ask what he's doing kidnapping me, but we'll get to that in a moment.

"You don't remember me, princess?"

Gah, the way he says *princess* makes me want to hurl.

"Let me up." I push against him and I'm surprised when he lets me go. I scoot over, placing distance between us. He simply stares at me and that creepy smile of his grows wider.

A quick check of my surroundings does nothing to ease my fear. There's nowhere to go. No place to hide. I'm in the back row of an SUV. Two massive men sit in the bench seat in front of me. Creepy Mr. Rogers sits beside me. And there's a driver. Also, male. Also, huge.

What is it with all these massively huge men?

Muscle. That's what they are. I take a look at my dress, not in the least surprised that it's the one I helped the man beside me pick out for "his woman." His words come back to me, and I can't believe I missed it.

I need to buy a dress for my... For a special woman.

Tonight's a surprise.

I plan on tying her to me tonight.

I've been chasing her for about a year now.

Wait? A year? That makes no sense. I mean, I get if he's been after me since my abduction in Santa Monica, but a year? That means he knows me from before; from when I was a slave to a man called Snowden.

I don't remember being lent out to this man. I know the face of every bastard who ever took me against my will. This is not one of them. I take a moment to study him and make no secret of the way I take him in.

"You don't remember me, do you?" He stretches his arm over the back of the seat and gives me a come-hither gesture with his free hand. I look at where he wants me to go and give a shake of my head.

No way am I cozying up to you, buddy.

The expression on his face twists. "Now, is that the way to behave?" He taps the spot beside him. "And after I've gone to the trouble to buy you that pretty dress? It looks amazing on you, by the way." His gaze sweeps to my bare legs and bare feet.

I'm not even going to think about *how* I got out of my clothes and into this dress.

He pats the spot beside him again. "Come now. Sit beside your daddy. I'm going to tell you how I'm going to be taking great care of you."

Daddy?

I just vomited in the back of my mouth. Men with daddy/daughter fantasies are the worst.

"You're not my daddy."

His eyes pinch. "Well, that's a decision you'll have to make now, isn't it, princess?"

"Huh?"

"Would you rather I be your daddy and take really good care of you, or…" I'm pretty sure I'm not going to like whatever it is he's going to say next. He certainly gives me enough time to think about it. "Do you prefer *Master?*" His lips twist into a snarl. "I have no problem tying you up and shoving you in a cage. A bit of fight can be fun, but I suggest we start off on a different foot."

"And what foot would that be?"

"A lovely little princess behaving like a doll."

Fuck. Now we're into the living doll fantasy. Whacked in the head does not do this man's crazy justice. But I'm not dumb. And I've played this game before. It twists my stomach, but playing the young little girl kept me alive for four years on the street. That sour taste in the back of my mouth returns.

I take a moment, weighing all my options, and I must say they are lacking. But for the first time in my life, I'm not alone. All I need is to buy time.

Time for Griff to find me.

Besides, if I'm too eager, Creepy Mr. Rogers will suspect something's up. I lift my bound hands to my mouth and pretend that I'm wiping my cheeks. His hawkish gaze follows my every move.

"Oh, don't worry. Your friends won't be troubling us."

"My friends?"

"Yes, darling. Those men who think to keep you from me." He points to my wrist. "I'm well aware of the tracking chips they put on you. That's why we stripped you down and removed anything that might be a bother."

A bother? To him maybe, but not to me.

"Who are you?"

"Princess." He pats the spot next to him. "I don't mind answering your questions, but I do demand an obedient little girl. You really don't want to earn a punishment." From the way his eyes gleam, I readjust my initial impression of the man. He's a sociopath, and this daddy/daughter thing is not what he's into. This is a man who likes to play games—mindfuck games in particular. He wants to play this little girl/princess routine until I grow comfortable with him and lose my fear. That's when he'll toss me in the cage and the real torture will begin.

Dude, I read you like an open book. And I want nothing to do with you.

"Now, princess…" The way he says that pulls my shoulders to my ears. "I'm going to ask you this once and only once. Your answer is important. Your truthfulness is vital. Do you understand?"

"No." I have no idea what he's talking about.

He pats the seat behind him yet again. This time when he looks at me, I see the madness dancing in his eyes.

"It's a simple question." His head cocks to the side like he's the most patient man in the world. "Are you carrying any other tracking devices?" When I begin to shake my head, he holds up a finger and shushes me. "Carrying them on your person, or in your person? I really don't want to have to carve you up so soon. I have a scanner at the hanger, but it's best if you tell me now. I don't appreciate little girls who tell lies."

Holy shit, but he's terrifying, and I have no doubt he doesn't appreciate that at all. I've known men like him before. I've served men like him before. But I've never been owned by a man like him before.

When I was a slave, it was common to be lent out to guests as their entertainment for the night. I've been forced to do some pretty sick and twisted things, but in the back of my head, I always knew I was only on loan. My Master didn't like his slaves returning to him damaged. That's probably the only thing that kept me alive for so long.

This nut job? There's nothing standing between me and his madness.

Nothing that is except my training and the plan we put together at Guardian HQ.

Skye's words come back to me. *One to find and one to hide.*

I gulp and look at the spot beside him. The place where, if I value my life, I will soon be sliding into. But not too fast.

Keeping my voice meek, I scoot further away from him, drawing up my knees and huddling into myself, just like a little girl would do. Damn, but this creeps me out.

I lift my bound hands and point to my left shoulder. "They put something in my arm."

"A tracking device?"

I shrug. "I dunno." Slowly, my speech patterns change as I take on the persona of my twelve-year-old self. "But there's something under the skin."

"Come here, princess." He leans toward me. "Let's see what those mean people did to you."

My brows knit together and I nibble at my lower lip. When I look at him, I do it from beneath the fluttering of my lashes.

"I'm not going to hurt you. You're daddy's little princess. All I want to do is take care of you."

I take my time, but slowly I take the bait and close the distance between us. I sit beside him, not touching, and hold my hands in my lap. Of course, I hold them. He's got them bound with a damn zip-tie.

He brings his arm down, curling it around my shoulders, and tugs me tight against him. Sickly sweet, there's an odor to him that makes me want to retch, but I tamp that down.

"Show me." His voice takes on an edge and I show him where the tracker is embedded in my arm. "Good girl." He finds the small lump under my skin. "George…"

He pins me viciously against him, I squirm in his grip, but I'm no match for him. The two men sitting in front of us spin around and lean over the back of their seat. One of them helps Crazy Mr. Rogers hold me down, while the other one flicks open a wicked-assed blade.

I scream as he pinches my arm and slices my skin. Pain rips through me as he digs the tip of the knife in my arm. I suddenly realize thrashing around may not be in my best interest.

My struggles cease, and I pant against the pain as he digs. Finally, blessedly, he locates the tracker and excises it from my flesh. Crazy Mr. Rodgers pats my shoulder.

"There now. See? That wasn't so bad. And you deserve something special for being so very honest with me." He holds out his hand. The man with the knife passes over a bandage, one of those big square adhesive things. Mr. Crazy places the bandage and even leans down to "kiss it to make it better."

I swear, if Griff and the rest of Alpha team don't get here soon, I'm going to hurl like there's no tomorrow. In fact, I'd love to barf on Crazy Mr. Rogers. I won't. Because, you know—self-preservation leads to survival, and survival is my jam.

I should be more terrified, but frankly, I'm pissed.

Been here. Done that. Please just for once, I'd love a surprise. I don't want the damn scars. I want a medal. A freakin' survivors' medal. And I want off this damn merry-go-round. I'm tired. I'm just tired.

The man with the knife opens a window and tosses out the tiny tracking device. My entire body sags in defeat. I have just the one tracker left, but I can only use it in extreme circumstances. If this crazy man really does have a detector at the hangar, I can't risk turning on the tracker behind my ear.

Hanger means airplanes. As much as it sickens me to think about it, I need to keep my last tracker in reserve for when we get to wherever it is we're going.

"Now, we don't have to worry about any of those men ruining our fun. Do we?" He hugs me to his chest, and I let him.

I curl against him like a little girl clinging to her daddy as my gut churns and acid rises in the back of my throat. Meanwhile, I plan my escape.

There are four of them and one of me. I see no way out of this mess, but I'm a survivor. Somehow, I'll find a way through this. We pull off the main highway and into a steady stream of people headed toward the airport. Prominent signs point the way to Arrivals and Departures, but we take an access road, heading to the private side of the airport.

We pass rows and rows of industrial hangars, some prominently marked with well-known shipping giants. Others are less well marked. The hangar we pull into has no signage on the front. The SUV pulls to a stop. The men pile out. Crazy Mr. Rogers gives me a little shove, and I slowly crawl out of the back seat and exit the vehicle. Tweedle-Dee and Tweedle-Dum bracket me the moment I'm out of the car. One grabs my left arm. The other grabs my right. They march me forward to let Crazy Mr. Rogers out of the vehicle.

He takes my arm. Tweedle-Dee and Tweedle-Dum step aside, and all civilized like, we walk toward a waiting plane.

The urge to run overwhelms me, but there's no way to activate the last tracker. I missed my opportunity.

I hate my life. Absolutely hate it.

The driver of the vehicle, who walks in front of us, suddenly smacks the side of his neck. He stumbles and pulls something looking like a feather out of his neck. He turns around, eyes wide, and collapses on the ground.

Tweedle-Dee and Tweedle-Dum draw their weapons, but then they slap hand to neck. This time, because they're closer, the tiny darts are visible. Their jaws drop. Their limbs twitch. They stagger and fall.

Mr. Crazy grabs me tight, pressing my back to his chest. He whirls around, facing the unknown threat, and puts a knife to my throat.

"I'll kill her!" He backs up toward the small jet.

The stairs are down. A man peeks out from the opening. I'm dragged backward.

Hot. Stinging. The knife slices my skin. I close my eyes and hold back a whimper. Blood drips down my neck. For now, it's only a flesh wound, but it won't take much for that to change.

"You're done, Townsend. Let the girl go." My eyes snap open with the unmistakable sound of Griff's voice.

Our gazes lock. He holds up a weird-looking gun and feeds me strength across the impossible distance separating us.

THIRTY-FIVE

Griff

DEAD COLD INSIDE, I ERASE MY EMOTIONS. ALL THAT ANGER? Banked. Fear for Moira's safety? Can't deal with that shit right now. Fury for the prick who has his hands on my woman? Oh, that's a boiling hot rage, but I sweep even that aside.

I hold my weapon steady.

Axel takes out the lead man with a tranq dart. The man drops like a load of bricks.

Fucking love that moment of surprise on his face. I shoot the man on the right while Axel takes out the other guard.

That leaves one man standing.

Julian Townsend holds a knife to Moira's throat. His arm wraps around her, pinning her arms down. He walks backward, eyes spitting venom, toward the waiting jet. No way in hell is that getting off the ground. Max and Liam have a bead on the open door. Anyone who so much as breaks wind gets a bullet between the eyes.

I'd shoot Townsend, except he uses Moira as cover. She needs to open up the shot for me. As much as we trained her, there is so much she doesn't know about how a team works.

Come on, Moira! You can do it.

We've practiced these moves hundreds of times. Over the past year, I worked her hard, teaching her Krav Maga with the rest of the rescuees at the Facility. She knows all the ways to escape a chokehold.

She knows what to do.

As for Townsend, the only reason he still breathes is because we don't have a kill order. That means we use tranquilizer guns.

Our mission objective is information. Can't get information out of corpses.

Axel stores his spent tranquilizer gun and draws his weapon. He's got a bead on Townsend's head. The little red dot holds dead steady. Axel is a fantastic shot.

One shot.

That's all it'll take to bring the man down.

Only, we can't.

I need him alive. He and I have a date. Just him and me. And Townsend is going to tell me all the shit he doesn't want to share.

Max, Liam, and Axel fan out to either side. There's no chance for stealth, so we didn't bother. We lost Moira's tracker a few miles back. From the bandage on her arm, I know why. Townsend will pay for that.

Wolfe and Knox are a few minutes behind us.

Come on, Moira.

I will her to read my mind.

Her eyes round with fear and she lets Townsend drag her back. How do I get her to understand?

Either she frees herself and gives me the shot, or Max is going to put a real bullet in Townsend's head. That will be followed by Axel and Liam. Then we have a corpse unable to spill any secrets.

Running out of time, inspiration strikes.

I take my left hand and place it at my throat. I keep a bead on my target with my free hand.

Moira's gaze tracks my movement.

Good girl.

Violently, I rip my hand away from my throat. If she doesn't understand, we'll have a dead man to interrogate. There are the three semi-stiffs on the ground. The tranqs will keep them down for another hour. More than enough time to mop this up. But I don't want them.

I need Townsend.

Fear simmers in Moira's gaze, but then her brows pinch. With her arms trapped in Townsend's grip, it's going to be difficult. But I've trained her.

She can do it.

Come on, minx!

I urge her with my eyes, hoping she understands.

Axel knows what I'm doing. Max and Liam get it too. But then, we work as a team and practically read each other thoughts.

Blood oozes from the cut at her neck, but it's not serious. She'll have to overcome her fear.

You gotta lean into that knife, minx. Come on…

I gesture again. Hand to throat. Then a sharp drop.

Moira's entire body stills. She blinks three times, deliberately, and with intention. No need to signal to Axel and the other guys.

They've been watching our silent exchange.

Moira's head snaps back. She clocks Townsend in the jaw. His head snaps back, and his grip on the knife loosens. Before he can compensate, she stomps on his foot and violently flexes at the waist. This frees her elbows. Moira jabs him in the gut.

One. Two.

She twists out of his grip. As his head whips forward, she clocks him in the jaw with the heel of her palm. His neck whips backward again. She takes the opening. Grabs his shoulders. Knees him in the groin.

Moira should move.

"RUN!"

Townsend stumbles back and cups his groin. Instead of retreating, Moira pushes him, using her body weight to force Townsend to stumble backward. She sweeps his feet out from under him. He cartwheels back and falls on his ass.

They finally separate.

Instead of running, she searches the ground.

I aim, but she steps in front of my shot.

"Shit."

Axel, Max, and Liam are on the move, sprinting across the tarmac.

Moira bends down. Grabs something. Then lifts her arm and points a gun at Townsend.

His eyes widen and he defends with his hands.

"Shit." With a curse, I lower my weapon and join my team.

Boots sound behind me. Wolfe and Knox are here.

"Moira! We need him alive."

My shout draws her attention. In that split second, Townsend launches forward. He grabs her ankles and yanks her off her feet. She falls flat on her back, and a loud *crack* sounds as the back of her head hits pavement.

Two shots go off.

No need to look.

Axel and Max disable Townsend, shooting him in his thighs. Another shot sends the weapon Moira held skittering across the asphalt.

I kick it further away as I race to my girl.

Axel stands over Townsend. Expression lethal. Face livid red.

Moira's my girl, but she's one of us now. She's a member of our team. Max and Liam sprint for the plane. We've encountered no resistance from there, which leads me to think Townsend left none off his muscle behind.

I kneel beside Moira and gather her in my arms. Limp, her head rolls back. I cup her head against my chest and feel sticky wetness in her hair.

Shit.

"Moira." I drag her back. Putting distance between her and the other men. Once safely away, I rock her in my arms.

Knox joins me. He does a quick assessment of her head. "She's good." He rips a bandage out of his pocket and gives it to me. "Hold pressure."

Max and Liam march the pilot from the plane. Hand on his head, he blabbers nonsense.

"How is she?" Max comes up to me, and I don't know what to say.

"Griff?" Moira's shaky voice is like a choir of angels singing from above. Something happens inside of me. My heart swells. And I crack a smile.

"Minx?"

Her lids flutter and she looks at me. "I want to kill him." She's not fooling around.

I let her go, but then grab her shoulders and force her to look me in the eyes.

"No."

"It's my right." She struggles, pushing me away. Frantically, she casts around. When she focuses on the weapon Axel kicked to the side, I realize she's not kidding.

I'd shake her, but she might have a concussion. Instead, I grip her chin and force her to look at me. "Let me bear this burden for you."

"He's mine."

"You've done enough. Look, minx, we need to get information from him. That's what I do. You don't need to carry the stain of his life on your soul."

"It's my right."

"And mine. Let me carry this burden. It's what a man does for the woman he loves." I implore her to let me carry that mark on my soul.

"I've killed before." Her voice fades.

"You take his life now, when he's been kicked to the ground, that's a different kind of mark. Trust me, minx, you don't want that blackening your soul."

"But you do?"

"To avenge my wife? You bet."

"Your wife?"

"You heard me." I take her hands in mine and draw her to me. "I thought I made that clear."

"I didn't think…" She wipes a tear from her cheek and looks at Townsend.

Axel, Wolfe, and Knox know their shit. It's not accidental that they block Moira's view. The last thing she needs to see is that man spitting venom in her direction.

"Me and Townsend are going to have a chat. And I promise, he'll never hurt another person in his lifetime."

Townsend's life is measured in hours. The faster he spills his secrets, the less he'll suffer, but if it takes days, I don't mind.

Right now, that's not my priority. I've got the woman I love in my arms, and I'm taking her away from all this shit.

"Wolfe." I bark out his name.

Wolfe doesn't bother to ask what I want. He knows. I catch the keys to the vehicle he and Knox drove and leave my team to clean up the mess. Moira and I have other, more pressing, things to take care of, such as how fast I can tie her to me and put a ring on her finger.

Once we're away from the guys, I grab Moira's hand. "How do you feel?"

"I'm tired of getting knocked in the head."

I press my lips together. "How about…"

"What?"

"You ready to become my wife?"

"Hell, yes! But there's one thing I need to know."

"Anything."

"Is Griff your real name?"

I throw my head back and laugh. Pulling her hand to my lips, I kiss the back of her knuckles.

"It is."

"Griff? Your name is really Griff?" She looks like she doesn't believe me. "I thought it was some cool-assed nickname."

"My first name is Griffen."

"Griffen?" She looks like she doesn't believe me. "And your last?"

"Morningstar."

"You're kidding me. Griffen Morningstar? Did your parents hate you?"

"No. They loved me very much. Enough to curse me with the worst name ever. When it came time to passing out names, nobody could do better than Griffen."

"There is so much about you I want to learn."

"Before or after I put a ring on that finger? Because I have to say, I've waited long enough."

Moira cups my cheeks. "I cannot wait to become Moira Morningstar, but you need to make me a promise."

"Anything."

Moira stops and turns back around. "I want him to suffer."

I hate the pain echoing in her voice. I hate everything she's endured. Moira deserves a happy life, and I vow to fill her life with more smiles than frowns. I want to hear her laugh. I imagine it's the most beautiful sound in the world.

"Don't worry about Townsend."

"Why?"

"Because I'm very good at that part of my job."

"Oh." She takes a long look at me, then smiles.

"Forever and always, you're mine." I take her in my arms and hold the woman I can't wait to make my wife.

"Yours, forever and always." Moira spins around and I take her hand in mine.

With Townsend ours, we have one more piece to the puzzle, but there's still much work to be done.

THIRTY-SIX

Eve

---

2 Months ago

Helplessness is my new normal.

If not for the protection of my Deverough name, nothing would separate me from the others trapped in this living hell. I walk around free, the *honored* guest of Tomas Benefield, a man who makes his living ruining human lives, while they endure horror upon horror. It's been five weeks of living hell and I don't think I can survive much more.

"Miss Deverough…" One of the guards pokes his head inside my room.

"Yes?"

"Mr. Benefield requests your presence."

Orders are given and I obey. I'm but one step from a slave. The other girls are slaves. I'm going to say that again, because I can't believe something like this exists.

They are slaves.

Those girls are trained and sold like chattel. They're nothing more than a commodity moving through the despicable industry of sex trafficking. There's no humanity in this godforsaken place. There's no escape.

I tap my foot and my knee bounces with nervousness. Sitting in front of the makeup mirror, I make myself beautiful for a monster.

I make myself beautiful… I give a sharp shake of my head, but it doesn't help. This isn't a dream. It's all too real.

This is my new life, a living horror show. Unlike the girls, however, I'm treated as a guest. Although an uncomfortable shift hangs in the air. It's been five weeks. Five long weeks waiting for the ransom demand to be met.

"I'm just finishing up."

The guard kicks his heel against the doorjamb. "Now, Miss Deverough."

"Of course." I deliberately set down my makeup brush, making it look like my compliance is my wish rather than Benefield's demand. "Where will I find him?"

"His office."

"Thank you." I glance into the mirror, catching the guard's eye in the reflective glass.

He holds my eye for a moment, then turns with a derisive snort. None of the guards are allowed to touch me, and it irritates them. It's a very small freedom, and I cling desperately to it.

For weeks, Tomas Benefield tells me he will let me go, yet here I remain; his *special guest.*

It's all an act, me getting dressed like I'm going out for a night on the town.

While the guard waits, I take one last look in the mirror and put on my game face. Turning with a false smile, I rise gracefully and walk out of my room as if it's my choice to do so.

The guard follows. He'll trail discreetly behind me, ensuring I don't make a break for it. Like there's anywhere to go.

Ignoring him, I begin the long trek to Benefield's office.

We pass a multitude of girls, all in training, performing their domestic chores; cleaning, polishing, vacuuming, and more. They do it without clothes. Clothing is a reward which must be earned.

They look at me, or rather through me, with heart-wrenching vacancy in their eyes. Their innocence fled, along with any hope, or any dreams they may have had for a life they will never get to lead.

Trafficked for their beauty, they're among the taken. I am too, but I was kidnapped and I'm being held for ransom. Those girls come from homes without the resources to buy their freedom. I, on the other hand, come from wealth.

The Deverough name is well known in the shipping industry, and my father commands the resources needed to break me free of this madness.

But something's not right.

The Retreat, which is now my prison, is beyond extravagant. It's a massive display of one man's wealth and the power he wields.

Luscious vegetation spills out of manicured flower beds set in interior courtyards. Fountains cast architecturally designed sprays of water into complex designs. Colorful birds squawk in their lavish cages. They're prisoners just like me.

Stone archways sit atop intricate columns and line the exterior of the courtyard. Between the columns, frescos of impressive artistic talent draw the eye. There's even a butterfly and hummingbird enclosure for the guests to enjoy.

So much money.

I thought the Deverough's commanded wealth, but this is beyond comprehension.

Outside Benefield's office, I take in a deep breath and brace myself. A knock on the door is initially met with silence, but then his gruff voice calls out.

"Come."

I push on the door, but the guard behind me places his palm on the rough wood and forces it open. I step under his arm and into Benefield's domain.

A sigh of relief escapes me. It's just him. No naked slaves with vacant stares.

"You wanted to see me?"

"Yes, my dear. Come over here, where the light is brightest." He points to a window. My stomach sinks when he grabs a newspaper.

I move woodenly to where he instructs and wait.

"Take this." He hands me the local paper. Everything's in Spanish. I don't know the language, but I can see the date. "Hold it up, just under your chin."

May 7th.

This marks the third time he's made me hold up a newspaper while he snaps a photo of me.

"Smile, luv." He holds up his phone. "You can do better. Your father will want to know I'm treating his little girl well."

I'm not a little girl. I'm twenty-two. I smile for the photograph while my hands shake and make the newspaper rustle.

"Ah, now that is a good shot. You have the most amazing eyes." He takes a step toward me while I force myself not to take a step back. Benefield thrives on fear and I won't give him any more than absolutely necessary. "Let's get a closeup of that date. Hold the paper next to your eyes and smile."

I do as Benefield commands.

"One. Two. Three. Say cheese!" He snaps more than one photograph, then takes a moment to look at them on his phone. "Yes, yes, this will do nicely." He holds his hand out, palm up, and I give him the newspaper.

I want to ask why my father isn't paying the ransom, but I keep my lips pressed into the best false smile I can manage. The first photograph was taken one week after my abduction. The second, I think they call it a *proof of life* photo on the television shows I watch, was taken after spending three weeks in this hellish place. It's been a little over a month now and I can't help but wonder.

Why aren't you paying the ransom?

I don't understand what's going on. My father might be many things. Our relationship is beyond strained, but he would never intentionally leave me in a place like this.

Icy tendrils creep down my spine. Is my father not meeting Benefield's ransom demands?

Is Benefield holding out for a larger payday?

I don't know what's happening and it's driving me insane.

Five weeks.

Too many days come and too many days go. Days turn to weeks and weeks turn to months. I'm the captive of a madman with a silver tongue speaking a mouthful of lies.

Five weeks is one week longer than the span of time a girl suffers beneath this roof. They spend one month being trained, sexually abused, and physically beaten, until any fight within them dies. Misery unites them, and maybe that gives them strength? Or maybe it steals their hope?

I wouldn't know. I'm not one of them.

Yet. I'm not one of them...yet.

Nevertheless, each day is a living nightmare and I wonder when my status will change. When will I become one of them?

The longer I'm here, the more I believe I'm never escaping this nightmare. But if I do, I'll make it my life's work to bring men like this down. Whatever it takes, I'll learn how to fight. I'll learn how to win. Justice will be served.

But first, I need to survive. I need to find a way out of here. If I don't, my future is written in the leering stares of the guards I pass, and in the frank admiration from the guests when I'm near.

The guests.

How to describe those lecherous bastards? Too rich and too bored, they'd rather destroy a life than find a woman willing to stand by their side. They're rotten people. Rotten men inside and out.

Reality is slowly settling in and I don't like my options. My heart rattles around inside my ribcage. Spurred to restless agitation by yet another ransom demand.

"You may go." With a flick of his wrist, I'm dismissed. Before I reach the doorway, he calls out. "Do not be late for dinner, my love. I expect you to be on time."

"Yes, of course." I take great care to be early to those hideous meals, but I was a minute late last night.

"My guests enjoy your company."

I'm sure they *do not*. His guests make my stomach churn.

"You should relax in the spa this afternoon. You look stressed." His brows pinch together, and if I didn't know better, I'd say he really was concerned about my mental state of mind.

He's not. Benefield is a monster.

As for me, tension swirls on every breath and surges with chaotic energy in my veins. It knots between my shoulder blades and climbs up the back of my neck where it settles, making my head pound with the beginning of a migraine.

"That sounds wonderful. Thank you."

I hate the spa. It's only ever used by the girls who are being put up for auction. Benefield wants them looking their best as he sells them to the highest bidder.

I'd refuse, but I know better than to upset my monstrous host.

As I make my way to the spa, I walk on pins and needles, doing everything in my power not to be noticed, which is silly.

Everybody notices me.

I've been singled out for special treatment, deference extended to me where it's not for any of the other girls.

Unable to get over the feeling my fortune is shifting from bad to worse, I'm on edge and the fear I battle each and every day takes on a sharper edge.

It digs in and takes root.

I feel it in the air—a change coming—it swirls around me infesting the cloying humidity that thickens each breath. It lingers in the oppressive tropical heat and saps my strength.

I cross an extravagant courtyard, guard in tow. Landscaped to perfection, my surroundings display the opulence and power of the owner.

I'm a captive within a secret compound, hidden somewhere in the forests of a tropical paradise. I believe I'm in Colombia. At least that's where the shipping container arrived.

The shipping container.

Thirteen of us endured a tortuous journey locked inside a cargo container. Opened once a day to provide meager rations of food and water, and to remove a foul bucket of waste, we survived only to endure what came next.

After making port in Colombia, half were loaded onto the back of one truck, and the rest were loaded onto the back of another. I have no idea what happened to the seven girls in that other truck, but I know what happened to the five who went with me.

We came here.

Over the next three weeks, those girls were tortured, trained, and forced to serve. They learned how to serve the needs of monstrous men and how to turn their anger, fear, and hatred, into docile obedience. One month later, they were sold and a new set of girls arrived.

This is how I measure the passing of time; each week a new shipment arrives, and a little piece inside of me dies.

The lingering effects of my summons throw my body into chaos. Adrenaline races around my body. My heart picks up its frantic pace, galloping around the inside of my chest as it feeds off my adrenaline-fueled fear. But while I may be shaking inside, outwardly I display the calm, cool demeanor of the socialite I was born and raised to become.

I hurry along, trying to ignore the beauty and elegance all around me. It's all a lie.

Breezeways break up the thick walls and pull the eye away from the multi-leveled turrets manned day and night by diligent guards. Designed to keep slaves inside, and outsiders where they belong, it's serves one purpose.

I'm locked inside a fortress. Wrought-iron gates give the illusion of decoration, but they are the bars of my prison.

Men with depraved tastes are entertained here. Tonight they'll congregate in the banquet hall for the finale of their weeklong depravity.

It's Auction Night.

The last week of every month, men descend on this lush paradise to sample the merchandise, and ultimately purchase the greatest indulgence; a broken woman formed into a docile slave.

I continue over the travertine stone of the courtyard, making my way around the fountains and weaving between the cages holding parrots, macaws, and cute little spider monkeys locked in cages.

I pass by the Oasis, a room designed to look like the inside of a sultan's harem, and hold my head high. The deep rumble of men's voices carries in the air. The lightness of feminine sounds layer on top, light titters that are fake but sound real. The girls are well-trained to please. Failure isn't an option.

To the uninitiated, it looks like a sensual paradise, but all I see are ugly men, rotten to the core, touching girls too fearful to pull away.

I endure the stares of our most recent guests. Their interest heightened only because I am untouchable.

Mr. H, in particular, can't keep his oily gaze off of me. An oil tycoon from Texas, he's absent morals and lacks basic human decency.

A shiver works its way down my spine as his hungry gaze sweeps over me. His slow blink churns my gut, and the way he makes a point to lick his lips brings bile rising to the back of my throat. His desire is quickly turning into obsession.

The guards never touch me. They're not allowed that privilege, and they're paid handsomely in the brothels outside these walls. I know because they speak of nothing else when they're around me.

Tomas Benefield is the man I fear. Master of this place, he holds supreme power over his domain. On his whim, I can be given to any of these men; guest or guard.

He's waiting on my ransom, and I wonder again what could be taking my father so long to meet this monster's demands. When does my time run out?

Eve is waiting for you!
To see what happens with Eve, get your copy today!
Get my Copy of Rescuing Eve

Please consider leaving a review

I HOPE YOU ENJOYED THIS BOOK AS MUCH AS I ENJOYED WRITING IT. If you like this book, please leave a review. I love reviews. I love reading your reviews, and they help other readers decide if this book is worth their time and money. I hope you think it is and decide to share this story with others. A sentence is all it takes. Thank you in advance!

CLICK ON THE LINK BELOW TO LEAVE YOUR REVIEW

Goodreads

Amazon

Bookbub

Ellie Masters The EDGE

If you are interested in joining Ellie's Facebook reader group, THE EDGE, we'd love to have you.

The Edge Facebook Reader Group
elliemasters.com/TheEdge

Join Ellie's ELLZ BELLZ.
Sign up for Ellie's Newsletter.
Elliemasters.com/newslettersignup

Also by Ellie Masters

The LIGHTER SIDE

Ellie Masters is the lighter side of the Jet & Ellie Masters writing duo! You will find Contemporary Romance, Military Romance, Romantic Suspense, Billionaire Romance, and Rock Star Romance in Ellie's Works.

Sign up to Ellie's Newsletter and get a free gift. https://elliemasters.com/RescuingMelissa

YOU CAN FIND ELLIE'S BOOKS HERE:

ELLIEMASTERS.COM/BOOKS

Military Romance

Guardian Hostage Rescue

Rescuing Melissa

(Get a FREE copy when you join Ellie's Newsletter)

Rescuing Zoe

Rescuing Moira

Rescuing Eve

Rescuing Lily

Rescuing Jinx

Rescuing Lexi

Rescuing Eden

The One I Want Series
(Small Town, Military Heroes)
By Jet & Ellie Masters

EACH BOOK IN THIS SERIES CAN BE READ AS A STANDALONE AND IS ABOUT A DIFFERENT COUPLE WITH AN HEA.

Aiden

Brent

Caleb

Dax

Patton

Rockstar Romance
The Angel Fire Rock Romance Series

EACH BOOK IN THIS SERIES CAN BE READ AS A STANDALONE AND IS ABOUT A DIFFERENT COUPLE WITH AN HEA. IT IS RECOMMENDED THEY ARE READ IN ORDER.

Ashes to New (prequel)

Heart's Insanity (book 1)

Heart's Desire (book 2)

Heart's Collide (book 3)

Hearts Divided (book 4)

Hearts Entwined (book5)

Forest's FALL (book 6)

Hearts The Last Beat (book7)

Contemporary Romance

Firestorm

About the Author

ELLIE MASTERS is a multi-genre and best-selling author, writing the stories she loves to read. These are dark erotic tales. Or maybe, sweet contemporary stories. How about a romantic thriller to whet your appetite? Ellie writes it all. Want to read passionate poems and sensual secrets? She does that, too. Dip into the eclectic mind of Ellie Masters, spend time exploring the sensual realm where she breathes life into her characters and brings them from her mind to the page and into the heart of her readers every day.

Ellie Masters has been exploring the worlds of romance, dark erotica, science fiction, and fantasy by writing the stories she wants to read. When not writing, Ellie can be found outside, where her passion for all things outdoor reigns supreme: off-roading, riding ATVs, scuba diving, hiking, and breathing fresh air are top on her list.

She has lived all over the United States—east, west, north, south and central—but grew up under the Hawaiian sun. She's also been privileged to have lived overseas, experiencing other cultures and making lifelong friends. Now, Ellie is proud to call herself a Southern transplant, learning to say y'all and "bless her heart" with the best of them. She lives with her beloved husband, two children who refuse to flee the nest, and four fur-babies; three cats who rule the household, and a dog who wants nothing other than for the cats to be his best friends. The cats have a different opinion regarding this matter.

Ellie's favorite way to spend an evening is curled up on a couch, laptop in place, watching a fire, drinking a good wine, and bringing forth all the characters from her mind to the page and hopefully into the hearts of her readers.

FOR MORE INFORMATION
elliemasters.com

facebook.com/elliemastersromance

twitter.com/Ellie__Masters

instagram.com/ellie_masters

bookbub.com/authors/ellie-masters

goodreads.com/Ellie_Masters

Connect with Ellie Masters

Website:
elliemasters.com
Amazon Author Page:
elliemasters.com/amazon
Facebook:
elliemasters.com/Facebook
Goodreads:
elliemasters.com/Goodreads
Instagram:
elliemasters.com/Instagram

Final Thoughts

I hope you enjoyed this book as much as I enjoyed writing it. If you enjoyed reading this story, please consider leaving a review on Amazon and Goodreads, and please let other people know. A sentence is all it takes. Friend recommendations are the strongest catalyst for readers' purchase decisions! And I'd love to be able to continue bringing the characters and stories from My-Mind-to-the-Page.

Second, call or e-mail a friend and tell them about this book. If you really want them to read it, gift it to them. If you prefer digital friends, please use the "Recommend" feature of Goodreads to spread the word.

Or visit my blog https://elliemasters.com, where you can find out more about my writing process and personal life.

Come visit The EDGE: Dark Discussions where we'll have a chance to talk about my works, their creation, and maybe what the future has in store for my writing.

Facebook Reader Group: The EDGE

Thank you so much for your support!

Love,

Ellie

Dedication

This book is dedicated to you, my reader. Thank you for spending a few hours of your time with me. I wouldn't be able to write without you to cheer me on. Your wonderful words, your support, and your willingness to join me on this journey is a gift beyond measure.

Whether this is the first book of mine you've read, or if you've been with me since the very beginning, thank you for believing in me as I bring these characters 'from my mind to the page and into your hearts.'

Love,

Ellie

The END

THE END

Printed in Great Britain
by Amazon

84318718R00230